HEIRESS
TAKES
ALL

HEIRESS

TAKES

ALL

EMILY WIBBERLEY &
AUSTIN SIEGEMUND-BROKA

LITTLE, BROWN AND COMPANY
New York Boston

Little, Brown and Company
Hachette Book Group
1290 Avenue of the Americas, New York, NY 10104
Visit us at LBYR.com

First Edition: June 2024

Little, Brown and Company is a division of Hachette Book Group, Inc.
The Little, Brown name and logo are registered trademarks of Hachette Book Group, Inc.

The publisher is not responsible for websites (or their content)
that are not owned by the publisher.

Little, Brown and Company books may be purchased in bulk for business, educational, or promotional use. For information, please contact your local bookseller or the Hachette Book Group Special Markets Department at special.markets@hbgusa.com.

Library of Congress Cataloging-in-Publication Data

Names: Wibberley, Emily, author. | Siegemund-Broka, Austin, author.
Title: Heiress takes all / Emily Wibberley & Austin Siegemund-Broka.
Description: First edition. | New York : Little, Brown and Company, 2024. |
Summary: Seventeen-year-old Olivia Owens plans an elaborate heist during her father's wedding to exact revenge for his actions, but things take a chaotic turn with unexpected wedding guests and obstacles.
Identifiers: LCCN 2023029149 | ISBN 9780316566759 (hardcover) |
ISBN 9780316566773 (epub)
Subjects: CYAC: Revenge—Fiction. | Stealing—Fiction. | Fathers and daughters—Fiction. | Weddings—Fiction. | LCGFT: Thrillers (Fiction) | Novels.
Classification: LCC PZ7.1.W487 He 2024 | DDC [Fic]—dc23
LC record available at https://lccn.loc.gov/2023029149

ISBNs: 978-0-316-56675-9 (hardcover), 978-0-316-56677-3 (ebook)

Printed in the United States of America

LSC-C

Printing 1, 2024

*To Katie, for believing in this one
from the beginning*

ONE

I REALLY SHOULDN'T HAVE WORN HEELS TO MY VERY FIRST HEIST.

They cost me only seconds on the stairs, possibly less. Seconds might be critical, though, in moments like this one. I reach the bottom steps, then the dark wood of the basement corridors, where I pause to pull off my pumps.

Ugh. More lost moments.

The instant they're in my hand, straps hung on my rubbed-raw fingers, I run.

Footsteps pound behind me. Not the ominous rhythm of two feet or even the hectic syncopation of four. This is a *crowd*.

The long passageways I've dashed into mock me with their formality, their elegance. White baseboards giving way to pink paint; deep, dark hardwood floors where the balls of my bare feet thump with every step; crown molding, which... I only know what crown molding is because Dad *would not stop* pointing out to guests that the *crown molding dates back to the 1800s.*

I don't fixate on their charms, though. Instead, I concentrate on how I know every inch of this house.

Like it knows me. The Olivia who learned to walk here. The wide-eyed girl who couldn't help imagining she'd inherited her very own modern fairy tale, complete with the closest thing to a castle Rhode Island possessed. The Olivia who invited over prep school classmates to experience its epic grounds because when she felt like she couldn't be interesting or important or loved, one thing she could be was rich.

The Olivia of now, who visits every week, quietly shocked by how quickly she could feel like a guest.

The Olivia of today, determined to steal from this house the way the past few years have stolen from her.

I hit the first corner in the hall, clenching my fist around what I've stolen, a reminder of why the footsteps won't stop. With every step, I fight to ignore the warm, wet sensation running down from my shoulder to my elbow. Sweat sticks the fabric of my dress to my back.

My ruined dress. It's probably the only pang of remorse I have for how the day went. The pink baby-doll dress my mom purchased, determined for me to fit into my dad's world, despite how his new bride's handbags cost what Mom makes every month. If I get out of here, I know how Mom's face will fall when she glimpses the present ragged state of what I'm wearing.

I understood that today would exact its costs, though. Every one of us did. If I'm caught, I won't be the only one going down for this.

Pushing my pace, I hit the next corner. Left, past the restroom with the white orchid. I wonder if even one single human being has used the white-orchid restroom this millennium. Then the next turn, right—

Wham. I slam my hand on the handle of the unassuming, unpretentious door. Behind it, concrete service stairs descend even lower. The walls of the hallway here have changed without warning from genteel Georgian to unceremonious, unyielding gray cement. The deepest inner workings of this home, where guests never come, hold the house's circuit boards, its mechanics, its nerve center. Mr. McCoy would point out how metaphorical the sharp change is, for capitalism or, I don't know, national history. *Every country club hides mazes of concrete.*

I race down the hall, passing the first door, then the first corner, then the second door. I played hide-and-seek down here once with my mom before the divorce.

The third door on the left is wide-open.

I rush inside, then slam it shut, chest heaving, my perfect home-made balayage now congealed clumps of brown and blond hanging haywire over my shoulders. In the center of the small, dark room, I pull my phone from my damp clutch. My heart constricts when the screen lights up.

The group chat is frantic.

Knight

> King, please respond!!!! THE hell is going on

Queen

> King seriously. Update now

Rook

> Someone please get a picture of the cake.

Knight

> ??? The cake RN ???

Assface

Yo the cake was poppin my guy.

I gotchu.

Rook

Can someone other than Assface get eyes on the cake?

Pawn

King, please confirm your status. Thanks.

Knight

You text so weird man

Pawn

I text like an adult, Knight.

With shaking hands, I key in my reply.

King

Everything is under control.

Stick to the plan.

The truth is, the message is for me, too. *Everything is under control*, I repeat in my head. *You're fine. No, you're incredible. You're ingenious. Okay, now you're getting hyperbolic. Rein it in, girl. You're good. You're fine.*

Everything is going to be fine.

Everything is under control.

Past the closed door, the sound of footsteps is now nearly inaudible. The wet trickle is reaching my forearm.

Everything is under control.

Slowing my breathing, I press on my phone's flashlight to investigate my surroundings for escape routes. While I might know every inch of this unwelcoming home, I don't necessarily know every conceivable hidden exit from its subterranean floor. Because—funny thing—none of the near lifetime of memories I've willingly or unwillingly made here included felonies.

Not wanting to draw my pursuers, I keep the overhead light off, which leaves everything outside the glow of my flashlight unclear in the dark. But there—near the ceiling, one small rectangular window reveals the deep blue evening outside. I just need something to climb on to reach it.

Swinging my light to the wall of high metal shelves, I search for pool equipment or boxes of gardening supplies or who knows what—

The door crashes open behind me.

In one of the most heart-stopping moments of my life, it occurs to me—the fact that the footsteps were dampened didn't mean *they weren't coming closer.* I whirl, the iridescent jewel of my phone's flashlight sweeping the room.

When my eyes reach the doorway, framing my pursuer in the light of the concrete hallway, I say nothing. I do nothing, except realize, for the first time today—

I do not have everything under control.

TWO

FIVE HOURS EARLIER

I STEP INTO MY HEELS. THEY'RE PERFECT, THE FINISHING TOUCH. IN the mirror, I look over my handiwork.

The first thing I notice isn't my outfit. It never is. It's the initials inscribed in the corner of the glass in the staff room of Vive, the superstore where I'm employed. The work of knifepoint, carved into the mirror that's intended to help us look professional on our way to the register, or, in my case, the custodial closet. *EH.*

Of course, I have no idea what they mean, which makes them the only interesting thing in the room.

Otherwise, the Vive employees' lounge is a gray underworld in contrast to the clean commercial aisles outside. Overhead lights humming with their depressing cast. Couches no one uses, wispy cotton protruding from the rips in their cushions. Lockers against one wall with empty loops for employees to place our own locks.

It is not, shall I say, the ideal place to get ready for my father's highest-of-high-society wedding. I don't need the openly judgmental glances of the coworkers who pass me on their way to their lockers to know my preparations for the day—my pink dress, my ivory heels—look, put gently, ironic.

I focus on the initials, letting them center me. *EH.* When I need to escape the reality of my work, I occupy myself by inventing possible meanings for them.

EH. Equine haberdashery, I note when I pass the hats with horse logos on them.

Exquisite handbags. The purses in the display case, fifty-dollar bags I walk past with embarrassment—not because I work here, but because I know I once would have, on price and misguided principle alone, considered them cheap and chintzy. I used to wear Gucci and Shinola to school. Now I can't afford what I used to mock.

Framed in the gray of the employees' room, I reach for the makeup I brought to work. The waver of weakness in my imprecise hand is from the hours I've just spent scrubbing the floor surrounding the refrigerators, where someone dropped a glass bottle of tea.

I need to work quickly, and not just for my own reasons. If the metal door on the other end of the room opens and my manager, Oren, emerges, he'll enlist me in helping Shaun shelve the deodorant. Yes, even though my shift ended eleven minutes ago.

Yes, even in my dress.

I'm what Vive calls "general personnel," which means I do whatever my manager wants. Rarely is it cash register. More often, it's cleaning.

I'm not ashamed to scrub floors, not when I know it's helping my mom with our finances. No, I'm ashamed by how much I *suck* at it. I have no intuition for the work, not to mention no musculature. Growing up on the Owens estate with housekeepers, I developed no finesse for what equipment or products to use, how much pressure each surface or stain demands, or countless other intricacies, leaving me envious of my more experienced coworkers. I'm Cinderella in reverse, the princess who discovered one day she was destined for drudgery.

I put on my concealer, smoothing out my skin, which no longer gets the perfect spray tan twice a month.

I miss my old life. I won't pretend I don't. When my mom divorced my dad, I was cast out of *everything*. His home, presumably his will... his world. The world I knew.

EH. Ex-heiress.

On my darkest days, I wish Mom had maybe... made it work. Not forgiven my father. Just... figured out how to live under our old roof instead of in the small home I moved into with her two years ago, when my father's prenup left her with nothing. Why should we get punished for his misdeeds?

The feeling never lasts long. I love my mom fiercely. I respect her conviction, her decisiveness, her self-respect, her courage. How hard she works to provide me with the narrow bedroom in our house, one the size of the closets in the Rhode Island mansion where I lived for most of my life. The way she decorated the room with reminders of what I loved, whimsically combining French art deco posters with a soccer pencil cup and the large purple mirror on my closet door.

It took more effort to make me feel like I was *home* than I'd ever imagined, or deserved, an effort I know my mom doesn't have in her to make every day.

It's something in her eyes. Even if she's up, moving forward, making the events of the day happen—only sometimes do her eyes look like *her*. Green, like mine.

Other times, when I look into them, I can see she's stuck

somewhere. In some shadowy, exhausting labyrinth she doesn't know how to get out of. Like she doesn't know if she's moving forward or if she's just still moving.

The employees' lounge's metal door rattles open right then. I whirl, panic rising, expecting Oren is going to criticize me for *something* related to the spill situation and consign me to shelving, and—

It's only Shaun, finished, I guess, with the deodorant. He doesn't glance over on his way to the lockers.

I face the mirror, with my chest rising more evenly, and inspect the pieces of my outfit. The dress I ordered online when Mom proudly insisted we pick out something nice. The heels. The gaudy wink of the plastic diamonds in my hair clip. The girl in the initialed mirror is Barbie come to life.

It's the perfect disguise. *Myself.*

Or the idea of me. The daughter of controversial podcaster– multimedia mogul Dashiell Owens. My father's made his fame on off-the-cuff impulsivity, on not overthinking, on deciding everything while considering nothing. Imagine what everyone in the entire universe thinks of *me*. Dress seventeen-year-old me up in pink with heels and shiny jewelry—nobody's going to double-check their first impression of Olivia Owens.

Which is, of course, essential to The Plan.

Reaching for my eyelashes, I push down nervousness. *The Plan.* Even if the notes I've meticulously made in the black notebook I requested for my birthday weren't neatly headlined with the two capitalized words, I would probably hear them with capital letters in my head.

The truth is, I haven't thought of much else since The Plan entered my head in one dark flash the day that we received Dad's

Save the Date in the mail. I've studied enough to keep my grades up, to dispel suspicion. I've helped out my mom however I could. I got this job, the least I could do when my mom works three, supporting us while struggling to stay on top of her medical debt.

One led to the other, like partners in crime—if she hadn't been chasing surge-priced ridesharing hours one Friday night, she wouldn't have gotten on the road exhausted from twelve hours of consecutive hostessing shifts. She wouldn't have nodded off for split seconds. Her car wouldn't have skidded on ice into the highway divider.

Wouldn't, wouldn't, wouldn't.

Her head hit the window hard. Her wrist crumpled from the impact. She was unconscious for fifteen hours. They were the worst hours of my life, in Rhode Island's Kent County Memorial Hospital, where I sat silently, holding her hand, waiting for her to wake up. Every detail of my surroundings engraved itself in my memory forever. The fluorescent lights, the white floors, the sterile hallways. The days were full of procedures, scans, metal pins, "we'll know more later," and incessant worry.

Incredibly, she made it through. She's fine except for pains in her wrist—and hundreds of thousands of dollars in debt forcing her to keep working. Even miracles can cost everything these days.

I honestly have no idea where she is right now. On weekends she does DoorDash or Instacart, which sends her from Coventry, where we live, into every corner of Rhode Island. I've gotten used to having the car only from Wednesday through Friday, when she walks to the grocery store that we're ten minutes from for her shifts.

Today, though, even with Dad's wedding, I don't need the car. The method of transportation is the first step. Starting in—

The clock on my phone counts up. 3:24.

With one false eyelash in my hand, I let nervousness overcome me momentarily. I don't fight the feeling. Here, now, I can permit myself the cold fear chasing through me. The rest of the day, I'll need to have everything under control, to compose myself into the exacting leader I know everyone needs. Right now, I can be fragile.

While I wait for my eyelash glue to set, I poke my phone screen with one sweaty finger. 3:25 p.m. Five minutes.

I exhale shakily.

I give myself seven seconds.

Then I meet my eyes in the mirror. Green, like my mom's.

Instantly, I iron every waver out of my nerves. Every hint of tremor out of my fingers. With unshaking hands, I press my fake eyelash perfectly into place.

I'm ready. For months, I've filled countless notebook pages with important research, checklists, schedules, diagrams, everything. No one ever counted on Cinderella wanting revenge.

Today, during my dad's third wedding, I'm going to execute the heist I've been planning for months.

I'm going to steal millions from my own father.

THREE

I GET A TEXT AT 3:28.

Early. Early is good. Exact is better, but early is good.

With one parting glance in the mirror, I return my makeup to my locker, knowing I'll never see it again. I leave the dismal employees' room of my job for what will be the final time, one way or another. In nine hours, I'll either be very rich or I'll be in deep, deep trouble.

In the parking lot outside the unassuming employees' entrance, I like how I look in my high heels, my pumped-up makeup. I stand out in the drab neighborhood I've called home for two years. Coventry is picturesque, kind of—not in the usual ways, the gorgeous homes or endless lawns of Rhode Island's expensive neighborhoods. But there's quiet endurance in this dull landscape. Concrete isn't charming, either, but it's strong. Impenetrable. Coventry looks like the town knows things—like the woods of exhaust-dusted trees hold secrets they'll never reveal.

Picturesque or not, however, this is not where one would expect to find the girl I'm pretending to be. The girl who could never mastermind today.

I lift my chin, drawing the crisp afternoon air into my lungs. There's no hint of rain. *Good.* I had contingencies for rain, but they were more complicated. I don't like complicated unless I'm in charge of the complications.

Everything is under control.

I walk to the white cargo van waiting on the pavement. The driver's mirrored sunglasses stay facing forward when the vehicle's sliding door rolls open to let me inside. Pulling the hem of my dress into place, I sit in the seat nearest the door, which I drag closed, sealing myself inside. There's no going back now.

Wow, you're being incredibly dramatic, I chastise myself. *Did you ever wonder if you might be less high-strung if you, I don't know, didn't think uberserious movie-voice-over things like "THERE'S NO GOING BACK NOW"?*

I put on my seat belt, my shoulders shivering involuntarily. It's not nerves this time. The van is freezing—exactly how I specified.

In my lap, my clutch clatters with the plastic sound of my lipstick, its own reminder of what I have planned. I stole the makeup on one of the *essentials-only* convenience store trips my mom sent me on. It's not the only time I've lifted something small in the years since my parents' divorce. The paperweight from my dad's attorney's office, crystal figurines from classmates' parties…I consider it "recreational petty larceny."

While my little habit might've offered me inspiration, however, it's nothing compared to the magnitude of today. Not even close.

The only other item in my clutch is my phone. They're my final props designed to turn myself into a character, the stepdaughter acting out because her daddy is getting married.

Shit, I mean, maybe it's the truth.

Steeling my nerves, I focus on my lock screen. The photo is of my parents and me from one of my dad's companies' fancy holiday parties. I'm fourteen, no idea what is coming for my polished life. My dress is expensive. My mom's earrings glitter.

It's a nice photo. Unsuspicious. Everyone, including my mom, would just assume I'm remembering my family in happier times.

No one except me knows what the photo really captures. The look in my father's eyes, the same way he regarded me in the limo on the way to the event. His favorite glare.

I learned to recognize the prelude to his vicious impatience from exhaustingly frequent instances, whenever I dropped something or had my iPad too loud or left the house late. I'd caught it then for FaceTiming my friends from the limo. I guess I was noisy or annoying or just young and a girl or who knows.

Do everyone a favor, he snapped when I'd hung up. *Keep your mouth shut tonight.* While indignation flashed on my mom's face, she knew not to provoke him further.

His glare in the photo is the perfect reminder of who he is. The careless cruelty—his unkind words were only a precursor to what would come next. Every way he would leave me needing to do what I'm planning. Every reason for ruthlessness.

The goal itself is simple. The passcodes to my dad's online offshore accounts—handwritten, to be unhackable—are in the safe in his office, just feet from where he will be getting married in a few hours. We get into the wedding, get the combination to the safe, then get the passcodes. Steal his money.

And, more important, get revenge.

While the driver wordlessly pulls out onto the highway, I face the other passengers, projecting calm. In the back seat, laptop open, scrolling silently, with the white light of the screen highlighting the dark circles under her eyes, is Cassidy Cross. It's the first glimpse I've gotten of the girl who will handle our technological requirements. Dressed entirely in black—which I did not require but very much respect—she's frowning as if the expression is her default. Wire-cutter-sharp eyes stand out from her cream-pale skin, her curly hair pulled back from her face.

I leave her be. Despite going to the same school, we've only ever met over months of emails, which I've decided speaks well of her, given the unique circumstances of our new friendship. She looks like how she writes—efficient.

Next to her, Deonte Jones is dressed in the uniform of kitchen staff, carefully modeled on the online photos I found of the wedding's caterers. The white coat with a precise black bow tie barely fits the present wearer's frame. Deonte is Black, six feet tall, probably well over two hundred pounds. He's built like a football player, which is convenient because he is a running back for East Coventry High, where I've gone since my dad punted me and my mom to Coventry—no football pun intended.

While we're not *friends* friends, Deonte spending time with the football crowd and me falling in with my revolving door of popular-ish girls, we chat whenever we wind up in the same class or party.

I clear my throat before I speak, not wanting to have phlegm from hours of not talking to anyone during my shift in my first remark to my crew. Heist leaders do *not* have after-work phlegm. "Do you have the asset?"

In response, Deonte just nods his chin toward the back.

I follow the gesture to a tall cardboard box tied down with bungee cords. Bungee cords weren't in The Plan, but they were the right move, I note. The box doesn't budge when our driver rounds the corner onto one of the several truss bridges crossing rivers through Coventry. I'm grateful for Deonte's improvisation.

"It doesn't look big enough," I say.

"That's because it's in pieces," he replies. "It wasn't safe to transport fully assembled."

I nod silently. Once more, his logic checks out.

"Drive very carefully," I tell the driver. Those bungee cords look sturdy, but one bump in the road and we're screwed before we even get to the wedding.

I'm pleased when we take the next turn even slower. Glancing out the window, I determine we're probably ten minutes from our next destination. Chitchat doesn't feel like the vibe while we drive. Everybody's probably hiding their nerves the same way I am, envisioning every moment, every step of the day.

I catch myself smiling from the dark humor of how jittery this wedding has us. I wonder if Maureen, my soon-to-be stepmom, is this nervous, or if self-involvement has entirely swallowed self-consciousness in the bride.

I *know* my dad isn't nervous. For months, he's been raring to convert this glaring evidence of his inability to maintain loving connections with women into his greatest success—a walk of shame spun into a victory lap. It's classic Dad, like when he got a comedy cable channel—I forget which—to foot the bill for his "Un-Grammys" when the Grammys ruled his collection of famous episodes ineligible for various categories. His capacity for manipulating failings into marks of pride is rivaled only by his fear of looking like the loser-jerk he is.

Yeah, Dashiell Owens is not nervous.

In fact, I'm counting on it.

FOUR

PAST THE BRIDGE, I WATCH THE VIEW OUT THE WINDSHIELD change while we move into the neighborhood of our next pickup, which is closer to the economic grade of where I grew up. Coventry's one-stories with chain-link fences cede to the endless green lawns of East Greenwich, where trees hide long driveways curving up to stately homes with white shutters.

It's September, the second week of my senior year of high school, the leaves giving up their green for the golden finery of fall. I imagine what my classmates must be doing right now instead of being crammed into this rental van. Waking up their summer-sluggish minds for the year's first calculus problem set. Planning parties in the victory-lap halo of our final year of high school. *College.* The applications. The interviews. The fairs in the gym. It's hard to imagine.

Will I even go to college? I don't know. Although my father might step in and pay to save face, it's not easy to contemplate leaving my mom with her debt, her lonely house. We're the only light in each other's days sometimes. With our present the way it looks, I don't know how to make sense of my future.

It's impossible to mock my compatriots' high school preoccupations without recognizing how, deep down, I'm viciously hungry for their comforting simplicity. Much good mocking comes from jealousy, and much jealousy comes from circumstances like mine. It's why I have such an effervescent sense of humor.

It's also why I'm spending my Saturday in pursuit of stealing millions.

While I contemplate whether I wish I were doing homework right now instead, the van slows on the preternaturally pleasant streets. Where one of the driveways ends, our remaining member waits.

Tom Pham is going to be famous one day. You just know it when you see him. Not because he's trying hard like most drama department prima donnas—but because he's *not*. Everything, from the precise wattage of his knowing smile in every conversation to the easy slant of his posture right now, standing on the corner outside his house with his hands in his pockets, feels naturally charming and charmingly natural. He's effortlessly cool, unflappably funny. Henry Golding meets Harry Styles in one sharply dressed chatterbox.

Right now, he looks ready to walk the red carpet. Like with Cassidy's funereal ensemble, I did not request the exquisite flash of Tom's outfit, the dark olive suit he pulls off with his nicely understated black tie on top of his crisp white shirt. The look is straight from GQ or *Esquire* except for the wide-petaled flower of his boutonniere, which is one-hundred-percent Tom Pham.

When the van pulls up, I haul the door open. Hands in his pockets, Tom cheerfully walks up to the car, where he flashes me one of his smiles. "Hello, everyone," he greets us with magnanimous charm, the way he's undoubtedly done in every play rehearsal he's ever waltzed into. "Could we please de-escalate the air conditioner situation in here?" he inquires while stepping over me to the only open seat.

"No," I say immediately. So does everyone else. Even Cass glances up to issue her denial.

"Sorry," Deonte continues. "We need this temperature for the cargo." The way he did with me, he nods to the trunk. Tom's eyes follow, finding the strapped-down box.

"Is that a *bomb*?" His question comes out mildly scandalized instead of genuinely fearful.

"Don't be ridiculous," I say curtly.

Tom's eyes rove over the box in the trunk.

"Okay, but, like," he says, "would you tell me if it was a bomb?"

"Would you freak out if it were?" I ask.

"*Me*? Freak out? Good heavens, no," Tom declares, then drops his voice gravely. "But for real, are we driving a bomb around?"

His eyes land on our driver. Incredulity explodes onto his expression.

"*Mr. McCoy*?" he nearly shouts.

"*Shh*," I hiss. "We cannot have heist crew members hollering the names of other heist crew members in residential neighborhoods on weekend afternoons."

Tom bobs his head. "Sorry. Sorry." He lowers his voice. "Mr. McCoy?"

Without glancing over his shoulder, our driver nods. "Hello, Mr. Pham." He sounds just like he used to in the classroom. Mr. McCoy, in his midtwenties, was one of the youngest teachers at our prep school. He addressed every student as Mr., Ms., or Mx., as if it were the only way he could cope with being called *Mr*. McCoy all day.

Tom rounds on me. "Why is *Mr. McCoy* driving us? And possibly explosives?"

"Rhode Island law requires minors to have their licenses for over one year before driving more than one teen," I explain calmly.

Tom's eyes remain huge. "I'm sorry," he says. "I thought the plan was to commit various crimes today."

"Man, shut up," Deonte can't help interjecting.

"I mean, we are, though, right?" Tom continues. "And we're worried about *traffic* laws?"

"Yes," I say, sterner. "I have no intention of being *caught* for any crimes today. Not now, not on our way home, not ever. Nothing we do can raise suspicion. Like, for instance, having a teenager in formal wear driving a utility van full of other minors. Now," I order, "please stay quiet. Given our cargo, it's really important for our driver to concentrate."

"*Our driver?* Olivia, it's not like you hired him out of Rhode Island's deep criminal underworld," Tom whines, pretty much ignoring me. "That's our *freshman English teacher.*"

This is, in fact, true. Due to unfortunate events during my freshman year, the only year I went to Berkshire Preparatory—where I met Tom—I guessed Mr. Peter McCoy would be interested in joining our crew. I was right.

"It's just," Tom implores, "he's a *teacher.* Do we trust him?"

"I thought the B I gave you on your C-minus Chaucer paper would've earned me your trust, Mr. Pham," McCoy comments.

Cass smiles. Tom has the good grace to do the same. "Okay, your notes were, like, unnecessarily mean, though."

"They were not mean. Your thesis was unsupported," our driver comments while checking his phone's GPS in the front cup holder.

"Guys," I cut in. "I remember reminding everyone to remain quiet to ensure Mr. *McCoy*"—I emphasize his name for Tom's benefit—"can concentrate."

Tom straightens his lapels in his seat. He heeds my instruction for roughly one-point-three-five seconds before he extracts his phone from his front pocket, the case emblazoned with some streetwear logo.

"Could I get the aux cord?" he pipes up.

I eye him in exasperation. "What did I *just* say?"

"This is a rental van from, like, 2000," Cass comments without looking up from her computer. "I don't think there's an *aux cord.*"

Tom wilts, crestfallen. It's a moment before he speaks. "I just... made us a little pump-up playlist," he confesses. He consults his phone, scrolling Spotify wistfully. "'Money' by Cardi B, 'Money Trees' by Kendrick—"

"Did you just put songs with *money* in the title?" Deonte interjects.

"Well, I'm not doing this heist for *fun*," Tom shoots back. I zero my gaze in on the pair of them, hearing impatience in Tom's plaintive tone. It isn't lost on me that most of the people in this car have never met. I carefully weighed the potential interpersonal hurdles of this versus the interest in keeping the components of The Plan under strict need-to-know secrecy. The second priority won out, but I really do not want the hurdles to trip us up seventeen minutes into the van ride.

Deonte shrugs. "If you got Cardi, I'm good."

"'Money' by Pink Floyd?" Cass inquires.

Now Tom cheers up. "Track five!"

"'Take the Money and Run'?" McCoy chimes in from the driver's seat.

The whole car goes quiet.

"Steve Miller Band?" our driver continues with eagerness verging on desperation. "*Fly Like an Eagle*, 1976?"

"I broke both hips the moment you said 1976," Tom replies.

Despite my interest in easing intracrew dynamics, I can't help smiling. McCoy, for his part, shakes his head with good-humored kids-these-days scorn.

"It's before my time, too, but point taken. Old guy driving the van," he says. "Not like I reviewed music for the *Yale Daily News* or anything..."

I realize I'm the perfect person to protect our dear driver from further musical embarrassment. "Everyone," I say sharply. "I do not feel I need to remind you of the stakes here, which rely on *precise* execution of *my* instructions without fail. When I say we need quiet, I mean we. Need. *Quiet.*"

Right then, my phone rings.

Cass snickers. I frantically jab the side button to silence the irritating marimba of the default iPhone ringtone spilling out of my clutch. Not gonna lie, it kind of ruins the effect I'd hoped my penetrating gaze would have over my crew.

Composing myself, I close my clutch, onto which I calmly place my hands. Straightening my posture, I face the crew, schooling my features into respectful contrition. "I'm sorry for—"

My phone rings again.

Heat shooting into my cheeks, I wrestle the button once more into compliance. My reprieve is short-lived. Not one second later—as if the caller expected my resistance—my perky ringtone pervades the van once more. Fully furious, but half scared something's happened to my mom, or Maureen's power tripping by demanding some weird errand of me, or I'm uninvited to the wedding now, or dozens of other unnerving scenarios, I have no choice but to slide my phone out of the clutch.

When I see the name displayed in plainspoken Helvetica on-screen, I decide I would've preferred Maureen's latest insult.

Jackson (DO NOT RESPOND)

Ugh.

I grit my teeth. "Everyone, for the love of god, please be quiet or I'm docking a hundred grand from your cut," I say. "I have to take this."

I pick up, knowing my ex-boyfriend will keep calling until I do.

FIVE

WHAT, JACKSON?" I SNAP INTO THE PHONE.

"Olivia. Okay. I'm sorry for calling you three times. Sincerely," rushes the voice of the only boy who's ever said he loved me.

If I weren't in the van, I would strongly consider explaining to Jackson Roese—*Pronounced like "rose,"* he says with his winning smirk upon even the faintest hesitation over his name's jumble of vowels—how calling me multiple times does not even scratch the surface of what he needs to be sorry for.

Then, though, the sterner part of me would prevail, the part I called on one Friday night with my phone in my hand, tearstains drying salty on my cheeks. The Olivia who'd closed out of her Instagram DMs, opened Jackson's iMessage conversation, removed the purple heart emoji from his name, and then sent, *I wish I had never trusted you. We're over. Please do not try to talk to me.*

In the three weeks since, I've held firm. I've refused to let Jackson "explain himself"—which I know with near certainty would look less like explaining himself than promising everything would be different, imploring me with those perfect brown eyes, pouring honeyed poison down my throat. Not going to happen.

The only reason I pick up now is present circumstances. Jackson has respected my privacy, never harassed me or pressed me with multiple calls like just now. With everything riding on today, with every intricacy requiring careful maintenance, I need Jackson off my back before I initiate the first phase.

"You're coming to the wedding, right?" he asks, his voice humming with urgency.

Wishing not to prolong this conversation, I give him the easiest answer. "Of course I'm coming."

"Okay. Olivia. Please," Jackson starts. He has this habit of prefacing significant things he says with staccato introductory sentences. *Okay. Olivia. Please. Olivia. Okay. I'm sorry.*

Okay. Olivia. I know you like your nickname.

Evading Jackson's efforts to win me over was only part of why I've refused contact with him for the past three weeks. The other is the memories I knew his voice, his face, his eyes, his manner, would summon up.

Jackson was my first friend at East Coventry High, the one who asked the "new girl" if she wanted to walk with him to third period two days into her transition from the hushed halls of Berkshire Prep. Every day, he provided the conversation, until, week by week, I opened up. Even while I did, I remained "new girl" to Jackson. It became our thing. We enjoyed the irony of the nickname, Jackson calling me "new girl" eleven months into our friendship, when I could walk East Coventry's corridors with my eyes closed.

I liked the nickname. I liked the way he said it, as if I were simultaneously the punch line and the one who told the joke.

I liked everything Jackson Roese said. I liked his smile, the diamond-cut grin set in his sharp jaw. I liked the curl of his hair. I liked everything he woke up in me when we would walk from class to class, laughing, Jackson regaling me with whatever outlandish thing he did over the weekend or passing me his headphones to share his newest musical discovery.

Which is how I found myself heading with him from class to our locker hall one day last year, listening intently after he announced he had "something he needed to discuss with me."

"I know you like your nickname," Jackson started.

I nodded, conceding. I did like my nickname. Was it original? No. It was something better—it was mine.

No, it was *ours*.

After reaching my locker, I shoved my econ textbook in, then grabbed the scuffed *One Flew Over the Cuckoo's Nest* for English.

"Which is why I'd understand your reluctance if I were to retire it," he said.

I stopped. Glancing up from my locker, not quite comprehending, I found Jackson leaning on the closed locker next to mine. He looked right into my eyes.

"The thing is," he said, "I'd really like to call you Olivia."

I'll never forget the way he breathed my name.

In our heist van with my phone clutched to my ear, the wound in my heart pounds while Jackson continues.

"I've given you space," he says. "Like you asked. You were clear, and I care. I promise I just—maybe in person we could—you could let me know what's going on with you. With us. I could—explain. Whatever you want me to explain."

I grimace. Needless to say, my plan does *not* include pleading from Jackson. The recency of our breakup is deeply unfortunate—if it had happened months before the wedding instead of weeks, he could've easily been uninvited. But Maureen sent her invites perfectly on time, and *of course* she invited her soon-to-be stepdaughter's (gag) boyfriend.

Which means I need this conversation over, now. "It's not going to happen. My father's wedding isn't the time. It will never be the time. If I see you in the next six hours, it will not be by choice. We're done."

"Olivia—"

Jackson is persistent. Which means I'll need to deal the death blow.

"I—I've moved on," I say. "I'm with someone new."

The line goes quiet. It's horrible. I know intimately the whirlwind I've just plunged him into. *Remember how* you *felt*, I remind myself. *Like the breath was ripped right out of your lungs.*

Miserable, I fill his silence. "I told you, Jackson," I say softly. "Don't try to talk to me." Then I end the call.

When I return my phone to my clutch, I glance up to find nobody looks like they want to heckle our driver or debate the Spotify playlist. Everyone is stiffly quiet, gazes elsewhere, until Deonte speaks up. "You good?"

I meet his eyes, gauging what he really wants to know. *Is he concerned for me personally or for the stability of the girl who holds his nonexistent criminal record in her hands?* Deonte goes to East Coventry with me and Jackson, which means he has context for the phone call I just hung up.

"I heard—" he continues, then cuts himself off, as if he's realized half a second late the car holding my heist crew might not be the place where I want to discuss my romantic misfortunes.

"*Heard what?*" Tom asks. There's no misinterpreting the shrewd hunger in *his* tone. While I did not know Tom well when we were

Berkshire classmates—even when we were freshmen, he was one of those campus celebrities who few really knew outside of his beloved TikTok—you didn't need to be close with Tom Pham to know he loves gossip, which is what he's caught a whiff of in Deonte's well-intentioned question. Even Cass glances up with guarded curiosity in her eyes.

I realize instantly the stakes here. I cannot have my crew thinking I'm going to be distracted when I'm not—I'm honestly not—or that I have some heart-throbbing ulterior motive.

"You heard the rumors." I finish Deonte's sentence. "They're true. Jackson cheated on me, and it broke my heart. It's in the past. I feel nothing for him. Him coming to the wedding has no involvement whatsoever with our plans today."

The group goes quiet. Well, Cassidy and McCoy stay quiet. While Deonte's expression doesn't change, somberness enters his dark eyes. I shift my gaze to Tom, for whom my speech was intended. I knew he would be the hardest to convince. Thespians tend to recognize most keenly when other people are performing.

I guess the firmness in my voice or the calm in my demeanor are convincing, though. Tom nods once, meeting my eyes with respect, maybe even contrition.

When Cass speaks up, I'm not certain I hear her right. "Okay, but who's your new BF?"

Glancing over, I find the ghost of her smile saying the question was ironic. I return the grin, relieved but unclear why she's ushering us past the fraught moment.

"Forgive me if I'm wrong," I say, using the opportunity Cass has given me. "But I don't think we're here to gossip. I think we're here"— I pause potently—"to get rich."

With perfect timing—which I didn't plan, but if the group wonders whether I did, then great—McCoy guides the van right into the
wide opening of the driveway I've pulled into countless times over
the past seventeen years.

In front of us, the gates of the Dashiell Owens estate loom, open
and waiting.

SIX

*T*HE DRIVEWAY WINDS UPWARD, SECLUDING US IN THE WOODS SUR-
rounding my father's home. It's designed for impressing guests,
not for easy ascent. On the curving climb under the vermillion cover
of fall leaves, I can't help remembering the dinners I've had here
every week for the past couple years—my dad's new way of pretending we're a family.

I get nervous every dinner, for no exact reason—only the unwelcome feeling of the home I once loved. The six or seven times I
brought Jackson with me, I felt calmer driving the Camry I share
with Mom up this foreboding driveway. Other nights, I find myself
fretful on the drive, uncommunicative during dinner, then frustrated
with myself, then restless when I go to bed because I know in a week,
I'll repeat the whole ugly riddle over.

I couldn't have known it would help me now. It does, though.
The funny thing is, driving up to my father's estate with nervousness
clenching my stomach, I feel…prepared.

The house is elevated—or the highest you can get in Rhode
Island. While the incline's grade is gentle, Deonte nervously watches
the box secured in the trunk.

When the road evens out, our destination finally in view out the windshield, we follow the valets' directions into the collection of Maseratis, Maybachs, and Porsches filling the otherwise needlessly large green lawn flanking one side of the house. The older I get, the more perplexing I find this feature of the grounds. What did Dad plan on doing out here? Play polo? Hold Coachella?

I direct McCoy to the very back. We'll need to walk farther, complicating hasty escapes, which is unfortunate.

On the whole, however, *seclusion means occlusion.* The more people, the more cars, the more everything distancing us from the house, the less memorable we'll be.

Yes, I found this pretentious-ass phrase in an online guide to robbing secure facilities. Yes, such content really exists. Yes, I promptly wrote the irritating rhyme into The Plan's notebook.

McCoy puts us into park. Everyone reaches for their seat belts. "Introductions," I say, preempting them. "Cassidy—our hacker." I nod to Cass, who does not respond. "Deonte, catering. Mr. McCoy—"

"It's okay to just call me Peter," he interjects. "People pretty much do outside the classroom."

"Mr. McCoy," I repeat. "Security. Driving. Tom," I continue, pointing two fingers to our remaining member. "Playing my date for the wedding. Yes, he's who I referred to on the phone with my ex. Our story needs to be consistent with what Jackson sees."

The crew exchange glances. I pause, giving them time to commit the configuration to memory. Much of this is new information to each of them. Like their identities, I've concealed from each member of my crew the parts of the plan they didn't genuinely need to know—until now.

I'm pretty certain I catch the moment it happens. The moment this becomes *real*. Everyone's expressions settle into mutual respect, then the realization of mutual reliance. Right now, from here on, we know each of us is depending on everyone else.

"This, of course, is the final time we will use the names we've just exchanged," I continue.

Everyone falters. Nobody received this part of the plan.

"We'll be using code names," I continue.

Pretty much from the outset, I knew we would need code names. If we're overheard or our communications over the course of the next six hours are discovered or whatever, keeping our real names clean is imperative.

"We will go by the names of chess pieces," I elaborate to the group.

"Ew, why?" Tom wrinkles his nose, evidently finding my code-naming scheme nerdy.

"Whenever I would go meet one of you, I used the same excuse to my mom," I explain. "I would say I was going to chess club." The excuse, I pretty quickly discovered, invited no curiosity, which was important when I would sometimes leave home for hours to drive to other neighborhoods or work with inconvenient schedules.

Cass glances up, catching Deonte's eye as if they're having the same thought. It's Deonte who speaks up. "Your mom...bought that? You in chess club?"

I frown, irritated by the insinuation that my presence would be unrealistic in chess club when I literally planned this entire heist. "Yes, she bought it," I say impatiently. "Besides, they're good code names. Easily memorable. Everyone knows the chess pieces." I read my crew's faces, searching for agreement. I find none. "Also," I add, trying one last angle, "I think they sound cool."

Everyone nods. I don't pretend I don't enjoy the group's validation of the coolness of my code names.

"I'll be Queen," Cassidy decides. "Because the queen can move wherever she wants." She places her hand on her computer.

"What about Olivia?" Tom asks.

Cass looks to me.

"Nah," she says. "Olivia is King."

I say nothing, meeting her eyes, grateful for the gesture from this girl who hadn't even met me this time last year.

"I'll be Pawn," McCoy offers from the front seat.

"'Cause you make the first move." Deonte nods. "Cool."

"No, because I was easily convinced by a group of children to commit several federal crimes," McCoy replies pleasantly.

Deonte laughs into his fist.

"I shall be Knight," Tom declares. "The well-cut suit is the modern man's shining armor," he notes as if he read the comment somewhere.

"Then I'm Rook," Deonte says. "Worth more points than the knight or the bishop."

Everyone pauses.

"Nobody here actually knows about chess, huh?" he says.

"Wait." Tom is eyeing our former English teacher, the hint of memory shining in his sharp eyes. "You got *fired* from Berkshire the year we had you, didn't you? Now you've turned to crime," he comments mournfully, as if everyone in this car hasn't just *turned to crime.* "And grown a . . . rather regrettable beard."

While I wasn't going to mention it, I'm not going to dispute Tom, either. McCoy looks halfway from winsome hipster to perpetually exhausted. Unfortunately, his new scruff is my fault. He was my first recruit because I knew he would need months to grow the beard intended to render him unrecognizable to the Berkshire parents invited to the wedding.

Whether driving the van or during the wedding, I knew we'd need someone like McCoy—someone who could move without the whiff of suspicious scorn reserved for teenagers in places of power. Besides, he's cool. Whether because he's precociously young or just nice, he treated students like we were important instead of like we were work.

"Say, Tom," he returns with the first hint of sarcasm, as if he's realizing we're now his coworkers, not his private-school pupils. "What's going on with you? Figured out your post–high school plans yet?"

Tom grins. "We're doing them right now."

"Could we please wrap this up?" Deonte interrupts. "I'm really concerned about the cargo."

"Everyone," I cut in. These little moments when we've veered close to bickering unnerve me. Bickering is *not* part of The Plan. "We will deal with the cargo when I say so," I continue, hoping what the situation needs is some good ol' fashioned leadership. "First, Queen will provide the documents."

Cass reaches into her computer bag. She produces a hard plastic badge with McCoy's photograph printed underneath the words *Millennium Security*, which she passes forward to McCoy. Cass doesn't speak much, but I don't need her to. In her black T-shirt and black jeans, she's the only member of the crew not coming into the wedding. No socialization required—only having her way with my father's online accounts, which she promised me was well within her digital reach.

I have no reason to doubt her. I recruited East Coventry's Cassidy Cross when I learned of her suspension from school for hacking the school's computers to delay finals by erasing teachers' exams. It was tight; I passed biology because of the extra week we got.

"Wait, McCoy's pretending to be security? In a tux?" Tom frowns when McCoy receives his badge, then nods respectfully to his former teacher. "Looks tailored, though. You just have that in your closet?"

"You have no idea how many weddings you'll go to in your twenties," our driver intones.

"For real, though." Tom faces me. "Don't you think he's going to look overdressed next to the other mall cops?"

"No." I smile without warmth. "I do not. In July, I went to my twenty-five-year-old *stepmother-to-be's* bridal shower for exactly one reason," I explain. "Which was *not* drinking my 'virgin mimosa' on the patio of the house my father more or less kicked me out of."

McCoy squints. "So—just orange juice?"

"Fresh-squeezed," I say. "No, I sat under the circusworthy complex of tents Maureen had put up on this very lawn like she could not *wait* to call this house hers so I could mine her for information on the wedding. The look, the details. The Pinterest boards. Oh, the Pinterest boards." I'm surprised her phone could still operate despite the overwhelming collection of inspiration photos stored within its rhinestone frame, which I have no doubt she's going to change out for diamonds the moment the marriage license is signed.

Maureen Grabe is twenty-five years old. I'm seventeen years old. She went to Berkshire Prep. My stepmother-to-be graduated three years before I got there.

Do I like Maureen? With her exaggerated "look over here, boys!" laugh, the collection of designer handbags she induces my father to buy but then never uses, the way she clicks her nails on the nearest surface whenever she's impatient with conversation or the house chef's preparation of her salad or the daughter of her fiancé daring to watch *Grey's* in the living room instead of chatting with her while Dad finishes up some interview before dinner? No.

Do I believe she loves my father? No.

But do I have some sympathy for her, this girl growing up fast into my father's world of wealth and power, to which she was drawn probably because of the lack of support or companionship in other realms of her life?

Still no. Maureen sucks.

"I got photos of the *ten* cakes she's serving," I continue. "I got details on dress code. White tie is expected of everyone. Including," I say, "the private security firm. My dad is way too afraid of bad press to ever, ever think of calling the cops. Instead they're using Millennium Security, but requiring even the guards to wear tuxedos."

I gleaned this detail when I pointed out to Maureen the comically stereotypical men in black suits with black sunglasses lingering on the periphery of the palatial pavilion tent where the bridal shower was held. Even the bridal shower "needed" security, Maureen insisted, I guess concerned nefarious elements would be drawn to the home by the promise of party games or delectable virgin mimosas.

Maureen, who was by then five or six very real mimosas deep, welcomed my follow-up questions. *Will you have them for the wedding, too? Oh, great idea. Like, what kind of clothing? Ooh, nice. Yes, I definitely think tuxedos will make the small mercenary force you've hired for your wedding look presentable.*

McCoy pins the plastic badge to the corner of his lapel.

Cass reaches once more into her bag, from which she extracts five sheets of ivory-white heavy-stock paper. When I gave her Maureen's full name, searching the file indexes of the print shops nearest to this house for the order to print the wedding programs was easy, I'm told. Downloading the programs was even easier.

Cass passes them to Deonte, who grabs one off the top. They're identical in every way to Maureen's programs except for one detail. "Program headers in bold correspond to phases of The Plan," I inform the group. There's no way for me to indicate out loud "The Plan" is capitalized, but I feel like everyone understands.

I'm proud of this innovation—cheat sheets no guest would ever question, because they look like misprinted programs. The first such item on the floral-decorated, needlessly embossed paper is *Arrival of Guests.*

"The first phase commences now," I say. "In thirty minutes, everyone except Cass, who will remain in the van, is to discreetly visit the ground floor's main restroom, where you'll receive your phones. We'll be using burners." In fact, when you combine tutoring money with Tom's ridiculous monthly allowance and McCoy's grown-up finances, used iPhones with new SIM cards are well within reach economically.

"Hold up." Tom pauses. "Why the restroom?"

I sigh. Not from impatience with Tom's perfectly reasonable question. No, on occasions like this one, I must sigh from the deep misfortune of being related to the humans responsible for the present problem.

"Phones are prohibited at the wedding," I say.

Tom's eyes widen. *"What?"*

"It's due to privacy concerns. Given the guest list, they want to"— oh, I'm fighting my grimace now—"'prevent the selling of photos to celebrity news sources,'" I say.

I could hardly comprehend this detail myself when I read it on Dad and Maureen's Save the Date. Researching this part, however, I found out they're not the first couple to ban phones over this concern. Nor could I deny that my father's fifteen years of media influence really will yield the sort of guest list certain publications would salivate over. I've stumbled on several posts for chichi blogs proclaiming today's nuptials the *social event of the season*. One even proclaimed the wedding "Gatsbyesque," which I showed McCoy to get the predictable rise out of him.

"Every guest enters through the metal detectors in front of the main entrance. Cameras, phones, iPads—they'll confiscate everything," I say.

"I'm very committed to this plan, but I'm not sticking iPhones into my bodily cavities," Tom notes.

"No need." I smile. "Rook," I say to Deonte. "Would you like to do the honors?"

Deonte nods.

While we watch from inside, he exits the van onto the carpet of grass outside. He continues to the rear of the vehicle, where he opens the heavy metal doors as if they're the cardboard flaps of the boxes waiting inside.

With everyone peering out, Deonte undoes the cords constraining the largest box. When he lifts the lid, the sides of the box drop open.

Inside, with condensation forming on its frosted sides, is the most gorgeous wedding cake I've ever seen.

SEVEN

*H*OLY SHIT," TOM SAYS IN DELIBERATE SYLLABLES.

The cake is exceptional. The cream-white frosting looks stone smooth, nearly reflective, with no hint of knife swirls or disproportionate distribution. It's flawless. Up one side, white roses splay out their petals in dewy displays. Gold designs in burnished foil entwine with them, imitating the intricate interplay of climbing stems.

It is the perfect cake.

Deonte puts on no false modesty. He grins widely, his round shoulders swelling, his posture straightening up two inches taller, which puts the edge of his close-cropped hair nearly level with the top of the van doors.

"I thought we were driving *a* bomb," Tom elaborates. "But this is *the* bomb!"

Nobody laughs. Not one of us utters the slightest expression of mirth.

"I'll workshop it," Tom promises contritely.

"It's incredible," I tell Deonte honestly. I knew his work would be. Deonte's role in the heist started to form in my head when I found the baking TikTok he'd started. First, he'd displayed his own designs, sculpting with frosting the way others do with clay or canvas. He'd gotten online hype with some of those "is it cake?" videos, crafting—of course—lifelike pebbled "footballs" with spongy chocolate inside.

Then, though, he'd gone semi-viral with a video where he'd re-created the cake from Harry and Meghan's wedding.

From there, incorporating him into The Plan was too easy.

For months, I didn't know if I could get him. I'd planned other, harder solutions to the problems I knew Deonte would knock out easily, not knowing if I'd have leverage to work him into my crew.

Until the cruel fortunes of the internet delivered him to me. Several colleges had recruited Deonte for football, I knew, but he'd declined. Instead, hoping to leverage his minor online stardom, he'd set up a Kickstarter for the funds he needed to open his own bakery in Providence.

It hadn't worked. He'd wound up significantly short of his goal. Tens of thousands of dollars.

I found the vlog he started in connection with the Kickstarter. I went through his videos, every single one. I learned *why* he wanted to open his bakery. I watched the time-lapse destruction of his dream on my narrow laptop screen. I felt the riddle of how I could recruit him resolve itself with neat clarity. Most important, I found what unified me with Deonte Jones. I don't need him to want revenge the way I do.

I just need him to be desperate the way I am.

One week later, I met up with Deonte in the East Coventry school library. Inconspicuously, as if we were studying. *If you could come into one million dollars without getting caught,* I'd said, *do you think you could open your bakery?*

By the end of the meeting, I was the first-ever heist leader whose crew included a baker.

Well, probably the first.

With the masterpiece in front of us now, what I love in Deonte's remarkable work isn't the cake's beauty. If beauty were what I wanted, I could be home watching *The Great British Bake Off* under my French art posters. I wouldn't be here with The Plan in motion in my head.

No, the wonder of Deonte's pièce (of cake) de résistance for me is its precision. This cake isn't only the Gucci bag of cakes, the Rolls-Royce of cakes, the Rolex of cakes, though it is those things.

This cake is the exact replica of the one Maureen showed me in her phone's camera roll.

She commissioned the cakes specially from the fanciest bakery in Providence. In hour three of the bridal shower, she spared me no detail. *See the gold leaf?* Swipe. *It's real gold. This cake costs what my dress does. Ha! Well, okay, not quite.* Swipe. *See the roses? Sixteen. Because we met on the sixteenth of January.*

Maureen of course neglected to point out this was *this* January. They've been together for, like, nine months. Maureen had been one of the TAs in the NYU journalism class where my dad had guest lectured on the media market. He'd been hunting for prospective employees, technically, but really, he'd been hunting for prospective Maureens. It turns out it's very easy for the iconoclastic number-one podcaster in the world to drop the name of the bar he plans to hit later that evening, then wait for eager grad students to show up.

On the patio with my orange juice in hand, I was delighted to indulge Maureen's explanation of every detail of the cake—which I promptly reported to Deonte. I even got Maureen to send me photos of the prototype cakes on the pretense of showing them to my mom. I knew it would thrill Maureen. With patient effort, Deonte developed the creation before us, which will fit right in with the *ten* cakes that Maureen's ordered for this four-hundred-person occasion.

While we watch, Deonte unboxes the three smaller cardboard containers belted into the back of the van. More marble-smooth frosting. More voluptuous roses. From the side of the van, he pulls the collapsible rolling cart I found on a restaurant-supply website, which he shakes into its intended form on the grass, then he carefully starts stacking the final cake layers.

Everyone watches with the hushed focus of those observing precarious skill, until, of course, it is Tom who speaks up. "Hold on," he says. "What does this have to do with—"

He pauses. Sucks in his breath.

When Deonte fixes the fifth layer of his creation into place, Tom literally leans forward, looking awed. I get flashbacks of his overwhelmed Macbeth in Berkshire's winter play.

"The phones are in the cake," he utters with near-religious intensity.

Deonte says nothing. One by one, the other members of the group turn from watching Deonte, who does not pause in his delicate completion of the cake, to me.

Wow, honestly, nobody told me how fun this revealing-the-phases-of-The-Plan part would be.

Of course, I pretend I'm not cat-on-the-windowsill pleased with myself. I keep to my demeanor from the drive—cool, collected, in charge. "Like I said, everything passes the metal detectors. Everything," I explain, "except the cakes. Too big. Too much gold."

The impenetrable functionality of this occurred to me the more I considered Deonte's skills, watching his TikTok, lying flat on my bed with one foot perched on my elevated knee, where I do some of my best thinking. Nobody—*nobody*—messes with the cake. Imagine some Millennium Security guard nicking one of those rose petals waving his detector wand near the frosting. I'm not sure who'd be hospitalized, Maureen or the guard.

"When I realized I knew one of the best bakers in the state, possibly the country"—I shoot Deonte the smile I'd hidden—"well, the plan for the phones was obvious. Now." I turn to my crew. "Any questions?"

In the van, the group faces me. The tuxedoed, bearded security impersonator. The baker ready with his creation. The debonair young gentleman. The black-clad infiltrator with her laptop. Watching them, I get the funniest, greatest feeling. Like they're not four individuals. *Pawn. Rook. Knight. Queen.*

They're one crew.

"Very well," I say. "It's time."

EIGHT

WITHOUT HESITATING, CASS JABS QUICK KEYSTROKES INTO HER computer. I don't recognize the interface she's working with, which my experience with hackers in movies indicates is promising. When Microsoft Windows disappears is when shit's going to get real.

In seconds, sound crackles from Cass's computer. Voices. Uniform, male. Discussing the "main entrance," the "east wing," positioning on the "garden terrace." Terms I know because they describe the house I called home for fifteen years.

Cass has hacked immediately into the Millennium Security's communications channel. She hands McCoy a walkie-talkie tuned to the same frequency. Watching her, her dedicated focus, her competency, I can't help respecting the quiet girl I'd never spoken to before today.

When I offered her the job—emailing her on the secure address she'd supplied me after I'd first reached out to her on DMs with an "exciting opportunity" connected to my father's wedding, the vague line I used in establishing initial contact with prospective crew members—she didn't even really seem interested in the money. I felt like she signed on just to prove she could do the job. While not *my* main motive for the day, it certainly is a compelling side effect of the revenge I'm out for.

In fact, if my father had respected me, had considered me worthwhile instead of the whiny, vapid girl he figures I am, I might not want revenge, either.

Deonte has finished assembling the cake, which he evenly relocates to the rolling cart. "Days of work," he laments. "Probably the finest frosting I've ever done. Can't even post a photo of it." He glances into the van. "I need the rest of you not to fuck up, because I cannot waste this cake on the heist going wrong. Cannot do it," he mutters to himself, starting to wheel the cake forward.

McCoy follows.

Then me and Tom.

We join the crowd of expensively dressed guests heading into the house's main entrance. The estate stands before us, imposing. Honestly, the house where I grew up is ridiculous. It's three stories of gray stone walls, sharply slanted roofs, and high windows, with sculpted rows of hedges and a front patio of smooth, latticed stone—everything speaks of monumental wealth dedicated to classical elegance.

Not that the design mattered to Dad. With his parents' wealth in his pockets, I'm pretty sure he'd just requested his Realtor pull up the most expensive listings in Rhode Island.

When I walk up to this house for dinner, I'm resentment knotted up underneath worry. Now one feeling consumes me.

Revenge. It runs deep in my chest.

Years before The Plan or this wedding, I was walking up these steps, heading unknowingly into the worst day of my life. It was a beautiful spring afternoon—I remember it perfectly. Mom was in Hartford caring for Grandpa, which she did often in my first couple of years of high school, so I Ubered home. I'd gotten out of school early because of some prospective-parents' event Berkshire was holding.

I guess my dad forgot, because I walked into the entryway to find him making out with Lexi.

Lexi, who was his publicist.

Not his wife, who was my mom.

I stopped in the entryway, stunned. I'll never forget how my dad responded. With one nod, his eyes on mine, not Lexi's, he dismissed her, leaving her to float past me on her violet perfume out the front door. Wiping his mouth as if he'd finished eating something, he sat me down on the white living room furniture.

Only then did my wounded confusion change into real fear. It was the way his gaze lingered on me, the look I recognized looming in his features. The look from the photograph on my lock screen of his company's party. My father's favorite glare. It meant the same thing every time—*I'm going to hurt you, and I won't regret it.*

Whatever was coming, I knew—I knew—it would not be good.

"Obviously, you won't tell your mother," he informed me.

When I paused, uncertain, which I know he intended, he went on.

"Olivia, you'll ruin everything. Your mother's whole life, our marriage. Everything we have here. No one needs to know what just happened." He leaned forward on the pearlescent couch. "Do you want to ruin everything? It'll be"—I remember how he paused, emphasis in the guise of consideration—"all your fault."

It was grotesque, putting the responsibility for his cheating onto his fifteen-year-old daughter. I knew it was wrong even then, yet I couldn't fight how convincing his words were. *Olivia, you'll ruin everything.*

Past the pressure of guilt, I understood everything else he was saying. *You'll lose your home, Olivia. You'll lose the life you've always known. You'll lose the only father you have.*

He knew what he was doing. He fucking knew it; I know he did. I've grown to recognize how people like my father operate. Wielding his money, his influence, even the roof over my head, like weapons. Using everything he has to hold on to everything he wants. Putting fault for ruining lives on people like me. The young, the powerless.

Painful weeks passed until, finally, I revealed what I'd seen to my mom, hearing myself gulping, starting to cry, my words coming fast. I got out everything, though. People like my father deserve deception. People like my mother don't.

Everything unraveled from there. My mom divorced my dad—who, I will remember every day of my life, never pressed for custody of me. Never.

His prenup with Mom to protect his inherited wealth—which is, in fact, *all* his wealth—left her with nothing except the minimum of child support, so to Coventry we went, into the house with my chaotic bedroom. I moved from Berkshire to East Coventry High for my sophomore year. My dad married Lexi—undoubtedly to save face because he never loved Lexi. What he loved was the flashy image of swapping his starter family for someone five years my mom's junior instead of looking like the ignominious divorcé he was.

My mom soldiered on, finding new jobs, managing hours, pretending she didn't notice the exhausting contortions of each week. I pretended I didn't notice, either. Figured out which days customers were rude to her from hearing the restrained edge in her voice. Explained the plots of our favorite shows after she started nodding off whenever we would watch them together—or, when she eventually stopped trying to follow the story, contented myself with sitting next to her while she slept.

Until the accident. Fate adding injury to insult, as it were.

When I got the call informing me of what happened, my vicious mind didn't even hesitate. It started in *instantly*. Reprimanding me for how she would have never gotten hurt if she didn't have to do everything for the daughter who destroyed her marriage. Feeding me whispers of how I could never possibly be worth the debts I'd put her in.

She could have died. Even while I knew everything was my dad's doing, his words stuck like invisible shrapnel in my heart—*Your fault. Your fault. Your fault.*

Nothing can quite remove them, even now, no repetition of how *it's* not *my fault, it's not.* I've spent countless nights with the irrational, unshakable conviction that I'm partly responsible for ruining my mom's life, agonizing over how I could possibly repay her. It's the only hope I have of quieting his accusations.

Eleven months after he married her, my dad hit Lexi with his second divorce. Months from then, Maureen showed up to dinner in my old home.

In the two years since I found him with Lexi, I've forgotten none of it. The look he gave me. The guilt. The pain. The manipulation.

Most important—my vow.

Packing up my room in the house I used to love during the week I moved out, suffocating with so much hurt I felt like I would die, I swore to myself one day I would steal something from *him*. Not just for revenge, either. I would prove I wasn't powerless just because he was powerful. I would cut into him long-overdue lessons. *I refuse to have everything put onto me. I refuse to have everything stolen from me.*

I would make him understand what it feels like when I—when *we*—stole something back.

On the huge marble steps of Dashiell Owens's home, Tom offers me the crook of his elbow as we'd planned. I put my arm in his.

For years, I've waited for the perfect opportunity to hurt my father like he's hurt me.

Today, it's finally here.

NINE

WE REACH THE ENTRANCE, THE METAL DETECTORS JUST IN FRONT of us now. "Ready?" I murmur to Tom.

"Pardon?" he replies.

From the way his voice sounds, my eyes snap to him. The detached frost in his inflection matches the regard he watches me with now, half impatient under the sleek facade of his expressionless features. It gives me exactly the confirmation I needed.

Because next to me, in the finest suit I've ever seen on someone in high school, is *not* Tom Pham, the charming class clown who joined us in the van. Replacing him is *Thomas* Pham. Sophisticated. Wealthy. Slick, with just the right edge of "bad boy" to make him utterly irresistible to the girl everyone expects me to be.

Okay, to the real Olivia, too.

I grin. "Oh, you're perfect."

Instantly, Tom's demeanor transforms. Drops, as if he's let slip the debonair curtain he's cloaked himself in for the occasion. It's the usual Tom in front of me now. "For real?" He preens smugly under my praise. "I'm thinking I might put him into my audition reel."

I nod in earnest. "You do that."

Tom was my final recruit, when I was considering the optics of

The Plan once I'd configured the mechanics. While we hadn't spoken since I left Berkshire, Tom is fortunately *very* up-front on his social media. He wants to move to LA for acting. His family—his parents a financier power couple who met on opposite sides of their firms' deals—has no problem with the idea. However, they insist he pay his own way, not wanting "acting" to wind up consisting of partying on the parental dime.

Tom is content to pay, no matter the means necessary. When I invited him in, I noticed hints of this dark resourcefulness hiding under his carefree humor. I found them intriguing. In fact, I found them impressive. I watch for them now, my own private fireworks show.

We reach the metal detectors, marching with the slow procession of women dripping in jewelry or wrapped in fabrics with French names while the men strut forward in shining leather shoes, reluctantly passing watches the size of house-arrest monitors into the scanner.

I step into the detector, which promptly goes off.

The guards notice the clutch I'm holding, which I open when one comes up to me. The tuxedoed Millennium man shakes his head. "No phones," he declares as if it's not his first issuance of this order today.

"Not even for *me*?" I stretch out the final syllable, pouting my pink lips. "I'm, like, *literally* Dash's daughter."

"No phones," the guard repeats, holding out his hand.

I let some spoiled-girl flash into my eyes when I surrender my phone in its pink plastic case. "Like, *such* a shame," I drawl. "Getting no selfies when I look this good is def ruining my hot-girl-wedding vibes."

The lingo is for the guests' benefit. If they've ever listened to even one of my dad's episodes, they're remembering callouts of *Gen Z with their internet-speak and no work ethic 'cause they can't live without their phones.* Paired with my little-princess pretense, I know I'll have everyone rolling their eyes behind my back.

Good.

The more people decide I'm just the shallow, vapid girl they expect, the better. Phoneless, I continue with Tom through the metal detectors. I told Maureen about my new boyfriend a week ago, and she was more than happy to add him to the guest list. I think she just wants to make sure I don't get in the way today. While my counterpart upholds his bored sneer perfectly, there's sincerity in his voice when he speaks under his breath. "Not bad," he says. "Performing the ditzy heiress. You might be as good an actor as me."

"I'm just playing the part they've already cast me in," I reply.

Tom says nothing to that.

When we pass the foyer, we can't help pausing. I understand Tom's quietly startled hesitation, which I recognize from every Berkshire friend I've ever invited over—the realization of exactly how much wealth I come from.

Even I'm caught up short, however, getting my first glimpse of how this wedding has remade my childhood home into this opulent spectacle. Complementing the high Georgian columns of the grand living room, where the chandelier hangs over the impeccable white furniture, flowers festoon the room in white petals. Silks draped from interior railings play up the whole "summer palace" effect. Guests fawn over one another's garments or delightedly exchange stories of recent weekend getaways to Fontainebleau or Florence.

We continue through the back doors to the terrace overlooking the grounds. The rose garden—where I hunted for Easter eggs when I was seven, read *The Giver* for school when I was eleven—is presidential, the fountains frankly royal. On one side of the stone deck, a string octet serenades the crowd. Past the roses, guests play lawn games.

Tom's brow furrows when he realizes how many people he recognizes. Not from Berkshire, either. The websites weren't wrong when they called this the event of the season. TikTok stars with bazillions of followers parade with petite entourages past the types of politicians you would *not* want noticed on your Instagram story. TV stars confine themselves to the shade of the enormous house, nonchalantly pretending they're not protecting their complexions from the September sun.

Immersing myself in the event means fighting familiar dissonance in myself. I want to disdain everything surrounding me, to remember the many who've silently suffered due to the way my father shaped his empire. I hate everything I see.

Yet...a small, horrible part of me remembers how this was nearly *mine.*

I don't know if one day it will be. When Dash kicked me out of this home, he cut me off so fundamentally from my former life that I guess I stopped thinking about inheritance entirely. Besides, complicated relationship or not, I don't enjoy thinking of the day my father is no longer here, even if it might leave me with the home that should have always been mine.

In a way, it doesn't really matter. I need money *now.* My mom needs money now. It's a right-now problem. The only solution for right now, instead of in however many years of life my father has left, is simple—steal it.

I continue with Tom down the back steps into the rose garden. We walk slowly, exchanging impersonal, gaudy pleasantries with guests—the point is for me to be seen with my eye-catching new boyfriend, Thomas Pham. Then I notice unforgettable brown curls on one of the heads in the crowd. Curls you could rake your fingers through forever, which then you decide to do, until fifteen minutes later, you have no idea what's going on in the Netflix episode and *oh hey, how did our shirts end up on the floor?*

Memories, I remind myself, fighting the yearning clench in my stomach. *Just memories.*

I entwine my fingers with Tom's.

"Hey," I say. "Why don't we go somewhere more private?"

TEN

THE EDGE OF THE ROSE GARDEN GIVES WAY TO THE LAWN'S SLOPE down to Narragansett Bay. The estate's boathouse sits surrounded by trees, solitary on the edge of the ocean cutting into the Rhode Island coastline.

Tom is not the first boy I've hooked up with in the boathouse.

He is, however, the first boy I've hooked up with in the boathouse in furtherance of complicated plans to steal my father's millions.

Tom kisses me while I fumble the door open. I won't pretend I wasn't looking forward to this part of the heist—Tom is objectively handsome, not to mention objectively very talented in this respect. *Olivia, you needed this*, I hear myself decide. Honestly, even without The Plan, this liaison with Tom Pham would be the perfect cure for the memory of my ex.

When I close the door behind us, my mouth on Tom's, the wonderful rush of my heartbeat very real even though our relationship is just for show, Tom pauses reluctantly, dragging his words over my lips. "How...how far do you want to..." He swallows. "Not that I'm not enjoying myself."

The dash of chivalry amid the charisma of his debonair-bad-boy vibe—how hard he's fighting himself to put me in control—yeah, it only makes it hotter.

In response to his question, I strut into the center of the room, leading him by the hand. Then I unzip my dress.

The fabric starts to fall to my feet when the door flies open. I snatch the dress to my chest and whirl around, exposing my bare back to Tom.

Jackson Roese is framed by the emerald backdrop of the lawn behind him, wounded fury covering his face like thunderclouds. "Olivia. Really? Now?" He steps in, slamming the door behind him. "Please. I just need to talk to you."

Playing his part perfectly, Tom cuts in. "Excuse me, we're quite in the middle of—"

Jackson rounds on him. "Who the *hell* are you?"

Either from experience onstage or, possibly, from experience dealing with jilted exes, Tom keeps his cool remarkably. "Thomas," he replies with disinterest. "Pleasure."

"Well, *Thomas*"—Jackson hisses like he thinks the name is fake, which, ironically, it is not—"you might've just waltzed in here for the day dressed like the green M&M, but I'd like to discuss something with my girlfriend in private."

"*Ex*-girlfriend," I snap. Jackson's eyes wilt like dead flowers.

Nevertheless, I don't let myself feel guilty. This is a necessary part of The Plan. I *cannot* be dealing with interruptions like this for the rest of the day.

Feigning reluctance, I face Tom, inclining my head to indicate the door. "I'll meet you later," I promise.

Tom doesn't react or question, only nods. He passes Jackson—whose eyes remain fixed on me—on his way out of the boathouse.

"I can't believe you," Jackson says quietly when Tom is gone. "Moving on so fast."

I meet his gaze. It's stunning how hard the wrecking ball right to my heart decimates the delight of kissing Tom. *Of course it does.* It's Jackson.

The Jackson I loved once.

Since we go to school together, this is obviously not the first time I've seen him in the three weeks since our breakup. He's there, every day, in the corner of the classroom in Government, or on the other end of the cafeteria when I eat lunch with Reshma and McKenna instead of holing up in the library by myself. But he's given me the space I demanded in my breakup text.

However, this is the first conversation we've had since. The first time I've looked him right in the face, into his gorgeous, heartbreakingly familiar features. The lips I remember whispering *I love you* into my neck whenever we had sex. *I love you*, I would repeat. The intense eyes from which he hides no emotion, ever. Jackson never hides—

Or I thought he didn't.

"You can't believe *me?*" I reply coldly, zipping up my dress with efficient formality. "At least I waited until we were over to hook up with someone else."

With the unconcealed emotion I used to think was his hallmark, Jackson's expression morphs. Surprise swallows his indignation entirely.

"Olivia, what?" he manages to say. "Is *that* what you think happened?"

"It's what I *know* happened." I was reading in my room on Friday night when the DM came in. I recognized the name, Kelly Devine, who goes to West Coventry High on the other end of the city. West Coventry is the nicer high school—nothing like Berkshire, just a little more upper-middle class. Crossover at West and East Coventry parties is pretty common, despite the uneasy collective economic chip on my classmates' shoulders. Which is to say, while I'd never spoken to Kelly Devine, I knew who she was enough to curiously open the DM.

It was a screenshot. Of a message from Jackson. Wondering whether she was, in unambiguous insinuations, down to hook up. Trying his very hardest to make illicit plans with Kelly, which she sent to me out of girl-code courtesy.

I didn't move from my desk chair for hours. I cried like I'd never cried in my life. I felt like part of me was dying, which I guess it kind of was. The truth is, I wasn't just in love with Jackson. With Jackson, I was something even more important.

I was happy.

Jackson's eyes have gone huge. "I did *not* cheat on you," he says emphatically.

I snort. "Oh, so Kelly Devine wasn't interested?"

"Kelly—" Jackson's expression clouds over with confusion, as if he doesn't know how I knew. The next moment, he pushes his uncertainty to the side, once more in control. "Olivia. I promise. I don't know what you've heard or from who, but it's not true. I—"

"Don't lie to me, Jackson." I cut him off. "You're no good at it."

Nothing he could say would change my mind. It doesn't matter. I never should have trusted him in the first place. I needed our relationship to remember what I should've known going into it—giving my heart to him was childish, something I should have outgrown by now.

Now Jackson just looks lost. Stranded in a maze of his own making. *Good.* It's where I needed this conversation to end. "Please," I say calmly. "Respect me *and my new boyfriend* enough not to bother me today."

I walk past Jackson toward the boathouse door. I think I'm in the clear until I'm reaching for the doorknob. Jackson's hand, quick but gentle, grabs my wrist.

His touch jumbles me up. Suddenly, it's the same hand, on the same wrist, over my head on my rose comforter with the lights off, the house quiet because my mom is working, my heart full of contentment I didn't know was possible. It's why I don't shake him off immediately. Why I look up with naked longing I know I shouldn't feel.

Jackson stares right into my eyes.

"I'm still in love with you," he says.

I open my mouth, feel my jaw working. Nothing comes out.

"I'll always love you," he continues. "And I will prove you can trust me."

Then he lets me go.

Unspeaking, I open the door.

I exit the boathouse rattled, glad Jackson didn't expect me to respond. I'll never give him the response he wants. While I wish I could forgive him, I can't. Every memory I have of us, no matter how wonderful, rings with the horrible echo of how my father ripped my life in half. Jackson *cheated*. I refuse to trust him.

On the walk up the sloping lawn from the boathouse to the rose garden, I refocus myself. The Plan is what's important. The deadline I gave my crew—providing Deonte enough time to remove the phones from the cavity he baked into a section of his cake, then smuggle them under his uniform into the bathroom—is coming up. Thirty minutes from entry.

I continue into the house, where I join the short line into the restroom off the living room. Hoping the rest of the crew followed my orders expediently, I'm pleased when I find only one phone taped to the back of the toilet.

When I click on the screen, I find the group chat with everyone's numbers I programmed in earlier this week before I drove the phones over to Deonte's during "chess club." Everyone has called out their code names, which I plug into each number's contact profile before supplying my own.

King

King signing on. Phase One is complete.

Pawn?

Pawn

On my way. Getting in position for Phase Two following welcome toasts.

The concise, organized confirmation is exactly what I need right now. I'm pleased with my crew, frankly. I shake off the memory of Jackson for good—today, I'm in complete control.

I stow my phone in my clutch, knowing no one will suspect it to contain contraband when security visibly searched it—and me—earlier. In the mirror, I check my hair, my heavy makeup. My lipstick is smudged, which is perfect. Slowly, I inhale, then exhale, controlling my nerves.

Heading for the door, I prep myself on what Phase Two entails. I'll need my crew to continue working as flawlessly as they have thus far. Feeling focused, I push open the door—

Only to run right into my dad, Dashiell Owens himself.

ELEVEN

HE ISN'T ALONE.

I pass analytical eyes over the people with him. It's important I consider them only parts of my plan instead of mere loathsome guests. Like...chess pieces. Very important ones in the game I'm playing.

Mitchum Webber is graying, brawny, his expression dour. My father's lawyer and best man. He seems uncomfortable in his tuxedo, as if celebration isn't his idea of fun.

His teenage children flank him. Amanda Webber is styled as I would be if I still lived in this house, her rust-red hair shining, her dress probably picked up at New York Fashion Week. She looks annoyed to be here. In contrast, Kevin Webber looks annoyingly happy to be here, his lacrosse-bro grin paired perfectly with his preppy suit.

"I need Jackson," Dash says.

I frown. *Hi, Olivia. It's wonderful to see you. I'm so glad you're here.*

I curtail my annoying brain's propensity to produce what I know my dad could have said, in another life, another family. I need to focus. Despite my planning, I did not expect my father to fling inane requests my way immediately.

"Which is my problem *how*?" I reply.

Is it petty of me? Yes. Even bratty? Yes. It's practically my birthright, like the money I'll be stealing. It gives me great joy to imagine my dad might recognize my reaction. No prenup could stop me from inheriting the sneer I'm giving him.

His eyes fix on me with more focus. I straighten on instinct, old muscle memory kicking in from when I once was the dutiful daughter. The one who wanted to please him, who learned his moods, who practiced avoiding getting caught in the cross fire.

Instantly, I scold myself. I let my shoulders slouch. Let him see the daughter he's already convinced I am. Lazy. Selfish. Superficial.

He scowls, looking like the pissed-off version of presidents' faces on money. My dad has the perfect haircut to make gray look stately, the perfect presumptuous grin to make his genteel features look earned.

Without them, he would not be notably imposing. He's of medium height and medium build. He works out often enough to stay in shape, which isn't difficult when four different personal trainers pay house calls to his private gym every week. His tux is flawless, of course. His shoes shine. He is wealth incarnate. The picture of success, rendered in other people's craftsmanship.

"Could you keep a lid on the teenage-girl thing on my wedding day?" he orders me.

"Sure, I'll keep a lid on the *teenage-girl thing*," I repeat, loving when the character I'm playing lines up perfectly with the sarcasm I want to deliver. "Jackson and I broke up weeks ago. I told you this. Twice."

He rolls his eyes. Whether at my facetiousness or something uninteresting I've said, I don't know.

Other instincts flare in me, unnervingly destabilizing. It's funny how rage and lost love strike the same sensitivities, places I can't afford having struck. In his quick response, I remember his reaction whenever my mom wanted to go out to dinner with one of her friends, or I said something he disagreed with, or obligations of my school or even parenting in general caused him the mildest inconvenience. They make me want to scream in his face the way I would when I was fifteen.

It would smash The Plan to smithereens, probably. I wouldn't put ejecting me from the premises past my dad. Or maybe he'd *send me to my room*, pretending he didn't enjoy the infantilizing irony.

Even so, for like one-point-five gloriously furious seconds, it would be worth it.

I don't scream, of course. I clench my jaw.

My father glances in irritation into the foyer, where guests file out to the gardens, heels noisy on the hardwood. The afternoon sun shines perfectly in every window as if it were paid to show up. I doubt Dash is impatient for the wedding per se—I'm guessing it's more his natural response whenever anyone doesn't oblige his every order.

"I'm aware," he snaps. "I figured you were back together by now."

It surprises me. "Why?" I ask honestly. I'm waiting for some jab about how girls like me love drama or are weak-willed or unhappy with independence. Podcast shit.

Instead, Dash eyes me, like I'm the surprising one. "Because you really liked him."

I open, then close my mouth. I don't know what to do with the insight. I hate that he's able to read anything real on me. He shouldn't have that fatherly right after all the paternal duties he's abdicated.

I feel sometimes as if his worst quality isn't his carelessness or his insipid greed. It's how, despite them, he's intelligent. Observant. Perceptive. It helps him when he needs it. The perfect gift to win forgiveness, the perfect nothing to say in investor meetings that sounds like something.

However, I don't want to debate *Jackson* in front of today's targets.

Next to Dash, Mitchum fiddles with the bridal party's white-rose boutonniere on his lapel. For the best man at the wedding, he looks bored to be here. I have a private theory that Mitchum personally hates my father, but as his lawyer, he keeps their relationship professional—which Dash has mistaken for friendship, having no real friends to compare to Mitch's constancy.

I used to find it cringeworthy. Now I find it invaluable. Because Mitchum being the closest friendship in my dad's life has earned him the dubious honor of being the only other person in the world who knows the combination to the safe upstairs.

Which makes him the centerpiece of The Plan.

The problem is on either side of him. For the next phase, Amanda needs to be far from her father, and Kevin needs to be far from… everything.

It's unlucky his family is key to my agenda, because the one year of prep school I spent with Kevin Webber is enough to last me for the rest of my life. He was the most annoying guy at Berkshire, a title with considerable competition.

Desperate for paternal attention in a way I find I can rightfully look down on, Kevin has been sucking up to my dad for years. Every Berkshire Parents' Night where students would represent their extracurriculars for groups of parents who just wanted to show off Porsches or watches, every party I held here because I understood the estate's grounds were a prerequisite for my popularity, there was Kevin, following my dad lapdog-like wherever he went.

Which is a problem. If Kevin gets wind of the heist, he *will* tattle.

I need to keep the conversation moving. It's what helps me push past the pang of my dad managing to peer right into my heart.

I shrug one shoulder with performative flippancy. "Why do you need Jackson?" I ask.

"Sam is *sick* today," my father says sourly. His emphasis says he finds the excuse either unworthy or unconvincing.

I wouldn't know who Sam Peters—the "SEO King," inventor of search-engine optimization algorithms, millionaire, Stanford grad, owner of homes in Palo Alto and Park City—is, except that when pulling a heist in the middle of a wedding, it's helpful to be familiar with the entire guest list.

Especially the groomsmen of the mark.

Hence my CIA-profiler knowledge of Mr. Peters, a recent friend of my dad's from the club where Dash golfs. I guess Sam was palling around with private-equity guys who wanted his money. He ran into my dad, conversation converted into five-hundred-dollar lunches, and months later, here we are.

Or, in Sam's case, here we're not.

Dash definitely does believe illness is often weakness, but in this instance, his skepticism that Sam is actually sick might be legitimate. A man who hardly knows my father could very easily realize he does not want to stand next to Dashiell Owens on his wedding day to a girl who's young enough to be his daughter.

"*Ooooo-kayyyy,*" I drawl, enjoying myself. I'm starting to understand Tom's interest in improv. "Well, last I checked, Jackson isn't a licensed medical practitioner who can help Sam get to the wedding, so..."

Dash narrows his eyes, frustrated with my lack of comprehension.

It used to get to me, in moments when the mistakes were genuine—forgetting which parent company owned which whatever.

Not anymore. I make my expression look even emptier.

"Maureen won't allow the wedding parties to be uneven," he explains stiffly. He shifts on his feet, the lines of his lapel crinkling with the movement. I smell the pungent sting of his aftershave. "I need a replacement groomsman," he says.

"And you...want Jackson?" I don't need to fake puzzlement now. "Why?"

When my dad stares past me, I notice a gaggle of guests posing for a photo in the foyer. *Emerald Schwartz.* Her real name. Star of *Family Fortune* on Fox. *Malcolm Schwartz*, her father. Political donor. Reason she's famous. Posing for the official photographer with Jenna Jurgens and Emilia Lin, friends of Maureen's.

The realization almost makes me laugh—Dash doesn't just want out of the conversation. He wants the publicity of his own wedding. The opportunity for famous people to say hi to him. The attention.

"Because I know he's coming, I know him, and he isn't *important*," Dash says. "If I were to ask someone else, they might wonder why they were only asked now, and I don't want to get into it."

I consider his reasoning with curiosity. It's exactly the kind of awkward social situation Dash considers himself above. I don't understand why he's submitting to Maureen's demand. So what if Maureen is upset that there are more bridesmaids than groomsmen? Or why doesn't he have her ditch a bridesmaid? The Dash I grew up with would never go out of his way for someone else's preferences.

"I'm not with Jackson. We're not even speaking, so I can't help you," I say. My performance requires less effort now. I can play the resentful ex easily. My DMs hold every scrap of inspiration I could ever need.

Kevin steps forward, hand held to his heart. He lowers his voice with forced confidence. "Dash, I can stand up with you," he says. "You've known me since I was born, and I'm not important, either."

Dash looks at Kevin, then looks back to me. "I want Jackson," he says.

Looking impervious to the rejection, Kevin nods. He's probably very used to it.

"Mitchum said he saw you with Jackson earlier. So if you're *not speaking*, I'm not sure what you were doing in the boathouse together," Dash goes on, his voice dark with the delight of pinning me using his lackey's information.

I purse my lips, hating his petty victory. I resist the urge to look at Mitchum, knowing I'm going to enjoy the next phase even more after his reporting on my personal life.

"We're fighting, not speaking," I reply. "If I'm the one who asks him to be your groomsman, he won't do it."

The familiar nonchalance of his shrug sets me on edge. "I can delay the wedding to give you time. Figure it out."

I stiffen, hoping it isn't visible. He has no idea what level of disaster he's just invoked. It's like when his dramatic gesturing during a phone call led to wine spilled on my ninth-grade science project poster board, except I could go to jail instead of getting zero credit. Delaying the wedding is to be avoided at all costs—even Jackson-related ones.

It leaves me with no choice.

"I'll ask him," I say.

Dash nods, satisfied. "If he's wearing a suit, have him change into one of my tuxes. The fit should be fine."

Quietly, I wrestle with my racing heartbeat. *It's fine*, I counsel myself. Yeah, it'll be frustrating. I can deal with frustration. I've gotten good at it at work. What inspires me is my mom, who I've watched neutralize frustration, handling shitty rideshare passengers and spills on aisle five. I have her resourcefulness—I just need to find her patience, her resilience.

Now that he has what he wants, Dash turns to leave.

"If he doesn't come through, I'm still available," Kevin calls after him. "I'll be on the bench, waiting to go in. On the waitlist. In the reserves. Groomsman understudy."

Dash ignores him, walking with Mitchum. They head for the foyer. Finally, his precious elbow-rubbing time with his guests.

Amanda, who has remained silent for the duration of the discussion, eyes flat as if she can't decide which of us she disdains the most, promptly makes off in the direction of the bar outside, where the hallway's windows reveal the green is filling up with guests. I seize my chance to separate the siblings.

"Kevin," I say, holding him back. "Have some self-respect. I know it's hard when you're...you, but just try."

If my words wound Kevin, he doesn't show it. I doubt he's one for hiding his emotions, which leaves me wondering if guys like him grow up physically incapable of imagining people might wish to insult them. He shrugs with loathsome cheer. "I want to be part of stuff," he says.

"Find some friends, then," I reply. "Don't be one of my dad's groomsmen. *God*."

"I have friends. So many." His defensiveness is plain now. He puts his hands in his pockets, squaring his shoulders petulantly. "If this were my wedding, there'd be twice as many groomsmen."

In my peripheral vision, I note Amanda has disappeared outside. It unwinds just the littlest fraction of stress coiled in me. "Kevin Webber's wedding. What a dark idea," I say. "Please don't invite me."

Having accomplished what I wanted, I walk off just like my dad.

TWELVE

IFIND HIM ON THE LAWN, PLAYING CORNHOLE WITH A GROUP OF children.

I pause a few feet away. He's shed his jacket, his sleeves rolled up in the afternoon light. The sun catches his curls in ways I really wish it didn't. I've had enough of admiring him, enough for a lifetime. Like the saying, an embarrassment of riches—I've had an embarrassment of Jackson Roese.

One year into our friendship, I was, quite honestly, infatuated with him. It felt good. I know it's not supposed to. Infatuation is supposed to vex me with prickling questions or make me fumble to get words out.

Instead, falling in love with Jackson made me feel normal, like I was who I'm supposed to be. With my dad, I'm the unsatisfying heiress, the child who has recently replaced her reverence of him with pesky outgrowths like a conscience. With Mom, I'm racked with guilt for the efforts she makes for me.

With Jackson, I was none of those things. I was just a sixteen-year-old girl with a huge, wonderful crush.

He points to the cornhole board, drawing his young charges' observation. "See, if you hit my bag off the board, then I'll lose points—yes, just like that. Exactly. Wow, I'm really losing," he comments, as if the development delights him. I chew my lip. His familiar speech pattern makes my heart pound painfully. "I might have to defer college," he goes on. "I need to up my cornhole game before I'm a freshman."

The girl near him giggles. "You don't need to be good at cornhole for college," she informs Jackson. "You just need to be good at math."

He sighs dramatically. "Yes, well, it's too late for math. Cornhole is all I have now."

The kids laugh. They're dolled up in wedding finery, their shoes getting dirty in the grass. The whole scene is miserably perfect.

It feels pulled from the life I'm not living, one where I'm the happy hostess who feels welcome on the lovely grounds. One where he's my date, where I walk up and entwine my fingers with his, feeling dizzy. It's funny. I'm glad I'm without them now, this house, Jackson—glad I've come to understand they're no good—yet the feeling that they were stolen hurts me just the same.

I exhale, shaken. *I can't watch this.* I can't let myself remember the sweet, charming Jackson who goes to every one of his sister's softball games. Who entertains the kids at a wedding. Who, when I was honest with myself, I thought was too good for me. I have to remember the real Jackson, the drop of poison in the honey. The Jackson I didn't see until it was too late.

I walk forward, heels plunging into the earth. "Jackson," I say.

He whirls, his features lighting with hope. *You have nothing to hope for,* I want to say. The reminder wouldn't entirely be for him. With Jackson, I wish I'd practiced hopelessness earlier. I'm certain it's preferable to heartbreak.

"Keep working on that toss," he says to the girl before jogging up to me. Jackson never walks when he can jog. The war of eagerness versus wounded pride is visible on his expressive features, unhidden in his eyes. "Where's your *boyfriend*?" He emphasizes the word as if he doesn't believe Tom's and my performance.

It pisses me off. Yes, okay, he's right. Tom isn't my boyfriend, but there's no reason he couldn't be. I'm very capable of rebounding. I mean, I'm capable of planning ingenious heists, of organizing the perfect crew. Rebounding is probably way easier.

I'm too smart to get defensive, though. I ignore him. "I need you to come with me," I say sternly. My job, I've decided, is simple. It's Heist 101. Get in, get out. Efficient. Easy.

Jackson's lips curl in what used to be my favorite half smile. "You'll get no complaints from me."

I congratulate myself on how little the smirk provokes in me. I say nothing, confident no unfortunate pink is stealing onto my cheeks. Under my impassive regard, Jackson collects his jacket from the nearby lawn chair where he's draped it.

I lead him across the lawn. Guests congest the deck steps. *Mindy Bunowski.* Maureen's Pilates instructor. *David Green.* Pennsylvania senator. *Rose James.* Pop-country superstar. I didn't need to do research on her. I'm honestly really excited to meet her, if heist-timing permits. I've loved her music since I was in middle school.

Now is not the moment. Jackson follows me up the steps and inside, where the formal living room is emptying out.

"I forgot to mention earlier," Jackson says, "but you look really beautiful today, Olivia."

I turn just enough to glare at him over my shoulder. In the momentary look, I catch—*ugh*. Genuine adoration in his eyes. No—adoration is a guise, I remind myself. Fake-diamond flash. It's not real. *It's not real.* For whatever reason, Jackson's whole devoted-heartthrob performance doesn't falter under my withering glance.

We're in the living room, continuing past the flawless couches, when Jackson speaks up again. "I'm pretty sure I saw Deonte Jones earlier?"

I falter. I prepared for the possibility, of course, the instant I learned Jackson was still attending the wedding despite our relationship's unanticipated demise.

Deonte is the only person in my crew Jackson knows. Tom and McCoy come from my Berkshire past. While he could conceivably know Cass, he didn't react when I dropped her name once, which wasn't surprising. East Coventry High is huge, with countless nation-states of classmates whose paths never cross on the expansive concrete grounds.

Deonte and Jackson, however, share school athletics—Jackson, soccer; Deonte, football—and the accompanying social community, as well as common interests and innate ease at making friends. I've heard them swap strategies for video games on occasion. I planned for the potential of them crossing paths.

Nevertheless, Jackson has me—well, flustered. I need a moment to summon my rehearsed response.

"I—hired him," I explain. "Or, I mean, I had my dad hire him. I know how much Deonte loves baking. He got to help out on frosting the cakes in exchange for serving drinks during champagne and cocktail hour," I elaborate, the deception coming easy now.

Jackson just inspires the liar in me, I guess.

"Wow," Jackson remarks, the resentment fading from his voice. "That's... really nice of you."

I say nothing, hating the feeling of him praising me in ways I don't deserve. He doesn't even know his admiration of me is fake. If he really knew why Deonte was here, he'd reject me all over again.

Part of me wants him to. It would be easier. Instead of dealing with the new regard in his eyes right now, I could accept how his carelessness for our relationship was inevitable. I could rationalize his rejection, even embrace it, the way I have on the darkest nights of the past few weeks. *A guy like you could never love a selfish, manipulative princess like me.*

Instead, he's watching me with the audacity to look lovelorn.

I hate it. I hate the little flicker of false hope in me. He decided I wasn't worthy of him. I *know* I'm not worth him. *Why can't we just hold on to what we know?*

"It made sense with the wedding," I say loftily. Jackson knows I give negative one million craps about my father's wedding, so he should know I'm pushing him away on purpose with the obtuse reply. "Deonte's good. With his videos, it wasn't, like, hard to get him the job."

Jackson evaluates the information. He still looks, infuriatingly, admiring of me. "Hope his grandfather's doing all right," Jackson ventures.

"He's not." Promptly, I wince, realizing the swiftness of my reply has revealed my attentiveness to Deonte's life. It's conspicuous in what I'm pretending is a professional arrangement...and one more reason for Jackson to pretend he considers me caring or nice or whatever shit I'm obviously not, or else he wouldn't have cheated on me.

Jackson goes solemn. "Damn. I gotta check in with him," he says, and it hits my heart how his immediate response is to reach out with kindness.

Not like you, you horrible girl, I remind myself. *You just wanted to recruit him.*

Deonte's grandfather is in declining health. The whole story is on Deonte's vlog on his defunct Kickstarter. Wilford Jones inspired his grandson's love of the culinary arts, although the focus on confections was one-hundred-percent Deonte.

Years ago, Wilford was diagnosed with dementia. The worse his condition got, the harder his family found communicating with him, Deonte explains, with one exception—the recipes they once shared. When Deonte fills the kitchen of his family's home with the scent of sugar, the light focuses in Wilford Jones's eyes, and his family gets a few good hours with him.

In such hours, Deonte first ventured the idea of opening his own cake shop, onto which Wilford grasped eagerly and asked after often—a hope changed into a promise. Knowing his grandfather didn't have long, Deonte launched his ambitious Kickstarter to open the bakery he wants to call Wilford's.

The final video on Deonte's Kickstarter is difficult viewing. It's his farewell, the culmination of his unsuccessful fundraiser. "I want to say I'm grateful for y'all, and it's not the end," he chokes out. "I don't know how—I just know it's not the end. I'm not going to let this make me a liar to my grandpa."

I knew how.

Deonte's not vengeful. He's not here for fun, although I doubt his sugar-shaped petals were drudgery for him. He's just dedicated. Devoted. He's here in honor of his grandfather's dying wish.

Which Jackson doesn't know I know. Or *shouldn't* know I know. Needing the precarious conversation over—and the adoration to end—I realize I need to reassert the Olivia he rejected, the heartless little princess. "I'll have my father add a little extra to his tip," I say, disaffected, as if it's the only response I could imagine to a classmate's hardship.

Now Jackson says nothing.

We head up the main stairs to the second floor, the sounds of the party growing quieter. With each step, I'm returning home from winter formal, feeling grown-up in my dress, ready to debrief with Berkshire friends who, when I switch schools, will stop speaking to me.

Or it's Christmas morning and I'm carrying department store boxes up from the foyer where I found them under the resplendent tree.

Or I'm helping the movers clear out the pieces of my room I'll need in my mom's new house.

I planned for the logistics of every imaginable facet of the day. What I didn't plan for was fending off memories with every step.

Honestly, I wish this were reflected more in my research, which consisted of reading Wikipedia pages on other heists and watching *Ocean's Eleven* repeatedly. I feel like other heist people— *heisters*? What do we call ourselves?—don't usually steal stuff from places where they experienced the overwhelming majority of their upbringing.

Jackson's words interrupt my recollections. "Your new boyfriend is Thomas Pham, right?" he says.

Hearing the edge in his voice, I smile. Looks like my dismissiveness worked as I'd intended. Excellent. Jackson disgruntled is one step closer to Jackson out of my way. "Tracked him down on social media already?" I ask.

"Your relationship looks pretty new," my ex notes. "No photos or videos with him."

He wants to play online detective? Okay. Of course, I've rehearsed responses to every question I could get regarding Tom. "I didn't want to rub it in your face," I say easily.

Upstairs now, we walk side by side past the white railing. Jackson studies me, and I know I'm halfway to selling him on my story. It quickens my pulse.

"How exactly did you get together?" Jackson presses. "You knew him from your old school, right?"

I could offer up every detail of the story I've invented of my "relationship" with Tom. However, sometimes overpreparedness is its own red flag. I sigh, opting for authentic impatience instead. "It's really none of your business," I say.

Heist notwithstanding, what I've said is not untrue. He honestly has no right to probe into my relationship. It's how I would feel even if I weren't, put delicately, in the middle of something. He doesn't get to care.

I quicken my pace to the end of the hall, where I open the door to my dad's room. Or my dad *and Maureen's* room, I realize, cringing. Jackson follows me in, the room's luxury fortunately distracting him. While he's come to the house for dinners when we were dating, he's never seen the second floor.

I won't say I don't understand his reaction. The room could probably fit half of my mom's entire house. The white rug on the hardwood is flawless, the furniture handcrafted. The vast windows frame the water reaching right out to the horizon.

When he glimpses the view of the bay, Jackson lets out a whistle.

I watch him dispassionately, the way his keen eyes rake over everything, the indescribable Jackson jaunt in his stride. I fight down how heartbreakingly *right* he looks here.

Not in this house. I mean...in my life. He feels right in my life.

No, I remind myself, *he doesn't*.

"Undress, please," I order him.

THIRTEEN

INTEND THE FLIRTATIOUSNESS OF THE COMMAND. I WANT TO REMIND myself how *un*flirtatious it feels to me, how coldly I can issue such demands. How little they spark in me. I want Jackson to listen hopefully for invitation in them while really I'm just screwing with him.

Jackson rounds on me slowly, looking as if he's found one view he prefers to the ocean. His eyebrows rise.

He doesn't question. Doesn't decline.

While not dropping my gaze, he undoes his tie and starts unbuttoning his shirt.

Objectively, it's sexy. Which is why I watch. I need to fortify my defenses. I need to know my enemy.

Of course, he notices I'm watching. His eyes darken.

With his shirt hanging open down his front, he steps forward, right up to me. I don't step back. Not when his scent hits me, intoxicatingly familiar. He smells like clichés—like safety and danger, like skin pressed to mine on my small couch far from here. Like kisses I want to lose myself in.

It means nothing to me.

Part of me wants to stop what's happening here, feeling my grip loosening on my composure. Part of me wants it to keep going, and not only out of the rigid desire to push myself into unfeeling. The weeks since I last touched Jackson have felt like forever.

He leans close to me as if he's going to kiss my neck the way he used to. Countless movie nights on my bed, school lunches when I'd pretend his flirtation didn't fill me with delight, minutes I'd linger in his car parked up the street from my mom's house when he was dropping me off.

"Olivia," he exhales. "Let me make it up to you."

His words wrench me out of the reverie. The fragile longing I'd started to feel shatters under the reminder of what he did. Glass ground underfoot.

I step back now, irritated. Embarrassed, even. While I'm glad I caught myself, I wish I hadn't had the feelings in the first place. The night I got Kelly Devine's messages, I decided in the deepest part of me I would never again let Jackson in. I won't have the heat in my cheeks make a liar of my heart now.

"I didn't bring you up here for *that*," I say sternly. "You're wearing a suit. You need to be wearing a tux to be a groomsman."

I walk into the bathroom connecting the his-and-hers closets. The room looks ready for a home-goods catalog, no shaving supplies or hair products in sight, everything fastidiously relocated by the housekeepers. It's palatial, the claw-foot tub shining ivory white, the ottoman's fabric flawless.

"What are you talking about?" Jackson follows me, understandably confused. "A *groomsman*?"

In the closet, I pull out hangers, looking for the right label on a garment bag. "One of Dash's didn't show," I explain. "He needs you to fill in." With perfect timing, I find the Ted Baker bag I'm looking for. I hold the dark plastic silhouette up in front of Jackson.

"No. No way." He looks aghast. "I can't be *Dashiell Owens's* groomsman. Are you kidding?"

"You're already at his wedding," I point out flatly. "What's the difference?"

Jackson watches me, pained. I hate the pleading written over his expression. I won't permit the risk of even one molecule of myself pitying him. "I'm at his wedding for *you*," he points out. "Being his groomsman would be for him. I hate him."

I fix my expression in place. I wish I was convinced the only reason Jackson hates my father is because Dash Owens is, well, Dash Owens. Public figurehead of entitled assholes. Except I know it isn't the full story. Part of the reason Jackson hates my father is because he knows how deeply my father hurt me.

Jackson doesn't deserve flirtation. He doesn't deserve updates on my relationship status. He *definitely* doesn't deserve to feel defensive of me.

He has, however, conveniently revealed the quickest way I can get what I want.

"Fine," I say, "then be his groomsman for me, too."

Jackson narrows his eyes. "Why? Why do you even care?" he asks. "If he's down a groomsman, he looks bad. Whatever."

I glance aside, frustrated. I don't welcome the direction of his interrogation. While Jackson is not calculating, he has natural savvy. He learns card games fast. He wins in-class debates with no prep. He figures out the plots of movies. I had to impose strict silent-watching rules following the disastrous guessing-the-ending-of-*Spies-in-Satin*-out-loud fiasco, although in fairness, silence often worked fine for what we ended up doing during movies.

While I want no one inquiring into my means, motive, and

opportunity, Jackson Roese is someone whose curiosity I especially cannot permit. He knows me too well.

It's just one more reason I don't want him getting close. "I don't care," I say. "Look, my dad told me to ask you. That's it. Be his groomsman or..." I pause, pretending I'm weighing my next words when in fact I've planned them perfectly. "Or there's really no reason for you to even be at this wedding. You're not my date anymore."

Jackson's eyes storm. Harried, he runs his hand through his hair, making the front stick up. Once, I would have smoothed it down for him. I don't.

"Olivia, can we just talk? I love—"

I cut him off, unable to hear the next word. "No. We can't." I look past him. "My boyfriend is outside, waiting for me."

It's time to make my move. The thing is, Jackson may know me, but I know him, too. He doesn't quit when he wants something. I walk past him, ready to leave. On my way out, I toss the tux onto the bathroom's plush ottoman, wondering for the millionth time why the room needs this particular piece of furniture.

In my head, I start counting. *Three...* My heels click rhythmically on the floor. Metronomic.

Two...

I head for the bedroom, not pausing in my pace.

One...

"Fine," I hear Jackson say.

I stop, hiding my smile from the mirrors. In their reflection, I watch Jackson collect the tux from the ottoman. He hasn't lost the half-desperate look in his eyes.

"*If*"—he emphasizes the word, walking up to me—"you save me a dance."

I frown imperiously. I don't like negotiating. I don't like conceding. It kind of negates the whole staying-in-control plan.

However, I'm not keen on wasting more precious minutes up here in present company. I have elsewhere to be, other machinations to put into motion. It's just one dance. I'll probably have fled the wedding when he comes to collect anyway.

"Fine," I say. "*One* dance."

Jackson grins his heart-stopping smile.

"Great. Hold this for me." He hands me the garment bag, then proceeds to unbutton his pants.

In front of me, close enough I could reach out with hands I'm determined to keep unmoving, Jackson strips down to his underwear.

I fight my renegade impulses, forcing myself to appear unaffected. It's one of the hardest feats I've ever managed. Jackson holds keys to places in my heart I didn't know could open, hidden doors in forgotten hallways.

He was my first in every way. The first time we had sex was perfectly planned. Courtesy of me, of course. I told him exactly when to come over if he wanted to do it. I made sure my mom was out of the house. I had protection. I had the right underwear. I'd done my research.

Jackson came over. I explained how much time we had and how I'd devised where in the house would facilitate the easiest exit if we were caught. I hit every contingency with efficiency, complete with backup plans and fail-safes.

"Any questions?" I asked.

He smiled. He walked up to me with the same softly adoring, half-amused look I always saw in his eyes when he was around me. *What a look.* It made me feel... precious and alive.

When he leaned in close, his hands found my hips, his whisper close to my neck.

"No questions," he said. "In fact, I know I'm in very good hands."

He followed my plans *exactly*.

Unexpectedly, the memory is what I needed. It makes me indignant. Right now, he's unintentionally doing the opposite. I unzip the bag and unceremoniously toss him the pants, then the shirt.

He pulls them on indulgently slowly, as if he's modeling. I hate how much he has to show off. With what once was pride, now protest, I'm faced with the familiar honest fact—Jackson is ripped. It's horrendously unfair. He couldn't content himself with helping his little sister with her homework, making me laugh until I cried with impersonations of our classmates, or listening intently to every song I ever said I liked, then including each with his own devotedly chosen picks on the "oLOVEia" playlist he made for our drives home?

He had to go and combine all this with the chest and abs of East Coventry High's star soccer captain, prize recruiting prospect of prestigious colleges? Not to mention his sweep of movie-star hair, his way of looking at you as if you've just pulled him into a closet, his devastating smile?

Honestly, it's criminal.

Shrugging on the dress shirt, he's practically flexing with every movement. He knows he is. He knows I know he is.

He extends one wrist to me. "Cuff links please?" He actually winks.

My mouth is dry. I say nothing. Instead, I set the garment bag down and open my dad's jewelry drawer. Inside, rows of cuff links sit neatly.

Jackson's gaze goes directly to the pair with crossed-dagger emblems. "Whoa," he comments. "Can I wear those? They're sick."

I roll my eyes, grimacing. "No. They were my grandfather's. The crossed daggers are a family symbol." Jackson isn't wrong, which I don't say. They are really cool. "My ex is not allowed to wear my grandfather's favorite cuff links," I inform him unequivocally. Instead, I reach for ordinary oval-shaped ones.

In order to put them on, I have to step closer to him. He hasn't buttoned the shirt, and I can see down the line of his chest all the way to his waistband. It's like a minefield. The flawless surface could prove fatal.

This is the problem with Jackson. He makes me volatile. He makes me scribble outside The Plan's clean lines. He is rogue flashbacks when I need clarity, uncooperative variables in my long-forethought formulas. He has the power to flip my chessboard right over, send the pieces flying.

When I finish with the cuff links, I step back. I need to reach a minimum safe distance.

Jackson chuckles, like he knows exactly what's going on with me.

I feel resentment's familiar flash. Him intuiting what his chest has done to me feels like—like something stolen. If I'm the one with the heist plans, why do I feel like the one robbed right now? Robbed of focus, of control, of every fragment of rationality in my head?

Goddamn Jackson.

He buttons his shirt with leisurely fingers. I hand him a bow tie, practically throwing it at him, and he grins as if I've told a joke.

"I have no idea how to tie that," he informs me.

I grit my teeth. Of course, I know how. I was raised here, in this place of closets with the dimensions of garages, personal department stores hanging in rows of shimmering fabric. Of my dad in hired cars, running late, prodding his phone in hasty distraction. *Here. Tie my bow tie. It's not rocket science.*

I step behind Jackson, lining my body up to his as I slide the silk around his neck. The proximity is overwhelming. It's just like hugging him, like lying next to him. Painfully right. I can't fight the waver of my fingers, the yearning hitch in my chest. It's horrible. Yearning does *not* fit into The Plan.

Jackson stands still under my ministrations.

"You can tell me you have a new boyfriend all you want, Olivia," he says, his voice vibrating from his neck into my fingertips. The feeling is devastatingly distracting. "But I know you're still attracted to me."

I pull the tie a little too tight on purpose.

"Easy now," Jackson responds.

Deciding I'm done with him controlling the conversation, I reach for the upper hand. Rebalancing the power. "Yes, I'm attracted to you," I reply. "In case you forgot, that's not why we broke up." The reminder swipes the charm right off Jackson's face. I guess I'm the one stealing again. The guiltless rush is wonderful, exactly what I needed.

I even out the bow. In the mirror, the newly dressed Jackson is polished. Precisely uniformed. He looks good.

Objectively, of course.

"Meet my father in his study with the rest of the groomsmen," I instruct my ex without emotion. I throw him the jacket, which he catches, then head out of the bathroom.

In the bedroom, with the endless views from the windows only emphasizing the room's expansiveness, I feel like I can breathe easier, if only barely.

I hear Jackson's voice behind me. "Don't forget about that dance."

FOURTEEN

I'VE ONLY JUST REACHED THE DECK WHEN I FEEL MY CONTRABAND phone in my bag vibrate twice in quick succession. I don't need to read the texts to know what they indicate. Phase Two is underway.

Every other day of my entire life, I've had zero interest in the Nassoons. The Princeton University a cappella group comprises precocious students who graduate into prestigious careers or, in some cases, into podcasting notoriety. They reunite for renditions of old favorites whenever one of them is getting married or for parties or other private events.

While I'm glad they enjoy their continued connection to their alma mater's singing group, ordinarily, I could not care less whether Fordham University Distinguished Professor of Comparative Literature Robert Ramos or Massachusetts General Pediatric Neurologist Jeff August want to spend their Saturday knocking out "Over the Rainbow."

Right now, however, they're everything to me.

This phase is coordinated to ten minutes before their performance.

I have two objectives. I need to reach the rendezvous point. First, however, I need guests to see me enter the house with my "new boyfriend" so they'll assume I've gone inside for a quick hookup. It was annoying when Mitchum saw me leave the boathouse with Jackson, but it also gives me confidence in my next alibi.

Everyone is gathered on the emerald grass. I have to hand it to Maureen—the event *is* impressive. Every detail feels planned, every placement of white roses, even every piece of crystalware and the precise white shade of the cocktail napkins. In the crowd enjoying champagne hour are more celebrities, politicos, and financiers; my memory pops off names rapid-fire in my search for one face in particular.

When I find him, though, I pale.

He couldn't have laid low? Introduced himself to some actress I'm sure he legitimately wants to meet? Sipped some champagne?

No such fortune.

Tom is with my Swiss cousins.

I have to rescue him. I slip forward, navigating the crowd until I'm close enough to thread my arm in his. He glances at me coolly, as if he weren't absolutely out of his depth.

Which I'm certain he was. Honestly, my Swiss cousins intimidate me. My grandmother's money comes from her mother, whose money ultimately comes from Swiss-noble fortunes. She eventually returned home to the family holdings in Switzerland when my grandparents separated. My father's siblings went with her.

In Europe, they've extended their richesse in ways quieter yet, per every indication, more impressive than my dad's little media empire. I knew it even in our infrequent visits when I was young, five-hour dinners when I would be left with my cousins. They made my clothes feel like hand-me-downs, my cultural references feel low-brow. Whenever our flight home lifted off the ground, I was grateful.

I smile, polishing on composure. "Mia, Finn," I say, "so nice of you to fly in for this."

Mia regards me, clocking right away how cheap my outfit is. Her impassive gaze is exactly like I remember. Of course, she looks stunning. Her perfectly blond hair is undoubtedly undyed, her shoulder-length cut shaped like fine sculpture. Her green silk dress snares the light in symphonies of shining curves. Finn stands beside her, six feet tall and formidable in a designer tux.

Mia smiles with tolerance. "Grandmother sends her love."

"Does she?" I reply lightly, eyebrow raised in challenge.

"In her way. She couldn't make the long flight, of course," Mia explains.

This is, naturally, a lie. Grandma Leonie has her own plane and flies for pleasure year-round. She has not, however, spoken to her son since I was a kid. I haven't seen the Swiss side of the family in years outside of social media, where they're not easy to overlook. Ski chalets, high-fashion events, nightclubs in every member state of the European Union. I'm guilty of assuming some of their posts were advertisements for Cartier or Dior on first glance.

"We were just meeting your new boyfriend," Mia purrs, placing one manicured hand on Tom's other elbow. "He's so cute."

I can't help possessively pulling Tom closer to me. The string of handsome European men in said social media posts has given me to understand nothing good comes of my heartbreaker cousin finding you cute. "Were you being nice?" I ask.

Mia eyes me innocently. "As ever."

"It's wonderful to meet more of your family, babe," Tom interjects into our subtle sparring. He's undaunted. I'm impressed.

What's more, I won't pretend I don't enjoy the low velvet of his voice when he says *babe*. I'm pretty proud of my choice of alibi. "May I borrow Thomas for a moment?" I inquire politely, heaping enough heat onto *borrow* for my insinuation to be unmistakable. They'll like the feeling of intuiting my intentions. People retain information more when they think they've figured it out themselves.

"Of course," Mia says. "I wouldn't dream of stealing him. Just remember to bring him to meet Grandmother before it's serious." Her smile shines like diamonds showing their sharp edges.

"That would be so fun," I say, matching her effervescence as if we're forgers etching out competing renderings of family friendliness. "Even with the long flight."

I revel in silent victory when Mia says nothing in reply.

I steer Tom up to the deck in the sunlight, picking up our pace when we're out of their eyeline. I lean in close. "Stay away from the Swiss," I instruct him urgently.

I fear my words have not set in sufficiently when my counterpart glances over his shoulder, his eyes admiring. "Your cousin is hot," he informs me. "And terrifying. Maybe hot *because* she's terrifying."

"Don't even think it, Tom. If you blow our cover by hooking up with my cousin, I will pin this whole job on you," I promise him.

"You know," he replies, "I don't respond well to restriction."

I pause, eyeing him. He holds my gaze. I heard the edge in his words, the reminder he enjoys playing dangerously. He *doesn't* respond well to restriction. He knows what I know—in fact, I have his renegade spark to thank for his being here today.

It's enough to compel me to change my strategy. I sweeten my voice. "Do it for me, then?" I urge him.

He probably knows I'm putting on indulgence, acting a little. He probably likes it. When he smiles faintly, I know he's satisfied with my redirection. "Is it time for the next phase?" he asks.

Exactly on cue, I hear singing. The opening notes of "Over the

Rainbow" in lovely male a cappella rise up over the lawn. People head in the direction of the music, the guests moving in one current while I continue with Tom the other way. The scent of probably hundreds of different perfumes, combining with the ivory petals of the roses, surrounds us.

I spin, smirking at him as we reach the house entrance near the bar. "It is," I confirm.

Tom reaches for me, and I let out a loud shriek.

The exclamation doesn't surprise him. It's one of the moments I laid out for him in the structured "run of show" I described during our private meetings in recent weeks. While much of his performance would, I emphasized, require improvisation, we would have to hit certain key moments for necessary effect.

He smiles while I put on scandalized delight. "Oh my *god*, Thomas," I say as if he's suggested something indecent. "*Shhh.*"

It works perfectly. We've drawn the eyes of everyone in our vicinity.

With their scrutinizing stares on us, I push open the door behind me and pull Tom into the house. As soon as it shuts, we drop the facade.

Knowing everyone outside is exchanging gossiping whispers about Dash's daughter hooking up in the middle of the wedding leaves me grimly gratified. I wish it weren't easy for them to jump to the conclusion I've engineered—wish every one of my dad's friends didn't project onto me the ready-made stereotype of the careless, obnoxious *girl*.

Even so, I'm using every resource I have. It's like the saying. When life gives you lemons, make millions of dollars illegally.

With Tom, I walk quickly and silently through the house. The hallways have emptied out, leaving them looking like they did when I lived here. Like they do when I visit. It's the fortifying reminder I need of why I've planned what I'm doing now. My dad's unforgettable domineering gaze glares from every mirror. The silence rings with the echo of his quiet cruelty. *Olivia, you'll ruin everything. Do you want to ruin everything?*

I feel my heart pounding. Flirting in front of strangers is easy. What's next is not.

I find McCoy waiting outside my dad's den. The adrenaline kicking into my system is fierce, uncompromising. I have to match its strength, wrestle it into my service. Especially when I know we've reached the point of no return.

When this door opens, I'll be a criminal.

FIFTEEN

I NOD. WORDLESSLY, MCCOY OPENS THE DOOR.

We step inside. The den is empty, as expected.

In fact, my dad's recreation room is comically in opposition to our designs. If I'm making myself into the stereotype of the ditzy daughter, this room casts my father in the role of the frivolous man-child effortlessly.

Wall-mounted screens host video game systems vintage and modern. The pool table in the center of the room pairs marvelously with the bench press against the wall, its presence inexplicable given the extensive gym elsewhere in the house. Leather couches complete the tasteless execution of male-pattern indulgence.

When the door is closed, I look to McCoy. "Is she here?"

"She's...detained," he says stiffly.

I raise my eyebrows in light incredulity. "Detained? Or kidnapped?" I press him. I can't permit caginess or errors of omission. Not here, not now. *Detained* in the restroom, puking because she's downed copious quantities of champagne? *Detained* hitting on cousin Finn or some damn thing?

Or detained because McCoy *kidnapped* her, as I very precisely ordered?

The question isn't low stakes. In fact, it's exactly the opposite.

Kidnapping Amanda Webber is *the* most important part of The Plan.

I can't ransom the combination to the safe from Mitchum Webber without the leverage of his daughter. It's the whole reason McCoy was recruited. He could pose as security and lead Amanda into the house under the guise of an anonymous threat to her without having to resort to measures that might traumatize her or draw attention. Simple.

"I'm really uncomfortable with that language," McCoy says, looking fretful.

I frown. "What language? The *K* word? That's literally what this is. You're the one who instilled in me the importance of words, *Pawn*. Now," I say as if I'm McCoy himself, lecturing freshmen who didn't do their reading, "did you or did you not kidnap Amanda Webber?"

He swallows. "I did," he confirms miserably. "She's downstairs in the theater. She found a Nintendo Switch on the couch in here and took it down with her. I gave her water and a tray of hors d'oeuvres, the lobster mac and cheese puffs, so I don't think she's distressed. She doesn't even know she's been detained."

I level him a look.

"Kidnapped!" he corrects. "She doesn't know she's been kidnapped."

Tom giggles behind me. I can't blame him. I would laugh at our despondent kidnapper, too, if I weren't trying to exhibit impressive leadership.

"Good," I say.

One could potentially wonder if I feel guilty for kidnapping Amanda.

I do not.

She's in the home theater with a Switch and lobster puffs, missing the Nassoons' overlong set list. From where I'm standing, she's coming out of today a winner. In fact, from the inception of today's kidnapping component, I was rigid in my resolve that no harm or fear would come to Amanda Webber. I'm vengeful, not vicious. I'm crossing off people who've crossed me. Amanda Webber isn't one of them.

If anything, I feel remorse for Mr. McCoy's discomfort. I'll simply encourage him to unwind in a lavish wellness resort with the fortune he'll make today.

I glance to the stairs leading down into the theater, chosen specifically for its private entrance. There's only one way in and out of the theater, and it's through the den. It allows Amanda to remain contained while giving us a private space nearby to make the ransom call without her overhearing—or, more important, even seeing me. Once we have the combination to the safe, McCoy will open the door at the bottom of this stairwell and tell Amanda the threat has been cleared and she's free to return to the party.

McCoy, however, is clearly not reassured by the harmlessness of his job. He collapses onto the leather couch. "I can't believe I'm doing this," he says to himself. "I'm an educator. Not a...kidnapper." He still struggles to get the word out.

"Are you actually, like, employed as an educator, though?" Tom asks. He walks around the room, looking at my dad's collection of framed nineties movie posters, morally unbothered by our hostage. As he should be.

McCoy looks up. "I have some job leads. But if I get caught as a *kidnapper*, I'll never even get another teaching interview again."

"McCoy, focus," I demand, dropping the code name in the interest of reaching him. He looks about one shallow breath away from a panic attack. "Remember why we're here. What are we doing?"

McCoy nods, struggling to center himself.

"Revenge," he says.

I notice Tom frown in confusion I don't have time to dispel. When I first met with Peter McCoy, I had in mind the motive I would play, chosen like a card from the shitty hand I was dealt. *Luxury? Desperation?* No. Not with McCoy.

Strictly speaking, Mr. McCoy was fired from Berkshire Prep for… a parent complaint. Less delicately, my dad had him fired. McCoy gave me a B and refused to change the grade after Dash called to complain.

I heard the whole story from McCoy when news hit the school he was being "removed." I went to his classroom the first passing period I could, heart in my throat, intuiting my father was responsible. McCoy explained everything. How he told my father my B in English was something to be proud of, not something to call to complain about, and how the fact that he was trying to change my grade would hurt my self-esteem far more than achieving a grade he deemed unsuitable. "You earned that B. I was proud of that B," McCoy said to me. "I still am."

I can't help smiling a little even now, remembering it. Mr. McCoy was my favorite teacher.

When I met him in the Starbucks in his neighborhood in The Plan's early development, I figured I would need to feel him out, assess the strength of his hatred of my father, and proceed with patience into the idea of revenge.

I swiftly realized I would not have to. McCoy was, in his words when we first met, having an existential crisis.

He looked it, haggard and haunted. My father was far from the first parent who'd wrenched McCoy's educational goals with their own narcissism and self-interest, he shared with me. And with every changed grade, every censored lesson plan, McCoy lost his faith in his work, his direction. He'd struggled for years, he admitted, feeling his life's purpose eviscerated by the whims of vapid manipulators like my father.

He wanted revenge. Just not only against Dash Owens.

He has a radical vigor for the idea of shaking a society like the high-class, low-morals one he encountered in his previous employment. If stealing from my father was one strike against Dash's wealthy world, Peter McCoy was in.

"Revenge," I repeat.

"Don't think of it like kidnapping," Tom chimes in. "Think of it like unauthorized detention."

McCoy stands. "You're right." He squares his shoulders with conviction I remember from his powerful *Catcher in the Rye* lecture. It's kind of great, watching his renewed zeal. "Let's get this *goddamn* revenge going."

I grin, and not only out of the unexpected delight of hearing him swear. In fact, McCoy's willingness to join me meant more than getting who I needed for the kidnapping. When I explained the full story, the situation my mom and I were in, I'd noticed the same righteous fury fill his eyes.

It had felt unexpectedly like the validation I needed in days where I could find so little. What happened to me *was* awful. I *deserved* the rage I felt.

With McCoy reinvigorated, I face Tom. "Knight," I say, nodding to the door. "Find Mitchum. Get him alone. Ask about internships at his firm."

Tom receives my request with instant focus. "New character," he replies. In the next moments, the change I watch come over him is almost eerie in its subtlety. He looks to the floor, then back up, his demeanor altered in exact incremental deviations. "Thomas Pham, high school senior and future lawyer," he introduces himself.

He walks up to McCoy, his gait gliding and eager, and holds out his hand.

"Thomas. It's a pleasure to meet you," Tom says, his voice changed into overachiever schmooze. "My hobbies include LinkedIn and acting like I understand the stock market. Ask me about my thoughts on crypto."

"Perfect," I confirm.

"You remind me of everyone I had to write college recommendation letters for," McCoy concurs. "You'd fit right in at Yale."

"Ha," Tom says, dropping into his own register. "God no."

"On your way," I remind him. "Keep Mitchum talking until the drop. Alone," I emphasize. "I'll give Rook the signal to look for you."

I pull out my phone and text Deonte three emojis in three separate texts. The chef, the champagne glasses, and the phone. He doesn't need to read them. Communicating The Plan doesn't hinge on iMessage pictography. The signal is in the number of messages so crew members don't need to get their phones out. Three vibrations for Phase Three.

Of course, I can't help having fun with my choice of emojis. I feel like I'm playing modernized Clue. *The chef. At the champagne welcome. With the iPhone.* Messages sent, I return my phone to my clutch.

Or I'm about to. Instead, it rings.

Not out loud, of course—no ringers was rule number one. I feel the phone's repeated vibrations in my hand, worry shooting into me. Rule number two was no calling unless immediately necessary.

Queen is displayed on the caller ID. It's Cass. "What?" I say into the phone, perfunctory.

She doesn't hesitate. "Security problem," she informs me.

"Okay." My palms start to sweat.

"On the comms I'm hearing them discuss positioning during the ceremony. They're allocating fewer guys outside, not wanting them in photos—Maureen's demands, I'm guessing—and more inside the house. For... heightened security of the house's valuables," Cass explains. "They're forming a, quote-unquote, walking perimeter around your father's study."

I say nothing, contemplating. Not surprised, exactly—while I did not anticipate precisely the concern she's raised, Cass's role was designed to incorporate moments exactly like this. Until she is needed to distribute the money from Dash's account, her job is ongoing surveillance of wedding security, with her proximity in the van important for accessing Millennium's localized network. I knew security surprises exactly like this one would require improvisation.

Nonetheless, the problem she's presented is inconvenient. My entrance into the study—and the safe—during the ceremony is a key step in The Plan. "Okay. Okay," I say. *Facts first*, I decide. "When? Have the guards gone inside yet?"

In the den, McCoy has evidently heard the low hum of nervousness in my voice. While Tom watches me neutrally, our kidnapper has started to fidget. "What's going on? It's—um, Queen, right?"

"Not yet," Cass starts to say in my ear. "They're—"

"Oh, shit. *Shit*." McCoy has once more started panicking, jumping to conclusions. He slicks his hair fervently, looking close to puking. "Please," he implores me. "Just tell me how bad it is."

"Wait," I interrupt Cass, unable to have overlapping conversations. "Pawn, it's going to be fine—"

"Can you put her on speaker?" McCoy pleads.

I'm tired of this impromptu game of telephone. "Queen," I say, taking pity on poor McCoy. "I'm putting you on speaker."

I hit the icon, and her sharp voice fills the room. "They're not inside yet," she says. "I see guards posted at the entrance...one in the restroom...and the rest outside for the welcome toasts."

McCoy exhales, realizing we have not, in fact, gotten caught.

"Okay," I repeat. "I'll...message you. I'll figure it out. Later." Every minute right now counts. This is a post-kidnapping problem. "I just need a new way into the study," I summarize.

"Yes," Cass confirms. "And when you get the paper codes out of the safe, you'll have to move fast. Like, *fast*-fast."

"Of course," I reply. "And thanks."

Cass hangs up.

Walking perimeter. Heightened security. I shake off the words, having meant what I said. The champagne toasts are winding down, and the upcoming phase is critical. I rehearse the next steps in my head, knowing they'll require unique precision.

It doesn't daunt me, exactly. I feel...I wouldn't know how to explain it. My heart is pounding in the best way, my veins rushing with the visceral thrill of the cogs moving in the invisible machine I've designed. While its mechanics came from me, they're operating outside me now, in the capable synchrony of my conspirators. Even the hiccup Cass has presented just feels like the next challenge to clear on our way to victory. I feel like I'm finding the new me.

Tom walks to the door. As he reaches for the handle—

The door opens from the outside.

The moment rushes into horrible focus. It's like watching something falling to the ground, something fragile. Something precious. My fine-china plans in midair, headed for the unforgiving marble of the foyer.

With the widest smile on his face, Kevin Webber enters our kidnapping control center.

"Hey, guys, is this where the real party is happening?" he asks as if he really hopes it is. He looks around the room. "What are we doing?"

I feel everything crash to a halt.

SIXTEEN

IN A MANNER OF SPEAKING, AN UNHELPFUL VOICE IN MY HEAD SAYS, *yes, this is exactly where the real party is. If, of course, you consider the "real party" gently holding your sister for ransom without her knowledge.*

I shut down said voice. I shut down my panic next.

Damage-control mode kicks on instantly. My mind promptly spits the list of what needs to happen. *Get Kevin out of here. Give McCoy privacy to make the ransom call. Waste no time.*

Cocking my hip, I slide into my wedding demeanor easily. "My dad isn't here, if you're looking to keep kissing up to him," I inform Kevin with unforced irritation.

Kevin shakes his head. "No, I know he's singing with his college group," he pronounces, continuing with hints of wonder and envy. "He has a very resonant voice."

The reminder of Dash's whereabouts is unwelcome, forcing me to remember the competing clocks I'm chasing. Champagne won't continue forever. I narrow my eyes. "Then what are you doing here?"

Kevin walks past us, admiring the den. *Predictable.* "I saw all the cool people were gone and knew there was a hotter party to be at," he explains, no hint of irony in his voice.

I gaze around the room. The *GoldenEye* poster next to *The Matrix* one, the dark screens on the walls. The harsh LED lights, no music. No one in here except me, Tom, and a random security guard. This is, in no way, the hotter party.

Kevin's expectant enthusiasm is undimmed, though. He makes no effort to hide how much he wants to be considered cool. I'd kind of respect his sincerity if it weren't so obnoxious. It's not unlike the room itself, I guess. While my dad's design is cringeworthy, it's *him*, not the genteel lord of Rhode Island every other room of the house pretends he is. I'm not sure which is worse.

He never wanted me down here. He didn't outright say so, which was uncommon reserve on his part. Even so, I just knew. I knew from the suspicious irritation he'd glance my way whenever I entered needing school forms signed or playdate permission. How young can you start feeling like an inconvenience without permanent psychological damage?

It makes our location exceptionally gratifying. While I was going to enjoy hitting him where it hurts no matter what, I'm really going to enjoy doing it from his moneyed man cave.

Unless Kevin Webber screws everything up.

Tom regards the intruder with disdainful curiosity. He says nothing, the silence of one with nothing nice to say.

It's generous, in a way. Tom is the one person in my crew who's withstood even more of Kevin Webber than I have. The fact that he's *only* glaring now, looking like Mr. Darcy styled for the GQ Men of the Year party, is commendable.

"Oh, hell yeah. Dash has a sick setup," Kevin says, evidently seeing with different eyes the same details I was just evaluating. He lies down on the bench press. "Want to spot me, bro?" he says to McCoy.

Nerves clench in my chest when he glances our security impersonator's way, then release. Kevin doesn't recognize the former Berkshire teacher. Why he isn't wondering what wedding security is doing
here is a mystery to me. Nevertheless, I'm grateful for his oversight.

"You...want to work out right now?" Tom asks. He's returned to
the droll demeanor of my date.

"Could be cool," Kevin replies. He sits up hastily. "Or whatever.
Maybe not. What were you guys doing?"

"Just showing security around the main floor," I say, improvising
fast. "It's still my house, you know. People shouldn't be wandering
into private rooms."

Kevin nods, not understanding I mean him.

"Well, we're heading back to the wedding now," I say pointedly.

My ushering gets me nowhere. Kevin rises from the bench press
and proceeds directly to the shelf of video games. "Come on," he goads
us cheerfully. "Let's do something fun! Cool-people-only side party!"

I watch him miserably, realizing the immense power of this place
over a person like Kevin. If only it weren't the one room in the house
with the perfect logistics for our kidnapping. Why couldn't Maureen
have converted it into her own personal massage room or something?
She probably will in, like, six weeks.

I control my frustration. "I'm not partying with you," I say firmly.

Kevin ignores me. "You haven't seen my sister, have you?"

In the corner of my vision, I catch Tom and Mr. McCoy exchange
a very incriminating look. I would reprimand them for the indiscretion if I could. "No," I reply, "I haven't."

Managing to withdraw himself from his examination of my dad's
PlayStation library, Kevin rounds inquisitively on McCoy.

"Funny," he says. "I saw you leading her inside."

Something shifts in the room. I remember when I was young, on the infrequent occasions my dad was left in charge of supervising me, I would end up down here. In hopes of distracting me while he played video games, he showed me how to make houses of cards. Young Olivia would stack geometric structures of queens and kings, clubs and hearts, precariously positioning the addition of each new card while *Halo* chattered away nearby.

If I wanted to find inspiration for my plans today in formative memories of my childhood, houses of cards would probably make the list. I remember the peril of each new card placed, of watching the paper pyramid in suspense.

It's how I feel now. Unsure whether everything is about to collapse.

Kevin waits. His expression is expectant. Not the expectation I'm used to on Kevin Webber, either—the zealous hope for someone to like him or agree with him or, say, help him lift weights in the middle of my dad's wedding. No, he's...evaluating us.

"I was showing her to the bathroom," McCoy says. While his gruffness is not quite convincing, I credit him for the logical explanation.

"Nah." Kevin shakes his head, resuming his perusal of the video game shelf. He looks only half interested, as if none of the contents are the game he wants to play. "She knows where the bathrooms are. We've come over for New Year's parties and stuff."

I decide to step in, worry weighing in the pit of my stomach. My house of cards is wobbling. "Kevin, let's go back to the bar. I'm sure we'll find Amanda there," I say, my voice sweet like it usually isn't. *Kevin is suggestible*, I reassure myself. *He's a joiner.* He'll want to do what I'm proposing.

Instead, he grins, and I realize this is much worse than I thought.

Kevin Webber is onto us. He knows I'm up to something. While I feel certain he doesn't know what, he suspects enough to use his suspicion as leverage.

I set my mind racing, combing overheard conversations of my dad and Mitchum, the hostage-negotiator show I got very into last year, and other heist research. *Leverage for what?* If I were in his position, I might extract information, money, or other advantages. I'm not him, however. Way, *way* not him. What does *Kevin Webber* want?

The realization hits me with instant certainty.

He's using what he knows to . . . *make us party with him.*

Wow. He's the worst.

The leading flicker in Kevin's eyes says he knows we're on the same page. "Dash has to have a stash nearby," he offers cheerfully. "Ha. 'Dash's stash.' You guys want to smoke?" When nobody responds, Kevin wanders closer to the stairs. "His private theater is downstairs, right? We could get high and watch *Kung Fu Panda.*"

In one part of my mind, I'm hoping Kevin never utters the phrase "Dash's Stash" in the company of my father, who would one hundred percent certainly start franchising cannabis dispensaries under this name. The rest of my concentration is focused on how close Kevin is coming to where we've hidden his sister. *Houses of cards. Ready to fall.* While I stand silent, recalculating, Tom interjects. "I don't smoke."

Kevin shrugs. "You could just watch the movie."

Tom eyes him dismissively. "Not if I don't have to."

Unfazed, Kevin nods as if he understands perfectly. "Not a fan of cinema's greatest franchise," he comments. "Well, what do you want to watch?"

"Nothing," Tom replies, clearly trying to end Kevin's cool-people-only party efforts quickly. To get us out of here.

"Everything's on streaming," Kevin presses. "What kind of movies do you like?"

"None."

Kevin glances up. His gaze is probing. I have the uncomfortable feeling he has improbably changed my crew from kidnappers into hostages. "Huh?" he asks Tom.

"I don't...like movies," Tom says, his performance finally flickering. Only my fake wedding date's dramatic panache renders the line half convincing. He continues, recovering his composure. "I'm incredibly boring. You don't want to party with me."

The look Kevin gives Tom startles me. He's patient, even confident, in permitting the pause to stretch. I don't know what's worse, or more surprising—the fact that Kevin Webber knows how to use leverage or the fact that he's employing it to force people he's not friends with to get high and watch *Kung Fu Panda* with him.

Finally, Kevin faces me instead.

"*He's* your new boyfriend? I don't see it," he says.

I decide I've had enough. Outside, with the champagne welcome winding down, I'm certain the Nassoons have knocked out "Diamonds on the Soles of her Shoes" and "Love Never Felt So Good." The clock is ticking. Furthermore, every minute we delay, we run the risk of Amanda getting impatient and wandering upstairs. I need to retake control.

"Kevin, stop acting like we're friends. You don't know me. We're going back to the wedding now," I order him. Keeping my voice unwavering feels like wrestling metal.

I grab Tom's arm and pull him with me to the door.

Kevin doesn't follow.

"The theater is down here. Right?" His emphasis on the final word has intentional edges. He's pushing us.

I whirl, finding him at the top of the stairs leading down to where we're holding Amanda captive. Sweat springs into my fingertips. I clench my grip on Tom. In front of my eyes flashes every night I needed to study for calc, or physically ached to watch *Downton Abbey* with my mom while she dozed, and instead holed up in my room meticulously planning this day.

It's McCoy who steps in. He grabs Kevin's elbow. "I'm going to have to ask you to return to the event. No one is allowed in Mr. Owens's private rooms," he reprimands Kevin.

Relief rushing over me, I mentally applaud McCoy for his ingenuity. He's fast on his feet. It shouldn't surprise me, I guess. I'm sure teaching high school students is a battle and a performance every day. With our counterfeit guard positioned in front of Kevin, I feel as if I can finally exhale.

Until Kevin gently yet firmly removes his arm from McCoy's grasp.

It's like the first card falling. On rare occasions, the structure will support the displacement.

On most others, collapse is imminent.

Kevin regards McCoy. Then he turns back to meet my eyes.

"You know, everyone thinks I'm stupid because I'm annoying," he says calmly. "I'm actually *just* annoying."

Every card, fluttering down instantly into my design's destruction.

Without hesitating, Kevin pushes past McCoy and descends the stairs.

SEVENTEEN

WHAT'S UP, AMANDA?"

Kevin's question echoes up the stairwell. I close my eyes, furiously searching my mind for fixes. My heart leaps into my mouth. McCoy has followed in pursuit of Kevin down the stairs, leaving only me and Tom. I can practically hear phantom a cappella ringing in my ears, reminding me of impending failure.

I pull Tom close. "Go outside. Get in position," I whisper, nearly frantic. "Wait for my signal. This is going to be fast and sloppy."

Exactly how I wanted my heist résumé to read.

"Okay, but how—" Tom starts.

I cut him off. "I'll figure it out."

With no one to play to, he drops his performance entirely. I doubt even his acting prowess could quite cover the dread I find in his eyes. While I did not need another reminder of how mine is not the only fate depending on this job, I have one in his ashen demeanor. I respect how, unlike others of us, Tom's motivation for joining my crew exists solely in shrewd impulsivity and lust for finery. But now that means he's realizing he's wagered everything for nothing except his own fearsome pride.

He heads out the door, glancing warily over his shoulder.

I don't hesitate to descend the steps into the theater. I honestly have no idea what I'll find.

McCoy waits in the doorway, his expression drawn with panic. I charge in and immediately notice Kevin reclined on the couch. Amanda, standing up as if she's stretching her legs, looks...kind of bored.

She shoots McCoy a glance. "Can I go now? Is the threat gone?" she asks. Her voice gives no indication she knows the danger is fabricated. She just doesn't care.

"No, you can't," McCoy musters.

Kevin's eyebrows rise. "Threat?" he repeats. He looks to me, lightly indignant. "Olivia, were you threatening my sister?"

I pause. "Of course not," I say when nothing else comes.

"Great," Kevin replies, laying his relief on heavily. "Amanda, you can go now."

His sister eyes him disinterestedly. "You're being weird," she states.

"Or you can stay," he offers. "Want to smoke with us? And watch *Kung Fu Panda*?"

Amanda's whole face scrunches up in disgust. "Ew. No."

She walks out. As she passes me, I consider grabbing her. Okay, *consider* may understate the reality. I feel my fingers itching, my mind roaring to reassert order. Instead, I restrain myself. I'm not a violent person—especially not in the presence of witnesses—and I won't upend my resolve not to put Amanda in my vendetta's line of fire.

Kevin doesn't move from his position on the couch. I think fast. Every minute in here, I find myself fending off discomfort I can't quite place, until I realize—it's because I haven't set foot in this room since I moved out. With my visits relatively restrained to dinners, I haven't had reason.

The underground theater is not exactly the local IMAX, with rows upon rows of recliners in the enormous dark. Nevertheless, it's nice. The low couches provide comfortable seating for fifteen-ish people, more if you want to get cozy. The projector mounted to the ceiling is state of the art. The screen occupies one entire wall.

I don't have many fond memories of the room. Finding my dad watching Comedy Central in here nearly every night when my mom would have me fetch him for dinner. Movie nights with classmates, where the pretense of watching whatever cult classic we decided on would devolve into everyone either hooking up or distracted on their phones.

Even so, the pull of the past lingers, reminiscences like whispers past closed doors. I decide I can harness them. Hold them hostage. Use the reminder of how wholly this place was ripped out of my life, consigned to memory. I can sharpen myself with the loss.

I press the anger in deep. I push myself.

Kevin. Inspiration strikes with wonderful immediacy. He's Mitchum's kid, too, and we have him alone in the very room where we were just holding our intended hostage. He wants to party with me? Perfect. I'll watch the first fifteen minutes of whatever he wants while McCoy places the ransom call. Kevin won't even know we've "kidnapped" him. The problem is the solution.

"You know what?" I say, recasting my demeanor. The daughter showing off her expensive home. I pull on the role with ease. "All right. You want to watch a movie? Why not?"

I walk forward, looking for the remote. Kevin doesn't move, his gaze following me into the low-lit room. Then he crosses his legs in relaxed satisfaction.

"Let's talk business, Owens," he says.

I feel my eyebrows rise. Reading Kevin's expression, I hope for wavering weakness or feigned certainty—or even self-consciousness over the drama of his opener.

I find none. Kevin Webber watches me like the high school Godfather. *You come to me on the day of* your father's *wedding!*

It keeps my gaze on Kevin, unflinching. I wait, refusing to prompt him.

"You had my sister down here. Why?" he asks. Without waiting for me to answer, he goes on. "You wanted something from her."

I shrug one shoulder. "Not from her," I say.

Kevin nods, evaluating the information. "I eavesdropped on your conversation," he continues lightly. "Or some of it. Paper codes in a safe...," he repeats.

I say nothing, furious. I put Cass *on speakerphone*, I realize, and I did it out of concern for McCoy, who was losing his shit. In the surprise of Kevin's entry, I hadn't even contemplated what he might have heard. It's damning proof of what compassion gets me.

Kevin's eyes light up. He flings his arms up, forming a headrest with interlocked fingers. "Of course!" he replies. "My sister goes missing in a flimsy *security risk*, and meanwhile all of you are discussing getting into a safe," he recites the pieces. "You were going to ransom something from my dad," he concludes.

I stare. I neither confirm nor deny. I'm a statue in fake eyelashes.

"I want in," Kevin says.

"No," I reply immediately.

Biggest possible no *in the entire universe*, I don't say, in the interest of poise. I've never uttered a *no* I've felt this deeply.

Kevin pouts. "Come on, I'm a way better kidnap-ee than Amanda!"

McCoy interjects from the doorway. "Hold on." He walks into the room, flanking me. "Are you *volunteering* to be kidnapped?"

"Is it technically kidnapping if I consent?" Kevin counters. He's gone from Godfather to Socrates in fifteen seconds flat, looking as if he very much enjoys the rhetorical deftness of his query.

"I mean, yes," McCoy replies, frowning. "You're a minor."

"Okay, well, whatever," Kevin says, undeterred. "I'm volunteering. Just give me a cut of whatever you're extorting my father for. I'll earn it, I promise. Amanda wouldn't have put on a show. She's unfazed by this shit. Whereas I'm happy to act very scared," he offers proudly. "I can pretend you're breaking my fingers or pulling out my teeth."

"God no," I say.

He shrugs. "I'm very convincing. I watch lots of movies."

I hit him with my harshest glare. I'm remembering he plays goalie in lacrosse, which is weirdly perfect. The position entails waiting, waiting, waiting, and more waiting, until one important moment. Right now, Kevin Webber understands his moment has come.

"Absolutely not," I say slowly.

He looks around expansively, pausing, I'm guessing, for emphasis. "I'm sorry, but do you have a choice?" he asks. He's matching my pace on purpose. "Your preferred hostage is probably doing shots at the bar by now." His expression changes. While his cheerful features haven't reached pleading, they're close. "I'm an excellent businessman. I'll negotiate for you."

While I'm not very convinced of his negotiating prowess, I hate how reasonable the rest of his point is. I'm weighing my response when my phone vibrates.

I need to check the message. New calculations scribble themselves on the crowded walls of my mind. Kevin heard me talking to Cass. He knows no one in this room has a voice that matches Cass's, which means he already knows I have a phone.

I pull it out of my bag. Predictably, Kevin's eyes round, smug. I ignore him for the moment, reading the screen swiftly.

Queen

What's going on? The Nassoons are on their final song.

I grimace despite my gratitude for Cass's update. Of course, she hacked the director's email and found the set list.

I don't have forever to make this decision. Either I give up everything or I work with Kevin.

Putting my hand on my hip, I pin him with the kind of look I usually reserve for the possums I've caught in our yard, rooting around in the garbage for the remains of discarded dinners.

"You are *not* a part of this," I start firmly. "However, if you agree to be a hostage, I will give you five thousand dollars."

The offer is ridiculously low given the amount we're planning on stealing. Especially to someone like Kevin, it'll mean next to nothing. I'm familiar enough with Berkshire kids' recreational weekends to know five thousand dollars won't get you very far. When you're hopping over to Italy or Ibiza on impromptu friend-cations every long weekend or visiting the Louis Vuitton store for retail therapy, five thousand is *nothing*. It's a starting place, one I'm willing to negotiate.

"I'm in," Kevin says instantly.

I close my mouth. Recovering, I smile.

Kevin Webber leans forward on the couch, rubbing his hands together with excitement. The world's happiest hostage. It really isn't helping my misgivings about cutting him in.

Kevin Webber, I remind myself, *who just pointed out I have no options.* Kevin Webber, who upset my precise schedule like chucking a grenade into the heirloom grandfather clock in the foyer upstairs. Kevin, who is the only cog I can fit into The Plan's faltering machinery.

Who is, unfortunately, right where I wish I didn't need him.

I swipe open my phone, where I fire off the text the thread is waiting for.

King

Go

EIGHTEEN

I MOVE TO THE WINDOW. THE ROOM IS HALF UNDERGROUND, THE rectangular panes level with the lawn. The grass is perfectly peridot in the daylight.

It's funny—despite the subterranean situation, it doesn't feel claustrophobic or constrained. Instead, it's protected. The vantage point I need. My fortress of operations, with cocktail tables laid out in front of me like chessboard squares. I have optimal surveillance of the guests on the lawn, their cheerful cliques in the pleasant sun forming in the corridors of my favorite maze. I realize I'm practically writing real estate listings in my head. *Expansive grounds. Perfect for polo, parties, and plotting.*

From my viewpoint, I wait for Phase Three.

"You look kind of familiar," Kevin says behind me.

"We've never met," McCoy replies.

I glance over my shoulder, finding Kevin eyeing McCoy. "Do a lot of kidnappings?" he asks pleasantly.

McCoy swallows. I notice sweat starting to sheen his forehead.

"Kevin, leave him alone," I say, scared McCoy is going to lose his nerve.

I turn back to the window. In my view is Mitchum Webber, easy to locate from his unsmiling solitude. Dude is practically wearing a sign saying *least fun person here*. Without his phone, without clients to email or news to half read, he looks uneasy, as if he's imagining places he wishes he were instead of here, sipping four-hundred-dollar champagne in the middle of Rhode Island's loveliest wedding.

Tom approaches Mitchum and holds out his hand as the final song is ending and people start to applaud. His demeanor is exactly right, winningly charming and high-school-valedictorian confident, with enough hints of humility for meeting one's hopeful career prospects.

They shake. With Tom's next words, Mitchum chuckles and claps my crew member on the shoulder. Knight has loosened up our mark's miserable demeanor effortlessly.

I feel like fist pumping. Obviously, I don't with Kevin and McCoy right here. I keep my eyes on the lawn, on the game I'm playing with the moves of others. Watching Tom is witnessing the clean magic of someone doing exactly what they're supposed to.

"What are we watching?" Kevin whispers, coming up next to me to look out the window.

I dart him a glare.

"In order to make a ransom call, Mitchum needs a phone," I say, knowing he's going to want commentary on every step. I'm stuck with him now. "Watch."

Okay, maybe I can't help showing off. Maybe I don't hate having a spectator. The point of a successful heist is for the audience not to realize what they're seeing. But with Kevin, I can flex a little.

In fact, I decide, maybe I *should*. Feeling included is Kevin Webber's kryptonite. If he considers himself "in on the scheme," he'll cooperate and will be less inclined to give us up later.

When Kevin leans forward, peering out the window, I leave him room. In front of us, my choreography unfolds.

Tom leads Mitchum to the table farthest from the crowd dispersing from the performance. It's littered with half-empty glasses. *Half-full*, Kevin would probably say. Tom is unhurried, his loping stride giving away none of his mission's imperative. While they chat, a server comes to pick up the glasses.

Only it's not a server. It's Deonte.

He sets his tray down to collect the glassware. He's expressionless, his efficient cleanup designed to be ignored. Of course, Mitchum ignores him. It was, I realized early in my planning phases, one of the upsides of the day's setting. The wedding came with ranks of people no one would remember—servers, chefs, security guards—into which I could insert my conspirators without notice.

When Deonte lifts his tray back up, he leaves behind the cloth napkin he placed on the table, using the tray for cover. The napkin looks forgotten, as if it was there when "the server" first came over, but it wasn't. Now it is. Right in front of Mitchum.

"The waiter," Kevin exhales excitedly. "Is he in on it?"

With stiff professionality, I nod. "Rook has made the drop," I confirm.

"Shit, you have code names? What's yours?" Kevin asks.

"King."

Kevin rubs his mouth in awe. "That's so dope." His eyes going round, he whips his gaze from the window to me. "Can I have one?"

"No."

While he deflates, I pay him no regard. Instead, I keep watching out the window. Tom laughs, shoving his hands in his pockets with rakish confidence.... The control freak in me wishes I could hear them. The silent cinema of Knight's charade past the heavy glass pane of the private theater is getting on my nerves.

Concluding the conversation, Tom hands Mitchum a card pulled neatly from his jacket pocket. It's a nice touch, not one I knew about.

"Knight is retreating," I say. "Pawn, are you ready?"

When I face McCoy, though, he looks as if he might be sick.

He starts pacing in small circles, muttering to himself. "Just remember, they're terrible people. Terrible. They deserve a lot worse," he counsels himself with urgency leaning into fervor. "Really nasty people."

He collapses onto the couch in dismay, evidently having not inspired himself.

I watch him with rising concern. Honestly, I'm starting to wonder if McCoy can even pull off the call. The guy is *nervous*. I figured years of lecturing ninth graders would lend itself to defenses against stage fright, even when the stage is his former student's opulent home and the monologue is a ransom demand.

Put gently, I may have misjudged him.

It's enough for my mind to start constructing ramshackle contingency plans. The next step needs to happen *now*, which means I'm out of opportunities to cut in Pawn's replacement. I guess I could—

"Oh yeah, my dad is awful! You really shouldn't feel bad," Kevin interjects reassuringly. "Just last week, he had a family evicted from one of his properties because their labradoodle was ten pounds over his dog size limit."

McCoy looks up. His eyes brighten as if someone's just requested his opinions on eighteenth-century poetry. I glance to Kevin, grateful for the unexpected help.

"What else?" McCoy asks.

"Um." Kevin presses his hands together, looking like he's scouring his memory for his father's misdeeds. While he obviously wasn't expecting to play such a pivotal role in his own kidnapping, the new straightness of his shoulders says the job exhilarates him. He snaps his fingers, seizing on something. "He made my sister change before the wedding because her first dress wasn't, quote-unquote, flattering."

"Asshole," I can't help saying.

"Perfect!" McCoy exclaims. He looks liable to hit Mitchum instead of calling him for ransom. Honestly, he's welcome to if it doesn't interrupt other plans. "One more," he prompts Kevin.

"He's never done pro bono legal work in his life!" Kevin says like he's shooting from the three-point line at the buzzer.

McCoy stands up, full of righteousness. "I'm doing this," he declares, staring out the window framing our field of combat, where the cocktail tables stand like soldiers.

Kevin exchanges a proud look with me. I don't bother to scowl in return. Kevin actually helped, and maybe *some* of his distasteful personality can be blamed on having a shitty dad.

McCoy pulls out his phone. He selects the contact I programmed into it last night.

It rings while everyone holds their breaths.

NINETEEN

OUTSIDE, MITCHUM LOOKS DOWN.

The phone we've dropped is on vibrate, inconspicuous. I watch him pause, making sense of the humming under the napkin. He lifts up the cloth carefully, eyeing what we've left.

Heart racing, I can practically feel the seconds pass, each one sliding past like drops of condensation on the champagne outside. *I need him to pick up the phone.*

Instead, my father's lawyer looks around. In the meantime, the phone stops ringing.

"Call again," I say.

McCoy does.

Mitchum looks down. I watch him double-check his memory, realizing what's happening here. Confirming the phone was *not* on the table when he got there with Tom nor left behind by Tom himself. Yet there it is.

The theater is getting hot, the unfortunate downside of our row of observation windows. The perfect wedding sunlight is streaming in, warming the room. The house is old enough that the retrofitted air-conditioning doesn't reach everywhere, including our semiunderground location. Watching Mitchum, I feel sweat forming on my neck, my forehead.

Once more, our mark lets the ringing lapse. I exhale in frustration. I counted on Mitchum Webber's curiosity and instincts for self-preservation to compel him to pick up the mystery call. Unfortunately, it seems he needs encouragement.

"Text it and say you have Kevin George Washington Webber," Kevin suggests.

"You're not serious," I say. "George Washington?"

He nods solemnly. "Information I would only share if my life were in danger. Or if I joined a sick gang of thieves."

I roll my eyes but catch myself smiling. Only a little. "Do it," I say to McCoy.

He sends the text. I watch the moment our planted phone receives the message, catching Mitchum's interest once more. His mouth flattens, his small features wrought with focus. Finally, he turns his back on the wedding to pick up the phone.

"Now," I order McCoy. The fresh hit of adrenaline in my veins is fantastic. "Nice work, George Washington," I concede to Kevin.

"Remember—the labradoodle, no pro bono," Kevin counsels our ransom caller.

McCoy calls. Mercifully, Mitchum doesn't hesitate. He answers, looking impatient, as if we were the ones making *him* wait.

"I want to speak to my son," he says without introduction or pleasantries. While the phone isn't on speaker, in the quiet room, I can make out the lawyer's curt words.

McCoy hands the phone to Kevin. I want to collapse onto the couch out of nerves. This is where Kevin could betray us. This is where I find out whether everything I've planned will disappear in disarray because I put my faith in someone who wears Italian-leather loafers to school.

"Dad, I'm scared but I'm okay," Kevin whimpers.

Promising start. His performance isn't up to Tom's—it's a little overdone. But it's fine. It'll work.

"Oh, Kevin," we hear from the phone. "Not again."

If Kevin notices my raised eyebrow, he doesn't respond. He shuffles his feet as if he really is sorry for getting kidnapped so often. When he speaks to his father, he keeps up his fretful delivery. "I know, I know. But these guys are really professional. I think they're mercenaries. Or the mafia. Or they're mercenaries working with the mafia."

I frown, indicating for him to shut up. I'm pretty sure he's just using *Call of Duty* storylines.

Getting the message, Kevin nods. "Just give them what they want and they'll let me go."

The entire room goes quiet until Mitchum sighs. "Put them back on," he says reluctantly.

Kevin hands the phone back to McCoy. "We want the combination to Dashiell Owens's safe," my co-conspirator says.

While his face has gone paler, his voice is firm. I'm kind of glad he makes no effort to sound mercenary-like or mafia inclined.

"And the keys to his Lamborghini," Kevin whispers.

McCoy does not pass along this request.

The line stays silent. When the moment stretches, I cross my arms. I can feel my heart hammering in my chest. I exhale slowly, the clarity of the sound underscoring Mitchum's nonexistent response.

"Is he . . . *hesitating*?" Kevin asks.

I don't have the chance to react before our "hostage" grabs the phone.

"Dad, seriously? I'm going to tell Mom you hesitated." He doesn't manage to hide the hurt under his indignation, or maybe he doesn't want to. "Is my life not worth the combination to *one* safe?"

"Don't be ridiculous. There's no need to tell your mother about any of this," Mitchum replies immediately. "Put the . . . mercenaries back on."

McCoy pumps his fist. I fight the same frisson of excitement.

When he receives the phone, McCoy flattens his expression. "The combination?" he prompts.

I catch Kevin's eye, noticing the somber tinge to his features. Quickly, he pulls his gaze from mine. In the span of seconds, he changes. The defeated slump of his shoulders rises. His good-natured half grin re-forms, like a conditioned response to other insulting conversations with his father, albeit probably not ones involving ransom.

While I would never willingly concede a place for Kevin Webber in my crew, I grudgingly recognize this certain commonality he has with my accomplices. We're each of us dealing in our own ways with hiding hurt or hope or confusion over our place in everything. We're good pretenders. We have to be.

As Mitchum recites the numbers, McCoy writes them on the notepad he's produced from his jacket pocket. I wait intently, fidgeting with the ends of my hair.

Finished, McCoy rips out the page and hands it to me. I stare at it, the neat sequence of numbers written in McCoy's whiteboard-ready handwriting.

It's . . . real. Eight numbers. One combination. Millions of dollars. Holy shit.

EMILY WIBBERLEY & AUSTIN SIEGEMUND-BROKA

We're halfway there. The realization hits me in a collision of joy and restraint. Halfway is nothing, I remind myself. Close is nothing. It just...doesn't feel like nothing. Moments like now are the only ones I did not let myself imagine while I worked out every other detail of my designs in my room. Obviously, I intended and expect to succeed, and I visualized the ways in which I would. Even as I did, though, I denied myself their psychological spoils.

Pride. Confidence.

It felt premature to laud myself for victories not yet won. It felt foolish when, these days, I'm really not used to things working out.

Distracting me from the afterglow of the achievement, Mitchum goes on. "Look," he says. "I really wish you hadn't threatened my kid, but if you're going to expose this asshole, do it. If my son is released in the next twenty minutes, I'll give you three hours before I report the safe has been opened. It should be enough time to find whatever proof you need." He hangs up.

I blink, not knowing what the fuck he's referring to.

TWENTY

EXPOSE THIS ASSHOLE. FIND PROOF.

The words ring in my head while McCoy and Kevin celebrate, while McCoy relays their success to the crew, while my phone blows up with excitement. I can't join in. I'm riveted, consumed. I feel as if someone has just carefully disassembled my house of cards and showed me how to win millions with the perfect poker hand instead.

Proof.

What Mitchum said implies that my dad has done something illegal. Something I could send him to jail for.

Would I send my own father to jail?

It's tempting. Very tempting. I designed this day because I want to hurt him. I want to make him pay for what he's done to me and my mom.

But do I want to ruin the rest of his life? Do I *want* him in prison? Ejected from the family? Desperate?

Why isn't the answer yes?

In my pounding heart, I wrestle with the conundrum into which Mitchum has unknowingly pitched me. The prospect of newer, deeper injury to my father should exhilarate me. The fact that it doesn't is pushing into pressure points I didn't know existed. I expected this day would test me. My intuition, my cunning, my improvisation, my persistence. How well I could withstand the emotional wounds every wall of this house inflicts. How deeply I wanted revenge.

In my every plan, I never expected *this*.

I never expected the day would force me to confront my capacity for *mercy*. How like a stain on my conscience it feels.

I remember furious nights under our new roof in Coventry, far from here, my eyes stinging from crying, my stomach sore from heaving. When Mom's physical therapy was hard, or when the stack of bills on the counter left her staring dejectedly into space. Or just when everything overwhelmed me, when the *new girl* struggled to fit into her new school, when I didn't know what kind of future the past year had left me.

Mitchum's unforeseen insinuation is pushing me, forcing me to reckon with the worst I wished for my father even then. I wanted him to know fear and remorse. I never wanted him to disappear from my life forever.

Why not?

Because I love him, even now.

He's my dad.

It's fucked up.

I feel the weight of reality crashing down on me now, the inescapable nature of what I'm doing here, the fatal feature of my heist. My victim isn't some faceless financial institution, my surroundings not the impersonal steel of meaningless vaults. It's my own father. My home. I want to wound my mark—not destroy him.

Does it make me weak? Disloyal to my mom? Cowardly?

I don't know.

Within it hides the final hidden piece of my motives, one I've concealed even from myself. Recognizing the figment of loyalty I still have for my father has exposed it like a message on my heart in invisible ink.

If I steal from him...he might even be impressed.

I read the financial press. I know his colleagues run empires of grift—stealing with fancy names like *high-risk*, *high-return*, and *speculative investing*—leaving people nationwide out of their money. If his own daughter, who for years he's considered only his empty-headed, worthless heiress, proves she's capable of the same machinations, he might just *care*.

Not if I falter now, though.

While I hate that any part of me wants his approval, the present is not the time to work through my issues. With the millions I'm planning to steal today, I'll hire a very, very good therapist. In the meantime, I decide, I won't let a stray comment from Mitchum derail me. I'll determine if I want to pursue whatever he's alluding to on a day when I'm not already in the middle of a heist.

Still, I file it away. In case.

I focus sharply on present company. They're enjoying our victory, McCoy shaking the stress out of his shoulders, Kevin grinning like he's won the state championship. We don't have forever to celebrate. While we're no longer facing the champagne welcome's deadline, the entire day is densely scheduled.

"Pawn," I say to McCoy, "get into position to escort Rook from the wedding after Phase Four."

McCoy nods, fully fortified now with no further kidnappings on his schedule. He leaves up the stairs to the den.

"What are you guys stealing from the safe?" Kevin asks, as if he's making friendly conversation.

Needless to say, I ignore his question. "Kevin, you can go now."

"Blackmail? Money? Diamonds?" Kevin presses. "Ooh, are you forging his will?"

I iron my voice into patience. "You were an excellent hostage, really," I say. "You've earned your cut. Now your job is to return to the party."

His smile doesn't change. I'd worry his face were stuck if his eyes didn't match his mirth.

"Come on," he urges me playfully. "I can do more."

I'm about to reply, saying I don't *need* more, when my phone buzzes repeatedly.

It's Cass again. I pick up, annoyance rushing over me alongside worry. Even with our strict policy of phones on silent, she needs to have a really good reason to call this often. Which, knowing Cass, she probably does. It's disconcerting, leaving me wondering if the security parameters have constricted further.

Or maybe she's devised the solution to the problem of the study.

No—I don't do optimism.

"Now what?" I ask.

"More radio chatter from security," Cass replies. "The ceremony is delayed. Something regarding the bride."

I close my eyes. *Maureen.*

I wish I could predict what's gone wrong "regarding the bride." Frankly, though, it's difficult to know with Maureen. She changes from welcoming hostess to chatty friend to judgmental socialite to domineering lady of the house with surprising speed. I can be in the middle of something like candor, explaining East Coventry gossip to her delighted inquiries, when she hits me out of nowhere with "Well, now I know why no one there likes you" or some other comically evil, eye-watering stinger.

I understand it, sort of. In this house, it's easy to not know who you're supposed to be. Still—Maureen put herself here. She's leaning into every contradiction of my father's cruel, kind, indulgent, depriving world. Giving herself over to its worst impulses.

Including on her wedding day, I guess. It's not out of character for her to upset her own Pinterest extravaganza.

"I'm on it," I say to Cass, steeling my will. "Stay ready."

"Always am," she replies.

I hang up, grateful for Cass's professionalism. It's refreshing compared to the last twenty minutes.

"Is Maureen getting cold feet?" Kevin asks. "Let's give her a pep talk."

I let out my breath. Irritatingly, I can't be mean to Kevin anymore, not after what he's witnessed. But I cannot have him tagging along to everything.

I look him right in the eyes, going for gently earnest when I speak. "Kevin, I really appreciate your help. We couldn't have done it without you." A lie. If he hadn't interrupted us, my original plan would have worked just fine, but whatever. "However, after successfully ransoming someone, you have to return whoever you've ransomed. Which, right now, is you."

Kevin pouts. I purse my lips, holding firm.

"I know valuable legal stuff. I eavesdrop on my dad all the time," he insists, hints of desperation stealing into his voice.

"I'm sure you do," I reply. "While we're on the subject of eavesdropping, I'm guessing you just heard him say he would call security if you weren't returned to him."

He slumps. "Fine, but my offer still stands. And"—he looks up, renewed—"we should celebrate when the job is finished. Movie night?"

"We'll see," I say.

I go up the stairs, ending the conversation. Returning to the house's hallways, I head for my father's office, where I know he and all the groomsmen are until the ceremony.

Walking the cream-white corridor, I prepare myself for contingencies. Surprisingly, the familiarity of my former home helps center me. On the polished hardwood, eyeing the patterns in the floor I've noticed hundreds of times, I can pretend I'm stretching my legs while memorizing the quadratic formula or rehearsing how I'm going to convince my mom I'm old enough to watch R-rated movies.

I feel my mind shift gears. If, as Kevin suggested, Maureen is getting cold feet, it's a problem. Not for Maureen or Dash, who really shouldn't be getting married. No, it's a problem for *me*. Without the ceremony emptying the house, I would need another way to get alone with the safe.

I'm not in love with either of my backup options, which involve arson or calling in a bomb threat. They're risky—very risky.

When I near the other end of the house, cigar smoke and the raucous laughter of drunk groomsmen greet me. With them come other flashbacks. "Investor meetings." "Deal-closing drinks."

I ease open the door. It moves noiselessly. The hinge, I remember, is oiled weekly. Inside, the room is disastrous. A frat house filled with fifty-year-old men.

And Jackson. Past the heavy smoke, he stands along the wall, looking uncomfortable and still heartbreakingly handsome.

Right beside him is the safe.

TWENTY-ONE

I ONLY LET MYSELF STARE AT IT FOR A SECOND.

Quickly, I shift my gaze to Jackson. When he notices me, his eyes lighting up with pleased surprise I can't stand, I crook my finger, urging him to meet me in the hall. He looks relieved for the excuse to leave the room, scrunching up his nose in repulsion while he walks through the smoke. None of the groomsmen watch him go.

"Olivia. Hi," he says, his staccato rhythm wrenchingly familiar. "What's up?" With his hip against the wall, he leans forward, everything in his demeanor eager to see me. Emboldened, I guess, by my promise of one dance. I feel I was pretty clear we were not on good footing with each other when we left my dad's closet.

Yet here Jackson is, looking like he did when he was pitching me on wearing matching sneakers to prom instead of dress shoes. His efforts, for the record, were unsuccessful.

I ignore it. I'll permit no patience for his flirtations, which is what's happening right now. For Jackson, leaning itself is flirtatious.

Obviously, I would prefer if he weren't anywhere near me today. However, having a man on the inside of the wedding party does have its advantages.

"What's causing the delay?" I demand. The harshness in my voice warns him I'm here only for wedding-related reasons.

If it registers with Jackson, my unflappable ex doesn't show it. "Maureen doesn't like her hair. They're redoing it for the third time. Dash and the groomsmen find this hilarious," he explains dryly.

I nod, my stress subsiding. *Hair crisis. Okay. No need for arson.* It comes as absolutely no surprise she's being a diva about her hair, what with her propensity for shifting personalities and her fundamental passion for ordering people around. Of course, nor is it surprising the men in the room past us have jumped on the opportunity to make fun of a twenty-five-year-old bride.

I spin on my heel, heading for the bridal suite to help move things along.

Jackson grabs my arm, stopping me. "That's it?" he asks. "Please don't send me back in there."

"Do whatever you want. I'm going to help Maureen."

He's still holding my arm, his eyes searching mine too intently. I want to look away, but I don't want to appear weak, not to him.

Finally, he lets me go. "Why?"

I shrug off his suspicion. "Why not?"

"You get me to be a groomsman just because Dash asked you. Now you're helping Maureen get ready just to keep the wedding from being delayed. Why do you care?" He places his words methodically, each following the previous as if he's putting together evidence.

I instantly realize I've walked—in heels, no less—onto very thin ice. Everything in my body screams out to panic, to flee in the opposite direction. But I can't. Not really. Running won't change what he knows. What he suspects. Running won't escape the danger I'm in.

One unfortunate reality I learned living in this labyrinthine house is how little it matters which pretty, perfect room you hide in. Problems will find you if they want to.

Jackson's eyes widen, his face reflecting the fear rising in me. "No," he says, realizing. "You're not."

I hold my chin up with defiant effort. "Not what, Jackson?" I retort, clenching my voice in iron.

He looks around furtively, then pulls me farther down the hall. While I resent every moment of contact, I'm prepared for it now. I feel nothing with his familiar fingers on my skin. Nothing except my wire-coiled nerves.

"You're not planning something at this wedding, right?" he hisses. "Revenge? Theft?"

"Don't be ridiculous," I say instantly. Extracting my elbow, I start walking again, pretending *everything is fine.*

Jackson catches up to me and places himself deftly in my way. "Tell me why you're helping Maureen," he demands, urgent now. "Why do you care about this wedding at all?"

"You've been out of my life for weeks. My dad and I have reconciled. I'm excited for Maureen to be my stepmom. We've grown very close." I can hardly get the words out. They're like regurgitating glass. I know they're not convincing.

"Olivia." Jackson pronounces my name in warning.

One I won't heed. I do nothing. Posture ramrod straight, imperious.

Jackson is undeterred. "Is *this* why you broke up with me?" he asks. "I told you not to do something like...this, and you—what? Wanted to cut me loose so I didn't stop you?"

I glare, my expression steely. He doesn't flinch.

While my gaze is full of spite, deep down, it's myself I'm furious with.

Of course I suggested The Plan to Jackson. Only in its earlier stages, when it was little more than the notion of stealing from my father. I got the idea as soon as I received the Save the Date, when Jackson and I were still dating. When I was still deeply in love with someone I thought loved me back.

The conversation has haunted me in every wayward glimpse of Jackson I've gotten in the cafeteria over the past weeks. The day I received The Plan's inspiration, several months into our relationship, was like every other. Getting home to my empty house, I went to check the mail. Jackson came over like usual, his used Jeep in my driveway, expecting we would do homework until other pursuits called us.

Instead, he found me rereading the Save the Date, fuming with intent. He figured I needed comfort, remembering the Olivia he had seen in drives home from godawful dinners here, in furious outbursts fresh off some wounding phone call with Dash.

I didn't need comfort. This was different. He mistook the dark fire of inspiration for hurt.

In my conjoined kitchen–living room, in the sunlight filtering past our cheap curtains, I explained myself calmly. I wanted to steal something back from my dad—what I deserved. My father had just given the perfect opportunity, in curly cursive with gold roses stamped into the edges. With the wedding invitation, he'd invited something else entirely.

In those first seconds, I was already fantasizing about Jackson and me pulling this job together. Us against the world.

Standing in the middle of the room, his backpack still slung over his shoulder, he listened with doubt warping his features. The idea unnerved him, I realized with the fast horror of miscalculation. I'd never heard Jackson criticize me until then. We nearly never fought.

Which meant I didn't recognize the disapproving stare he fixed on me.

He told me I shouldn't get wrapped up in revenge. I should live my life and forget about my dickhead father.

I was *better* than this, he insisted.

He was wrong.

"I broke up with you because you cheated on me," I remind him, my voice venomous.

"Except we both know I didn't," he replies. He speaks every word slowly, charged with indignation.

I've had enough. Without hesitating, I walk past him into the chandeliered foyer. While I hear him following me, I couldn't care less. Honestly, I get madder with every passing instant. How *dare* he look for other reasons I dumped him?

I find refuge in my fury, my only reward for the end of our relationship. I continue out the front door, out to the ridiculous circular driveway, knowing Jackson is on my heels. The daylight is dazzling enough to hurt. In front of the hedge spires flanking the portico, the valet staff has parked the fanciest cars, their hoods shining.

Jackson's betrayal had proven convenient, in its own way. I didn't know how I would explain to him I *needed* to go through with my plans. It wasn't me not letting go of the idea. The idea wouldn't let go of *me*. The DM I received freed me from having to justify myself to Jackson.

And if I'm really honest with myself, it was almost a relief.

If he had discovered the depth of bitterness, jealousy, and ruthlessness in me, he would have abandoned me for good. In my guiltiest moments, I'm convinced it's *why* he cheated.

Maybe I even deserved it.

Heartbreak and the guilt for my mom's injuries and my parents' divorce have left me without much faith in my own goodness. The heist is my chance to use everything Jackson couldn't love in me— my vengefulness, my uncompromising retaliation—for something like redemption.

If I can be the one in charge, I won't only be…everything else. The daughter who needs providing for, even when it endangers her mother's life. The jilted girlfriend. The one who ruined everything, according to my father. Olivia the ruiner.

If I'm successful, I won't just earn millions. I'll prove I'm someone worth respecting.

I head down the idyllic stone pathway leading from the driveway through the grass to the guest cottage. Yes, the grounds have a freaking guest cottage. While it's designed like the main house, with stately white-framed windows set under the gently sloping roof in Georgian gorgeousness, the purposeful unobtrusiveness of the structure changes the feel of the place entirely. It emerges from the greenery like a secret among friends.

I ignore the heartstring pull of just seeing it. "Look," Jackson says behind me. "How can I prove it to you? You said I hooked up with some girl?"

"Kelly Devine," I correct him. "I don't know the particulars of what you did together. I just saw the DM."

"DM," Jackson repeats, inexplicably relieved. "Perfect. Can you show me the screenshots?"

"Sorry, can't," I say with mock remorse. "No phones at the wedding."

I hear my ex's forced patience in his next words. "Right. I mean when the wedding is over. You can even go through my phone. Read every message I've ever sent. I honestly don't care. I don't have any-thing to hide."

"No thanks," I say. "I don't need to spend hours looking for a message you've had weeks to delete."

Unfortunately, fate won't let me have my perfect comeback. The moment the reply has left my lips, I stumble on a rock in the path. I pitch forward, hands flying up—when Jackson catches me, his grip gentle on my waist. The hot shock of him holding my hips is merciless, supplying me with memories like notes shoved under locked doors.

His hands linger a little long. He drops them when I straighten up, impatient with him, impatient with myself.

"I don't understand where this is coming from," he says with shattered hollowness. "What I do understand, though, is you're done with me. Fine. But, Olivia, *please* don't do what you're doing."

I'm not certain what exactly makes me face him in the middle of the garden path. Or...I wish I weren't. The fact is, the fervent con-cern in Jackson's voice unlocks a few of the doors in my heart I would rather remain closed. I find desperation written everywhere on his features, filling his eyes.

It makes me do what I've promised myself I wouldn't. I hesitate.

He continues. "Your dad isn't just an asshole. He's powerful. Even dangerous. Same with the rest of the men in his circle. If any of them finds out what you're up to," he says urgently, "they'll crush you. They'll ruin your future—they don't think you have one in the first place. But I know you do."

I know you do. I know you do.

I hate how his validation works into me. It's like every interac-tion I've unfortunately had with him the past couple hours. Painful reminders of pleasure gone.

"You can't risk it for whatever revenge you're chasing," he finishes. "You're more than what he wants you to be."

His words hurt worse than falling on the rocks would have.

There was a time I wanted to be the girl Jackson thought I was. Good. Noble. Above the shitty hand I was dealt. There was even a moment I thought about calling off the heist, held comfortingly in Jackson's arms. The poison my dad dropped into my heart, the conviction that I'd ruined everything and would ruin everything for my mom, went quiet, and with it the hunger for revenge, my sweet antidote. With Jackson, I glimpsed a future perfect enough that I could maybe escape the unforgiving pieces of my past. I just remember feeling terrifyingly *happy*.

I'm glad I didn't give up the heist. Happiness is like anything—it can be stolen.

I step away from him slowly, careful with the path. "You're right," I say, dropping heavy gates over my demeanor. "I *am* done with you. I didn't need Kelly Devine to know I was never the girl you wanted."

I don't wait for his reply. I walk into the cottage and close the door on him.

TWENTY-TWO

I HAVEN'T VISITED THIS PART OF THE HOUSE SINCE I MOVED OUT. Not in dinners with Dad and Lexi or, recently, Maureen. Not when my dad found it easier having me come here for custody-related court filings we needed signed.

Never.

It hasn't changed. I don't know whether I wish it had. The carpet is incomparably soft where the hardwood cedes to cream. The furniture is comfy, worn in where I, myself, sat hundreds of evenings. The windows capture the sun just right, fully yet not straight on, leaving the room lit with natural light.

The light. She loved the light.

I held no fondness for my father's den or the home's half-entrenched theater. What I feel walking into the gorgeous guest cottage is different.

I *hate* it here.

Once, I felt the opposite. *Once upon a time.* The fairy-tale phrase fits the first memories I have of the welcoming, elegantly designed outpost on the periphery of the grand house's grounds.

My mom would paint here. I would watch her. Here, in the middle of the sitting room from which the other rooms extend. When everything was normal. When I didn't know what my dad was capable of. When I didn't know what my *mom* was capable of. What resilience, what care. She would paint the house, the gardens, flowers, even occasionally me.

My mom hadn't grown up with much. Public schools, suburban homes with chain-link fences, new neighborhoods when her father's managerial job for a vacuum company had sent him to new offices. My mom, intelligent and in love with culture, had gone to Queens College in New York City, supporting herself with jobs like the receptionist-slash-assistant position at the art gallery where, the story goes, she'd met my dad with a "spirited" conversation.

I could read between the lines of the fairy tale. He'd stumbled in with Princeton friends classier than he, stinking of money and who knows what else. When she'd chastened his incivility or his disrespect for the art, one would have expected the young media heir to sneer or, worse, wield his influence over the meager gallery assistant.

He hadn't. It's the one part of the anecdote of my mom's I've had to accept on faith. In her description, my father had been . . . different when he was younger. Playboyish, yes. Narcissistic, yes.

Nevertheless, my mom says he had been self-conscious, considerate, even noble in ways it is impossible to imagine now. Dashiell Owens had found himself charmed when my inconspicuous mother snapped at him, and he had charmed her in return.

While my mom knew he'd enjoyed the rebellion of spurning his family's expectations and marrying outside of high society, she hadn't minded. She'd even appreciated his willingness to act for himself instead of the Owens family's plans. The unlikeliest of matches had been made, and the daughter of interchangeable suburbs had wed the son of Rhode Island's wealthiest dynasty.

Whenever she speaks about how she met my father, she ends the story there. Over the years, I've learned more and more how to interpret the sadness in the silence following the fonder reminiscences.

Those years warped the integrity out of my father. Some combination of monotony, age, and his changing role in his family stole the spark of selfless zeal my mom says he once had, leaving only the man I know—from charming heir to cunning, cynical patriarch.

His podcast didn't help. My father has stumbled into the admiration of the internet's worst people, self-worshippers and iconoclasts who hide misogyny and entitlement under pretenses of reasonableness, or sometimes don't hide it at all. Desperate for his venture to succeed, and with no character of his own left, my father indulged their views, assimilating more and more of them.

And my mom stayed. I don't know whether she felt like she could catch glimmers of the good in him, or if she held on out of some admittedly misguided resolve to keep my family whole, or if sometimes the momentum of life just makes swerving feel impossible. Days stretched into decades as she embraced her unlikely, impossibly indulgent life.

Out here, I could understand why. I can only imagine how the freedom to learn to paint, in this landscape fit for framing, would have felt for her. Here, she was *happy*.

Until everything changed. Of course, the memory of her painting is not why I hate it in the estate's guest cottage. When my dad cheated, my mom moved out of the main house. I went with her. While she looked for a new place to live, dealt with the divorce, everything, we stayed...here.

I know the symbolism was not lost on my mom. Her studio, her former place of fulfillment, was changed into the only home she had for months. It was like living in the perfect representation of everything my dad's actions had stolen from her. Not just the square footage. He was robbing her of the freedom and joy she'd never had when she was young.

It reminds me I'm not pulling this job only for myself. I'm not the only one who lost everything. Who felt the stab of deception from someone she'd loved, only for the pain to earn her nothing except the loss of the life she knew. This home—the entire miserable mansion, not merely the guesthouse—wasn't stolen only from me. My mom has the same right I do to wanting my father to pay. Revenge just isn't her thing.

Unlike Jackson, she has no idea what I'm doing here. I explained without explanation. *I just want to go,* I repeated. Of course, my mom assumed righteousness in my motives, probably figuring I wanted to maintain some semblance of my relationship with my father or maybe even remind myself of the feeling of my old life.

I didn't disillusion her. I didn't want her to worry. I can carry out her revenge alongside mine without her ever knowing.

I just have to get past this part. The logistical headache I'm dealing with is enough of a problem. Dealing with it in my least favorite part of the house is adding injury to inconvenience.

In fact, only one thing could make the experience worse.

Maureen reclines on the chaise longue, sipping her champagne in her twenty-thousand-dollar Oscar de la Renta gown, hand sewn with thousands of crystals. They glitter in the painting-perfect light, looking like winking intruders. Her engagement ring sits waiting on her hand.

Her hair is perfect.

None of the bridesmaids are doing hair or makeup, actually. Instead, in the cottage's open room, they're all posing for photos, laughing as if *this* is the party and the wedding is an afterthought. I recognize them from my research. Unlike my dad's group, it is my understanding they're Maureen's real friends. They're wearing ivory satin dresses, voguish pieces handpicked by Maureen. While they're loud, each woman a few drinks in, I'm glad for the lack of cigar smoke in their festivities.

I plaster on my shiniest smile.

"Maureen," I say, "you look beautiful."

Noticing me, she stands and places her glass delicately on the end table. She rushes over to wrap me in a hug. "Oh, Olivia, you should have been in our pictures," she gushes. "I can't believe I forgot."

I don't let my smile slip. Maureen didn't forget. She knows I know she didn't forget. She scheduled every minute of the event. She decided how many cakes to have, what the centerpieces should look like, how the napkins are folded. She's planned every last detail of today as meticulously as I have.

Maureen doesn't want me around, and I can't fault her. When you're marrying an older man for his fortune, why worry about getting to know his estranged daughter?

"I would have loved that," I say.

"We'll get some just us later," Maureen promises.

"Definitely."

We're both lying.

"I heard there was a hair emergency. I came wondering if I could help," I say innocently, looking around as if I haven't already figured out no emergency has arisen.

Maureen grins with put-on guilt, confirming the suspicions I had the moment I walked in the room. "Our cover is blown, girls," she calls over her shoulder. "Looks like it's time to get hitched."

The girls whine. I can't help noticing how Maureen herself, despite her playful show, looks momentarily disappointed. Of course she does. Everyone she wants to spend the day with is here, not on the lawn, and certainly not in the smoky study. She wants to hang out with her friends. Once more, I can't fault her.

"Great," I reply cheerfully. "I'll let my dad know you're ready."

I'm on my way to the door when Maureen interrupts me.

"Actually," she says.

When I look back, I find something new in her eyes. The shrewd sparkle looks unsettlingly like inspiration.

"There is one thing I need before we start," my stepmom-to-be says.

I wait, suppressing frustration under my mask of innocent accommodation. "What is it?" I ask. I notice Grace Winters—law student, high-powered New York internship this summer—and Yungmoon Lee—works in programming for a fitness-app developer, just got dumped—observing me from the counter where I would cry over my geometry homework when my mom wasn't looking. They're not-so-subtly measuring my patience for Maureen.

"There's just something missing from my look," Maureen muses.

She walks to the floor-length mirror near the bed. With pursed lips and evaluative eyes, she takes herself in.

Head slanted to the side while she observes, she addresses her cohort. "Don't you think I need a necklace?"

It's Hannah Chapman—former president of the Stony Brook

sorority, where Maureen was recruitment chair—who replies unhesitatingly. "Oh my god, *yes*."

"I was just thinking that," Yungmoon joins in.

Maureen turns from the mirror and faces me with her hand on her unadorned neck. Wrestling with impatience, I preempt her. "Sure, a necklace will definitely complete the look. Do you have a few in your room you want me to grab or what?"

She's messing with me. It's not surprising, honestly. I resent playing errand girl for her, but if the power play is what she's delighting in right now, cooperating will move the proceedings forward. I can suffer her little indignities. I've had *plenty* of practice.

And after all, it occurs to me in the moment, by the time I've gotten into the safe, Maureen and Dash will be legally married. Just as the guesthouse has reminded me I'm not the only one I'm stealing *for*, Maureen has just reminded me my father is not the only one I'm stealing *from*.

I straighten up, enjoying the new motivation—until I notice the way Maureen is smiling.

"I was thinking," she says softly, "of the diamond necklace in the safe." Her voice is casual, but her eyes watch me carefully.

The light perfectly filling the room instantly ceases to warm me. Cold dread pushes deadly quick from my heart into my fingertips, my cheeks, my lips. It's so, so much worse than being Maureen's errand girl. But I can't react, not when I know exactly why Maureen has her eye on the piece in particular.

The diamond necklace in the safe is mine.

Or it will be. In my grandfather's will, he left the heirloom for me to inherit when I graduate from high school. He inherited it from his mother. While valuable, the necklace is far from the flashiest piece in the house, its diamond nowhere near the clarity of the one on Maureen's finger.

I rather liked my grandfather on Dash's side. He was nice to me when the rest of the family wasn't. I was a kid when he died, and I remember the will reading—my feet wedged into unfamiliar formal flats, my new dress itchy. Grandpa gave half of his fortune to charity. The family was irate. Even in first grade I knew they were.

The other half went to the siblings, with my father, the firstborn, in the role of executor. I've never forgotten Mia's grimace when I got the necklace. The fact that Grandpa chose me out of all the cousins always made me feel special.

The necklace is the only thing in this house that remains legally mine, or it *will* be mine. It's why Maureen wants it. Rubbing her ownership of the house in my face.

I have to handle my reaction delicately. If I resist, Maureen will know she's won her petty psychological game, and any resentment she sees in me will look like a motive when the rest of the day goes down.

I school my face into magnanimity. "Of course," I say. "I'll get it for you."

Turning my back on Maureen's victorious grin, I head for the door.

Outside, I find Jackson is gone.

TWENTY-THREE

I'M WALKING UP THE GARDEN PATH WITH LONELINESS AND FRUS-tration when I feel my phone vibrate in my clutch. In the solitude of the greenery, I check the messages hurriedly, worry lancing into me.

Rook

> Yo quick question

> When I was doing the phone drop I noticed Walker Harris is here. My brother and I have watched Undead Nation every Friday for literally years and walker plays his favorite character. it would be cool as hell if someone could get his signature for my bro

> He knows I'm at a fancy wedding. It would really mean a lot to him

Queen

> Seriously?

I pause, recalibrating in relief. While I'm not in favor of over-use of our contraband phones, I'm not against the crew refocusing and letting off steam on the group chat—especially Deonte, whose present assignment is to sequester himself in one of the downstairs restrooms, the one with the white orchid, where no one ever goes. I want him waiting in there until his next phase so the caterers don't scrutinize him or, worse, assign him non-Plan work.

However, I do not need infighting. I wait, ready to defuse.

Queen

> I LOVE UNDEAD NATION

> Your brother is cool.

> I want an autograph too.

Knight

> I think I can make that happen. Not sure he deserved the Emmy, though. He could bring a little more Shakespearean theater to some of his scenes imo.

Rook

> Bro, it's a zombie show. Shut the fuck up about Shakespeare. (Thank you for the autograph though.)

Pawn

> A Shakespearean reading is actually interesting. A little Macbeth, a little Lear.

Queen

> I want off this chat. I'm watching for the gore, not so
> I can write an essay. Shit.

I have to smile. I shut my clutch, deciding I'll only request they restrain their conversation if they're still discussing the world's favorite zombie show when I reach the main house in five minutes.

As I reenter the Owens house's corridors, the cast of my new obligation returns with every step, closing over me like rain on a wedding day. When I push open the door to my dad's study, I discover Jackson has come back to the smoke-filled room. He's seated next to Dash, looking much chummier. He doesn't even glance up when I enter.

Good. Maybe he can let it go now. Let *us* go.

I approach Dash, passing groomsmen who either ignore me or eye the interloper with distaste. When I reach my father, he doesn't glance up, either. He looks content, cigar on his lips, surveying his slick kingdom.

The faster I can get the conversation over with, the more easily I can keep the day moving. "Maureen's ready," I announce. "She just wants to wear the diamond necklace."

At this, Jackson whips to face me. "But that's Olivia's," he says to Dash.

I clock his instant defensiveness of me. It ruins the impassivity he feigned when I came in. Not surprising. As it happens, Jackson excels at giving himself away.

He knows about the necklace, of course. The deeper our relationship got, the more of my childhood I shared with him. I opened up fully, exposing even the unholy combination of pride and resentment, shame and longing I felt about my immeasurably wealthy upbringing. He knew I cherished the very idea of the necklace, the little glimmer of good in my ugly history with my dad and his family.

I don't fall into Jackson's eye-contact trap. Pretending he's looking out for me? Pretending he cares? *I'm still in love with you. I'll always love you.* What game is he playing when he's the one who threw us away?

Dash stands up from the edge of his desk. "Olivia can loan it to her," he says with practiced comfort in distributing other people's property. "Whatever my bride wishes, right?"

I hold in my vomit.

While I watch, he walks to the safe, where he enters the combination. Although he hides the dial from the room, I know what numbers he's whirling in, having just ransomed them out of Mitchum Webber. Mitch, who I notice frowns with the uncomfortable reminder of his double-dealing.

Dash opens the safe with the heavy *chunk* of the metal door.

Immediately, his phone, which he clearly hasn't been made to relinquish in his own home, beeps with a notification that the safe has been opened.

I knew it would. The safe is programmed to message him whenever it's opened, the second the lock disengages.

He swipes the alert away. "Probably time to surrender this," he says, holding up his phone. "Don't miss any messages, but make sure you silence it, Quinn. If Maureen sleeps in another room tonight because my phone went off during the ceremony, you're fired."

He laughs grandly as if the punch line isn't his assistant's livelihood. Quinn approaches nervously, rightly uncomfortable with the responsibility. I don't know Quinn personally, despite him having worked for my father for years now. I don't know if he likes Dash's podcast or if he's interested in media or if he just needed the job. He's wiry, probably five or seven years out of college, and quiet-looking. He's not one of the groomsmen, but he's being made to stay by Dash's side.

Pocketing the phone, Quinn retreats.

I ignore him. The safe consumes my focus. Inside, like the spoils of war, sit folders, envelopes, watch cases, jewelry boxes, keys, and other items I'm not familiar with. With the security surrounding the Owens estate, the house itself is like a safe. The safe within the safe is reserved for items of the highest value—or the utmost secrecy.

Dash swiftly finds the jewelry box he wants. He takes out the diamond necklace—*my* diamond necklace—and holds it up to me. In the dull light of the hazy room, the pendant is dead rock.

I take it, not letting my gaze linger on it for long. Without emotion, I leave the room.

My blood roars in my ears. I head down the hall on my way back to the cottage, hardly even processing where I'm going. My hand is clenched on the chain.

I remember the day my grandfather first showed me the necklace. He was sick. He knew he didn't have long, and he told me that even though he wouldn't be there for my graduation, he had a special gift picked out for me.

Young Olivia was flattered and moved in ways she couldn't express. I loved my grandfather, and I admired him. I could even then discern he was the kind of person I wanted my dad to be. Newspaper magnate and New York–socialite Andrew Owens had made his fortune with publications in nearly every major city in the United States. When he and his wife, my grandmother Leonie, divorced, he remained in New York. In the high society of the eighties, their separation was slightly scandalous. Neither of them cared. It's kind of the Owens way.

Grandma Leonie received custody of my aunt and uncle, who went with her to Switzerland, while my grandfather got Dash, the firstborn son, presumably on some old-school socioeconomic grounds of him learning to run the family empire or whatever.

In fact, my dad is still the CEO in name of the Owens media portfolio. He is *not* the kind of company head I understood my grandfather to be, opting to sell off many of the firm's components and only visiting the office four or five times on a *good* year, instead devoting his efforts to his iconoclastic podcast.

Whenever I expressed curiosity about Grandpa's company, I would only get cheap platitudes about "new media" and "dying industries." However, I've long suspected Dash's podcast is one part intergenerational disinterest in Grandpa's work, and one part fear he'll fall short of his progenitor.

Honestly, I miss Grandpa. Even a decade later, the heartstring pull remains. I remember when he let me hold the necklace, which he'd had one of his many personal assistants deliver to the hospital. I gazed into the glassy facets of the pendant wrapped in my hand now. It was my favorite gift I'd ever received, and I hadn't even gotten it yet.

I don't have to reach the cottage before I find Maureen. Right outside the high front doors in the portico's shade, she's heading up the stone steps, bridal party in tow.

Forcing my smile, I hold up the necklace.

Maureen blinks. As if she'd forgotten she even requested it. As if she wasn't even waiting for it. In overdone delight, the excitement of someone used to feigning excitement, she claps her hands.

It makes my stomach roil in new ways. Maureen is pointedly

acting like my prized possession is one more wedding gift that she won't use.

"Put it on me, won't you?" she asks.

My fingers go cold on the diamond.

Maureen gestures to the photographers. "I want you to capture this moment," she orders them, eyes remaining on me. "Stepmother and stepdaughter."

Her voice is a sugared sword. She turns slowly, moving with precision in her low heels, exposing her bare neck to me. Making herself vulnerable because she knows she can. In just hours, she'll be the lady of the house. She'll have all the power.

Or so she expects.

She has no idea what I have in motion.

While the cameras flash, I step forward and put the necklace around her throat.

TWENTY-FOUR

TOM WAITS FOR ME IN FRONT OF THE FRENCH DOORS LEADING TO the deck. His back is silhouetted against the glass.

He turns when he hears my footsteps. "Hello, date," he says, his voice full of the smile dancing over his features. "Ready to steal the show?"

I find myself smirking in return. As I recompose myself from the Maureen episode, Knight's mischievous cheer is exactly what I need. I put my hand on his arm, and we exit out the elegant doors.

The champagne hour is winding down. Guests have enjoyed themselves—I notice glassier eyes, pinker cheeks, louder laughter. Only the younger contingent, the social media stars in flashy outfits, look bored.

They won't have long to wait. With Maureen mollified, the wedding is officially underway once more.

With relief, I clock Kevin standing with his sister, inserting himself shamelessly into conversation with impeccably dressed guests our age. Business as usual.

I avoid catching his eye as I head with Tom to the bar, where I order sparkling water with lime. The drink is my excuse to linger here in the bar's high visibility while I canoodle with my new boyfriend.

His hand lowering to the curve of my hip, he leans in close, whispering in my ear. "Five hundred dollars of Nobu sushi," he whispers with sultry promise. "My very own Patek Philippe Nautilus."

I smile for real when I realize he's naming purchases he's going to make and stuff he's going to do in Los Angeles with all the extra money the heist will leave him.

"Nights in the Viceroy L'Ermitage whenever I feel like it," he murmurs. "Room service and everything."

While I laugh—of course he has his luxury watch and hotel picked out—the French doors open, spilling out the groomsmen. Jackson hits the stairs with force until he sees me. His gait falters. His face crumples.

Tom's arm still hugs my hips, my hand still resting on his lapel. It's not enough, though. I need to rub this in. Past Tom, my eyes meet Jackson's across the flagstone. I lean in closer to my date to whisper in his ear. "You wouldn't happen to have expertise in dresses or women's jewelry, would you?" I ask. "A celebratory shopping spree is sounding pretty good right now."

I feel Tom's laugh down my whole body.

When I look back to Jackson, his face is resolutely turned in the opposite direction, the muscles in his jaw visibly tight.

Good.

Today is about revenge, and maybe not just on my dad.

It would have been easier if Jackson hadn't come today. If he'd spent the day with Kelly Devine or whatever other girl he's trying to hook up with. But now that he *is* here, I realize I'm glad. Jackson deserves to see this. To know how I felt.

Satisfied, I sweep my eyes over the men behind him. Mitchum emerges. Then tech bros and wealthy men who've bought their sons spots on *Forbes*'s "30 Under 30." Then the person I'm searching for. Quinn.

"Phase Four," I say under my breath when I turn back to the bar.

I don't have to wait long. Rook was prepped for this. While he was hired for his baking expertise, his athleticism will help with what comes next. Deonte sweeps through the crowd, champagne tray held high.

Right on schedule, I hear a loud crash behind me. The musicians stop playing. Gasps race across the patio.

I smile as I sip my sparkling water.

"Holy shit," Tom murmurs, his head still near mine. "Was that—"

Looking like one of the startled guests, I whirl to take in the carnage by the steps. Quinn is drenched in an overfilled tray's worth of champagne while Deonte stands in front of him, his posture contrite despite having just thrown the scoring touchdown in The Plan.

"The safe is programmed to text Dash's phone every time it opens," I explain to Tom. "His phone is . . ."

Tom's eyes widen in impressed comprehension. "Let me guess. On the young man now wringing champagne from his suit?" he asks.

I bite the inside of my cheek to keep from grinning. "My father's assistant," I confirm, waiting for the rest of Phase Four to unfold. Instead of the head caterer arriving on the scene and reprimanding the waiter he definitely didn't hire or train, McCoy will swoop in. He'll discreetly but professionally escort Deonte off the premises, looking to the crowd like security taking care of the disruption. Except in reality, Deonte will join Cass in the van.

Which . . . isn't what happens.

I sit, going rigid, while Quinn Rhodes instantly explodes. Whether because he's past his limits due to my dad's demands or he knows he probably no longer has anything to lose employment-wise or he's just an asshole—I know my vote—he starts shouting at Deonte.

We're close enough to hear everything said, and from a lot farther we'd still be able to hear Quinn's screams of "fifteen hundred dollars' worth of iPhone" and "What is wrong with you?"

It is not discreet. It is not efficient.

I'm rising from my seat when circumstances worsen. Quinn has gotten in the face of the impressively impassive Deonte, seething. "You will reimburse the cost of the destroyed item," he orders. "It's nowhere near the cost in data loss, so you're getting off easy. *Fifteen. Hundred.* I'll sue you in small-claims court if I have to." Deonte is wisely silent, correctly intuiting I'll handle the Quinn situation later, one way or another. After tonight, fifteen hundred dollars will be nothing to all of us.

But into the fray steps... Jackson.

I pale. Jackson has no idea what he's interrupting. He does, however, know his classmate is dealing with family difficulties.

"I'll—I'll pay," he interjects. Even Deonte looks openly startled now. Jackson continues, gaining confidence. "I was in his way. It's one iPhone, man. I'll pay."

He wasn't in his way. *Not good. Not good.* Not only is it horribly messy from the planning perspective, it's one more reminder I don't need of how revenge against Jackson is something I desperately wish I didn't want. After all, Jackson doesn't have fifteen hundred dollars. Jackson mowed lawns to afford the pair of Adidas I really wanted for Christmas.

He's just offering out of reckless kindness. Shameless generosity.

It's a viscerally painful reminder of the difference dividing us like a diamond knife. The reason he could never want me, one I can't even argue with.

I steal, while Jackson gives.

His offer mollifies Quinn, who's realized he's making a scene. "I'll find you," he promises Jackson, who nods with the same glorious, ridiculous confidence. In the ensuing moments, I note McCoy moving in. The relief I feel when he escorts Deonte off, according to plan, is immeasurable.

"Awful little man," Tom remarks. "Not your ex," he clarifies with admittedly amusing reluctance. "The assistant."

"He's nobody." My voice is raw and unapologetically flippant. "He'll be fired soon."

Tom angles his body to look at me, his eyebrows furrowed in curiosity. "I mean, he clearly sucks, but I'm guessing he was a jerk about the phone because your dad is a jerk to him. Now he's going to lose his livelihood because of our scheme?"

I shrug.

"You don't feel bad about that?" There's no judgment in his question, only interest.

My lack of guilt is not something I would show anyone else. Tom is different, though. As the only member of my crew who is currently enrolled in a private school costing fifty grand a year, his motives are...murky. Like mine.

When I reached out to Tom Pham, having seen his social media posts on looking for funding for his Hollywood foray, he invited me to the new "gourmet frozen yogurt" place in his neighborhood. It had special high-end flavors like Colombian chocolate and rosewater raspberry. I'll never forget starting the recruitment meeting with Tom eyeing me over his white cup of salted caramel–vanilla, sunglasses perched on his head.

Unlike with other members of my crew, I opted to come right out with my plan. When he inquired why we were meeting, I said, "I know you're looking for funding for LA. I want your help stealing millions of dollars from my shitty dad." If he wasn't interested, I'd pretend I was screwing with him. I'd pass it off as a droll, elaborately constructed joke. Pretend I was filming a TikTok prank. The drama kid in him would accept my premise. I'd then ask him to tutor me in French, which he would decline.

Instead, when I pitched him on the heist, he stuck his plastic spoon into his Froyo. "Fun," he said. "I'm in."

He wasn't joking. He knew I wasn't joking. His eyes were hungry. *Fun.*

Fascinating.

He watches me with the same exact expression now, waiting for the rationale for my remorselessness for Quinn.

"He helped cover up the affair my dad had while married to my mom," I say flatly.

Tom receives my explanation. "You really hold a grudge," he remarks.

I shoot him a look. "Obviously," I reply. "If I didn't, you would end the day a lot poorer than you will."

His smile catches the glint of something delicately knowing. "While I'm very grateful for the opportunity for my personal gain, I do want to flag how your stone-cold drive for vengeance may not be the healthiest coping mechanism."

I straighten in his arms, surprised—and suddenly annoyed. I

wanted us on the same page. Thomas Pham is the one person in my crew, the one person in the world, on whom I could rely for freedom from judgment or inquiry, even in the midst of my inaugural heist. What I need from him is a co-conspirator, a dashing decoy, not someone to help me soul search or question my motives. "Thomas," I say, noticing my fingers worrying the condensation on my glass in the sun. "Why are you doing this, exactly?"

"I'm just pointing out you might want to consider—"

"No." I shake my head. I want to make him say what I need to hear. To repeat what's ringing in my own ears. I wrap my voice in vicious velvet. "Say it. Don't lie to me. Why are you doing *this job*? You don't need a million dollars to move to LA and start auditioning."

Tom grins. "No one *really* needs a million dollars. Doesn't mean we don't want it. I'd rather audition from a home in Santa Monica instead of the back room of a house I found on Craigslist."

It isn't enough. He's evading. Playing with me, probably. He's him. I lean closer, holding his gaze. I'm sure only he can see what's hiding in my sweet expression.

"You can admit it, you know," I say. "To me."

"What?"

"You like this," I declare in knowing victory. "As much as I do. The thrill of it. The feeling of proving just how much you're capable of."

Tom's smile grows. His eyes spark like fireworks in the night sky, explosions of enchanting danger against the darkness. In the distance, the musicians start heading toward the water, where the ceremony will take place.

He eyes me intently. I don't know whether he's looking for something or just looking.

Finally, lowering his gaze, he speaks kindly. "I guess what I'm saying is," he replies, "hold your grudge. Get your vengeance. Wonderful, as long as it's not...against yourself. None of this is your fault."

Feeling as if I'm pulling myself from the grip of his words, I look away. Instead, I focus on the greenery in front of me, the grounds done up in Maureen's voluptuous vision.

In this very garden, I would play games with my mom. Somersault contests. Horse pretend, which was exactly what the activity sounds like. Paddleball and, of course, my favorite. *Hide-and-seek.* In the hydrangeas, I would crouch, feeling as if I were fleeing not only my indulgent pursuer, but the entire world.

It's how I feel ignoring Tom's insight. Like I'm fleeing. Hiding.

Except it isn't fun now.

He presses gently. "Olivia, do you hear me? What your father did, what Jackson did to you—"

The warning glare I flash him stops the sentence on his lips. We are *not* discussing my disastrously failed relationship. Not in the middle of Phase Four, not ever.

He doesn't flinch. I watch him reevaluate, design some new rhetorical path forward. I prepare myself for graceful generosity or guilt or concern—*oh, the concern*—or whatever other well-intentioned response will just make me feel worse.

Instead, because he's Tom, he only smiles.

I'm spared having to interrogate why he's eyeing me like he knows something I don't when security approaches us—

No, not security.

McCoy is only just managing to hide the panicked skip in his stride. His ungainly facial hair twitches with his nervous chewing of the inside of his lip.

He looks scared.

On the periphery of the champagne-welcome festivities, he halts, waiting near the low stone steps up to the deck. He covertly gestures for me to come join him. I hand Tom my drink, giving him a cautionary glance saying we will *not* resume our discussion later, then head for where McCoy stands urgently.

Keeping my composure casual, I walk until he's close enough to speak to me and not be overheard. He leans in, preserving what looks like event security informing the groom's daughter of some routine goings-on in the house.

What he whispers to me is nothing routine, however.

"*Cass and the van,*" he says, "*are gone.*"

TWENTY-FIVE

IJAB THE NUMBER OF HER PHONE CONTACT AGAIN, COLD SWEAT coating my fingertip.

I'm in the same restroom where I collected the phone a little over an hour ago. My heart slamming in my chest won't slow. My fifth call has just gone to Cass's automated default voicemail. Frustrated, I hang up.

I know we don't have long. If Cass was caught, it's only a matter of time before the wedding is searched for co-conspirators, whether because she gives us up or they go through her phone. The wise move would be to ditch our tech in the Atlantic and call the day off.

Without Cass, I don't even know how to transfer the funds. The Plan is useless. Inert. It's excruciating—I don't *want* to call off the heist, not when we have the combination to the safe in hand. Not when the only part remaining is the easiest one.

I look up, leaning over the polished porcelain sink, and meet my own furious eyes in the mirror.

No, I'm not feeling wise, I decide. I'm feeling vengeful.

I can't just return to this wedding and watch my father marry yet another woman who isn't my mom. I can't see Jackson at his side, like an incarnation of history repeating. I can't return home, where peeling paint and medical debt wait for me. I can't just be a bystander to the hurt in my life. *I need this.*

The white porcelain in front of me dazzles in the crisp lighting. Straightening up, I hold on to my resolve. I'll figure out something. Mitchum mentioned evidence in the safe. If that doesn't help me, I'll steal Dash's watches if I need to.

I just have to move fast. No more calling Cass in vain. It's time to act.

Quickly, I exit the bathroom—finding my crew waiting for me in the hall. A security guard, a server who just spilled champagne everywhere, and my date. A completely expected group of people to be waiting by the bathroom.

"What the hell?" I demand, referring to their utter inattention to their suspiciousness.

Emphasizing my point, a woman walks past our unlikely foursome to use the restroom before the ceremony. When the door closes, I raise my eyebrow, wanting an answer.

It's Deonte who speaks up. "Look, I don't want to be here, either," he says levelly. "But my ride is gone."

"I'm just with my date," Tom offers.

I swing my gaze to McCoy, who's fiddling with his forged badge nervously.

"Oh, I don't have a good reason," he says when he realizes I'm waiting for his excuse. "I'm just stressed and want to know how we're avoiding being cau—"

The bathroom door opens.

"No one is being *coddled*," I say, improvising. "I promise my dad will fire anyone not at their posts." The woman passes us, looking oblivious, I'm relieved to find. When she's out of earshot, I continue, lowering my voice. "We proceed as planned. It'll be fine."

McCoy's eyes round. *"How will it be fine?"*

While I respect his paranoia, I don't need his doubt. "It just will," I reply hotly. *I'll figure it out.* It's like the puzzles I make on an app Jackson showed me, which I enjoy so much I cannot delete it despite the end of our relationship. What pieces do I have? Where do they fit?

"Ten minutes until the ceremony."

I look up, distracted from my problem-solving by the usher who has entered the hallway. Despite the whirlwind in my head, I manage to fix on a smile. "Finally," I say. "Thank you." When the usher exits, I lower my voice. "Just go," I direct McCoy and Deonte urgently.

They glance over their shoulders questioningly, but they obey, walking stiffly into the living room. I don't care *what* they do for the next thirty minutes, as long as they don't draw attention. All I need is for someone to notice me stealing off once more with my dashing alibi. I'm reaching for Tom when the perfect opportunity arises.

Mia walks into the hallway to use the restroom.

"Kiss me," I say to Tom under my breath.

He needs no further prompting. He really can kiss. The way he presses me up against the wall, the dark heat in his eyes the perfect contrast to the cool paint behind me, has me feeling like he could offer classes.

As Mia is reaching for the door, I pull my mouth—reluctantly— from Tom's. "Sorry," I say breathlessly to my cousin.

I'm not surprised when Mia laughs, nor when she gives Tom the sort of appraising glance no one could misread. "Don't apologize. I sincerely get it," she says.

I smile wanly, pretending not to notice her flirtatiousness. His handsomeness aside, I know what's happening here. He's another diamond necklace in a family obsessed with them. I have him. She wants him.

When Mia enters the bathroom, I push Tom away lightly. "Thanks," I say.

"Anytime," he replies.

Despite myself, I pause, wondering if he means it.

My phone buzzes, recapturing my focus. While pulling the phone out in the middle of the hallway is risky, I have to with Cass unaccounted for. After glancing each way down the familiar corridors, I whip the phone out, determined I'm safe for the moment.

Queen

> Sorry. Some security started looking around. I moved to the garage.

The relief is intoxicating. Overwhelming. I feel like I'm flying over the stately sloped roof of the house, high over the Rhode Island coastline. *Of course.* Security would patrol the parking. The van is more noticeable staying in one place when other vendors have come and gone. I wish I'd thought of the detail, honestly.

I show Tom my phone. His reaction mirrors mine.

"Phase Five?" he asks.

"Phase Five," I confirm. The words taste sweet like wedding cake and fizzy like champagne.

When Mia emerges, I have my arms back around Tom's neck.

"You coming outside for the ceremony?" she asks expectantly.

"You know, I've seen my dad get married before. I'm not sure it improves on second viewing," I reply.

Mia permits only the smallest of perfunctory smiles, as if she recognizes my humor while finding no joy in it. "Certainly not when you have someone like Thomas here to amuse you instead."

I put a hand on Tom's chest, half in possessiveness, half indulgence. "You won't tell anyone, will you?" I ask conspiratorially.

Her smile sharpens. "Your secret is safe with me."

It's not, of course. I know it's not. Mia exchanges family secrets like currency. In fact, I'm counting on this delightful tidbit—*Dash's wayward daughter missed most of the ceremony while hooking up in the bathroom!*—to make its way back to Switzerland before the bouquet has even been tossed. She's the perfect witness.

Mia heads outside while the sounds of the string octet drift through the doors. It's the beginning of the processional, which means we have twenty minutes or less.

Phase Five. It's my personal favorite phase, I have to say. High risk, high reward.

Very high risk, though.

The wedding itself is the diversion on which the entire Plan was founded. In the next fifteen minutes, we hit the safe. We have the length of my father's nuptials to get in and out while the ceremony keeps four hundred pairs of eyes on the bride and groom. If we don't leave the office in time, we will be caught by Dash, Maureen, Mitchum, Maureen's maid of honor, and their officiant, Reverend Arnold, who will enter to sign the marriage license.

We'll be out in time, I reassure myself. All I need are the account passcodes, and then Tom and I will be back at the ceremony in time to catch the vows.

We wait, wanting the house completely clear. Except it won't be clear, I know from Cass's phone call earlier. Just clear of *guests*. In the meantime, Millennium Security's walking perimeter is forming on the ground floor of the house I once called home.

When Pachelbel's Canon in D begins, Tom and I exchange wordless glances. While it would have been ideal to let Deonte and McCoy handle this part so I could sit in the front row of the ceremony with a stronger alibi, I couldn't let them take the risk. If I'm caught opening my father's safe, I can pass it off as wanting earrings to match my necklace. If Deonte or McCoy is caught, they're going to jail.

And...I *want* to do this part.

I didn't orchestrate a heist just to sit on the sidelines. *I* will be the one to open my father's safe. To steal from him. To take what should have been mine.

I pull out my phone.

If security sees me in the next five minutes, everything is ruined regardless of the cheap iPhone in my hand. I move between the windows to call Cass. Without a word, I put the phone to my ear. "Hello, King," she drawls, no hint in her voice of remorse for the collective heart attack she just caused us.

Of course, I say nothing.

"Okay. No one in the foyer," she informs me, commencing the strategy I pitched her on the path up from the cottage.

When Cass called us during the kidnapping, I noticed how, in describing the guards' positioning during the champagne welcome, she knew exactly where they were. She could see their positions. I asked her for elaboration, and she explained, with pride visible even in iMessage, how she'd figured out she could locate the receiving signatures of their earpieces and map them onto a layout of the home and grounds.

Including now. Including the "walking perimeter" in the hallways surrounding the study.

I knew I would need Cass as my eyes and ears. With my phone clutched to my face, Cass is going to guide our way.

I proceed through the foyer, Tom on my heels. "Stop. *Stopstopstop.* Go back," she orders urgently. We withdraw until Cass continues. "Okay. Living room is clear now."

Silently, I steal forward on my way to the study. When Cass commands, I slip with Tom into the hall closet, evading the next oncoming guard's notice.

In the darkened quiet of the closet, only inches separate me from my counterpart. It's...intimate, charged in a way I had not anticipated when I planned our approach with Cass. His eyes meet mine, his cologne unreasonably sophisticated for our age, an expensive aura of confidence. While Cass is silent, waiting for the moment to issue her next instruction, it's impossible not to feel the heart-pounding proximity with him.

Knight, I remind myself. Our chest-to-chest closeness right now is for nothing except the job. Just business.

This business for which no one appears to share my dark love like he does. The business of deception. Of ruthlessness, danger, indulgence.

"Now," Cass says in my ear.

I wrench myself out of the moment, knowing I can't hesitate, and continue down the hallway, feeling how Tom clings to my every step. I'm getting a sense for the guards' pattern. The study is nearing, if slowly.

"Hey, I can kind of say whatever to you and you can't reply, right?" Cass asks out of nowhere. When I don't, she goes on. "Ooh, fun. I guess, um..."

I quell my irritation. She's not wrong. In the echoing, empty hall-ways, I literally cannot reply without risking detection.

"I have to say," she goes on, "I admire you adding a whole fake boyfriend into your plans just to get back at your cheating ex. It's inspired, honestly." She laughs, half sympathetic, half something else. Her ruefulness is hard to read. "People suck. Guys suck. I just want you to know I get it."

I don't know what I would say if I could. The rare flash of commiseration from Cass leaves me wondering who cheated on her. Of course, Tom offers no reaction, having heard none of her commentary.

"Wait," Cass says.

Despite myself, I'm distracted. Her mention of Jackson waylays me for split seconds.

"Wait, shit." Cass speaks fast, snapping me into focus. "Olivia, *get back to the hallway closet. One of the guards changed direction.*"

I don't even have milliseconds to spare on resenting how her little monologue nearly cost me everything. I hustle as fast as my heels will carry me, Tom close behind. When I enter the closet, compacted in with him once more, I hear no commotion from the hallway, no quickened footsteps. Only my pounding heartbeat.

We made it.

With my pulse slowing, and gambling on the sturdiness of the door, I whisper firmly into the phone.

"*No more distractions,*" I say.

"Right," Cass replies, sounding uncharacteristically chastened. "Okay, um. Wait. This is weird. Hold on..."

I want to ask what is going on, but I hear footsteps outside.

Cass continues. "They're all retreating. Radio chatter is calling them down to the entrance, where paparazzi are trying to get in. You're, uh, yeah, you're in the clear."

It feels impossible for something to have actually been *convenient* today. I head out into the hall, making a mental note to click whatever links promise leaked photos of Dashiell Owens's private wedding in thanks to my savior, the intrepid paparazzi downstairs.

In front of the heavy study door, I hang up the phone and slip inside.

Except, when I open the door, the room isn't empty.

TWENTY-SIX

DASHIELL OWENS'S SECOND WIFE, MY STEPMOTHER FOR ELEVEN long months, the woman who ended my parents' marriage, stands in front of me in a dark red gown.

Lexi.

She wasn't invited to the wedding.

She definitely isn't supposed to be in Dash's office.

And she absolutely should not be standing next to *the open safe.*

Impossibly, Lexi grins. She gives me a playful wave, like we're downstairs during cocktail hour. Her whole vibe is enviable, honestly. Her makeup is bold, her dark hair perfectly curled. Everything from her red lip to the thigh slit in her dress to my father's most personal documents in her hands is screaming *revenge.*

There is no way my dad ever gave her the combination to the safe. If he had, he would have changed it the second Lexi was legally no longer Mrs. Dashiell Owens.

"*How—*" I start, then whirl.

Kevin steps out from behind the door I just opened. "I told you I was a good businessman," he says, far too smug even for Kevin Webber. "You didn't want to work with me. *She* did."

I dig my nails into my palms, furious with myself. I should have had McCoy make the ransom call in the other room—or pulled Kevin away, distracted him, done anything to ensure he didn't overhear the combination to the safe. Clearly, he memorized it, which, yes, I did not think Kevin Webber and his 2.0 GPA paid for by Daddy was capable of.

If I'm going to save today, I chastise myself harshly, *I need to stop underestimating Kevin.*

What a horrific realization.

I face Lexi, deciding I'll handle Kevin later. "Lexi. What are you doing here?" I keep my voice even, as if I have all the time in the world and not eighteen minutes now.

"Such a funny little mix-up. I think my invitation got lost in the mail," she says sweetly. "I simply *had* to come and give my blessing to the happy couple."

"In Dash's office," I reply flatly.

She tosses her hair over her shoulder, unfazed. "The night is long, Olivia."

No, it's not. I have one window of opportunity, and *Lexi* is in my way. I don't know how she managed to get into this wedding without an invite or how she got past the guards. *Did she call the paparazzi to clear her escape route?*

There's no denying she's done some planning of her own.

Planning *what*, though? If I can answer that question, I'll have the upper hand on her.

While the race to the bottom in my bracket for worst stepmother is quite competitive, if I had to choose a winner, it would be Lexi. Maureen is young, naive, and marrying Dash for his money. While it's gross, it's at least understandable. Lexi actually loved him. She's a monster, obviously.

It offers the first hint of explanation into why she's here, or one possible reason. While Dash may have cheated on my mom, I know part of him did love her. No part of him loved Lexi. She was face-saving for him, pure and simple. He wanted his circle to consider him the winner instead of the divorcé—wanted everyone to know he could replace the job of "wife" as easily as he could replace anyone on his payroll.

With characteristic lack of restraint, he made his absence of genuine affection for her evident. It was startling to notice him apply to someone else the deliberate disregard he'd started directing at me—the refusal to ask questions, the quickness to frustration, the looking past you or scanning his phone when you were speaking. For Dash Owens, it was a marriage of inconvenience. It lasted eleven months.

Those eleven months were . . . war.

I didn't care how my dad regarded Lexi. I was hurt, and I was furious. I did everything in my power to make her uncomfortable in the house she stole from me and my mom. I undermined her at every dinner, spoke ill of her whenever I could. Dash never once reprimanded me. Which is how I know Lexi was no one to him.

The split was almost as acrimonious as my parents'. Lexi did not go quietly. One time I came over for dinner to find she had put one of my dad's suits in the oven, destroying the suit, almost starting a fire, and ruining the twenty-thousand-dollar Wolf French Top. If I didn't hate her, I would admire the vigor of her vengefulness.

I step forward, summoning some self-assured swagger. "What do you want, Lexi?" I ask. "Come to steal the marriage license so my dad can't officially replace you? What sad and pathetic plan have you gotten *Kevin*"—I glance at her annoying accomplice out of the corner of my eye—"to help you carry out?"

Lexi's mouth flattens.

I prepare myself. I haven't spoken to Lexi in a year. She has no reason to meet me with charity or cooperation. Whatever she's up to, I'm probably inconveniencing her as much as she is me.

"We could have been friends," she says instead, her eyes wistful. "Livy and Lexi. Dash's girls."

I gag. Lexi doesn't notice, or pretends she doesn't, occupied with her domestic fantasy.

"No one calls me Livy," I inform her. "And no, we couldn't have been *friends*. You literally helped my dad cheat on my mom. The only thing we have in common is we both used to live here."

Warning fire flashes in Lexi's expression.

"Well," she says sharply, "and we both want something in this room."

The change in the register of the conversation is palpable. We're not running into each other. We're facing off. I hold my ex-stepmother's gaze until I hear Tom shift on his feet. The meaning in his movement is clear. Our window is closing.

The safe isn't. It waits, inviting me like no pretty foil on cardstock ever could.

So I gamble. *High risk, high reward.*

I walk past Lexi to the open safe, my heels clicking on the hardwood. "Excuse me," I dare to say.

Lexi's eyebrows rise. She watches me in undisguised curiosity.

I'm wrestling with curiosity of my own. "How were you going to get into the safe without Kevin?" I ask casually. It's just…extracting the combination to my very own father's safe cost me months of planning. If Lexi had her own means of infiltrating the lock—well, I consider the point one of professional interest.

"I figured I would be able to guess the combination," she replies innocently, evidently delighted with her own confidence. "I know every important date in Dash's life. All his lucky numbers. I wasn't *sure* I could crack it in the time it took him to marry that girl outside, but I knew I had a chance. Still"—she smiles—"it was fortuitous when I found this young man lurking downstairs. Waiting for you, he said."

I purse my lips while I peruse the safe. Lexi probably didn't know Dash's phone would receive a notification if the safe was opened. In dousing Quinn, I unintentionally *helped* Lexi.

Great.

Fending off frustration, I focus on my search. In seventeen years, I've never observed the contents of my father's safe up close. It's full of obvious valuables—watches of ludicrous size with interchangeable European names, jewelry dripping with gems, crystal figurines. Handcuffs, which is weird. Heirloom-looking pieces whose discoloration doesn't detract from the intricacy of their old craftsmanship.

Realistically, I could probably smuggle one out in my clutch and sell it for hundreds of thousands of dollars.

I'm not here for hundreds of thousands, though.

Under the luxury items, I find something more promising— paperwork. Physical stock certificates of shares in the Owens media companies, trust documentation with pages initialed in unassuming pen ink. I rearrange the pile, sifting around, searching for what I need.

It isn't here.

"I believe you're looking for this," Lexi says.

I round on her, dread forming in my stomach. She pulls a folded piece of paper from her dress.

"The passcodes to his offshore accounts, right?" Lexi preempts me. "I know you and your mom have stumbled upon rough times. Medical debt, not to mention single parenting with no résumé. That little two-bedroom, one-bathroom must be cramped."

Her every pretense of friendliness for her former stepdaughter has vanished, spiked in the heart under her stilettos.

I keep my face impassive, straightening up. Inside, I'm the opposite. I'm flat-out panicking.

"I'd be happy to give it to you, Livy," Lexi drawls, "if you do something for me first."

TWENTY-SEVEN

WHAT?" KEVIN COMPLAINS.

I look over, finding him regarding us from the door, hands planted petulantly in his pockets. "*You,*" I rage, realizing why Lexi knows what I'm here for. *Paper codes in a safe....* Unfuckingbelievable. If five seconds of overheard conversation I let happen out of momentary weakness led *Kevin Webber* to ruin my entire enterprise—

His concentration is on Lexi. "You want to work with Olivia? I thought *we* were partners," he whines.

I recognize myself in the glance Lexi gives him. I grasp on to the opportunity. Kevin has messed enough up. I resolved I would deal with him later. Now, it seems, is later. I need him out of the way, eliminated from whatever dangerous equation Lexi is offering me.

"Sorry, Kevin," I say with sarcasm dialed up to eleven. "It looks like no one wants to work with you. Again. You really are an atrocious businessman."

"Dude, come on," Kevin implores.

"Need I remind you, you did double-cross us," Tom points out. "*Dude.*"

While Kevin sulks, I walk over to my dad's desk. I sit down in his maple-and-leather chair, needing to rest my feet and also wanting to look cool. I cross my legs calmly.

"Tell me what you want for the passcodes," I say.

Lexi's eyes dance with delight. Her rouge lips curl. She slips the folded paper into her bra, which is gross. Can't wait to hold it later.

Opposite me, she seats herself languidly on a chesterfield couch while Tom and Kevin remain standing near the door, our audience. Everything in the room has the same feel of unearned luxury and stately entitlement. Sitting on the soft leather, Lexi fits right in.

"When Dash and I got married, we signed a prenup," she begins.

I stay silent. I've watched my dad enough to know forcing the other person to do the talking is the position of power. Nevertheless, I'm sweating. Eighteen minutes have wound down to fourteen.

"I knew I would have to sign it," she continues. "I knew I wouldn't get any of his money should we divorce. However, I also knew your father's...proclivities."

"You mean how he's a dirtbag who cheated on my mother with... Who was it again? A real piece of work she was," I interject. *Forget the position of power.* With Lexi, I can't help indulging familiar instincts for spite. Old habits die hard, I guess.

Unlike insincere marriages.

The campaign I waged against my ex-stepmother over the months of her and Dash's marriage was, in honesty, not only out of resentment for Lexi. It was my coping mechanism. In the early days, when I moved from the guest cottage into my mom's new home, I would spend every dinner here racked with conflicting emotions. I felt guilty for how much I missed this house, when it represented my dad and his cushioned cruelty.

Even deeper down, I hated how much I missed *him* or even the idea of him. I wanted to hate him fully—I did. Driving up the winding path in Mom's and my crappy shared car, I just knew I didn't yet.

Lashing out at Lexi was my release. I could hide from how complicated my feelings on my father remained—from how difficult I found disentangling my heart from the parent who rejected me. If I couldn't fully hate my dad, hating Lexi was very, very easy.

Granted, she did herself no favors. She loved playing house. Playing *mom*, plying me with syrupy questions whenever I was here for dinner. *How's your new school? When's prom? Do you have your dress? Who's Jackson?*

Loathing my father got easier, of course. I no longer had need for her when my father replaced her with Maureen.

Lexi doesn't flinch under my insults, likely leveraging muscle memory of her own. She examines her flawless manicure. "Yes," she replies. "I suspected he would cheat again. Our sudden divorce nearly confirms it."

I cannot fault Lexi's logic. Cheaters never change. Not when they're your dad. Not when they're your ex.

"Wow. I'm so sorry," I say dryly. "How awful. You didn't deserve it at all."

Lexi narrates on as if I haven't spoken. "Like I said, I suspected he would cheat, so when he handed me the prenup," she says, "I had him add an infidelity clause."

Now I lean forward onto the desk. *Interesting.*

I remember Lexi's persistence. I remember her vicious marital ambition, her lack of guilt for upending my parents' relationship and ruining my life. I remember her immediate, almost-oblivious entitlement—her greatest similarity to my father. Where my mom unashamedly never entirely got used to the privilege surrounding her, and where Maureen overcompensates, preening and showing off how she feels she owns this place, Lexi acted like she simply *did*.

I do not, however, remember Lexi for cunning or intellect. The "infidelity clause" is worth credit I would not have assumed she deserved.

"He agreed that if I ever got proof of him cheating, I would receive five million," she explains unceremoniously.

I feel my eyebrows rise. I'm honestly surprised my dad agreed. Yes, he's gauche, he's selfish, he's cheating-inclined. He is not, historically, stupid.

"In order to collect, I need proof," Lexi continues. "And I want to collect. Here, tonight. At his wedding."

Folding my fingers in front of me, I stare. "You think *I* have proof my father—who *kicked me out of the house* for telling my mother I caught him cheating on her with you—is cheating again?" I recap, my insinuation clear. I'm the *least* likely person Dash would let evidence of his adultery reach.

The point doesn't perturb my former stepmom. "I think you can get it," she says. "Everyone in Dash's life is here tonight. His office is empty. I know you have . . . sticky fingers." Her smile sparkles without warmth. "Find it," she orders me.

I grit my teeth, not pleased she's mentioned my shoplifting in front of Tom and Kevin. I was only ever caught once. The convenience store called my mom, who I guess felt obligated to relay the news of my unconsummated lipstick larceny over to Dash. While Mom, who picked me up from where the store detained me, was upset, she let me off easy punishment-wise. I know she understood what I was dealing with, how confused and on edge I was.

When I came here for weekly dinner, Dash yelled at me, obviously. It was easy to ignore—I knew he just wanted to feel dominant and warn me against messing with his reputation.

Lexi, however—Lexi was worse. She wanted to *mother* me about it. Even while I gave her nothing, her questions sharpened into scalpels, probing how I must've needed to act out with everything I was facing at home.

With her expectant eyes on me now, I push aside the resentment. I can't let it interfere with solving the very serious problem I'm facing. I need to figure out a faster way to obtain the codes from Lexi. I can't just interrogate every guest and ask if they've slept with my father.

"Look, Lexi," I say, exhausted. "The codes in your bra will get us into Dash's offshore accounts. How about I just give you five million and skip the recon into my dad's sex life? Everyone wins. Except him, I guess."

Lexi grimaces. "It's not about the *money*, Olivia," she replies. It's small comfort she's dropped "Livy" for the moment. "I thought you would understand better than most. It's about him. I want him to *pay* me because he has to. Because I was his *wife*."

My head hurts; my heart pounds. I'm glad the emotion painting my cheeks isn't visible under my foundation. I stand sharply. "I'm sorry, but I can't help you."

Lexi rises, startled. "Why? You would just give up the little heist you planned over something this simple?"

I nod. "I'm not helping you. Ever."

Heading for the door, I ignore the look on Tom's face. I understand his deep alarm, I do. I'll need to explain our defeat to the rest of the crew or reconfigure The Plan or I don't know what. It's ninety-nine percent certain the day will end with our phones in the ocean.

"What about Mr. Peter McCoy?"

Lexi's question halts me immediately.

The next moment, my gaze flies to Kevin. He shuffles his feet defensively. "I mean, come on," he offers. "You didn't really think I wouldn't recognize a teacher, did you?"

I glare—no, glower, hot indignation filling me up. Dealing with Lexi, I felt resentment. I understood her despite the world of inconvenience she's caused me. Knowing Kevin's put my co-conspirator *and friend* on the line, what I feel is rage. "You're desperate for people to like you," I seethe. "But have you ever done anything worth liking?"

His face falls. It earns him no sympathy from me.

I turn back to Lexi, recovering my composure. "McCoy did nothing illegal," I inform her.

When Lexi frowns, I recognize finally the stepmother I once knew. Gone is the voluptuous negotiator holding my heist in her hands. Instead, her concern is coated on heavily. She's not mad, just disappointed.

"He planned to, though, didn't he?" She shakes her head mournfully. "Kevin here was just so chatty when I was searching the office. Kidnapping, Olivia? I know you've had your indiscretions, but this is really bleak."

"Olivia," Tom interjects, the wavering note in his voice impossible to ignore, "who knows what else Kevin has said?"

Unfortunately, he's very right. *Deonte. Tom. Cass. McCoy.* I won't let them go down for this, not when I'm the one who brought them into it. The chess club code names feel ominous now. I've just realized the fundamental danger they imply. In chess, you play an opponent who's out to knock each of your pieces from the board. Right now, the queen in front of me is poised to claim all of mine.

Except it isn't checkmate. Not yet.

"Proof Dash cheated on you," I say slowly, "and you'll give us the codes and not say a word about what we've done?"

"You'll never hear from me again, sweet stepdaughter," Lexi confirms. "I guarantee it."

I chew my lip. What she's demanding of me is near impossible—like stealing millions from one of the most prominent men in media, like doing it while in high school. Like surviving half the shit I've dealt with. Impossible is my brand.

I hold out my hand.

When Lexi smiles, Kevin storms from the study, cut out once again.

With manicured fingers, my ex-stepmother shakes my hand on our deal.

TWENTY-EIGHT

I NOD TO THE DOOR. "STAY ON KEVIN," I SAY TO TOM. "MAKE SURE he doesn't talk to anyone else. He's done enough damage."

Tom hesitates only momentarily, darting concerned glances at me and Lexi, then follows Kevin out.

Returning to the couch, Lexi picks up the file she was holding when I walked in. "Do you know who Abigail Pierce is?"

Without deception, I shake my head. I've never heard the name. Lexi hands me the file, which I open. Inside, I find Dash's will, signature pages labeled with the name of my grandfather's trust, and other vaguely legal items I don't recognize.

The final piece of paper is a printed email from my dad to Mitchum, asking him to prepare updates to the will to include his new wife—and Abigail Pierce, with no further details provided.

I read on, searching the included email correspondence for clues on the identity of the mysterious Ms. Pierce. Yet when I reach the summary of recipients my father requested and received from Mitchum five months ago, another name stuns me. It isn't Abigail Pierce's or Maureen's or Lexi's.

It's...mine.

Even now, years after he made clear I ruined his marriage and caused his divorce, Dash has not removed me from his will. He has not revoked my entitlement to my share of his fortune.

I'm still an heiress.

Distantly, I recognize the irony in the circumstances of my discovery. Only while literally stealing from him do I learn he has not removed me from his financial future. Will he after I pull my heist?

I honestly don't know, I realize. I expect he will, of course. Stealing millions of dollars does not historically endear one to one's family. However...I assumed he'd removed my name when he cast me out of his house. Yet here I am, listed next to Maureen and Abigail Pierce.

Suddenly, I remember Mitchum's invocation of *proof* and *exposure*. At first, I hesitated to pursue them, hating the perverse protective loyalty I still have for Dashiell Owens.

Now I have an excuse I can live with. The stakes are much, much higher—*my* inheritance is on the line if my dad has committed fraud or some other crime to be exposed. Yes, it's less moral than loyalty to my father, but I've never cared for a clean conscience. Obviously.

In the worth of my father's name, I now have something to lose.

Which means I have something to protect. *In love and ruthlessness, Dad.*

With new determination, I decide I need to learn what exposure Mitchum Webber feels my father is vulnerable to. Not to exploit it, but to control it. Whatever place I may one day inherit in the Owens dynasty—or whatever dynasty I'll forge on my own with this surname clinging to me—will carry any stain shed onto Dash. If he goes to jail, if courts or the IRS come to collect his wealth, I'll be losing just as much as him.

My mind starts to whirl. Is Abigail involved in the proof Mitchum mentioned? Is she someone he's paying off, concealing whatever it is Mitchum wants "exposed"? Or is she just another mistress in a long line of his infidelities? It's statistically the likeliest option.

"Whoever Abigail Pierce is," Lexi remarks, as if following my logic, "she's not family. Not someone who works for him. And yet he's giving her a third of his fortune? I'd start with her."

Lexi is right. I need to focus on the heist, which now rests in my ex-stepmother's manicured hands. I can handle the potential Mitchum fallout later. While seeing proof I'm still in the will has shifted some of my plans, it doesn't change today's main objective. I still need money now. I still *want* money now. Whoever Abigail is, she's my clearest opportunity, my hottest lead. I need to figure it out in order to finish what I started.

With her usual presumptive comfort in the rooms of my father's house, Lexi collects her clutch from the couch. "I'll be attending the wedding. Find me when you have something," she says pleasantly.

I glance up, not sure I've heard her right. *Attending the wedding?* "Maureen will throw you out."

Lexi laughs. The sound is like the fine ceramics in the kitchen crashing down the staircase in the foyer. "I'd like to see the future Mrs. Dashiell Owens try," she says pleasantly. "I imagine she'd like to know who Abigail Pierce is as much as we do. Maybe this marriage will be over before it starts."

TWENTY-NINE

Meet in the garage after the ceremony.

I put away my phone after texting the chat. The estimated window is down to four minutes. I need to get out of here or risk an unplanned encounter with Reverend Arnold and his happy entourage.

I have nothing, of course. Lexi's departure left me mere minutes for the cursory search I conduct of Dash's office. It yields only unnerving evidence of how many cigars one man could possess. After shutting the safe, I slip out of the office unseen.

The vacant hallway leads me out onto the lawn overlooking the ocean, where the ceremony hasn't ended. Rows of white chairs face a botanical arch in front of the glassy water. The light glitters on it like pearls of mercury. On the grounds of the Owens estate, even nature feels the irresistible need to show off.

I find Tom and Kevin seated in the back row, where I slide into the empty seat Tom's holding for me. I earn reproachful glances from the nearest guests, which I welcome.

Or I pretend I do. In fact, on the lawn—past the white roses whose cultivation interested my mom, in front of the water where we would skip stones into the mirrored horizon—it's unexpectedly a little much.

As I mentioned to Tom, I'm only playing the part every guest imagines is real. *Olivia Owens.* Heiress without a clue. The daddy's girl whose dad didn't want custody. But under their glares in the midst of my father's wedding, the reality of my reputation starts to hurt. *I'm* the interloper? *I'm* the problem? I used to *live here.* Not them. Not the social media girls on the end of the row. Not the financiers whose Ferraris occupy the driveway.

It isn't the indulgence of my dad and his guests' lifestyle I'm jealous of. I'm pissed to hear Lexi's words ringing in my head. *It's not about the money.*

It's them feeling they deserve to be here. It's easy for them to sneer and whisper for one ugly reason—they feel like they're worth this world, this house, this opulence, and I no longer am. *The estranged. The starter family. The reject.*

Under the arch, Maureen recites her vows. Clichés performed with practiced pathos. The expression on my dad's face rubs in everything I'm feeling.

It's funny, realizing I planned for every part of this wedding except the wedding part. The part where my father marries his new wife. Where he pushes the girl sitting in the last row—and her mother, working multiple jobs and probably feeling grateful photographs of this event won't find their way onto her Instagram—further into the past.

I shouldn't care. Dashiell Owens is the worst.

Shouldn't leaves me with nothing except shame, however, when the reality is, I can't escape the hurt of how easily my dad has moved on from me and our family. It's vexingly inconsistent. I can get multimillion-dollar combinations out of highly paid lawyers. I can smuggle phones past private security. Why can't I pry open the locked safe of my own heart and extract this feeling with the same precision?

He looks *happy*, damn him.

Maureen will want kids. When she has them, I'll mean even less to him. Just a memory of what was. Instead of walking the hallways of this house like a guest, I'll walk them like a ghost.

Unless.

Unless I cut a hole into my father's life so deep that he can't help feeling my presence every goddamn day. I want him to know it was me. I won't need the Owens home then. When I'm done here, I'll buy my own house with *Live, Laugh, Larceny* written on the wall.

Pain startles me—I glance down, noticing how hard I'm clench-ing gelled nails into my palm, the synthetic pink sharp in contrast to the deep red of my sore skin.

I relax them. I just need to find Abigail Pierce.

While the officiant continues the proceedings, I survey with new evaluation the judgmental guests surrounding me. *Opportunities.* Really, I couldn't have asked for a more perfect venue to dig into Dash's personal life.

I see business partners current and old. The CFOs of his media companies who do the more hands-on work for him. Rivals he keeps close. *James Fontaine.* Provocateur host of *The Jimmy F. Hour. Walter Peterson.* Eagerly stepped up into the C-suite role when my father announced the "demands of fatherhood" led him to shift into an executive chairman role. Ha. More like the demands of increasing podcast episodes per week while my mom cared for me.

I pass my eyes over famous guests. Neighbors and friends. Family.

Someone at this wedding knows who Abigail is. I just have to find them.

Well, no. It's more complicated than that. I can't just orchestrate a second ransoming on the fly. Whoever it is, I'll have to get close to them. Charm them. Convince them to tell me who Abigail is or, ideally, get them to let it slip without them even realizing it.

Logically, I'll need to start with the people closest to him. His groomsmen.

When my father seals his new marriage with a kiss, the audience erupts into cheers. I divert my eyes, letting my gaze wander down the line of groomsmen. Jerry Hausman stands next to Mitchum, whistling while my dad—*barf*—dips Maureen.

Jerry was my dad's roommate at Princeton. He's his oldest friend, even if their relationship more often leans competitive and manipulative. I'm pretty sure Jerry has unsuccessfully pressed Dash to invest in one of his various funds or cryptocurrencies for years. Dash refuses. Still, once a year they'll take some disgusting boys' trip to Vegas or Abu Dhabi or Monaco.

Who knows what Dash has confessed while drunk out of his mind?

I put Jerry down on my "mark list." I just need to find a reason to be near him during dinner.

My eyes stray farther down the line of tuxedoed men until they land on Jackson. His hair is windswept in the salt spray, the flower of his boutonniere fluttering against his lapel. He's standing straight, his hands clasped in front of him like he's cut from marble.

He's looking right at me, his expression a mixture of concern, longing, and hurt.

I don't drop his gaze, getting an idea. The beginning of a new plan.

Phase Six.

THIRTY

STEP ONTO THE CEMENT OF DASH'S SIX-CAR GARAGE, AND IT'S AS if I've walked into a new world.

There's no wedding finery here. No floral arrangements or crown molding or crystal centerpieces. Instead, only the unglamorous utilitarian components. Trash cans, coolers of ice, extra linens. When the door shuts behind me, the sounds of cocktail hour are drowned out. I hear only the hum of the massive lights hanging from the ceiling and the harsh clicking of my heels on concrete.

I walk swiftly. The garage doors are open, revealing the golden hour outside. Catering vans and security trucks occupy most of the spots, but there's no one loading or unloading. I know from Maureen's run of show that while she is legally becoming Mrs. Owens in the office right now, the wedding staff is circling with hors d'oeuvres and frantically flipping the grassy cliffs from ceremony seating to dining arrangements. It gives me a window before I'll be expected at dinner.

Before Phase Six begins.

I enter the van parked in the corner. Inside, my crew waits.

The moment I roll the door closed, everyone speaks at once. "Where are the codes?" Cass demands. "We need to know what's going on—"

"I'm pretty sure the other security guys are onto me—" McCoy frets.

Deonte rounds on Cass. "Oh, and you couldn't have given us a heads-up you were moving the van? I had to sneak my way back into the wedding."

"What are we doing about *Kevin*?" Tom asks resentfully. "How are we supposed to get your ex-stepmom the proof she needs—?"

The cacophony continues. Everyone shouts over one another, filling the van with accusations, questions, fears, and complaints, exchanging the information the others don't have. I don't cut them off. In the echoing metal cage of the vehicle, I let the clamor of their debate rush over me.

Everything they're saying is a real problem. I can't even keep up with the string of unsolved variables. Each one on its own is vexing— all together, they add up into one undeniable reality.

The Plan has imploded.

Deonte and McCoy are stuck here until the other vendors start leaving. I have no idea how I'll handle Kevin, frankly, short of the enticing possibility of tying him up and leaving him in one of the closets in the basement. Lexi—Lexi is a whole handful of problems in herself. Assuming I procure the evidence she wants, how will I even orchestrate the exchange without drawing attention?

The crew is not helping. Like, *very* not helping. While I reflect on everything going wrong, their "discussion" has unraveled into infighting over whose role is more important. While McCoy mediates with unsuccessful if valiant educator-ly effort, Tom feuds with Deonte. "I'm *just saying*, you get to sit in the van while I have to—"

"I *did* my part," Deonte protests. "You glad for those phones? Then why don't you say thank you—?"

"The phones were Olivia's idea. You made a cake, and it wasn't, like—"

"Gentlemen, I'm one insulted cake away from a hard-core migraine," McCoy chimes in.

"Ridiculously immature." Cass passes judgment from her seat, arms folded over her chest.

I sympathize with McCoy's headache. It's kind of like the drive up, except for one crucial difference. I'm not in control.

Not yet.

"Don't say shit about my cakes," Deonte warns.

"Everyone." McCoy glances up urgently.

"Okay, I'm sorry, man," Tom says, sounding genuine. "I was out of line. The cake was lovely. Sincerely. Flower game was unreal. Still—"

"*Everyone.*"

When McCoy holds up his phone, the infighting ceases. The strategy no one can agree on, the complaints of our present hope-lessness, the futility, the frustration—it all stops. The van goes silent except for one insistent sound.

McCoy's phone vibrating.

The screen is lit up with an incoming call. The caller ID displays *M*, one of the five numbers programmed into the phones.

M for *Mitchum.*

"Well, shit," Deonte says.

"I concur," Tom adds solemnly.

THIRTY-ONE

EVERYONE'S BREATHING SEEMS TO STILL AS FIVE PAIRS OF EYES FIX on the phone in McCoy's hand. Disaster scenarios tornado through my mind. Mitchum is calling. Mitchum has handed the phone to security. Security has turned the phone over to the police. The police have already called in the FBI.

Is this a federal crime?

I feel like I should know the answer, but I didn't want to dwell on the consequences for something I had no intention of getting caught for.

"Did no one remember to pick up the ransom phone?" Cass asks, her tone low with accusation.

Deonte whips his head toward her. "Maybe if the *van* had been where we thought it was, McCoy would have been able to return for it as *planned*. Instead, we were completely stranded, trying to figure out what the hell had happened."

"I'm sorry," Cass replies, sounding anything but apologetic. Her pale skin is tinted pink, with bright red splotches growing on her cheeks. "Would you rather be in handcuffs right now? Because if I hadn't moved the van exactly when I did, I guarantee security would have found me. Which would have led them to all of you. I think I'm owed a *little* appreciation for my quick thinking."

"Appreciation?" Deonte repeats. "Man, I don't even know who you are. So far you've hacked a local print shop or something? Their password was probably *printshop*."

Cass sets her laptop down as if she's about to climb out of her seat. I have to regain control, reinstate the new plan, avoid getting caught.

"Enough!" I call out.

The phone's buzzing stops, leaving the garage eerily silent.

"Maybe it was a butt dial?" Tom suggests hopefully.

"Pray tell, *whose* butt?" McCoy replies.

Deonte rolls his eyes. "Be serious."

"I would never joke about butts under these circumstances," McCoy says.

Before I can end this inane debate, the phone starts ringing again. We don't have many options. Even fewer when we don't know who has the ransom phone. I meet Cass's eyes. She rubs her chin as if she's running through the same mental checklist I am. When I glance to the phone then back to her, she nods, understanding my silent question. Our move will depend on who we're up against. Which means—

"Answer it," I tell McCoy. "If it *is* Mitchum, he already knows your voice."

McCoy brings the phone closer to his face, his hand trembling. "What do I say?"

"As little as possible," Cass supplies.

He doesn't look stoked about his new role. Slowly, he hits accept on the call, then he quickly shifts the sound to speaker. "Hello?" he says stiffly, his voice unnaturally flat.

I hold my breath, closing my eyes as if I can better hear who holds our fate in their hands if I can't see the interior of this van.

Sound explodes into the speakers. "Hey, where you guys at? Another party within the party?"

I massage my brow, feeling physically ill with relief and annoyance at once.

Kevin.

"How did you get this phone?" I ask with resignation. It's not the worst possible outcome. It's, like, the fourth-worst possible outcome. Competitive ranking.

"I went back and picked it up after the ransom call," he explains proudly. "*Duh.* Pretty quick thinking on my part. You wouldn't want this phone falling into the wrong hands."

"No, we wouldn't want that," I say dryly.

"Where are you guys?" Kevin presses, dropping his haughtiness. "What's the new plan?"

I consider informing him we're on our way to catch some mid-wedding weight lifting in the house's gym. I wonder how long he would wait.

Unfortunately for my nascent plan, Tom interjects. "We're obviously not going to tell you."

"You might as well," Kevin replies, undeterred. "I've searched the whole house. If I can't find you, there's nothing stopping me from"— he pauses for emphasis—"pointing out your absence to my father."

I groan. I don't know whether what is happening here is comical, infuriating, or sad. Probably some of each. I muster patience I didn't even know I had—forged in the East Coventry High lunch line and the DMV—and formulate my reply.

Before I get the words out, I hear the door from the house open. Footsteps enter the garage.

It could be security or catering. I fall silent, leaving the entire van in vacuum-sealed quiet. I can practically hear heartbeats echoing within the metal cavity of the interior.

"Man, your dad has some sick cars," Kevin says. "Let's take one for a spin."

His voice comes from the phone—*and* from three feet away.

I feel like screaming when the van door rolls open. Framed against concrete is Kevin, looking incredibly pleased with himself. He grins in exultant victory, the winner of the highest-stakes game of hide-and-seek any of us has ever played.

"Perfect!" he says. "The gang's all here."

THIRTY-TWO

SCOOT OVER, SCOOT OVER."

Kevin pleasantly addresses Deonte while clambering into the van. Deonte, appearing to not entirely understand the situation, nevertheless recognizes its volatility. He repositions, offering Kevin only inches of space, which, of course, Kevin seizes. Our interloper puts his hand out in Deonte's direction.

"What's up? I'm Kevin," he says.

Deonte regards Kevin Webber for a moment. Then he looks at me, his eyes saying, *Fix this.*

As if I needed the encouragement.

"Kevin, just fifteen minutes ago, you screwed us all over massively. We do not want to hang out with you," I say, reaching for the right combination of rational, retaliatory, and understanding. He's not wrong—he is the only person outside the crew who knows our whereabouts, which is powerful information. I certainly don't want to emphasize how powerful it is, which kissing up to him would do.

I also just would never want to do that.

Kevin only shrugs, not stung in the least. Honestly, his resilience for rejection is some kind of superpower. I wonder if he was bitten by a radioactive loser. "Whatever. I have information you may find interesting, though. Plus, you really can't trust me. I've seen all your faces now," he points out. "Kinda have no choice except to include me in the friend group!"

"This isn't a *friend group*," Tom explains witheringly. "We're here for a job. One you just made way harder."

Unlike Deonte and Cass, he has classmate experience with Kevin Webber. It sharpens his eagerness to lash out at Kevin when he doesn't have to play my effete paramour in front of Lexi.

"You hang out a lot, though," Kevin argues.

"Dude, we're working," Deonte says more gently.

"I would like to state for the record I don't hang out with teenagers recreationally," McCoy adds.

Kevin shakes his head with confident skepticism. "Nah. You're all on a group chat. I saw it during my kidnapping."

"It's a work group chat," Cass clarifies.

"I saw *emojis*," Kevin replies, the prosecutor with his key evidence.

"It's code," Cass says slowly. Her voice is a glass knife, fragile and deadly. I feel for her with acute guilt—her part of The Plan was intended to involve no guest contact, unique among the crew.

Of course, *none* of The Plan was intended to involve quite as much Kevin Webber as has occurred.

Kevin frowns doubtfully. However, he lets the point drop, looking to me instead. "I'll give you some information free of charge," he offers. "So you know I'm legit."

Oh, great. More negotiating. "Kevin, how many different ways do I need to say—"

"Dash and Maureen don't have a prenup."

The volunteered information silences me instantly.

In fact, my mind nearly shuts down under the weight of comprehension. "There's no way that's true," I get out.

It's wildly unrealistic, almost flat-out impossible. My father, media emperor and intergenerational wealth hoarder, wouldn't overlook this procedural detail when marrying an obviously money-hungry woman decades his junior.

Kevin crosses his arms, cocky. He's messing with me, I decide. He's worked out exactly what kind of fake reveal would entice me. "It is. I don't know if my dad really realizes I listen when he complains. Of course *he* doesn't want Dash's money going to Maureen when they divorce. It's less for him."

While lying isn't beneath Kevin, if what he's offering is true, it's something I definitely need to look into. *Why would he marry Maureen with no prenup?*

Past the possibility's obvious illogic, I can't help wrestling with how he insisted on the legal protection, with its inherent suspicion, even when he married my mom. *There's no way he loves this girl more than her, right?*

Right?

Kevin watches me, oblivious to the information's emotional impact. While I'm caught up in contemplation, Cass speaks.

"Is it possible Dash cheated on Lexi with Maureen?" she asks slowly. Her demeanor is completely changed. I recognize the image of myself in how the riddle has consumed her. "Could it be that simple? Is *Maureen* the evidence we need to give Lexi? Maybe he's pined for her for years. What if he's just so confident in the marriage he doesn't even want the prenup?"

I consider her questions. It would fit Dash's pattern, no doubt. Cheating, marrying, cheating, marrying. But it feels too neat.

Still, the lack of prenup means *something*. I don't want to reject possibilities out of hand, not when I have nothing else to go on right now.

"New plan," I announce.

I look around at my crew, my chess club, cataloging our recent setbacks. Regret hits me in a flash of clarity. Not for the mess we're in, not for my lack of foresight. No, I regret how, in all my rerouting and recalibrating, I've forgotten something essential. I have the greatest asset I could ever want right now—*them*.

Knight, Pawn, Rook, and Queen have risen to challenges and executed everything I expected and more. While The Plan is mine, the heist is ours.

"McCoy, ditch the security cover," I say. "If they're onto you, you're in trouble anyway. You have a new job."

He visibly braces himself. "Please don't make me take anyone hostage."

"You'll be attending the rest of the wedding as a guest. A beloved teacher of Maureen's," I elaborate.

His face clouds. "But I didn't teach Maureen."

"And as long as you don't talk to the bride herself, no one needs to know. You're a Berkshire teacher. Formerly," I amend apologetically. "Get in with her parents and try to get a more detailed timeline on the happy couple's courtship. You will, um"—I hesitate, working out the logistics—"have to shave your beard."

"Oh, thank *god*." Tom exhales.

I look to Deonte. "You're stuck at the wedding for now. Lose the jacket, go inside, and avoid catering staff. You're here to personally apologize to Quinn for spilling on him. Make the inroad."

"*The inroad?*" Deonte repeats. "The guy is an asshole."

I nod, anticipating the objection. "He is. And he most likely was just fired because of what you did. Explain to him the champagne incident got *you* fired, too. Complain about Jackson since he so eagerly took the fall for it. Commiserate. Get a drink with him, et cetera, et cetera. From one unemployed guy to another."

Deonte evaluates. I see it in his eyes—he knows the premise would work. He just needs to sell it.

"You're popular. People like you," I press him. "Loosen Quinn up. Chat with him. Get what you can on Maureen from him."

"I only agreed to bake and spill some champagne," he reminds me plaintively.

"Well, if money isn't incentive enough," I reply, "if you stick around, you'll get to taste your cake."

Now I know he's convinced. As if it's just occurred to him, he glances up, speaking to the crew. "Y'all better get slices and leave me good reviews on Yelp when I open my shop."

I face Cass. "I'll investigate Abigail Pierce online," she says, pre-empting me. "See what I can find. But I'll need to change locations— I can't stay in this van with catering coming back soon."

"Right." I follow her point, chasing the solution from the garage's concrete walls into the elegant corridors of the estate. "We'll have to move you into the house. My former room should be sufficiently private," I say.

"What about me?" Tom asks.

His enthusiasm is welcome. "I'm so sorry, Tom. We have to break up," I inform him dryly. "Loudly and in public."

He puts a hand over his heart, mock wounded. Romeo in a storage van. "Olivia, why? We were so happy."

I can't help laughing a little. "I need a seat at the head table," I say regretfully.

Tom's eyes widen. "You . . . sure you want to involve him?" he asks.

"Involve who?" Kevin interjects, intrigued.

"No, but it's my best option," I say to Tom. "As Dash's daughter, I'm relegated to the family table. I need a promotion in the wedding hierarchy."

"And I'll get more info from my dad on the prenup if I can," Kevin offers.

I narrow my eyes at him, although honestly, I'm conflicted. I don't like him inserting himself in The Plan. However, I can't deny the value in what he's proposing. Grudgingly, I nod, and Kevin fist pumps.

"After I'm kicked to the curb, I'll keep an eye on Kevin," Tom reassures me.

I don't hide my relief. "Good."

Kevin isn't offended. In fact, he looks delighted. "Sweet, we're partners," he exclaims. "Like Batman and Robin. Mario and Luigi. Master Shifu and Po."

Tom gives him a blank look.

"My guy," Kevin responds urgently. "We have *got* to watch *Kung Fu Panda* after this."

I don't want the discussion to devolve further. "Okay, everyone knows what they're doing?" I interrupt them.

The crew nods, including Kevin, who looks as if I've just signed him up for the Avengers. I guess I'm glad he's committed.

"Perfect," I go on. "While it pains me, I'm adding Kevin to the group chat."

"Yes!" When Kevin claps in excitement, Cass winces. "What's my code name? You're all chess pieces, right? It's perfect," he enthuses. "Six pieces, six people. Which one haven't you used?"

Deonte shakes his head firmly. "No way. You have to earn Bishop by not betraying us," he reprimands Kevin. "You can be Assface."

"Okay, okay," Kevin replies unflappably. "A little hazing is often part of a new friend group. Assface, I shall be," he declares.

Tom presses his mouth closed on repressed laughter. Even I'm having difficulty remaining stone-faced.

"I'm pumped," Kevin says to the group, as if we've just offered him the entire multimillion-dollar score. "I've always wanted to be in a group chat."

THIRTY-THREE

WINTER FORMAL MY FRESHMAN YEAR OF HIGH SCHOOL WAS money themed. Not literally, of course—the dance committee named the event something frivolously idiomatic like "Nights of Splendor." It didn't really matter what they called it. The point of the event was showing off. My classmates in Prada and D&G, the hotel done up *almost* as opulently as this wedding, everyone eager to flaunt.

Like me, in the photograph on the white shelf over my old desk.

Walking into my childhood room, I meet my own eyes in the small image. Me, dolled up and glittering, with Berkshire friends I no longer speak to.

The rest of my surroundings strike me similarly. The crystal souvenirs from European vacations. The signed poster for the Dream Team concert my dad got VIP passes for when I was in middle school. The other photos, impromptu "photo shoots" with old friends and views from faraway hotels. None of the old ones of me with my parents, which I destroyed when I moved out.

I'm shocked by how much my room no longer feels like mine, as if I'm an intruder stealing into my own life. It's the room of a younger Olivia, one from whom I feel impossibly disconnected. It's part of why I don't come up here often, even when dinner delays leave me downstairs with nothing to do.

I remember exactly how I felt getting dressed for the dance in the photograph. I was excited, yes. Happy, sure.

Did I *want* to go? I don't know. What unnerves me is the memory of how the younger me just...did stuff because it was there to be done. Because it was the expectation for the cute role of heiress I'd grown up into. *The one I thought I was demoted from,* I remind myself, *until an hour ago.* Standing here in my childhood room, I find I'm wrestling with how it makes me feel. *Was I forsaken, or was I freed?*

It's the gloriously messed-up part of everything. Looking around at the luxurious icons of my old life, I find I'm *not* jealous of the Olivia who lived here. The delighted, directionless girl who trusted her family to be there for her. Who imagined the future would look like the past, but better.

I pity her. She had no idea what was coming. She didn't know to protect herself from heartbreak.

And she didn't know what she was capable of. I'm proud I'm no longer her. While a knife can sparkle in the light even if its edge is dull, the past few years have made me sharp. With resourcefulness, with purpose.

I close the door behind Cass, who walks in, evaluating the room. She's clearly awestruck by the furnishings.

"No wonder you want to steal from your dad," she comments, her eyes rising with the high ceiling. "Must have been hard to give this up."

I cross the room to my dresser. It's bare now, cleared out of everything I took with me when I left. Only clothes that no longer fit remain. I open a drawer, see old sweaters and jeans, then close it. "I don't think this stuff is me anymore," I reply.

Cass scoffs sharply. "Who cares if it's *you* anymore? I would never give up anything like this."

The hungry immediacy in her voice catches my curiosity, despite everything else whirling in my head right now. It's the first comment I've heard from her that isn't deserved dismissiveness for other crew members or objective efficiency. The first volatile glimmer of... want. Intention. Motive.

She runs her fingertip over the rooftop of the palatial dollhouse in the corner. Then she moves to the bookshelf. There aren't many books on it, but Cass pulls out the richly bound hardcover copy of *Oliver Twist*. Only now does the irony of its presentation strike me, the famous story of a gang of thieving street-urchin children, packaged in gold-edged pages with a velvet bookmark.

"I loved that one," I can't help remarking. "Fitting, I guess."

Cass flips the pages, something unreadable on her face.

"Me too," she says. She closes the heavy copy. The fleeting emotion vanishes from her porcelain features, her usual efficiency returning. "These accommodations will be sufficient," she informs me, plopping onto the bed, where she opens her laptop.

I laugh. "There might be some ancient Skittles in the nightstand. Help yourself."

"Appreciated," Cass replies.

I head for the door, then turn back, remembering the way her eyes looked roaming over the lovely detritus of my old life. "Don't give it up," I find myself saying.

Cass glances up in guarded confusion. "What?"

"When we get paid, whatever it is you want," I elaborate, fumbling to put into words advice I don't entirely know how to give. "Whatever it is, don't give it up, because people *will* try to take it from you."

She meets my eyes for a long moment.

"I won't let them," she says finally.

I nod. When she returns to her screen, I leave her in my old room, kind of wishing I'd put my foot through the dollhouse in the corner.

THIRTY-FOUR

I FEEL LIKE WE REALLY HAD SOMETHING HERE," TOM SAYS TO ME when I put my hand in his.

I found him waiting for me on the stairs, our next stage. He's the picture of preparedness, his suit unruffled, his hair dramatically perfect.

I roll my eyes. "You'll survive," I reply.

We hear voices at the bottom of the stairs and the office door opening. Dash exiting the office where he executed yet another marriage license, new wife accompanying him in the celebratory postlude. It's our moment.

"Three...two...one," I say under my breath.

Right on cue, Tom starts our scene.

"*Fine*," he says loudly, with pompous retaliation. "I didn't even want to come anyway!"

"Then why did you?" I wail. While it's not as if I were expecting loads of fun from the day, the past hour has offered nothing except frustration. It's nice to indulge in the easy over-drama of Heiress Olivia.

"I don't even know." Tom glowers. I have the distinct impression I'm not the only one enjoying the pretense. "You have major issues."

"Oh, *I* have issues?" I retort. "*You never loved me, did you?*"

Now he can't help almost smiling. Admittedly, I'm not just revel-ing in my character. He's a perfect scene partner. It's fun, challenging him to follow my lead.

"I loved you!" he cries.

"No," I fire back. "If you loved me, you wouldn't be saying this now. I should tear up the *poem* you wrote me."

His character falters just momentarily, the span of one raised eye-brow. Recomposing himself, he levels Shakespeare-meets-the-CW hurt into his voice. "You destroy our poem, and this is really over."

"I thought it already was," I reply in my own imitation of wounded rage.

Inside, I'm dancing with delight. Our audience has gathered. Guests have entered from the garden, drawn to the foot of the stairs in unsubtle voyeurism. Exactly the way I imagined when I re-scripted the heist's second act in the van. I rip my hand from Tom's and stare at the light behind him until my eyes water. The opulent chandelier glitters painfully, prickling my vision.

Tom, a better actor than me, manages to summon real tears. They fill his brown eyes beautifully.

"You just don't know how to be loved," he says, his voice so quiet, it commands the room. "You wouldn't even know how to recognize it when it's right in front of you."

I blink, my performance caught on something in his expression. He looks...*real*. As if his words aren't just a line in this show we've enacted.

You don't know how to be loved.

How could I, when half the people who have loved me have bro-ken my heart? The question is the reminder I need to shrug the accu-sation off—to remember why we're really here.

"Right in front of me?" I ask, scoffing. "No. Not anymore."

I walk past him, down the steps. Out of the corner of my eye, I note the occupants of the office have emerged into the foyer. My dad and Maureen look around the room, confusion on their faces.

I've done what I need to. Plenty of people have witnessed my dramatic breakup. Word will spread across the wedding by dinner. What I do next isn't part of The Plan. It won't help me get the codes to Dash's accounts or find out who Abigail Pierce is.

I do it for one reason only. Because Dash has done his best to relegate me into the shadows of his life. I don't live here, in my childhood home. I wasn't in the bridal party. I'm not even seated at his table.

Right now, though, I'm not in the shadows. I'm center stage. I'm the main attraction, and I can't help using that spotlight to cast darkness on Dash. To make his day look just *a little* worse.

"Screw you, Thomas!" I shout at the top of my lungs. "I never should have slept with you."

I hear gasps ripple through the room. Heads turn in my father's direction. Whispers spread. Hopefully about how shitty a parent he must be to have a daughter acting out like this.

"You don't mean that," Thomas says from the stairs, valiantly charging forth despite the change in our audience.

I raise my chin in haughty indignation, glowering the way I imagine my cousin Mia would. While I don't know where I'm going with the performance, I don't care. The farce has gone from the means to my devious end to the end itself.

"Oh, I—" I start to say.

I don't react fast enough when I notice Tom's eyes flit past me. The hand I feel clasp my elbow is unforgiving.

I whirl, finding my father himself.

Dash is livid. His face, which has started recently to show wrinkles like the soft creases of dollar bills, is warped with fury. The vein in his forehead is visible, spidering out over his silver eyebrow. His lips only control his snarl with effort. *There it is,* I notice. Dash Owens's favorite glare, reserved for his darling daughter. It startles me, catching on old instincts for repentance, ones I've fought and reassured myself were gone.

Their reappearance is unwelcome. Will I *never* get free of the urge to seek my father's forgiveness? I have enough opponents—Lexi, Dash, the entire Millennium Security squad posted up in my childhood home like it's the Pentagon. I can't waste one moment of hesitation, one scrap of effort, fighting *myself.*

Dash pulls me off the last step of the stairs and into the study, moving fast. I don't resist, distracted and in my head.

He slams the door, sequestering us in his wood-paneled place of power. "What the hell is wrong with you?" he demands.

His reaction...hurts. I stiffen, surprised by how wounded I am. Yes, I know my "breakup" with Tom was only for show. My dad doesn't. What if I *were* feeling everything I loudly pretended? Humiliated, disappointed, used?

Is *this* how my father would react?

While his parenting wasn't exemplary when I was younger, he was only dealing with the small stuff. Forgotten homework, loud sleepovers with friends, the dimensionless difficulties of childhood. Moments like right now give me rare glimpses of how he would have reacted if I'd needed help with harder parts of life, the dangerous grays of adolescence. Dating. My future.

I shrug off the feelings, literally. "Nothing. I was just ending a relationship," I drawl. "Surely you can relate."

Dash grinds his jaw. It gives me a dark hit of relief. *Good.* I can get under his skin just like he can get under mine. The joy of family.

"You're embarrassing me. At my *wedding*," he emphasizes, as if I'd somehow forgotten my surroundings. "Knock it off. I kicked you out of this house once, and I can kick you out again."

Without offering me the chance to respond, he storms out. I don't dare hope he's fleeing from the guilt of the cruel invocation of my living situation, which was low, even for him. No, he just wants nothing more to do with me right now.

Forget him, I reprimand myself sternly. I don't need to defend my feelings. I owe him nothing. I deserve to have human emotions even if they're inconvenient to my father. I'm not just an heiress or a reject. I'm a person.

I'm surprised to find my eyes watering. Dash's words were quick, the moment only seconds long, but their sting remains.

What dries my lashes is the sight of the safe behind his desk. The perfect iron reminder of my resolve. I sniffle once, sharply, flattening my mouth. Even if I have to help Lexi, I *will* get the codes I need.

He can kick me out then. I won't care.

THIRTY-FIVE

I HEAR THEIR BICKERING BEFORE I REACH MY DAD'S BATHROOM.

"At least wash it first," Tom implores.

"Tom," McCoy replies patiently. "It might surprise you to learn I have a few years of shaving on you."

"Which is why what you're doing should horrify you."

I open the door, hating the headache I feel pulsing in my temples. I reach in vain for my favorite cure—vengeance. The room yields ready material. I remember when my mom lived here, the care with which she chose every painting on the walls. I remember when one day, during Dash's marriage to Lexi, they were gone. I imagine Maureen's eagerness to redecorate, to erase the past.

It…doesn't work. For once, fury doesn't erase the hurt or the stress. I need something stronger. I need a win.

"Is there a problem?" I ask irritably.

McCoy stands at the sink, his jacket thrown over the ottoman. His beard is half shaved off. It's hilariously ungainly, or it would be, if I were in the mood for humor.

Tom perches on the pearl-white tub. His distress is visible. "Yeah, there's a problem," he says, gesturing with urgency in the unkempt

McCoy's direction. "He's just *using* your dad's razor. You can get infections, or even, like, hepatitis. I don't know," he elaborates hastily. "But you're definitely not supposed to share razors."

"We're doing a lot of things we're not supposed to today," McCoy remarks.

"Not unhygienically—" Tom starts to plead.

I interrupt him, impatient. "I meant a *real* problem."

McCoy halts his shaving. His eyes find mine in the mirror. Tom turns to me, his objection dying on his lips while his expression shifts from surprise to concern.

Only with their reactions do I realize how harshly my words rang. It embarrasses me. Worse, it makes me feel guilty. The people in the room with me now have done nothing except perform excellently in the ways I've requested of them. They don't deserve the worst of me. It's poor leadership.

"Sorry," I say hastily. "Look, if it makes you feel better, I'm ninety-nine percent sure Dash doesn't have hepatitis."

I'm hoping to make the moment light. Instead, the joke falls heavily to the marble.

Tom's expression doesn't waver. "What did your dad say to you?" he asks.

"Nothing," I reply.

He just waits. When he raises an eyebrow, it isn't prying or judgmental. It's . . . kind. He's inviting me to confide.

"Knight, I need you on Kevin," I say.

Tom watches me, no doubt noticing the impersonal use of his code name. It's not a closed door—it's a slammed one.

"Whatever you want," he says after a moment.

He strides out, letting his hand linger against my side when he passes me. It's kindness I don't need and kindness I don't deserve. The half smile I muster is forced, imitation like my shouting on the stairs.

I move farther into the bathroom, the walls echoing the buzz of the electric razor. Little by little, McCoy transforms back into the teacher I used to know. Right down to his expression, the inquisitive sensitivity flickering in the glances he darts me. His knack for knowing when a person was having a hard day never failed to impress me. While he might be the world's shittiest kidnapper, he was a wonderful teacher.

"You know," he ventures, "I'm always here if you need someone to talk to."

I walk to the ottoman and sit, putting distance between us. "You shouldn't want to help me," I remind him.

He puts down the razor and wipes the shaving cream from his face with a towel. "Olivia, what happened to me wasn't your fault. I did my job, and I would do it again."

I kick the leg of the ottoman, feeling like a child. While McCoy inspired me and was encouraging whenever he called on me in class, even when I wasn't always prepared, neither his lectures nor his kindness were what I valued most.

He pushed me. No one ever pushed me. Not in the right ways. Everyone else pushed me to shut up or acquiesce when I irritated them. He pushed me because he believed in me.

The problem was, I was his student in the worst year of my life. The year my parents split up, the year I was kicked out of my own home. The year everything changed. The semester at Berkshire was already paid for, so I was allowed to stay until the end of the school year, but I knew it would be my last before I transferred to East Coventry.

I walked the halls feeling like their pretentious stone was

crumbling around me. Like every marble staircase would collapse under my feet, leaving me in some sinister underside. *Of course* my grades suffered. I wasn't good about doing readings or homework, not when I was focused on surviving the ruin of the life I knew.

McCoy was the only one who cared. He knew something was going on at home, but when he scheduled a meeting with me and my parents, Dash didn't show. He was confident the donations he'd made to the school would ensure my grade point average.

It was what the rest of my teachers were doing. Practically Berkshire tradition.

The entire school was pretend, right down to its design. With stately walls designed to emulate impressive schools of England, when really, it had been constructed in Rhode Island in the eighties with investments from rich parents just like my dad. The place was a master class in hiding ambition and indulgence under facades of pretty propriety. The halls emulating Ivy League institutional legacy, the dances offering veiled excuses for debauchery, the promises of how we were future world leaders and entrepreneurial visionaries when everyone knew grades were cheated for and purchased. It was pretend, pretend, pretend.

I wanted no part of it.

I was determined to earn whatever I could. For weeks in the guesthouse, I stayed up studying while my mom worked late shifts. We woke up exhausted together. She quizzed me over instant-noodle dinners. Our final English exam was a comprehensive Shakespeare review worth twenty percent of my final grade. Even if I got one hundred percent on it, the best I could do was pull my C-minus to a B-minus.

I did.

I cried when I saw it, and for the first time in weeks, my tears were happy. That exam taught me I could do whatever I set before me. It taught me what I was capable of. Without it, I never would have planned something like today.

Is it kind of ridiculous to attribute my heist aspirations to *The Taming of the Shrew*? Yes.

Is it the truth? Yes.

I was incredibly proud of myself. Proud in a way I hadn't ever felt in my entire life. McCoy was proud of me, too. He'd never had a student get one hundred percent before.

My dad was . . . not.

When Dash saw my transcript—saw the single B-minus I *earned* in a string of A-minuses I decidedly did not—he was furious.

In the end, donations don't control just GPAs. McCoy was fired the very next week.

"I'm serious, Olivia," McCoy says, turning to face me. "You are not to blame for what happened to me."

I meet his eyes, hating how his kindness to me is only a reminder of the kindness he can no longer give classrooms of students. "It was because of me, though," I say, letting emotion crack my voice.

"It was because of your father," McCoy replies quickly. His tone is decisive. "I've met a lot of fathers over the years. Yours isn't a good one."

His judgment makes me incomprehensibly, immediately angry. "You don't know him," I retort.

McCoy reads me, like I'm Ophelia or Anna Karenina or another of his doomed heroines. When I see his gaze settle into calm scrutiny, I know what comes next. I remember it from the open discussions he would encourage in his class.

"Why do you defend him?" he asks patiently.

Why? Why do I jump at chances to defend Dashiell Owens? Why do I come to weekly dinners here while I feel like an intruder in my old life? Why do I want to impress him? Why do I even care?

I feel myself fighting to evade the questions, reaching for the one I find more comfortable. *Why is McCoy asking?* It's hard enough to wrestle privately with my relationship with my father. Why did he have to invite the conversation out into the open? Why did he have to expose the way daughterly loyalty has its grip on me, like a little marionette—hating her strings, yet knowing she'd collapse without them?

"Maybe I'm misunderstanding," he continues, conceding, explaining himself. "Misunderstanding you or him... Olivia, do you have fond memories of him? Was there a time your relationship was good?"

I seize on the opportunity he's offered, the search for the empirical proof. The scientific, statistical measure saying, *You, Olivia Owens, were loved.*

I search and I search and I search.

It would make it so easy if I could just find what he's asking for, I know. It would quell the conundrum in me. It would *make me make sense*—my hesitation for vengeance, my hunger for Dash's admiration.

Yet with every passing second, my silent struggle growing more frantic, I find nothing. I scour Easters when he grimaced at the egg-dyeing colors little Olivia got on her hands or her meaninglessly expensive dress. I hunt every dinner I can remember for encouragement or interest instead of sarcasm and scrolling his phone. I scrounge for signs of companionship, finding only weekends when his absence for "investor events" prompted neither surprise nor loneliness. I pillage my own past, looking with sticky fingers for valuables, yet come up empty-handed.

When I look up, McCoy knows I have failed.

I have no *real* explanation for why part of me clings, even now, to Dash Owens.

I have to, I want to say. I don't know how to get the words out so that he understands. *I have to or else my soul would split and my whole self would fall into the chasm left in its midst.*

"I'm just saying," McCoy replies softly. "You deserve never to doubt your parents love you, Olivia."

I have the windpipe-crushing urge to cry again. To let McCoy comfort me. To listen to his words of encouragement and share with him everything my dad just said to me. *I kicked you out of this house once, and I can kick you out again.* It would be so easy to let him help me.

Then what?

I'll have only given one more person the power to hurt me. To reject me. To betray me. If not today, then one day.

I can't do it.

I decide I'm past accommodating his miserable kindnesses. The anger finds my words for me, clean like fire, changing my marionette strings into dynamite fuses.

"He's the only father I have," I snap. "You're certainly not my dad."

Immediately, McCoy's expression falls, wounded. Still, he's too good, too unlike Dash. He hears the recoil in my voice and meets me with understanding instead of retaliation. "I know that," he says gently. "I can still be here for you, though."

No. No, you can't. "What you can do is the job." I stand up.

McCoy studies me, pausing, then nods. He turns back to the mirror to wipe the rest of his face.

I walk to the door, resisting the urge to meet his eyes in the mirror.

I'm grateful to Mr. McCoy. He taught me I'm a good student. I'm capable of learning. I can pull myself out of anything if I set my mind to it.

I learned my lesson well this last year. I won't give anyone the power to hurt me again. Even if it means pushing away the people I care about.

THIRTY-SIX

I STAND BESIDE MY FATHER IN FRONT OF THE BAY WHILE THE SUN descends. In the light of golden hour, he holds me close, smiling with his dear daughter on his wedding day.

The drone whizzes in front of us, firing off shots. The hovering camera and four photographers surround us, a platoon devoted to capturing every angle. Over the softer sounds of the water, the robotic hum of the drone's propellers fills the day.

My heart is still pounding from his words in the office, but I keep my expression serene, as if I'm a wanted part of this family. I guess I'm smiling, the feeling not unlike sculpting stone with my hands. The photographer issues us directions I can't hear past the roar in my head, and Dash laughs, pulling me closer. As if nothing happened.

It didn't, to him. He probably barely remembers it.

But to me, it's everything.

Part of me wants desperately to forget it ever happened, to let my dad hug me for the cameras and pretend it's not a show. To hold this up as proof to McCoy, to anyone, that there's something worth saving here.

Not even I can lie to myself that well, though.

When the photographers tell me to exit so they can get shots of only the couple, I welcome the chance. I walk out of view of the cameras, feeling stress and sadness aching my back. I gulp down the clean scent of the ocean, free of my father's cologne. It's ironic, how houses with everything can make you wish you were anywhere else.

"Olivia? Are you okay?"

It's Jackson's voice, reaching into my heart in ways my exhausted head can't fight fast enough. Regaining control of myself, I turn, finding him watching me. The bridal party waits nearby, on hand for photographs. Jackson has wandered away from them.

His expression is rich with compassion, his favorite counterfeit currency. It unfortunately only makes the handsome lines of his face more undeniable. I hate how much it hurts to see him look so... *loving.* Like he cares about me.

Not for the first time, I find myself asking *why.* Why did he throw away what we had? Am I so easy to toss aside?

Of course I am.

My own father has done it, hasn't he? Why would Jackson have ever wanted to stay?

The fool I was, I remind myself. Jackson Roese had everything I could have wanted. Popular-guy charisma matched with quirky streaks and an unpretentious, joyous sense of humor. He cherishes mundane details like they're in the Louvre. He looks... like he does. He smiles as if you're the only person in the world.

None of it was what stole my heart. I fell for how caring he is. *Hey, new girl. What do you say we walk together?* I fell for how much patient kindness fills the soft space under his renegade charm.

Except, when I was falling for him, I was really just falling for his lies.

Jackson made me notice the phrases' similarity. Falling for some-one is loving them. Falling for some*thing* is getting conned.

I was falling for him, in the end. Just not the way I expected.

I close my eyes hard, settling into the hurt I can never escape. Tears fill my eyes again. This time, I don't fight them. I look up at Jackson, letting him see how they glitter on my lashes.

I have a job to do here. I might as well make the most of my pain.

He rushes to my side. "What happened?" His voice vibrates with low fury. He darts a scathing look at Dash.

I wish he hadn't. I don't need the painful reminder of how much I let him into my life. Of course he's correctly guessed my dad has done something to hurt me.

"Tom and I broke up," I say.

When Jackson pulls his gaze back to me, startled, I revel in the neat misdirection.

"Oh," he replies hollowly.

"It probably doesn't surprise you," I continue. "You know better than anyone how easy I am to get bored of."

He reaches out as if he wants to take my hand—then stops himself. *He's respecting my wishes*, part of me says. *He's out of patience*, part of me replies.

"I was never bored of you," he says firmly.

I look to the side, only half acting now. The wrenched feeling in my heart provides exactly what my performance needs. Yes, I engineered this conversation in order to have Jackson invite me to be his plus-one in the dinner seating arrangement—filling the space intended for the wife of the absent Sam Peters. The position will put me in proximity to other groomsmen, namely Jerry Hausman, who I'll probe over filleted cod for information on Dash's infidelities.

Even so, part of me needs to have this conversation with my ex.

"I wish I could believe you," I say to the water. "I just really loved you, you know. Tom was...a rebound, obviously." I laugh wetly. "But ending things with him is still just..." I let the tears flow harder, using the reserves of real feelings exactly the way I need them. My own heart is my co-conspirator now.

It works flawlessly. Jackson pulls me into his arms and strokes my hair soothingly.

"Hey," he whispers. "Hey, there, new girl. I'm here."

The tenderness in his voice cracks my heart wide open. I let myself cry into his shoulder, something I've wanted to do for weeks and am only permitting myself now because it furthers my goal.

The fact of its objective doesn't change how it feels, however. It's wretched heaven. When I'm in his arms, he feels like he's still mine. I pull back, wrenching myself from his intoxicating magnetic field. Despite how much I want to, I know I'll implode if I stay. Instead, I smile bashfully as I wipe my eyes. *Remember The Plan. The objective.*

Jackson's warm eyes make it very difficult. "How can I help?" he asks.

I breathe in through my nose, preparing myself for the sting of what I'm going to do next.

I reach for his hand, entwining my fingers with his. He looks down, startled, then grips my fingers tightly, as if I'm his life raft after he's been drowning for days.

"Olivia." He exhales my name desperately. It steals the air from my lungs. "You believe me now? You know I didn't cheat? That there's *no* one I could want but you?"

I stiffen. I don't want to say it. But I need to be at that table.

"I believe you." I force a smile and lean in to brush my lips against his. *It's only for an hour,* I tell myself. I can end things with him again when the cake is cut, when I have the information I need.

Jackson leans in, his gaze on my lips, his hand rising to cup the back of my head. *It wouldn't be so bad.* Letting myself pretend for just an hour I'm everything Jackson once made me feel. Loved. Important. *His.*

If it's for the job...

Even if everything else fails, I'll have stolen something. An hour of my old life.

A breath away from his lips, I feel his hand grip my hair, halting me. I open my eyes and find him watching me, his expression stern.

"You're lying to me," he says. "Why?"

He releases me. I step out of his embrace, the facade shattered. While I'm relieved for the excuse to drop my act—forcing my reassuring words felt like chewing glass—I'm frustrated by how easily he figured me out. Jackson's goodness makes it easy to forget he isn't guileless. He's maddeningly savvy and strategic when he wants or needs to be. Less golden retriever, more German shepherd.

Embarrassed he caught me in the deception, I cross my arms. While I mean it to look indignant, I end up feeling like I'm just defending my heart. "What gave me away?" I ask, surrendering myself to the irritating reality instead of the painful ploy.

"I know you. You can't lie to me," Jackson replies evenly, as if he's remarking on the weather.

It snaps the fragile filament of desire in which the past few minutes have wrapped me. The heat in my cheeks contorts my features into fury. My voice comes out scathing. "If only I could be more like you, then."

He looks exhausted by the reminder. His eyes smolder like hot coals after the fire has gone out. "What is it you want, Olivia? It's obviously not me."

I glance to my father, then back to Jackson, weighing my remaining options. I go with the direct approach. "I want your plus-one's seat at the head table," I say flatly. If playing him won't work, negotiating might.

"Okay," Jackson agrees.

I falter, eyeing him curiously. "Okay?" I repeat.

The photographers behind him call for the bridal party to join the photos. "You could have just asked. You didn't have to try to seduce me or whatever," Jackson says. He starts walking backward, talking to me while heading toward the edge of the bay. "I'd do whatever you asked of me."

Without waiting for my reply, he turns. He leaves me watching him, the black outline of his jacket receding into the dying light.

I should be happy. I got exactly what I wanted. Instead, I'm stuck with Jackson's words ringing hollowly in my ears. The truth is, the one thing I ever asked of Jackson Roese—in stolen kisses, shared confidences, and hopes I only ever dared with him—is the one thing he wouldn't give.

THIRTY-SEVEN

INALLY, MY WONDERFUL DAUGHTER, WHO I WANT TO THANK FOR welcoming my new bride," Dash declares. "What a beautiful family we have."

I raise my champagne flute, my feigned smile matching the performed love in my dad's words. I hate how easily he lies, the cheap fakeness in his invocation of me. Remembering how differently he spoke to me in his office, I set down my glass without sipping.

With the groom's toast concluded, dinner commences. The lawn has been transformed for the post-ceremony festivities, Phase Two of Maureen's own operation. In the center of the green, under the deepening light of dusk, dinner is held in a palatial white tent. Inside the structure's white folds, lights strung from end to end dazzle overhead. There's even a chandelier. It's the fanciest tent I could ever imagine.

Dash and Maureen start making their rounds, greeting their guests. I know what my father's really doing, of course. He regards every one of them for what they can give him, or why he needs to keep them close, and he charms them.

His performance, as on the lawn for our photos, is infuriatingly perfect. The winking charm, the fratty candor when he needs, the fawning. He's a world-class schmooze. It's his only genuine gift—and, I admit, the only moments in which I catch glimpses of the man my mother said she married. The Dash Owens who could make people feel like the diamonds amid displays of lesser jewels.

I'm seated at the large rectangular table reserved for the wedding party. The sweetheart table with the happy couple is behind me. And with the wedding dinner laid out for my watch, I do what my father inspired in me.

I examine the guests as if they exist only for my machinations. I pass evaluative eyes over them, looking for weaknesses to exploit or incentives I can offer. I view these people as opportunities, the way they do one another. Lifestyles of the rich and shameless.

I made sure I was the first one into the tent in order to rearrange the seating, placing myself across from Jerry Hausman and his wife, with my back to my father. Next to me is Allen Chang, another friend from college, a member of Dash's old Princeton Eating Club.

I'm poised, prepared. With the neatness of the silverware in front of me, my next move is set. While Lexi might have interrupted me, I've recalibrated. Everything is in place.

Or nearly everything.

The only problem is, as ever, Jackson.

He watches me seemingly without even blinking. It's the frustrating flip of happier moments when Jackson's stare on me felt like devotion instead of inconvenience. Now I can't have the conversations I need to without raising his rightful suspicions.

I keep waiting for the woman next to him to engage him in conversation. No such luck. Jackson has picked now to debut the first antisocial aura he's ever given off in his life.

Servers deposit strawberry salads in front of us with elegant coordination. With Jackson's eyes on me, I reach for my fork. I slant my head to him, smiling politely.

"Are you going to count how many times I chew before I swallow?" I ask.

He doesn't look like his obvious scrutiny of me embarrasses him at all. "You're the one who wanted to sit with me," he replies levelly. His voice holds flat notes of *your problem, not mine.*

I stab a strawberry. I plop it into my mouth. I deliberately chew three times. When I swallow, I grin at Jackson like I just put on a show. If I were standing, I'd curtsy.

He looks as if he wants to laugh. Instead, he restrains himself.

"Riveting," he remarks.

I roll my eyes, but I'm smiling a little, the hidden mirror of his own repressed expression.

It's fun. Irritatingly fun. *Fun,* I remind myself, won't get me what I need. I have to wrench matters into my own hands.

I peer past Jackson to the woman to his left. *Trish Parris.* Wife of Lamonte Parris, the CFO of the Galmont Group, Dash's company's largest newspaper portfolio. Founder of her own nonprofit dedicated to restoring and protecting centuries-old houses in East Coast cities.

Pursing my lips, I comb my recollection of the research I've done on her. I can't make convincing conversation about Philadelphia mansions or whatever. Recreational golfer...Mother of twin ten-year-old boys.

Yes. Perfect. My angle.

Reaching behind Jackson, I tap Trish on the shoulder. When she looks over in polite incomprehension, I nonetheless notice her gratitude for how I've delivered her from sitting in silence while her husband discusses "the markets."

"Trish, how are the boys?" I ask enthusiastically. "I haven't seen them since the holiday party. Aren't they into soccer?"

Trish brightens. "Both boys are playing club this year."

However delighted Mrs. Parris is, she's got nothing on me. I grin. Forget recalibrated, I'm feeling victorious now, and it's a rush. While designing the perfect conversation isn't much, momentum starts with small wins.

"Oh my god," I gush. "You have to talk to Jackson. He goes to East Coventry High, and his coach says he's, like, definitely getting a likely letter from UPenn for soccer."

I predicted exactly the way the light in Trish's eyes sharpens. The favorite subject of these parents isn't their children—it's how to get those children into Ivy League colleges. I should know. All of my dad's colleagues have asked me what prestigious campus I'm planning on making mine next year. While my enthusiasm for the subject is fake, my lack of real answer is honest—I'm kind of preoccupied. With my mom, with my divided household. With my heist, which unfortunately I cannot put on my application.

Jackson darts me a glance, like, *low blow.* But it's too late. Trish engages him instantly. "Likely letter?" she repeats. "What's a likely letter?"

Smiling to myself, I put another strawberry into my mouth. I can let myself enjoy the flavor now. Its sweetness is exactly how I'm feeling. I face Jerry, my mark, who's laughing at something Allen has said. I wait for a lull in the conversation.

"Jerry," I interject. "Do you know if Abigail is here tonight?"

Execution of days like this, I'm learning, is ninety percent planning and ten percent instinct. Here, my instinct is to hit the question head-on.

Jerry startles, surprised Dash's daughter is speaking to him. It almost looks like he needs a moment to remember who I am, even though I'm pretty sure he's my godfather. "Abigail who?" he asks.

I plunge forward. "Pierce."

Jerry furrows his brow. "Abigail Pierce...," he repeats. "Who is she again?"

I dig my heel into the grass beneath me, hiding my nerves. "You don't remember Abigail?" While I keep my voice friendly—the over-enthusiastic questioning of Dash's gossipy daughter—inside, I'm flailing. Jerry's nonrecognition looks genuine. He doesn't seem like the type who would cover for my dad, or who would do it well if he intended to. I look for winking references to shared confidences or glib flickers of glee. I find none.

"Can't say I do," he replies disinterestedly. His gaze returns to his friend. "Hey, Allen, remember that one ex of Dash's? Alice something? I wonder if she's here. I wouldn't mind running into her again."

I can't help glancing at Jerry's wife. In conversation with the woman next to her, she looks as if she didn't hear her husband's remark. Still, it's pretty cavalier of Mr. Hausman.

Allen laughs. "She's definitely not."

I hear the hint of unsavory indication in Allen's voice, as does Jerry, who straightens.

"Oh shit," he starts. "She wasn't the girl he—" He falters, his shrewd eyes flitting to me. Remembering present company, he has the unfortunate grace to look mortified. "Sorry, never mind," he says.

"Please," I reply, hoping he can't hear my desperation. "Don't get shy on my account, now."

"It's not appropriate," Jerry insists decisively. "What's going on with you, Olivia? How's your mom?"

I don't credit Jerry with concern. Instead, I'm forced to wonder whether the pivot to my mother is Jerry's logical leap to one more hot ex of my dad's he wishes he could *reconnect* with. In fact, I'm certain my mom could get it if she wanted to date. Jerry Hausman wouldn't be the hundred-millionth runner-up, even if he weren't married.

"You'd know if any of you guys checked in on her," I reply, no longer caring that I come off withering.

Jerry's eyes flash with retaliatory fury. Not surprising. Getting called out is what people like him hate most in the world. He takes a sip of his wine, passing a veil of discretion over his emotions quickly. "You're very right," he says, then turns to his wife—finally. He inserts himself into her conversation, unambiguously ending ours.

I chew the inside of my lip, frustrated. Nothing from Jerry. *Nothing*. With the first course winding down, I'm empty-handed.

"He deserved that," Allen says next to me.

I look over, not expecting the resolute reprimand from the man who was just joking with Jerry. I shift tactics. If insulting Jerry Hausman wins me Allen Chang's alliance, I won't object. "I don't know how you all are still friends," I remark, hopefully just dismissive enough for Allen to want to justify himself.

He scoffs. "*Friends* is not really the word for it."

While the server collects his salad plate, I consider my approach. Asking about Abigail outright didn't yield anything, and I can't press the subject again without raising suspicion. I decide to proceed more broadly, gather whatever information I can and piece it together later.

"Why are you here, then?" I ask.

Allen studies me. I meet his gaze, unwavering. When the corner of his mouth lifts, I can practically see the moment he realizes

I'm smarter than his "friends" assumed. He leans back in his seat, delighted.

"Dash owes me money." His voice is quieter now, but his words are enunciated so I don't mishear. "I would very much like to be paid back one day."

I don't even consider my next question. It flies out of my mouth. "My dad needed *money*?" It feels ridiculous when I say it out loud, here in front of his multimillion-dollar mansion, during the most expensive wedding Rhode Island has hosted in years.

He tips his head ever so slightly toward me, conspiratorial. "It was a decade ago. I'd prefer not to go to court to collect, so"—he gestures to his engraved crystal nameplate next to his place setting—"I keep up appearances, hoping the next time I bring it up, Dash will write the check. So far, it hasn't worked." His eyes fix on me with renewed interest. "Maybe I'll collect it from you one day, heiress."

The words don't feel friendly. A chill creeps down my neck despite the warm fall evening. Smiling stiffly, I'm relieved when Allen's wife pulls him into her conversation.

Wanting to look unaffected, I return to my salad. The servers are gradually collecting them, preparing the tent for the next course. I can only handle four bites before I feel my stomach resisting. Is Dash's debt connected to Mitchum's insinuation? Or Abigail Pierce? Do any of these pieces have *anything* to do with the others? I'm starting to feel like I'm holding multiple threads in each hand and none of them tie together.

Did he not get a prenup because there isn't money to protect? Maybe *Maureen* comes from money. She went to Berkshire, after all. I always assumed she was the gold digger—maybe it's the other way around.

Worst of all, if Dash hasn't paid Allen back, does he even have millions in his offshore accounts?

He must, I reassure myself. He has his inheritance from his father. His portfolios of companies. He's probably just being a dick to Allen for the power trip.

We just have to stay focused. Stick to The Plan.

I glance around the tent, clocking my crew. McCoy is standing at Maureen's family's table, talking genially with the mother of the bride. Tom is next to Amanda, seat stealing at Kevin's table, a hand clapped on his shoulder. Deonte is nowhere to be seen, but neither is Quinn.

Everyone is doing their jobs. I need to do my part.

I stand, determined to speak to the groomsmen at the other end of the table.

Jackson's hand on my wrist stops me.

THIRTY-EIGHT

THE FOUR HUNDRED OTHER PEOPLE IN THIS TENT DISAPPEAR.

My focus narrows to where Jackson's fingers grip me, holding tight enough that the skin of my arm whitens. It doesn't hurt—it's just unexpected. Jackson's touch was always painfully gentle. He pushed strands of hair behind my ears, held the small of my back when we were going through doors or up stairs, slid dress zippers down so slowly, I would shiver.

His fingers now aren't gentle. They're frantic.

"Tell me what you're doing," he demands, his voice shaking. Not with anger.

With fear, I realize.

Why does he still care so much and not enough? Never enough.

I rip my wrist from his grasp, realizing I can't deny it any longer. He knew my plans. He could destroy me if he wanted.

He already did.

"You can't seriously think you could"—he looks around, lowering his voice—"*steal* from these people. You're just a kid."

Indignation fires through me. I straighten. "Why not?" My voice is sturdy, my gaze challenging.

His eyes widen with shock at my confirmation. "This isn't you."

He shakes his head in disbelief. "Olivia, talk to me, please. Something is going on with you, and I just—"

I cut him off, not able to hear him tell me one more time I'm better than this. "No," I say firmly. "This *is* me, Jackson. Maybe you didn't really know me, or maybe you just wanted me to be someone I wasn't. It doesn't matter. You don't have to worry about me anymore. You're not my boyfriend. You're not anything to me."

The words hit him like punches to the softest parts of him. My heart cracks with his pain, an instinct I need to outgrow. Just because he seems like the boy I loved—just because it's impossible to remember his betrayal alongside the way he texted me good night every night—doesn't mean this is real. It never was.

Which is what makes my feelings right now incomprehensible. Inscrutable. A cipher without a key.

No matter how much Jackson hurt me, I don't like hurting him. I wish I did, but I don't.

I feel my phone vibrate in my purse and seize desperately on the distraction. Maybe someone in the crew has turned up a lead. Direction. Phases. The job.

That's what's real.

I just need to get away from Jackson.

"Look," I continue, letting my voice soften with the guilt I shouldn't feel, "if you want to start making amends for what you did to me, then stay out of this, Jackson."

His gaze, cloudy with hurt, suddenly clears. He fixes his eyes on me, and fire unfurls in them. "For the last time," he says, his voice low and furious, "I didn't do anything. If you loved me the way I loved you, you would believe me."

I know what he's doing. I hear the ultimatum in his words.

He's using months of make outs, of movie nights, of the soccer practices on East Coventry's patchy field that I spent happily ignoring the history reading I meant to do, of ice cream dates when I was discouraged—strawberry for me, chocolate-chip cookie dough for him—like weapons. Plans I could hardly comprehend myself whispering—*maybe one day we'll go to Paris and see the Eiffel Tower from our window and sleep in the same bed every night*—like incriminating confessions.

Love like leverage.

He wants me to soften or retreat. I've wondered in these past weeks whether he ever really understood me. Now I'm certain he didn't.

If he had, he would know Olivia Owens doesn't retreat.

I look right into his eyes, where the chandelier reflects like dewdrop diamonds. The effect is not unlike the half-pleading pain in his expression. It's not the real thing—it only looks like it.

For once, I hide nothing in my heart. For the fastest moment, I unleash into my voice all the hurt, the anger, the longing I've felt for weeks.

"I think it's clear," I say, "we never loved each other at all."

Without waiting for Jackson's reaction, I leave.

THIRTY-NINE

IN THE REFUGE OF THE HALLWAY RESTROOM, I CHECK MY PHONE.

Rook

> Quinn quit

> Hasn't left the welding

> *Welding

> **Wedding god damn

> Currently getting wasted at the open bar

Yes. Perfect. I welcome the logistics like I'm collapsing onto a hotel comforter after a long flight. The job is what I can cling to in the chaos.

I collect myself, gazing into the mirror, letting my shoulders unwind. I want to look at ease for what happens next. Comfortable in power. When I'm ready, I exit into the hallway.

King

I'm on my way.

In the dark of night, the patio is deserted. Everyone is in the tent for dinner, where the servers have started carrying out the main courses. No one occupies the bar except the people I need.

I inspect Quinn Rhodes, realizing, while I never wanted to know my father's assistant—former assistant—familiarity with the gangly thirtysomething would have helped me now. Instead, I have to rely on the characterization I can construct from quick observation. *Generic undercut.* No creativity in execution despite wanting to look cool. *Cheap tux.* Here for business. No interest in or sense of opportunity for wedding hookups, not while leashed to my dad's whims.

Drink in hand. Not his first, from the dull abandon in his eyes.

Acceptable conditions for information extortion, I guess.

Getting closer, I notice he doesn't just look drunk—he looks like he's having fun. Deonte does, too. Despite their conflict earlier, he's clearly sold Quinn on commiseration over their recent unemployment. He's relaxed, palling with Quinn as if they're playing pickup football on the lawn instead of ignoring the wedding celebration.

The fact that Deonte has managed to make friends with someone he just doused in champagne does not surprise me at all. From the cake to the flawless phone drop to the incident with Mr. Rhodes here, Rook is shaping up to be the MVP of my crew. I understand it, motivationally. While McCoy is here for revenge, Cass and Tom for their own dark whims, Deonte is the only other person here out of devotion to the person he cares for most in the world. I note to cut him some extra.

Assuming there's money in the account.

I can't even contemplate what I'll do if there isn't. How I'll pay my crew.

Sidling up to the bar, I shut out the idea. Quinn does a quick double take when he realizes who I am, then leans away in unambiguous displeasure.

"Nah, she's cool, man," Deonte interjects. "Olivia's the one who got me this gig."

Quinn eyes me in concession, clearly not convinced I am "cool." He still smells like champagne, I note.

"Olivia," he greets me, his voice like curdled milk. "Congrats on the new stepmom."

"Quinn." I match his introduction. If he's spoiled cream, I'm cotton candy laced with arsenic. "Rough night?"

"Don't pretend you're not pleased."

I laugh lightly, reaching for the peanuts in the dish on the bar. *God, I'm hungry,* I realize. Jackson and freaking useless Jerry Hausman have cost me the miso-marinated black cod everyone else is enjoying right now.

Quinn is right. I've never hidden my resentment of him. We cross paths when I'm over for dinners and he's finishing running down the podcast guest list with Dash or planning my dad's next whatever. I would often outright glare.

How could I not, when every glimpse of him reminded me of how he helped and covered up my dad's cheating on my mom?

He knew everything. Every plan. Every schedule. He helped my father make them. He didn't hesitate.

Well, here's hoping his insider status helps me now.

"I did hear you quit," I say, making a mockery of sympathy.

He knocks back his amber drink. "He was going to fire me, but after all these years"—he shakes his head like, *no way*—"I had to be the one to leave. It was past time. Your dad kept promising me a job at Hub, but I doubt he ever meant it."

"He didn't," I say honestly. Why Quinn would ever want to work at the online "listener companion platform" my dad developed for his podcast, which has devolved into a few hundred of his wannabes ranting at one another, I'll never understand.

It doesn't matter. I have my angle now. I know exactly how I'll play this conversation.

"He said you were support-staff material," I recall, "and nothing more."

Quinn's lip furls.

Even Deonte winces. "What a dick."

"Hey, I didn't ask to be born to him." I shrug. "Quinn actually applied and interviewed to be his little minion."

My insult glances off—exactly as I'd hoped. Quinn is preoccupied, fuming. "Well, I guess I'll have my revenge in drinking as much top-shelf liquor at his wedding as I can," he says.

Deonte's eyes flit to me.

"What if you could do more?" I ask innocently.

Quinn's gaze moves to me. *Perfection.* Not even hotel sheets compare to the exquisite indulgence of plans perfectly executed. Yes, Quinn Rhodes is sniveling and selfish. It doesn't mean he's senseless. Even inebriated, he understands I'm offering him an invitation I haven't yet opened. His silence is intended for me to continue.

I do. "Lexi is here tonight."

His expression slackens a little. "*Lexi* Lexi?"

I can't resist. "What, surprised Lexi is somewhere she's not supposed to be? I can't imagine," I drawl.

Although the corner of his mouth pinches, Quinn doesn't reply. *Good.*

He waits, and I continue without my sarcasm. "She wants to collect on her prenup's infidelity clause. What with how you covered for Dash with my mom"—I say, casually bringing into the open the ugly source of years of resentment I've had for the slight man in front of me—"I figured you might have done the same when he and Lexi were married."

The look Quinn gives me is no longer displeased. It is, however, incredulous. "You're helping your stepmom get money from your dad," he recaps, "by proving he cheated on her."

I crunch down my peanut dinner. "Oh, is that unhealthy? Do you think we need family therapy or something?"

Quinn laughs—not ruefully for once, I notice. "Why are you even here?" he asks with humorless incredulity. "You hate your father. I doubt you have fonder feelings for Maureen."

I shrug, projecting nonchalance despite how his question has levered open complications I'm working desperately to ignore, ones Mitchum's revelation have only heightened. "He's my dad," I say. "Where was I supposed to be?"

"Family, man." Deonte nods—in support, I recognize, of my insubstantial cover story. "Family means everything."

I catch his eye, understanding his comment comes, like the sharpest strategies, from somewhere genuine. The anguish of family has driven us here, in our separate ways. "For better or worse," I reply. Deonte lifts his drink in agreement.

Quinn's gaze goes distant while he considers my inquiry into Dash's infidelities. Hope speeds my heart rate until he frowns as if I've struck out. "There wasn't anyone else I knew of during Lexi's short-lived reign as Mrs. Owens," he replies. "I think getting caught really shook him."

While I catch Deonte's face fall, I won't admit defeat. I grasp on to the only opportunity Quinn's response provided. *Getting caught.* As if he was used to not getting caught. As if—"So he cheated on my mom with more women than Lexi," I say.

Quinn studies me. "Do you really need to ask?"

It's funny—I'm no longer hungry. Not when my stomach has dropped straight to the patio stone.

I'm not just hurt, I realize as I reassemble my composure. I'm angry at myself. I won't easily forgive my own naivete. Cheaters never cheat just once.

I push past the pain of the realization. I need to focus on the objective. "Who's Abigail Pierce?" I ask, the night's new multimillion-dollar question.

Quinn finishes his drink. "How do you know that name?"

"I'm Dash's daughter," I reply, hoping the non-answer is enough.

It isn't. He narrows his eyes, as if he's half appalled, half impressed. "You really are," he says, his voice hollow.

The words douse me. He doesn't mean them complimentarily.

I push the comparison aside. If I have to be like Dash to steal from Dash, then fine. "You know who she is," I say, pressing my point.

Infuriatingly, Quinn Rhodes only shakes his head.

"I don't," he replies, his voice devastatingly genuine. "I just know she's your competition."

FORTY

WHILE MY FATHER WALKS MAUREEN INTO THE CENTER OF THE tent for their first dance, I walk into the dark night.

What I need is to get on the group chat, but I can't justify another trip to the bathroom without faking a UTI—which I did consider, but Tom came up with the solution.

Cornhole. Our cover.

It's perfect. The boards are in complete view of the tent, yet too far away to be heard over the ten-piece band's ABBA covers. Who needs phones when you can have real live conversation over the East Coast's favorite bougie outdoor game? Anyone who happens to notice the four figures tossing beanbags in the dark will assume the teens at the wedding have grown bored and decided to goof off.

Honestly, I note as I approach my crew, they've really committed to the bit.

Deonte and Tom are squaring off against Kevin and McCoy. From the very elaborate high five Tom and Deonte exchange, it appears they are keeping score. Nothing like a competitive cornhole match in the midst of a high-stakes heist, I guess.

Kevin picks up the four beanbags at his feet. "You think you can discourage me with your victory?" he says to his opponents. "I'm a born underdog, baby. Losing is where I win."

McCoy looks down at him, startled. "That was very nicely put, Mr. Webber."

Kevin straightens his shoulders at the praise. He notices my arrival and waves. It's ridiculous, but I find myself waving back, rolling my eyes for good measure. I should cut into the game, begin the meeting.

But I don't know. I guess I wish I'd seen some of the game.

"Bro, you haven't even gotten one on the board. Spare us the inspirational speeches," Deonte says, laughing with Tom.

Kevin starts swinging his arm, miming his shot. "If I sink all four in the hole, my group chat name changes to Bishop."

Deonte and Tom exchange a look. "All four, Assface," Tom confirms.

Kevin carefully lines up his toss. The lawn goes silent.

While we wait, holding our breaths under the starry sky, I almost forget why we're here. Maybe in some other universe, Olivia Owens invited her friends to her father's wedding. Maybe her father meant it when he toasted her. Maybe her boyfriend never cheated. Maybe tonight is about her family, her friends, her life full of hope and possibility—

Kevin's first two shots go wide.

Everyone groans sympathetically. Kevin, however, isn't deterred. He picks up the next beanbag. He tosses it. This time, it hits the board. There's too much force in the throw, though, and it slides clean off. Before it hits the grass, he's already throwing the final one.

It goes clean into the hole.

The four of them erupt in cheers. Even I, on the sidelines, can't help smiling. Kevin looks as startled as the rest of us. He jumps into the air, pumping his arm.

"You're not Bishop, but good job," Deonte says, high-fiving Kevin.

Part of me wants to join in the moment, to linger here, to see the rest of the game even.

"Has anyone connected with Queen?" I ask instead, hating my own formality.

The cheering dies instantly, everyone turning to me with smiles slipping from their faces. It hurts more than I expected, even though it's my own fault. It's just been a while since I was part of a friend group. I miss it.

I shake off the sentimentality. No distractions. No weaknesses. I need to focus on what I'm good at. Which isn't making friends.

"She's on her way," Tom replies, his tone neutral. "She said the options you gave her were...challenging, and no one is allowed to make fun."

"Make fun?" Kevin repeats. "Of what?"

Answering his question, Cass emerges from the house's patio doors. She's braided her hair simply down her back and managed to find some lipstick left behind in my room. Instead of her black-on-black hacker ensemble, she's now outfitted like the Olivia of freshman year, complete with the silver-black dress I wore to winter formal. It doesn't really fit Cass, and it's obviously not her style, but somehow, she's honestly pulling it off.

Who cares if it's you anymore? I would never give up anything like this. I smile, appreciating the living proof of her words in my old bedroom.

There's something so unapologetically confident about Cass, the coder taking this job just to prove she can, that makes her look almost as if she were made for dresses like these.

The heels, less so.

She stumbles on the grass on her way to us.

Looking relieved to have made it to us with intact ankles, she stops. "Laugh and I'll hack your search histories," she says gruffly.

Her threat doesn't exactly have the intended effect. Tom swallows a snicker. McCoy hides his mouth in his hand.

Before my crew can turn on one another, I interject. "I think you look pretty."

Cass looks torn between immediately pulling up my late-night searches of "how to get over your dirtbag ex" for public ridicule and being touched. Before she can decide, I steer this meeting toward its intended purpose.

"Updates," I say quickly. "Go around the group." I nod to McCoy first.

Ever the straight-A-student-turned-teacher, McCoy is ready to be called on. "Maureen's parents are polite, but they don't seem happy about this wedding. Her mom told me the newlyweds haven't been together long."

"It's not like she would have told her parents if she was sleeping with a married man," Cass says. "That doesn't negate the possibility of infidelity in Lexi's marriage."

She has a point, but we need proof, not possibilities.

"No," Kevin agrees, "but what I found out does."

Unfortunately, we all turn to look at him. The sudden attention goes to Kevin's head. He grins like a child with a new toy.

"It wasn't easy to get out of my dad," he goes on, preening in the spotlight of our attention. "I didn't want him to know what we were up to, *of course*, so I had to be extremely deft in the conversation. I knew I had a couple of routes, but ultimately I chose a lateral approach to the subject, which naturally—"

Tom cuts him off, sparing us the unnecessary editorializing. "Mitchum did a background check on Maureen when he found out there wasn't a prenup. She was living with a boyfriend in California in her year between college and journalism school, during Lexi and Dash's marriage."

"Well, that feels conclusive," I say, pinching my nose. Another dead end. We don't have time for dead ends, not with the wedding progressing. Mitchum gave us three hours before he has to report the safe has been opened. If we haven't gotten into the bank account by then, every password will be changed, and we'll have nothing.

What do we do if Dash didn't cheat on Lexi with Maureen? It's not as if we can search the *wedding* for other suspects. If there even is anyone to find. I'm starting to suspect my father was somehow loyal to his second wife.

Which is just perfect. It's maddening—the one instance in which I'd welcome my father having cheated on his wife, and he manages to disappoint. Nice work, Dash!

I grasp for other loose ends, desperate.

"Why isn't there a prenup?" I ask.

This time Kevin answers quickly, before Tom can steal the stage. "Dad doesn't know. He did imply that Dash's podcasts cost more money than they make...but even so, he says it's highly out of character for Dash."

I file away the observation. There's nothing I can do with it right now. Turning to Deonte, I gesture for him to take the floor.

"Quinn believes Dash never cheated on Lexi," he says, then glances meaningfully at me, a question in his eyes.

I shake my head, appreciating the kindness. I don't need everyone knowing just how broken my parents' marriage was.

Deonte goes on without missing a beat. "He referred to Abigail Pierce as Olivia's competition."

"That's not surprising," McCoy muses. "Her name is on the will. Another heir."

"Please tell me you found out who the hell we're dealing with," I say to Cass.

For the first time, Cass looks ill at ease in my hand-me-downs. "I don't know," she says to the ground. "There's nothing. I've pulled census records, local clerks, and...less public records. Credit card databases. Everything. As far as I can find, Abigail Pierce doesn't exist."

I swallow the scream of frustration clawing at my throat. There's a solution here. I can find it. I'm good at this—at *only* this. If I fail today, if I go home with nothing to my mom's debts, to a school where I have no real friends and now no boyfriend—

I can't. I refuse.

"You know, you talk a big game about hacking our search histories and such," Tom says, frustration evident in his tone, "but you can't even find one person?"

"Why don't you open the Safari app on your iPhone and check my work?" Cass replies flatly. "Or you can save yourself the time it takes to use *Google*, and trust me when I say, whoever Abigail is, someone paid a lot of money to have her digital footprint erased."

"Why would someone do that?" Kevin asks.

"If they're trying to cover up something," I say, thinking out loud. I return to Mitchum's words. To Allen's. My father has debts, probably more than I know. He's done something that can be exposed and used against him. Abigail is somehow the root, but of what?

"What's interesting is that you said she hadn't been added to the will yet," Deonte muses. "This is something Dash has recently decided."

Tom's eyes sharpen. "Maybe we're thinking about this in the wrong direction. What if Abigail isn't someone he's covered up? What if—"

"Abigail knows something and is blackmailing him," I finish, catching on to the idea's momentum. That would make her worse than my competition. A threat.

The idea surprises me. Are my father's enemies my own? I'm stealing from him, but are others allowed to? Now that I know I'm in the will, I know I'm intended to inherit part of what he will pass down one day. Is it weird for me to feel vindictive and defensive at once?

Or is it just family?

"This is all fascinating theorizing," Cass interrupts, "but none of it helps us get into the bank account."

McCoy reaches up to stroke the beard he no longer has, then lowers his hand. "She's right," he says. "We need to deal with Lexi first, which means we need something to trade her for the codes."

"But we don't have any proof Dash ever even had an affair," Tom replies.

Everyone falls silent. We're stuck. I can't find proof of something that might have never happened. I work my exhausted imagination for what other kind of leverage we can offer Lexi, but with time running out, I'm not confident in my efforts.

Is this it? The ending?

"No," Cass says slowly, as if she's working through something. "I could make some, though."

The second the words have left her, she stands straighter in her heels. It's oddly meaningful, the rare glimpse of the person under the cutting efficiency, dark curls and discomfort in formal wear. Cass, I intuit, isn't a girl comfortable with failure. It bothered her more than us that she couldn't track down Abigail Pierce online. With this new direction, however, she's returning to herself.

I trust her conviction more than I have reason to. Still, I have to ask. "How?"

Cass smiles, the idea clearly coming together perfectly in her mind. "I'm in Dash's house. On his network, his VPN. I have *everything*," she explains—crows, really. "I could easily use his computer to fabricate an incriminating email to Maureen, then change the sent date so the email client thinks the email is old. From during Dash and Lexi's marriage."

"Would that work?" Deonte's voice is wary.

I gnaw the inside of my cheek. There are holes in the strategy. It's not ideal, but we've run out of time for ideal. Perfectionism is more often a weakness than a strength.

"It wouldn't hold up in court," Cass continues, "but Lexi will buy it in the moment. She doesn't know I'm here, doesn't even know I exist. She would have no reason to suspect Olivia is capable of complex digital forgery on hours' notice. She'll give us the codes before she realizes the email is fake."

Interrupting us, cheering drifts over from the tent, a reminder of the time we're losing.

"They're bringing out the cake," Deonte comments, his gaze

snapping to catering staff. "I'm not missing this. I think they're serving mine."

While I'm supportive of Deonte's hard work, I'm a little less motivated by the cake itself. Jackson's nosiness if he finds out I missed the cake-cutting, however? *That* I find compelling.

"Do it," I say to Cass. "Tom, Kevin, go with her. Get the email, then make the exchange." I furiously start checking off logistics. "Shit, has anyone *seen* Lexi? Is she just lurking somewhere in the wedding?"

Kevin shuffles his feet. "She, um, gave me her number when we were working together, before she ditched me for you."

"Of course she did," I remark dryly. "Get the codes. Return them to Cass. I want this wrapped up before the father-daughter dances."

Everyone nods. For the first time since sitting down to dinner, I feel in control. We're not just reaching into the dark, hoping our fingers catch on something useful. We have a plan. When I'm twirling prettily in my dad's arms while he plays the doting father, I'll have something steadying me against his hypocrisy. The knowledge that I've stolen millions from him.

"Love this direction, crew," Kevin says, football-clapping his hands. "One quick question. Do you think we can finish our cornhole game first?"

We all reply in unison. "*No.*"

"Why would you even want to?" Tom goes on. "You were obviously going to lose."

McCoy raises his eyebrows sternly. "Don't be so sure, Mr. Pham. Cornhole is a finnicky game."

"Look, we don't know who was going to win. So we can agree it was a draw," Kevin suggests hopefully.

Deonte frowns. "No way."

"I propose a rematch later," McCoy says.

"Whoever wins plays me and Olivia," Cass replies, darting a conspiratorial glance at me.

Sudden warmth spreads in my chest at the inclusion. None of us are friends in real life. There's no reason to ever meet up again. Still, part of me wants to.

"No way would Olivia deign to play," Kevin says.

McCoy meets my eyes, his expression somehow supportive despite how I treated him upstairs. "I'd like to see it."

I should walk away, remind everyone we're not here to play games.

Instead, I pick up four beanbags from the ground and line myself up on the court. Muscle memory comes alive in me instantly. One after another, I toss them onto the board. One after another, they all slide perfectly into the hole.

No one makes a sound.

"You all forget," I say, turning to them. "This used to be my house. I grew up at this board."

McCoy cracks a grin first. Then Tom laughs. Deonte slow-claps. Cass just nods in approval.

Kevin, of course, *whoops* loudly, then hoists me on his shoulders, chanting my name into the night sky. I'm laughing too hard to reprimand him for drawing attention. Besides, if my dad were to come over right now, he'd think I was playing cornhole with friends.

It wouldn't even be a lie.

Winded, Kevin sets me down. "No wonder you're King."

FORTY-ONE

I SHOULDN'T HAVE ENTERED THE RECEPTION TENT WITHOUT MEN-tally clocking where every person of interest is. I shouldn't have forsaken focus, occupied with delusions of friendship I can't write into crisp checks. I shouldn't have forgotten I'm here to steal a future, not relive a past long ripped from my fingers.

If I hadn't been smiling when I walked in from the lawn, still reveling in my silly victory, I wouldn't have let my father get the drop on me.

"Where do you keep sneaking off to?"

I whirl, finding him standing behind me, eyes narrowed in suspicion.

My mind blanks. Every cover story and contingency and backup—gone. Scrambling, I will my thoughts to focus. Tom was supposed to be my cover. But with our change of plans necessitating a public breakup, I can't lean on him. There's only so much waffling Dash will buy, even from a teenage daughter.

The problem is, he shouldn't have even noticed my disappearances. The fact that he has, that he's even paying attention, is unnerving.

I open my mouth, praying something coherent comes out.

Instead, I feel a hand on my elbow. "Sorry, sir. It's my fault."

Jackson's voice comes from my right. He deftly places my arm on his, as if we're together. I would correct him, but between Dash and Jackson, one is an annoyance, the other a catastrophe. I close my mouth and smile like a lovestruck girl.

It works. Dash looks from Jackson to me, his expression smugger by the second.

"What did I tell you?" he says, gloating. "A father always knows his daughter."

The irony is so beautiful, I'm half tempted to tell him exactly how much he doesn't know about his daughter. I don't, of course. I just lean into Jackson. "You were right," I say, knowing my sarcasm is lost on him.

"Just keep it respectable, please," Dash says. "My guests saw you with another boy not an hour ago."

I bite my teeth hard, a grimace hidden in my smile.

"Of course," Jackson promises.

Unsurprisingly and infuriatingly, Jackson's word satisfies my father. It's not like he needs to hear his daughter speak on the subject of her own body.

When he's gone, I round on Jackson. "Why did you do that?" I demand, furious with him for the crime of being nice to me after I was awful to him at dinner. Why didn't he take this chance to hurt me back? To tell my dad exactly what he knows I'm doing?

Why is he always *good*?

Jackson runs a hand through his hair, leaving it roguishly mussed in heart-sickening contrast with his tuxedo. "I'm sorry he thinks we're back together," he says, sounding defeated. "It was the only explanation I could come up with on the spot. We can just tell him things didn't work out."

I shake my head. I don't love that I'm now fake-dating my ex, but I can deal with it, especially because it saved me, the heist, everything. "No, why did you help me?" I ask, meeting his eyes.

His face softens. "I'll always help you." He says it simply, as if he's surprised I even have to ask.

Why did you cheat on me? Why isn't this Jackson the real Jackson?

He goes on, sincerity painfully splayed across his features. "Even if . . ." He takes a deep breath and lowers his voice. "Even if you're doing what you said you would do tonight. I don't like it. I think it's dangerous. I worry about you. But these weeks without you have taught me that if you need help—*ever*—I'll be there."

I can't lift my gaze from his. His words hurt worse than any accusations he's thrown at me tonight. I crumble, remembering the night I told him I wanted to steal something back from Dash. He tried to convince me not to. Now, months later, heartbreak sharp between us, he's supporting me anyway.

"Stop being nice to me," I say. Pleading, weak, vulnerable.

Jackson's lips lift in the start of a smile, the one I traced with my fingertips once. "Sorry," he says, unapologetic. "I think I'm just going to be *more* nice."

I can't help it. I laugh. "So mature."

He looks delightfully caught off guard by my giggle. It makes his smile grow, boyishly exuberant. "Dance with me," he says.

His invitation tears me into pieces I don't know how I'll ever put back together. I want to be in his arms. I want to forget what he did to me. I want to keep him far away.

"We made a bargain, did we not?" he reminds me. "I'm collecting my one dance, hard-earned by listening to foreign-market speculation and '*unfair*' taxes on the rich for an hour in the grooms-men suite."

When he holds his hand out to me, I stare at it, knowing every-thing his touch promises.

I stop resisting. Threading my fingers through his, I let myself want this, just a little bit.

"*One* song," I say, not sure if I'm reminding him or me.

FORTY-TWO

UNDER THE CHANDELIER, HE PULLS ME INTO HIS ARMS.

I've fought the menace of memory in every corner of the house, the painful reminders of everything I lost. Yet, on the grounds where I grew up, in Jackson's arms, this is the first time today I've felt like I'm home. We spin, his gentle grip guiding me while he caresses, his practiced athleticism capturing the grace of a guy who is exactly where he wants to be.

With me.

I fight the feeling. I fight it hard.

It doesn't help when Jackson starts softly singing along to the song in my ear. I'm pulled, shaken from here to headphones shared on the steps of East Coventry High, or drives home when he would sing out loudly to whatever pop song was on the radio. With Jackson whispering lyrics in my ear, I smile despite myself.

And, surprising even me, I speak.

"I didn't mean it. What I said earlier."

Jackson stops singing. "You're going to have to be a little more specific."

"When..." I swallow. I hate how Jackson hurt me. How he deceived me.

Still—while maybe I'm just weakening in his embrace, right now I feel like I shouldn't write off every day and every way he was good to me. Which means not lying the way he did.

I make the leap. "When I said we didn't really love each other," I clarify. "It wasn't true. Not for me."

Jackson doesn't dare speak. The moment stretches, suspended like the chandelier over us.

"I loved you," I finish. "So much."

He stops swaying. Withdrawing, he looks straight into my eyes.

We stay motionless, surrounded on the crowded dance floor. No plan, it occurs to me, have I ever inscribed in my head the way I did with Jackson's every feature. The precise swirl in his chocolate-colored eyes. The fraught line of his mouth.

"I still love you, Olivia," he pronounces with unwavering conviction. "I didn't cheat on you. I swear. Why can't you believe me?"

I look to the side, evading his earnest sincerity—and my gaze lands on my father dancing with Maureen. Maureen, who's wearing the necklace I was promised was mine. My father, who not long ago pretended I wasn't someone he threw away, toasting me in front of his friends with words I would have given everything for him to have meant.

I know how dangerous it is, accepting the assurances of people you love just because you want to. What are pretty words, no matter how much I need to hear them, in the end? Nothing but weapons aimed at my heart.

"You could never deserve someone cheating on you," Jackson says, holding me close. "No one does, but you...I would *never* do that to you."

He has no idea how much his words break me. Wasn't that my

deepest fear? That I somehow deserved deception because I'm not *good* inside? That Jackson cheating on me was just an...evening of the scales?

"That's not true," I say, my voice warbling with tears.

"Olivia." He strokes my face, his features twisted with pain for me. "Olivia, no. You deserve to be cherished."

I look into his eyes, wanting to believe him. My mom didn't deserve to be cheated on. I know that above all else. Maybe...I take a breath. Maybe I didn't, either.

"I'm not going anywhere. I'll wait until you believe me," Jackson goes on. "I'll wait forever."

Forever. Forever. The syllables pound in my ears. Poem, promise, or prison sentence?

As if I'm determining escape routes or planning new phases, I fight my raging heart rate, forcing myself to evaluate his offer emotionlessly. Okay, not emotionlessly. Rationally. I can manage rationally. He would wait forever? Obviously hyperbolic, yet...Is there an amount of time after which I could forgive him? Trust him, even?

I'm not sure.

Part of me really wants to find out, though.

If we had forever—

I'm opening my mouth to reply when my eyes land on the security officers posted in a corner of the tent. When my dance with Jackson last directed my eyeline their way, they were alone, stern in their complacency. Now they're not. The man with them is—

Mitchum Webber.

If we had forever...

Embarrassment rages under my flash-fire panic. *Foolish.* Why even wonder if I could eventually forgive Jackson? I never have enough time. Not enough in this house. Now, not enough in this heist.

How could I have forgotten the time? In the arms holding me, I have my answer. Jackson distracted me. No—I distracted myself with Jackson. In the day's critical minutes, I let heart-aching hypotheticals and hopes suspended under the chandelier divert me from the harshest of realities.

Three hours have passed. Mitchum is about to report the safe was opened.

Time is up.

FORTY-THREE

I RUN THE SCENARIO IN MY HEAD WHILE I DANCE WITH JACKSON.

When the safe is reported open, security will move into the house to inventory what was taken. They'll find Dash's possessions intact and realize the document with his bank information was stolen. The codes to his accounts will be changed.

We'll fail.

None of this would have been a problem if Lexi hadn't derailed The Plan. We'd have sat down to dinner as millionaires, and security would have a suspect list of four hundred guests, none of whom Dash would have wanted to question and thereby reveal his losses to.

"Are you in trouble?" Jackson asks, spinning us so he can follow my eyeline to the cluster of security guards conferring with Mitchum.

I frown, hating having to admit that the fears Jackson had for my heist are all coming true. "I'll figure it out," I say stubbornly.

His grip tightens on me just slightly. "How can I help?"

"Jackson..." I chew the corner of my lips.

"No." He shakes his head. I recognize his earnest, resolute look. *No.* It's the Jackson who refused to let his sister walk to her friend's house after dark, the Jackson who replied encouragingly whenever I said something negative about my grades or my appearance. "No.

You do not have time to convince me I shouldn't." His expression softens. "Please, Olivia. Just let me do this for you."

I do *not* want to let Jackson do anything for me. But he's right—I *don't* have time to debate my ex. He's had numerous chances to turn me in tonight and wreck our plans. While I can't trust him with my heart, I think I can trust him with my heist.

Scanning the tent, I find Deonte sitting at an empty table on the edge, waiting for our next cue. I nod in his direction. "Spin me over there," I direct Jackson.

Jackson nods as the song changes to "September" and everyone who wasn't already on the dance floor surges to their feet to groove. I resolve to anonymously tip the band for their perfect timing if I get rich tonight. With the hardwood crowded with dancing bodies, it's easy to slip unnoticed to the other end of the tent. While the chandelier, now projecting rotating lights, masks us in spinning purple and blue, I whirl, beckoning Jackson.

He plays his part easily, a natural dancer. In the tux, I can't deny he looks particularly good while he moves to the beat, his bow tie slightly askew, his shoes shiny, the line of his waistband visible beneath his open jacket. When our path is blocked by bridesmaids, Jackson places nimble fingers on my hips and cuts a line through the women until Deonte is close enough to see us.

Understanding the urgency in my eyes, Deonte rises and dances his way to join us.

"Mitchum is alerting security," I inform him, my voice low, my grin fake. If anyone notices us, they'll think they're watching only gossipy Olivia with her friends. "The safe," I continue, "will be searched in minutes."

"*Shit*," Deonte hisses, the exclamation in cutting contrast with his upbeat dance moves. "Well, it...," he starts, as if he's searching for hope. "It'll take them a while to realize what's missing. Maybe we have enough time before the passwords are changed," he ventures.

"Here's a wild idea," Jackson interjects into our impromptu dance circle. "Why don't you *return what you stole?*"

I glance up, ready to remind him I have no intention of giving up now. *Olivia Owens doesn't retreat—*

When I realize what an idea he's just offered us.

"Yes," I hear myself say. "Yes, exactly. We'll put the page Lexi stole *back* before they ever find out it's missing. We'll already have the codes. We won't need the physical piece of paper, and they'll have no idea we have the information."

"*Codes?*" Jackson repeats, alarmed. "What exactly are you stealing?"

I guess he assumed I was after diamonds or crisp stacks of hundreds or perhaps very expensive cigars. If I were capable of amusement right now, I'd find his quaint surprise funny. I yank him closer to me in the guise of dancing, recklessly welcoming the heat wave the proximity rushes over me.

"Enough," I say, "to cover my mom's debts."

His expression softens—momentarily.

"And that's all?" he presses me.

His narrowed eyes make me...sad. They're the reemergence of his judgment, of the Jackson who rejected me instead of the guy who, moments ago, only wanted to help.

I remember what I felt when I decided I would share my plans, *The* Plan, with him. I wasn't ranting or lashing out. I imagined Jackson might, I don't know, sympathize. He might want what I want. Jackson is smart, he's resourceful, he's never had opportunity handed to him, and his righteous streak runs deep. I assumed he might understand why I needed to do what I needed to, and how. It didn't have to be a fight or an ending.

It could have been a dance.

Instead, he's helping only grudgingly, reminding me in pinprick glances how he really—still—sees his ex.

I cover the emotion coyly. "Well," I reply. "Maybe a *little* more."

Jackson's mouth pinches. I know he wants to lecture me. Instead, he restrains himself, to his credit, only breathing in deeply while he watches the security staff in undisguised concern.

Feeling the music, synchronizing my racing mind with the rhythm, I gaze to the main house, where the footlights under the hedges cast imposing conical shadows up the walls in the night. I wait until—there. Tom and Kevin emerge from the French doors onto the deck.

Kevin flashes me a thumbs-up. Relief races through me.

"Deonte—"

I could have guessed I wouldn't need to explain to Rook what needs to happen next. Extricating himself from our dance circle, Deonte preempts me hurriedly. "I'll take the page to the safe now and get Cass the codes."

I nod. Moving fast, he hits the steps, where he greets Tom and Kevin, then slides something into his jacket. He enters the house, the whole maneuver costing us only minutes.

"September" shifts into the swing of "Everybody Wants to Rule the World." Tom and Kevin join us, our dance circle re-forming, providing the perfect cover for our conversation.

When I notice Tom's eyes lingering a little long on Jackson's hands on my hips, recognizing the dark charge of noncommittal jealousy in them, I raise an eyebrow at him. *Staring, Knight?*

He shrugs in reply. *What if I am?*

"We should leave, right?" he asks abruptly. The same edge of resentment flashes in his voice. "I mean, even if security doesn't find anything missing, they're going to want to figure out who opened the safe in the first place. We have everything we need anyway," he continues, glancing at me. "Right?

I meet his locked-and-loaded gaze. "We can't," I reply. "You're exactly right. Security will start looking for the perpetrators. Leaving now will make us the obvious suspects."

Tom's frown could cut paper.

"Okay...," Kevin interjects, concentrating. "We're just hoping Cass can get into the account before the codes are changed?"

I press my lips flat, hating how much I understand Kevin's skepticism. While the chorus hits, I do the frantic math in my head. How many minutes until security has concluded that what was stolen was information? How many minutes to get Dash, the groom, to lock his accounts?

How long does Cass need to untraceably move the funds?

I remember our earliest conversations when she first signed on. She said she would need five minutes at least. Ideally, she would have more. In my head, I can practically replay her voice on the phone.

It's...going to be close, I realize. With security closing in, we may not have five minutes. Forget *ideally*.

McCoy awkwardly shuffles over. When he reaches our dance circle, he drops his efforts. "I can't," he says. "There's no way not to be creepy dancing with students. But I think everyone needs to know Lexi appears to be on her way to confront Dash with the fake evidence. Right now."

I spin myself on Jackson's arm to look behind me, where I see

Lexi storming across the tent. Dash is bent over the Owens family table, no doubt making small talk with one relative or another. Lexi can't see him yet, but she'll find him soon.

"Olivia," Jackson says, fear fusing with warning in his voice, "what have you gotten yourself into? How many schemes are you juggling?"

"A lot," I reply, only half paying attention. And they're all about to come crashing down.

When Lexi confronts Dash, he'll reveal the email is fake. Even if his denials don't convince her, she'll probably blow our cover, which won't help us keep a low profile when security starts looking for who opened the safe.

Lexi. It's darkly, dismally ridiculous. The woman couldn't content herself with ruining my life once. She had to return for more.

In a way, we're locked in a horrible ring of fate. The person who set me on the course to this heist will now prove its unraveling.

What we need is to stall the search of the office, where Deonte is finishing hiding the evidence of our heist, *and* stall Lexi. We need a distraction.

"McCoy," I say, "move the van somewhere safer." I look around, evaluating my options. There's the obvious. Pretend to be drunk, crash into a table. Embarrassing but effective. Or I could have someone tip off security that Lexi isn't supposed to be here, but then Lexi would expose us while she's escorted off the premises, taking us down with her. I could rush the stage and make a dramatic toast. Or—

My eyes fall on Maureen. In the chandelier light, her neck glitters.

My diamond.

I look to my crew, unnerving calm descending over me. "I know what to do," I say. "Stick to the plan. No matter what happens to me."

FORTY-FOUR

I CUT OFF LEXI ON MY WAY TO DASH.

He and Maureen are engaged in conversation with one of his cousins, Rupert, my grandfather's sister's only son. Doing research into my own family was, surprisingly, one of the most complicated pieces of heist prep. Stare at the diagrammed lineage of a legacy like the Owenses for long enough and you'll feel like you're reading an epic fantasy novel. Dash is playing the genteel, grinning groom, his schmoozing powers on full display.

I can't hesitate. Can't give Lexi room to grab his attention.

I interrupt him bluntly. "I want my necklace back," I demand.

Dash blinks, surprised. I put on a pout. Now more than ever, I'm playing the overemotional, impulsive, reckless daughter, who would do something disruptive but could never plot a multistep heist.

I recognize the shift in his expression even though his smile doesn't change. In front of cousin Rupert, he's controlling himself. It gratifies me to note how poorly he's pulling off his restraint. While I might have learned how to pretend from him, I've surpassed his lifetime of practice.

He keeps his voice low. "What the hell has gotten into you?" he hisses, darting glances at the family, all listening into our conversation eagerly.

Mia smirks from the other end of the table. I know the Swiss faction is fully enjoying my show. Yes, they'll lose more respect for me. Who cares? They've never really been my family anyway.

Maureen's hands fly to the diamond—the one she practically forgot she requested when I fetched the heirloom for her. Notably, she doesn't offer it up.

"My necklace," I prompt. "Grandpa left it for me. Not your third wife."

When Maureen's eyes narrow, her skin going white, I quietly revel in how well my words have hit their mark. Calling Maureen out for wearing my grandfather's heirloom *in front of the assembled family* is unexpectedly perfect. Where relation itself demands no loyalty, family diamonds are the closest indication of cachet. I've just made Maureen the outsider, the pretender.

Let's see how you like it, Mrs. Owens. Care to make a scene?

"Stop being so childish," my father snaps.

I hear the force in his words, how they summon feelings he's not having for the first time. Years of judgment, of disappointment spoken and unspoken. I let the hurt roll over me, cleansing me in fury.

"Why?" I challenge him. "I'm seventeen. Or did you forget when you kicked me out of your house that I'm still legally a kid?"

Rupert's eyebrows fly up.

My father's face flushes. He looks, for once, lost for words, called out on his behavior in a setting he can't manipulate. It's incredible to watch, silence from a man who once podcasted for forty-five minutes on how movie streaming represented the socioeconomic collapse of the country.

Silence, however, won't save me. It's not enough.

With security descending, moving in on the periphery, and Lexi undoubtedly lying in wait, I feel my window closing like the front door on the day I moved out. I need to act. Now is the moment.

I reach forward and rip the diamond necklace from my stepmother's neck.

It doesn't come off easily, the motion jostling Maureen so much, she spills her glass of champagne on us both. I slip when the necklace comes free, landing hard on the grass. Gasps echo up from the family in unison. Instantly, four hundred pairs of eyes fall on me. The band stops playing. It's kind of amazing how quickly a party can change into a disaster area.

While I have the entire wedding's attention, I start running— passing just feet from security, making sure they see the diamond necklace dangling from my hand. As I'd hoped, they change directions, no longer approaching Dash.

Now they chase me.

FORTY-FIVE

I REALLY SHOULDN'T HAVE WORN HEELS TO MY VERY FIRST HEIST.

They cost me only seconds on the stairs, possibly less. Seconds might be critical, though, in moments like this one. I reach the bottom steps, then the dark wood of the basement corridors, where I pause to pull off my pumps.

Ugh. More lost moments.

Until now, adrenaline has driven me, obliterating the pain in my insteps and narrowing my focus while guests gawked and security pursued me. If my heels are my unfortunate impediment, I have one very real advantage over the costumed guards chasing me. I know *exactly* where I'm going. I've literally played hide-and-seek within the walls of the corners I'm rounding right now.

Champagne runs down my shoulder in a garish parody of sweat. The strap of my dress got ripped somehow, I don't know—maybe someone reached out for me on instinct when I fell, and fingers found fabric. The dress is ruined, which splashes a shot of remorse into the fear filling me.

I understood today would exact its costs, though. Every one of us did.

My frantic run, diamond necklace in hand, is the only way I might spare us costs none of us can pay. *Might.*

When I reach the room with the pool pump, I check in with the group chat, then hastily hunt for means of escape, using my phone's flashlight to guide me. There—on the other end of the room, one small rectangular window. I search the shelves for something to climb onto. I no longer hear the hammering clamor of footsteps, which is good.

Or I assume it's good, right until the door slams open. I whirl, the frantic floodlight of my phone illuminating the figure in the doorway—

It's Jackson.

"What—?" I start to say. Relief and confusion and panic detonate in me in a combination I can't handle. I'm cut off when Jackson shuts the door behind him, rushes forward, and places a firm hand over my mouth.

We're pressed together in the dark storage room, our gazes locked. His heartbeat is racing with mine. Not like they're competitors—as if they're fleeing the same disaster hand in hand. We wait while footsteps pass us, then double back at the sound of voices from upstairs.

"I think they're leaving," I say, managing to keep my voice level. Not prepared for proximity with Jackson, I step away hastily. "*What,*" I demand of him, "*are you doing here?*"

I'm grimly glad when he looks frustrated with himself. It means I'm not the only one.

"I...don't know," he says.

No way. I'm not letting him off with easy vagueness. I shake my head. "When I first asked you if you would help me steal from my dad, you said no," I press him. "Now you're hiding from security with me. You don't need to go down for something you weren't even part of."

"Well, maybe I should have been!" Jackson exclaims.

His admission startles me into silence. Not just what he's said, either. It's the way he's said it, the *fact* that he's said it. While Jackson is forthcoming with apologies—kind of absurdly chivalrous about them, in fact, loading his messages with contrite emojis whenever he ran fifteen minutes late picking me up—he isn't often one for self-doubt, for uncertainty instead of confident charm. It's surprising, watching him conflicted.

He paces the room, one hand wringing his hair, equal parts indignant and defensive. Readying himself for a fight where his only opponent is regret.

"Look, what you're doing . . . isn't what I would choose on my own, but part of loving someone is expanding your world to fit theirs," he explains feverishly. "I should have when I had the chance." His eyes find mine, imploring.

I swallow down the emotions rising in my throat. "No. I don't need to drag you down with me," I reply. "I'm probably going to get arrested by the end of the night." Pushing him away is perverse enjoyment. I reach for it, clinging on to it. It's all I have. If you can't revel in victory, you can at least revel in defeat.

"You could never drag me down," he says, his voice low.

He's nearly invisible in the dark, the sharp lines of his face the only constellations in the starless night of the room's shadows. Hating how futile the effort feels, I let my heart reach out. I want to believe him. Part of me even does. I *do* have good reasons for what I'm doing. My mom needs this money.

But . . . it's not the whole truth. I won't pretend I don't enjoy what

I'm doing, the dangerous rush of it. The high stakes. The vindication of vengeance no one thinks me capable of. I suppose I'm more like Tom, whose dark recklessness I recognize from my own reflection.

Jackson has no idea how far down I can drag him. If he imagines nobility is my only reason for being here, he's wrong. Maybe I should work harder to show him, but I like the way he looks at me. Adoringly.

He smiles, worsening matters. His grin could light up entire rooms, even ones where we're hiding in the dark from pursuers. It is infuriatingly endearing. "Also. Olivia. Come on," he says, "I highly doubt you'll get caught. I don't know what your plan is, but I know you have one. Probably a detailed one, with, like, *steps*."

"Phases," I correct him.

His grin widens. "Phases," he repeats. "Right. Of course. You'll get out of this," he promises me.

I know I should consider promises from Jackson worthless. Honestly, though, in his unflinching help, his kindness, his support...I don't know. He insists he never cheated. I haven't figured out how to reconcile what I saw, what I *know*, with the Jackson I've encountered over and over in the past hours. I just know the deepest part of me, the one I've pushed myself to call naivete or weakness, is no longer convinced he's lying.

I'm surprised how much his faith in me means. I feel unexpectedly encouraged. "Thanks, Jackson," I say, meaning it. In this day of lies, it's nice to say something real.

Suddenly, I shiver, chilled by the champagne dampening my dress.

"Here," Jackson says. Too quickly for me to object, he takes off his jacket and wraps it around me. He holds the lapels closed in front of me, our foreheads pressed together while I'm wrapped in his scent.

I only pull back when my phone buzzes in my hand, and I look down to read the text message. Queen has sent the dollar bills emoji.

It's the perfect little pictogram I've envisioned for months. It's even materialized in my dreams on occasion. I established this code for the crew with one unambiguous meaning.

It's done.

We're rich.

I look up at Jackson. The fireworks of elation must be visible in my eyes because he beams. It makes me want to laugh, how it's exactly the look he would give me if my senior year of high school were normal. If I made honor roll or got into my first-choice college or scored the winning goal on the field or something. Instead, I'm standing in the dark, celebrating robbing my father of millions of dollars. It's surreal. It's perfect.

"Did you do it?" Jackson asks.

I nod, letting my grin finally spread. My heart pounds in my weightless chest. I feel like I leaped out of an airplane without a parachute and landed on my feet. Powerful. Invincible.

Happy.

The feelings well up in me, urging me to keep chasing the emotion. Without hesitating, I press my lips to Jackson's, operating on pure impulse.

He's stunned for a moment, his mouth caught in an exhale. Then, as if he's made entirely of rogue hunger, he kisses me back fiercely. He clings to the jacket he wrapped around me, pulling me close.

It's like none of our other kisses, which is saying something. It isn't just passionate or desperate. It's greedy. Unrelenting. The consummation of need, the key I sought when I contemplated my heart's deepest-hidden doors. Desperation and satisfaction in unity. My heist is worth millions—this kiss is priceless.

And everything priceless is dangerous.

I pull away from him far too late, raising my hand to my lips, an investigator looking for evidence of crimes of passion. I can't believe what I've just done—how risky, how uncalculated. How unlike me.

"I—" Jackson starts.

He releases his hand's grip on the jacket. I face away from him, heat pounding in my cheeks. Desire changing into embarrassment on close examination. *How could I? How could I have let him in?* I shrug off the jacket, my indiscretion's prelude, and fling it to Jackson, not caring if he catches the expensive garment. Vigorously, I tear my focus to what I need right now. Escape routes. From the room, and from the questions.

Scanning the dark space, I grasp on to the possibility I noticed earlier. The rectangular window under the ceiling opens onto the grass outside.

"If—" Hearing the wobble in my voice, I swallow, then stand up straight. "If you lift me," I say, "I can climb out that window, then pull you up. We don't know if security guards are waiting in the house."

I walk to the window, ignoring the hurt reflected in Jackson's eyes. *Just because something is priceless doesn't mean it won't cost you everything.* He follows me after hesitating, and I'm glad he isn't pushing or objecting. I don't want to discuss what just happened. Reaching the wall under the windows, he kneels and cups his hands with interlocked fingers for me to step onto.

In preparation, I place a hand on his shoulders to steady myself.

He looks up, directly into my eyes.

"Give me a chance," he implores. "Let me prove I never sent that message. Just five minutes. Please, Olivia."

I meet his gaze. The pounding of my heart holds me in place, fight-or-flight impulses wrestling in stalemate. Even while I hesitate, I know what I'm going to say. Maybe it's the ecstasy of victory sending recklessness coursing through my veins—or maybe I'm just desperate for a reason to forgive Jackson.

I step forward, placing my foot in his hands carefully. "What did you have in mind?"

FORTY-SIX

WE COME OUT ON THE SIDE OF THE HOUSE FARTHEST FROM THE wedding. Music echoes distantly into the night. Quickly, we wipe the grass from our knees in the dark.

Jackson takes my hand and leads me around the house, heading for the front. The house's high walls look somehow somber in solitude, grandeur with no one to impress.

I don't pull my hand from his. While Lexi remains a problem, the money in my account makes me feel like I can spare the five minutes Jackson wants. Besides, the longer I stay away with the necklace, the longer I'll keep security distracted.

It's pragmatic. Smart planning.

When we reach the front, Jackson continues to the check-in desk, where he asks the woman on duty for his phone.

While she rummages in the plastic containers for the iPhone I know she will eventually retrieve, the one with East Coventry soccer stickers on the case, I eye him doubtfully. "Jackson, I'm not stupid. Even if you show me your messages and there's nothing there, you could have easily deleted it," I say.

"You can look through everything," he insists, unwilling to let his hope falter. "Every text I've ever sent. Every photo. Even the deleted ones. Anything."

The woman hands him his phone. Immediately, he passes it to me.

The device lights up with the movement. "I need your password," I say, fighting the waver in my fingers.

He has the audacity to laugh. "It never changed."

Something flips in my stomach. I guessed his password early in our relationship—just joking around, I racked my memory for meaningful digits. Jersey numbers, locker codes, even his "lucky number," which is fifteen. He didn't mind when I figured the combination out. After I knew, he would often hand me his phone while he was driving and ask me to message his parents saying he was on his way.

I assumed he changed it when he started cheating. If he never did...

Circumstantial evidence, I counsel myself harshly. Weak circumstantial evidence.

With reluctant keystrokes, not wanting to recognize the password's implications, I input the six familiar numbers. Like every day in his Jeep with the roads of Coventry flying past us, the combination unlocks the phone. It's a vexing variable, unsettling the picture I've formed in my head of the past few months.

Past the lock screen, his wallpaper startles me.

It's...us. The same photo from when we were dating, us on the beach—the day we drove out to Sandy Point over the summer. I'm smiling, caught halfway to laughter. The sunset lights our faces in gold. Jackson is kissing me on the cheek while he holds the phone.

He couldn't have known I would look at his phone, could he? Couldn't have prepared the right wallpaper to fake dedication?

Could he?

If he didn't...

In the entryway, marble framing the night where a valet waits for guests who no doubt enjoyed the dramatics of my exit, I feel the world constrict. Not even Lexi's presence in the study or Cass's disappearance scared me quite like Jackson's phone has. If he was honest with me—if Kelly Devine lied—and I distrusted my own boyfriend, the boy I loved...how can I ever repair the damage I've done?

Jackson watches me. The elegant lighting plays over the contours of his face, emphasizing every emotion. Defiance, devotion, and desperation joining in my ex-boyfriend's eyes.

No more hesitating, I tell myself.

I open his DMs and scroll through them until I find the date my heart broke.

Exactly as I expected, Kelly's handle waits for me. My heart tight like a fist, I click kellsbells816 to find...

Hey. Was thinking about you. You up? Would love to go out sometime if you're free

The message I memorized, right in front of me.

I look up at Jackson, feeling like I'm going to throw up. Was this just a cruel joke? Did he want to watch me hurt in person? When he meets my eyes, though, not even I can keep up my guarded distrust. He's...reading me, just as I'm reading him. When he recognizes my wounded confusion, his expression changes to mirror mine.

He grabs the phone from my hands. No one could fake the frantic puzzlement in his face as he reads.

"Olivia. I swear," he says. "I've never seen this before. I *swear*. I promise I didn't send this."

I stand, struggling in the doorway of the home I lost when my dad cheated, when he wanted me to lie for him. In fact, I'm practically in the same exact *place* I was when I saw him with Lexi. I'm ready to retreat to where it's comfortable—where I put my trust in no one but myself.

But the pleading written everywhere on Jackson's face won't let me.

"Olivia," he repeats, imploring. His eyes light with wild inspiration. "Why—why would I hand you my phone if I thought this message was here? I know you see the holes in this. You're you."

I feel myself shaking my head.

I...I won't. I can't.

"I'm not your dad," he continues. "God, Olivia, please. You have to know I'm not him."

I don't know what to say. No, I'm not fully convinced Jackson cheated. I just don't know how to give myself over to the faith he's asking of me. But before I can reply, the woman working the phone desk walks over to us, security with her.

Shit.

"Olivia Owens?" the guard asks.

In my peripheral vision, I notice movement. I look to the parking area in front of the house, of which the valets are no longer the only occupants. Millennium vehicles maneuver into position, blocking road access, leaving everyone at the wedding trapped. In minutes, we've gone from guests to prisoners.

Hiding my panicked pulse, I put on my spoiled heiress demeanor. "Don't tell me all this commotion is just for me." I roll my eyes. "It's a necklace. I was joking. Jeez."

The guard frowns. He doesn't hold his hand out for the diamond, however. He grabs Jackson's phone, which he returns to the woman at the desk. "You both need to come with me," he orders us. "There's been a security breach in the house. So far nothing of your father's appears to be missing, but every guest will have to be searched before leaving."

"So we're all, like, stuck here?" I manage indignant sarcasm despite the desperation driving the question.

"I'm afraid so," the guard confirms.

Double shit. Diamond-encrusted, multimillion-dollar shit.

"Why?" Jackson asks. "If nothing was taken, then what are you looking for?"

"Cybersecurity threats," the guard replies.

I know exactly what he has in mind. Phones—like the one in my bag, the ones every member of my crew has. Computers—like Cass's laptop on which she wired the funds.

With my pouting veil of impatience in place, I grab Jackson's arm and start to head for the wedding.

"Olivia?" I hear the guard say behind me.

I turn back, fighting panic. I can't be searched, not yet. I need to ditch my phone.

The Millennium Security guard holds his hand out. "The necklace please?"

I wish I felt relieved. Instead, withdrawing the diamond from my bag, I only feel like I've lost something.

And I'm about to lose much, much more.

FORTY-SEVEN

MAYBE I'M NOT GOOD AT HEISTS. IF I WERE, I WOULD TAKE THE perfect opportunity in front of me.

To return to the wedding, we pass through the house. Security doesn't follow me. Why would they? I'm Dash's daughter. Whoever stole from Dash stole from me, too. It would be incredibly easy to run up to my old room. To ditch my phone in one of the drawers of things I left behind in the move. Just another relic from my childhood about which no one would think twice.

When security finds phones on my crew? Different story.

They would take the fall. Sure, they would pin the operation on me, but without any physical evidence, no one would listen. As agreed, Cass has wired the money to the Swiss bank account I opened to distribute to each crew member once we have returned home and everyone has carried out their jobs completely. I would walk away with the entire payload—one more gilded liar in my family's legacy.

It's sort of perfect. It's what a real heist leader would do.

I pass by the stairs, the window of opportunity closing with my every step.

I can't take the out. I can't betray my crew. I think they might be my friends now.

God, what a depressing thought. Two of them, I barely talked to before today, another is the most annoying guy I've ever met, and one of them is a *teacher.*

Even so, I want us all to leave this wedding with million-dollar party favors.

Jackson at my side, I exit the house onto the patio and head for the tent, where the festivities are still going in full force. Clearly, security hasn't decided to disrupt the dance floor yet. There's no rush. We're roadblocked in anyway.

"What's your plan?" Jackson asks while we cross the grass.

A tuxedoed Millennium Security officer covertly guards every corner of the tent. It'll be impossible to get one crew member, let alone all of them, out of the tent without drawing attention. Despite the odds, I keep walking. "Making it up as I go," I say.

Out of the corner of my eye, I notice Jackson smirk. "That doesn't sound like the Olivia I know." His voice is teasing.

I cut him a half-hearted glare. While I want to focus on the rather dire situation in front of me, I can't deny there's comfort and confidence in approaching this with playful flippancy. I find myself feeling grateful to him for the opportunity to joke. "Last chance to walk away," I warn him. "Stick with me any longer and you'll be an accomplice."

"Do I get a cut if I stay?" he replies immediately.

I can't help smiling, surprised by him. "That doesn't sound like the Jackson I know."

He takes my hand, his expression suddenly serious. "I'm staying. No matter what."

Tonight has been full of mysteries. My father's cover-ups. His debts. Abigail Pierce. Above all else—Jackson. I don't know what I *should* think, but I know what I believe. I don't pull my hand from his. He's standing by me when he has every reason not to. It means... something. I know it does.

"That sounds more like you," I say softly.

My words admit to more than I meant to reveal, a tenderness in me I never could cut out despite how many nights I wished I could.

Still, I don't take it back.

Jackson smiles. His hand in mine, we enter the tent together.

I clock Lexi quickly. From the way she stands, arms crossed in the corner, her gaze fixed on Dash with relentless focus, I know she hasn't had the chance to confront him yet. The reasons are the three security guards Dash is currently conferring with, heads tipped together in hushed conversation.

"Find my crew," I direct Jackson, not taking my eyes off my targets. "Tell them we need a way to destroy the phones and get them out."

"Wait, what?" Jackson falters. "Where are you going?"

"I need to tie up another loose end," I inform him. The edge in my voice invites no inquiry. Jackson offers none, leaving me to cross the dance floor in the direction of my former stepmother.

Watching Lexi's eyes, I wonder how the day makes her feel. Her intrusion into the office did not put her in proximity with the party, only the hallways of the house empty of guests or ceremonial focus. Now, out here, she's experiencing the full finery of her ex-husband's next wedding.

I know she notices the contrast. Her own wedding to Dash was nice, don't get me wrong. Dash's event staff know how to plan the loveliest thirty-person ceremony my father's favorite Hamptons club had ever held. Nevertheless—it was nothing like the epic event we're in the midst of.

I know from Instagram. I'd spent the day watching old movies with Mom, forgetting the world with Doris Day and Edy's Neapolitan ice cream.

When Lexi notices me approaching, her frown deepens.

"Whatever you're going to say," she preempts me when I come close, "don't bother."

I smile, enjoying the imitation of the charmless expression she would often give me. "You have no idea what I'm going to say," I point out.

"I'm collecting my money. Tonight," Lexi insists. Her eyes flit to Dash—hungrily defensive, practically paranoid in her focus. "He has to know I was here," she continues.

The glimmer of hurt in her voice forces me to falter. While I may have mirrored her shallow smiles on purpose, it's disconcerting to hear in her voice the echo of the reminders I've privately issued myself often in the past hours. *I want him to know it was me. Cut a hole into my father's life.*

The display is unsettling. Despite every way I rightfully resisted Lexi's presence in my family, I found her intimidating in one frustrating respect—she refused to be intimidated herself. The way she flung coats on the furniture, left glasses on the table, held work meetings in the living room—she continued to coordinate publicity for various Owens portfolio companies even into the marriage—everything projected the assumption of entitlement to her new role in my father's life.

It's something Maureen hasn't mastered. My new stepmom eagerly postures like she's this house's owner. Lexi acted like its empress.

She's clicking her acrylic red nails now, worrying the skin of her fingers.

"How have you not been thrown out yet?" I wonder aloud. Honestly, the guards could probably question her right now on the grounds of her whole Lady Macbeth vibe alone.

She spares me a look. Half pitying, half dismissive. "I was his publicist," she reminds me. "His wedding planner is the same woman I hired for his five-million-listeners party."

I can't help cringing, remembering. I was in middle school—for months, my dad talked about nothing except his New York night-club event celebrating how his data people determined five million people consistently streamed every episode of his podcast. What do you get when you mix one vain CEO intent on cross-platform re-invention with the money for unlimited alcohol? Very gauche, easily Googleable pictures and one *very* long fight with my mom about the example his debauchery set for his daughter.

"She owes me one," Lexi comments.

I huff a laugh. Of course Lexi has her own resources. Her own people on the inside.

"Look," I say grudgingly. "I...understand why you want to confront him, but you can't. Not right now."

"Why not?" Lexi demands.

"See the security he's with?" I pause indicatively. "They know the safe has been opened. When you confront him—when you reveal you're here when you shouldn't be—they'll arrest you."

Understandably, the revelation pulls her focus to me. Her gaze narrows. "How do they know the safe was opened?"

I roll my eyes, impatient, needing to return to my crew instead of negotiating the favor I'm doing for my ex-stepmother. "If you don't want to trust me, fine! Enjoy getting arrested for nothing," I say. "Look," I explain, "Dash didn't cheat on you. We fabricated the evidence. You're *our* pawn. You're in the middle of *our* plan. If you confront my father, he'll say the same. Do you want to go down for nothing?"

"Dash...was faithful to me?" She sounds impossibly *happy*?

It annoys me. "Congrats," I say dryly. "You were the wife he actually liked, I guess. It only cost you five million dollars. Listen to me," I go on. "You should leave. Your very presence here is incriminating. If we had worked together from the start"—I shrug—"maybe we could have avoided this."

Lexi has the gall to grin. "We could have," she offers.

"No," I say. "We couldn't."

I watch my words reach her with the insistent ebb of resignation. The fervor in her eyes clouds.

"Why are you helping me now, then?" she asks.

Fixated on my father, she weighs the reality in front of her. The man she wants to confront who has no idea she's here. The security surrounding him.

I study her, reckoning with how *little* I recognize the Lexi before me, the one I expected to encounter during her and my father's short marriage and never did. Insecure. Daunted. The Lexi who understands how fast one can lose love and luxury in the corridors of the Owens estate. The sight feeds my forming suspicion that Lexi has spent years in disguise, playing wife like I'm playing heiress. Only now I'm glimpsing the sad shadow of the person past the veil.

I guess it...makes me want to show her the same.

"Because," I say, "I know what it feels like to be tossed aside and replaced."

Lexi faces me now—and she actually looks ashamed. Another first. I intended my words' combination of accusation and commiseration, and her expression says I've hit my mark.

She folds the paper I notice she's holding. Our forged email. She slips the sheet into her clutch.

"Thanks," she says. "For the warning…and the insight. I guess I'll slip out."

"The road is barricaded," I say.

In her catlike grin, I glimpse the usual Lexi returning. Presumptuous. "I didn't park on his property," she replies patronizingly, like, *oh, duh, of course not*. "You want a getaway ride?" she offers.

"From you? I'm good," I reply.

Instead of leaving, the way I felt my dismissal very much invited, Lexi pauses. "Olivia, I just want to say—"

No. No way. Understanding, fine. Reconciliation?

I cut her off. "Apologize to me," I snap, "and I'll call security over here right now."

The disguise drops again, long enough for me to catch surprising hurt staining her features. Just as quickly, she replaces the facade. "You know," she starts, and I masochistically welcome the return of the voice she would use when she was playing "mom" with me, "sometimes apologies are better than payback."

"If you really believed that, you wouldn't be here right now," I point out.

Lexi huffs a laugh.

"*He*"—her eyes move to indicate my father—"doesn't ever apologize. Ever."

In the echo of her parting words, I have no reply, and Lexi offers me no opportunity for one. She spins on her heel and leaves the wedding, a streak of red in the white night.

FORTY-EIGHT

MORALE IS PERILOUSLY LOW WHEN I RETURN TO THE TABLE. I sit, apprehensive. "I know we're not in an ideal position," I start, "but we can figure this out. I can talk my way out of being searched. Cass is inside. She'll be fine. I'll...I'll pass my clutch around and we'll fit as many phones in it as possible," I propose. "I'll toss them with the catering trash."

No one speaks. McCoy arranges the silverware on the finished dinner in front of him.

"I listened in on my security walkie," he says hollowly. "They're doing a complete search of the house, prepared for the suspect to have hidden items inside. Everyone will be physically searched before leaving unless they object. If they object, they'll be added to a list of names to be passed to the police for the formal report and investigation."

I do not enjoy the feeling rising from my stomach. The cold in my cheeks. The devastating effects of this unwelcome role reversal. I entered this wedding more huntress than heiress. Now I'm the hunted.

I'm the prize.

"Hey, Rook," Tom says hollowly. "I got the autograph you wanted.

The Walker Harris guy." He slides Deonte a cocktail napkin. "I just went up to him."

Deonte's gaze is fixed forward, presumably on our collapsing futures. "Great. I'll mail it to my brother," he says. "From prison."

Even Tom's wry glimmer has gone out. He gives no sharp or snappy reply.

"But seriously," Deonte says, with softer genuineness, "I appreciate it." He offers and receives a half-hearted fist bump from Tom.

It cracks me. They're not coworkers. They're good people, kind people, people with whole lives and families they've entrusted to my failed plan.

No. I refuse. Olivia Owens doesn't retreat. "I don't care if security is closing in. Whatever," I reply, hating its frustrated insufficiency. "I'll try anyway. The guards don't know this house like I do. I'll—I'll find a way."

Tom meets my eyes, somber.

"And if you don't?" he asks.

The dark quiet of his words unnerves me like it wouldn't coming from any other member of my crew. I'm used to voices of reason, even doubt, from everyone else. When *Tom Pham* feels like the fun has run out... I force myself not to waver, holding his gaze. "Have I let you down yet?" I return levelly.

His face falls, his reaction almost pitying. "You can't do everything, Olivia," he says softly.

"Hey," Jackson cuts in. "Don't underestimate her."

Tom's head swivels. He regards Jackson with distant surprise. I watch the instant it happens—when, with failure's weight pressing down on us, he decides against good grace. "I'm sorry," he replies, his sneer lethal. "When did we start listening to cheaters—?"

"I *never*—" Jackson rises from his seat, the chic folding chair wobbling under him precariously.

"*Jackson*," I hiss, grabbing him and wrenching him down. I'm about to reprimand them when movement across the dance floor catches my eye. It's cousin Finn, his stature and flaxen hair unmissable even in the chaotic scene. *Interesting.* He's arguing with a security guard, and the commotion has started to attract stares like mine.

Or like mine except in one important respect. Mine has come with an idea.

I face my crew. "Phones in my bag," I order. "*Now.*"

No one hesitates, not when my urgency sounds like hope.

I pass my clutch to Deonte under the table, where the linens conceal it. He covertly removes his phone from his pocket and slides it in, then passes the clutch on to McCoy. Kevin is next. Everyone is quick, coordinated.

"Another phone isn't going to fit," Kevin informs us quietly.

"It won't need to," I reply. "Tom, you're coming with me. Jackson"— I look to my ex, his eyes expectant—"I need you to play groomsman. Distract that security guard with bridal party concerns. Ask him… whether it's going to be a problem if *substances* are found in the study where the groomsmen were partying."

Jackson doesn't question me or critique the morality of my plan. He nods and gets up, heading for the guard cousin Finn is confronting.

I wait, then follow him at a distance with Tom. While I notice occasional eyes on me, it looks as if the security presence has largely distracted guests from my necklace stunt.

Next to me, Tom does not look encouraged. "You're seriously back together with him?" he asks. His voice is unreadable, which for him, is unusual in itself.

I dart him a glance, surprised. "I'm not sure. Do you care? I thought you were just here for a job," I comment. If it's coy he wants, it's coy he'll get.

"I am," he says. "I don't care."

His delivery is convincing, but of course it is.

In front of us, Jackson nears his mark. Unable to fight my curiosity, I indulge the opportunity to press Tom. "If you did care, would you say anything?"

He looks at me now, gaze narrowed.

"I don't know if you would," I go on calmly. "If you're capable of it. I think you're like me. We keep secrets from everyone. Most of all, ourselves." I face forward, finding my newest co-conspirator's figure in the crowd. "Jackson . . . is different," I finish.

"You sure about that?" Tom asks.

I'm not expecting the certainty of the reply I hear come out of me. "Yeah. I am."

When Tom nods once, the gesture is quiet confirmation. He understands. He knows I'm right. We could never risk ourselves with each other.

While we watch, Jackson moves in on the guard. He engages him while the man is already dealing with Finn, understandably overwhelming the officer, who calls for backup. More Millennium Security personnel congregate, offering our window of opportunity. In the commotion, we steal past the guards.

The boathouse waits in the distance. It's not far, really. Just one dark runway separating us from salvation. Once we get inside, we can drop our phones in the ocean.

I pick up my pace down the incline. Tom understands our objective intuitively. After reaching the waterfront outpost, we duck inside.

I unzip my clutch as I approach the dock. Far from the party, it's hushed in here except for the gentle ripple of the water in the night. It's kind of nice, honestly. I feel like I can breathe.

Until the door opens behind us.

Mia enters, her eyes falling directly on the phones.

FORTY-NINE

W HAT A LOVELY LITTLE FAMILY REUNION," MIA DRAWLS.

She walks into the space as if it's hers, or it will be one day. Of course she does. The leverage she's just gotten could destroy me.

"You have seconds to put those away before security arrives," she informs me. "I'm not going to let you drop them in the ocean like you were obviously intending. If, however, you'd like to zip up your discount-rack clutch, now would be the time," she says with flippant impatience.

"Why would security come in here?" Tom inquires. I have to laud him for the disaffected lack of panic in his voice.

It delights Mia. She flashes him a sharp smile. "Because I'm having Finn tip them off about suspicious activity in here as we speak." Her innocent delivery sparkles like fake diamonds. She's playing with us. Mocking us.

I zip the clutch slowly, watching her. While I intend to project confidence, I doubt I'm mustering anything except surprise. Mia strides farther into the room. In the clicking of her heels on the wood, I hear clock hands and courtroom gavels.

"I know you're the one who opened the safe that's caused all this commotion," Mia continues. "I'm half impressed, honestly. Up until now, I wasn't even convinced you were really an Owens." She gives me the same smile, her voice playful as if we're gossiping. As if her insinuation of my family inauthenticity is the kind of joke one might exchange over lunch in the cafeteria. "I wouldn't even really care, except I'm not getting in trouble for *your* sloppiness. If you want to live up to our name, you're going to have to do better in the future."

I'm stunned. Nothing she's saying makes sense. *I'm not getting in trouble?* In trouble for what? How does Mia know I opened the safe?

How does opening it make me an Owens?

Right on cue, security enters, flashlights on. Their harsh floodlights fill the room, sweeping every dark corner. Past the rushing in my ears, the water has started to sound restless. "Hey, you can't be in here until you've been searched and cleared. Return to the tent, please," the guard in front orders us. He holds the door open, waiting for us to file out. I'm faintly grateful for our youth—despite how suspicious we're acting in the middle of the security crisis, the guards are disposed to write us off, presuming we're smoking or hooking up instead of literally in the middle of a heist.

As we leave, I'm conscious of my every step away from the concealing ocean. The clutch in my hand makes my fingers sweat.

I find myself next to Mia on the incline returning up to the party. With her words circling in my head, I say quietly what I've figured out. "You have something you don't want security to find, either."

With the guards still searching the boathouse behind us, Mia smiles once again. It's remarkable how many different flavors of insult her pleasant expression can hide. I wonder if they have classes on the subject in Switzerland.

"You know," she begins, "I was surprised how opulent this wedding is. Especially since the trust has run out."

I whip to face her, then hide my startled reaction in embarrassment. Everything she's saying fits into place, pieces of the puzzle I didn't know existed to solve until today. The debts. The trust. The prenup. But there was clearly money in Dash's personal account. Otherwise, Cass couldn't have made the transfer.

I don't know what it all means. Despite the pieces in place, the picture eludes me.

Mia doesn't overlook my—okay, incredibly obvious—surprise. "You didn't know," she says, realizing. Enjoying herself immensely, she nods. "I suppose not, what with your unfortunate living circumstances."

While I grit my teeth, wanting to extract further information from Mia, her words explode indignant fury in me. It's the way she says *unfortunate*. Yes, my mom's debts stress me out. Yes, the reasons for our living situation were painful. *Unfortunate*, however, disregards everything my mom has done for me and every joy we've found in our new life. Mia doesn't get to call ice cream movie nights, Saturday-morning Eggos while we do the crossword, and my weird, wonderful room *unfortunate*.

We've arrived back at the tent, where security is making their way from table to table, searching the guests. "Look," Mia says more seriously, "what I don't want the guards to find doesn't concern you."

She opens her purse, pulls out her lipstick, and reapplies. I don't know why—her lips look perfect—until I notice the flash of silver inside her bag. *The crossed-dagger cuff links.*

"They should have been my dad's. It was in the will," she says softly. "Dash kept them instead."

I meet Mia's eyes, frankly shocked to recognize the grim resolve in them. Everyone in the Owens family has been reduced in my head to fortunate villains, caricatures of wealthy cruelty. It's funny to stumble into reminders that my relatives have their own wounds, losses, and regrets. Even so, her choice of vengeance leaves me with questions.

"You're sneaking around a house full of diamonds and secrets," I say, remembering the necklace I was forced to lend Maureen. How young Mia had listened with visible jealousy at the will reading. "And you're here for...cuff links?"

Mia frowns. "I'm here for the piece of the legacy we're owed. The cuff links were *my* family's in the will, and I'm not giving up what's supposed to be ours. As for the rest"—she shrugs—"what claim do I have to what's yours? Honor among...among whatever we are, I guess." She chuckles. "Honor among us."

Mia, my cunning, moral cousin. "I don't understand wanting this family's legacy," I say finally. "I do understand wanting what you deserve."

She grimaces stiffly, the closest to commiseration I imagine we'll ever get. "Your table is set to be searched first," she informs me. "The search better be over before they get to mine."

Her parting glance is a favor wrapped in a warning. She could have given me up in the boathouse—it would have ended the search, and she wouldn't have been caught. The fact that she didn't was...an unexpected kindness from my cruel cousin. Instead, she's telling me to find a way to end this search so neither of us have to be caught.

However, if it comes down to it, she's made plenty sure I will go down before she does.

"Your former stepmom. Your cousin. You," Tom says next to me, his eyes following Mia with more interest than I'd like. "I'm starting to think everyone in your family came here to steal something tonight."

I can't help following his eyeline to Mia as she returns to the Swiss family table. She sits. It would be imperceptible to those who aren't looking. I'm looking, though. Everyone at the table exchanges glances. Mia nods.

Like the leader of her own crew, I realize.

My cousin's words come back to me. *Up until now, I wasn't even convinced you were really an Owens.*

I'm not sure what I'm the heiress to anymore. A dried-up fortune? Or a legacy of thieves?

FIFTY

THE GROUP CAN READ FAILURE ON MY FACE. DOWNCAST GLANCES and slumped shoulders from the rest of the crew greet us when Tom and I return to our table. With how intensely Kevin is fidgeting, I'm surprised his fingernails remain intact. Security is approaching, about to arrive.

"You tried," McCoy reassures me. "Sometimes that's all you can do."

I can't manage a smile. My whole family has done nothing but get in the way at every turn. This is *my* fault. In the end, I didn't factor in the variables. I didn't understand the extent of the risks.

I picked the wrong people to steal from—my own kin.

What's the word for *mastermind*, except not? *Mediocremind?*

I don't want to cry in front of the crew. I just feel like fate is repeating. Since my parents' divorce, I've developed the habit of imagining life in endings. The end of the home I knew. The end of high school, which will—without the day's heist—leave me with no certain future. The end of my relationship with Jackson, more devastating for how it felt like proof my pessimism was well-founded.

Except, in the months of planning the heist, I felt like...everything wasn't just endings. It felt like the *start* of something.

I was wrong, I guess. I'm the queen of endings.

"You did your jobs perfectly," I say, knowing it's what I owe them. Honesty is, ironically, my final refuge. It's the inversion of the euphoria I felt when we ransomed the safe numbers out of Mitchum. *We've failed.* "I'm so sorry. You probably—"

"Hey," Deonte interrupts me. His voice, like his gaze, is gentle yet firm. "We're a team. This is on us, too."

"Yeah." Tom joins in immediately. "We made our choices. You can't blame yourself."

It only makes everything worse. Their kindness wrecks me, reminding me how much I care about the people at this table, more than everyone here who shares my last name. The realization would feel like finding the fortune I never expected, except for one little problem—I've already destroyed it. I've ruined everything. *Olivia the ruiner.* Like I ruined my parents' marriage. Like I ruined my relationship with Jackson, vindictive and distrustful. I'll earn nothing from my first heist except the consolation prize of caring for the people I've put in handcuffs.

My first and *only* heist.

"You guys are my best friends," Kevin says.

For once, no one laughs or makes fun of him. While we've only spent a handful of hours together, Kevin isn't entirely off the mark. I've put my trust in each of them and been rewarded for it. They didn't betray me as others have in the past. Instead, they stood at my side, saw my worst impulses, helped me even when I pushed them away.

They make me think maybe there are people who...stay. I lift my eyes to Jackson's with fragile hope.

McCoy pats Kevin comfortingly on the back.

"Looks like we won't get to watch *Kung Fu Panda* together.

Unless they have it in prison," Tom says. "I was sort of looking forward to it, for real."

Impossibly, I smile. I'm legitimately impressed Tom's sense of humor endures even now.

His words reach Kevin differently, however. Our newest crew member stands suddenly, determination etched on his features. It's startling, yet weirdly captivating. "No, we're *going* to hang out," he declares as if he's his middle-namesake, George Washington himself. "I owe it to you after what I did with Lexi."

Deonte claps a hand on him, trying to pull him back down. "Man, don't do anything foolish."

Shaking him off, Kevin remains determined. "I have to do this," he says.

I'm watching him with wide eyes, inspired if uncomprehending. "I appreciate the sentiment," I say slowly. "But what exactly can you do to get us out of this?"

"Give me my phone," Kevin requests.

I evaluate. Yes, handing over evidence to Kevin Webber is not, conventionally speaking, wise. How much more do I have to lose, though?

Under the table, I open my clutch. Kevin grabs the burner from inside.

He stands sharply, staring into the distance, resolute. "I'll go down for the team," he announces. "And afterward, we're having a movie night."

FIFTY-ONE

I THINK THE GUY'S INTENTIONS ARE GOOD, BUT DO WE REALLY trust him to not make this worse?" McCoy wonders aloud.

We watch Kevin stride up to his father. Mitchum Webber sits with the other groomsmen, impatience emanating off the finely dressed group. I wonder how Maureen is doing—the death of the party is pronounced, the wedding having entirely devolved into the paranoid atmosphere of the security inquisition. Without music, the hum of nervous small talk pervades the tent. The chandelier hanging over us hovers like a guillotine.

"I don't know if it matters," Tom replies. "What's worse than prison?"

I can't help my reaction. Possibly I've gone soft or having friends has made me an optimist. "I trust him," I hear myself say.

Jackson's hand finds mine under the table.

Kevin and Mitchum are too far for us to hear what they're saying, but Kevin's words have an immediate effect on his father. Mitchum frowns, then his face reddens. He grabs Kevin roughly and drags him over to the security guards nearest to us.

"Tell them what you told me," Mitchum orders Kevin.

Kevin doesn't falter. In fact, his contrition is remarkably

convincing. "You can call off the search," he says. "I pretended I was being kidnapped so I could get the combination to the safe from my dad. I faked the kidnapper's voice."

The security guards exchange looks. "I better get Mr. Owens," one of them says before walking off.

"Why?" the other guard demands of Kevin.

Kevin shrugs, the perfect picture of embarrassed defensiveness. I glance to Tom, noting the grudging respect hiding in my co-conspirator's expression.

"I thought it would be cool, I guess," Kevin replies.

"You thought it would be *cool*," Mitchum repeats, visibly irate, "to go into Dashiell Owens's safe?"

It happens fast—the flash in Kevin's expression. I wouldn't recognize it if I hadn't felt it play out beneath my own fake eyelashes hundreds of times. Kevin is seeing his explanation fit into place with the image of him that his father has. He's realizing how, while leveraging others' assumptions of your vanity or unintelligence is useful, it is not fun.

Dash comes over, Maureen with him. He isn't frayed or stressed the way one might expect in the middle of this derailment of his wedding. Instead, he's practically preening. It's unsurprising in hindsight. Of course he's enjoying the power of subjecting his guests to this intrusive process. Maureen, on the other hand, is not sharing his enthusiasm for the disruption to her carefully planned wedding.

"Yeah," Kevin confirms. "I knew he has dope watches in his safe. I wanted...a pic of me wearing his Audemars Piguet for my profiles and shit. Ladies love an Audemars Piguet." With oblivious confidence, he winks at my father. "You know how it is, man."

I grimace. I hate how much Kevin has probably correctly guessed my father's convictions about impressing women with watches.

Maureen interjects. Fury has made her pallor clash with her dress. "So all of this was because you wanted a photo? You don't even have a phone."

After reaching into his jacket, Kevin pulls out the burner.

"I snuck one in," Kevin says. "Sorry."

Now Dash's demeanor darkens. He rounds on the security guards. "I was promised no one would be able to get a phone in."

The guards exchange nervous glances. Kevin, however, spares them, needing to explain. "Look." He holds up the iPhone. "Here's the proof."

While I can't glimpse the screen, I very much suspect Kevin really does have a selfie of him wearing the Audemars Piguet, from when he and Lexi first opened the safe. While expertly employed, his cover story wasn't a story at all. I have to smile. I hear McCoy stifle a laugh. Deonte shakes his head, amused.

Dash hands the phone to security. "Put this with the other guest phones," he orders. "He's not to receive it until he leaves."

"Which means we can call the search off, right?" Maureen cuts in with the usual edge in her voice. "Not that this whole fiasco hasn't already become the centerpiece of my event."

The guards nod. "We're very sorry for the inconvenience," one of them says.

For one single second, I swear my dad's eyes flash to me. His gaze narrows. Then he faces the guards, looking somehow smug.

"Call off the search. Fix this," he directs before returning to his guests.

Mitchum doesn't appear pleased by the resolution. "Go wait in the car," he tells his son. "Obviously, you're grounded."

Kevin bobs his head. "But...you're not going to delete the photo, right?"

A vein throbs down the center of Mitchum's forehead. It's captivating. "Go," he says.

On Kevin's way out of the tent, he walks with shoulders slumped, his head bowed for his father's benefit. But when he passes our table, the crew quietly applauds him. He flashes us a smile and a covert thumbs-up before resuming his solemn march off the grass. The victorious hero, returning to his dad's Lamborghini with the heist's outcome owed to him.

"I have to admit it," Tom says. "The guy has really grown on me."

I laugh, not disagreeing. Very little unexpected is ever good. Kevin Webber's selfless collaboration is the sterling exception.

"I think he's earned the title of Bishop," Deonte adds with fitting gravitas.

While I nod my confirmation, I catch sight of McCoy. He's wiping his eyes. "Are you crying?" I ask.

"It's okay, Pete," Tom reassures him. "We're going to be fine. You're not going to prison."

McCoy shakes his head. "It's not that. It's just...as an educator, it's really beautiful when you see the weird kid finally find his people."

Deonte groans, but I notice his eyes have likewise gone dewy.

In perfect punctuation of our celebratory moment, the band resumes playing, ending the depressing pall over the gaudy celebration. It is, incredibly, "Don't Stop Believin'." I don't know whether the pick is cliché or perfect. Probably both. Dash grabs a mic from the band. "Search is over, everyone. The security issue has been

Relief falls over the crowd, who rise with the music. It feels as if the past hour never happened. Everything is ridiculously, wonderfully *normal*.

I meet the gazes of my assembled crew, one after another. My friends. My people. Wow, McCoy is really in my head.

"We did it," I say softly.

We did it. We infiltrated my father's world-class safe. We fended off intrusions from unexpected interlopers. We stole millions of Dashiell Owens's money. We evaded detection. It *wasn't* the heist I've planned for months. It worked anyway, which makes me even prouder.

The reality of our victory is reaching everyone. Giddy smiles from Tom and Deonte. Quiet wonderment from McCoy. "I say we tear up this dance floor," Tom says.

McCoy raises a glass. "For Kevin!"

His rallying cry lifts everyone from their seats. "Don't Stop Believin'" continues into the epic chorus, and McCoy raises hands of victory while Deonte and Tom groove. It's oddly moving, watching them enter the dancing throng. Just a group of world-class criminals celebrating something no one else knows happened.

Instead of joining them, I hold Jackson back. He looks to me, delicate uncertainty in his eyes. His hesitation says he would wait forever. It renders him devastatingly handsome. Under the glittering lights, I do the exact opposite of what I've done for months—I don't overthink.

"Thank you for trusting me," I say to him. "I trust you, too."

I pull him into a tender kiss, feeling like I'm stealing one perfect moment for myself.

FIFTY-TWO

I DON'T JOIN EVERYONE ON THE DANCE FLOOR. INSTEAD, I EXCUSE myself to go find Cass.

I enter the house. In the night, its silence is haunting. The fine furniture has the reserve of unused objects. As if it's waiting without knowing what for. Past the now-closed French doors, the muffled music pulses in warped throbs.

I do not continue upstairs to my room, where I left Cass. Slowly, calmly, I walk down the hall to the study.

The lights from the disco ball shine in the windows, painting me in dark blue. When I reach for the doorknob, my fingers do not waver. I open the door, and I'm unsurprised to find Cass standing in front of the open safe.

She's changed back into her own clothes. It makes her imposing in ways it's difficult to describe. While pretending has its utility, looking like yourself signifies strength. Power.

My voice is steady, my question sure. "Why did you really come here today?"

Cass whirls. The delicate gears of meshing mechanisms move in her eyes. I'll give her credit—she's very fast.

"Olivia, hey. I was just making sure—"

I hold up a hand to silence her. "Spare me the lies," I say. I shut the door behind me. The latch of the lock resounds into the room. My pace leisurely, I walk to one of the leather couches and sit, folding my hands in my lap. "What I want to know," I go on, "is why you actually wired the money. If you were here to betray me, why not just fail to do your job?"

The change in Cass now is slow. Her face shifts into something I don't recognize. Gone is the girl who opened up to me in my bedroom, who supported me and shared glances with me all day. In her place is a stranger.

She straightens. Her chin rising, she looks down on me. "How did you figure it out?" she asks with deathly patience.

I unzip my clutch. I returned my crew's phones to them earlier—inside the bag, only one phone remains except for mine. I swiped it at the check-in desk while the guard was handling my necklace. Jackson's. When I toss the phone to Cass, the East Coventry High sticker reflects the light.

She catches it, her eyes widening with realization.

It's gratifying. I feel as if I've wrenched a few gears out of her incessant mental machines. "If Lexi hadn't sent us on that wild-goose chase, I would never have put it together," I remark. "I guess I owe her one. But it was just too coincidental. Jackson was framed for cheating in the same way you suggested we frame Dash for Lexi."

I put together the pattern when Jackson showed me the message. He wouldn't have unless he legitimately didn't know they were there, which would be the case only if *he* didn't send them. Before returning to the wedding, I checked my bank account, fearing the worst.

The money had been there, though. I disregarded the question while we dealt with more immediate threats, although it was why I never particularly feared the security sweep apprehending Cass.

Cass lowers her hand holding the phone. I wait, expectant. With the study's heavy door separating us from the rest of the house, no music pervades the inner sanctum. Our confrontation's ornamented cage is whisper-hushed.

"Oops," Cass finally says. She shrugs, unbothered.

"I started thinking," I go on, not interested in indulging childish sarcasm. "Why would you break up me and my boyfriend?"

Cass crosses her arms. "Clearly you've figured it out," she prompts me, meeting my impatience with her own.

"You're the one who named me King. You shouldn't be surprised," I chastise. "The obvious explanation didn't fit. It's not like you wanted to get with Jackson yourself. You haven't even looked at him the entire day. Which meant your target was the other person in the relationship. Me."

She says nothing. It's confirmation enough. She grips the phone, glaring.

"You made it clear on multiple occasions how easily you can and have hacked my phone," I go on. "You read my DMs to him, didn't you?" I remember what she said to me over the phone on my way to the safe. There wasn't someone who cheated on her. She wasn't commiserating. She was...gloating. Glorying in the reminder of what she'd wrought.

The venom in her stare flattens into resolve. It is a look without regret. "You were on the verge of giving up the heist," she explains. "All for him. His account was laughably easy to hack. Password *newgirl* with his jersey number."

I revel in my deductions even while the pain of yet another betrayal is quietly ripping me up on the inside. Just when I was ready to trust, to let people in. I can't dwell on it right now. Right now is for *why*.

I put the question to her directly. "Why did you need me to go through with it if you were going to betray me in the end?"

"Have I betrayed you?" she replies. Her posture is poised, wound tightly. She doesn't look uncomfortable, however. It's like the edge is home to her.

"You're here for the handcuffs, right?" I ask. "In the safe, I mean."

She grins and pulls the handcuffs from her back pocket. I knew their presence was suspicious the moment I saw them. If Dash possessed something to defend himself with, I'd have found a gun inside with the watches, heirlooms, and gold jewelry.

Handcuffs aren't dangerous enough to be locked up. What if they weren't hidden to defend oneself against potential intruders? What if... they were *left for someone to use*? Right now? What if someone— somehow—knew *I* was coming? What if I wasn't the only person planning ahead for my heist? What if others were maneuvering just like me?

I stand. Figuring everything out feels like stretching every muscle at once. I walk to the safe, where I pull out my father's will. I speak softly, knowing my opponent is hanging on to every word. "I started wondering. Maybe Abigail Pierce isn't someone Dash had an affair with. Maybe she's the product of an affair. A daughter."

Cass goes very still. I circle her, then position myself in front of her to look her right in the face. The color has fled her skin. Her eyes have gone from gears to knives.

"Abigail Pierce," I repeat. "The girl you conveniently couldn't find online, because you didn't need to, did you? Because she was already at the wedding. Already in my crew."

She meets my gaze. I'm staring at my reflection in a shattered mirror.

I hold my hand out.

"Hello, sis," I say.

FIFTY-THREE

ABIGAIL REACHES FOR MY HAND AND, INSTEAD OF SHAKING, SNAPS a handcuff onto my wrist. Acting with quickness I don't anticipate, she hooks the other handcuff around a leg of Dash's massive wooden desk.

It's what I get for a greeting, I guess. Instantly, I feel foolish for my formality.

"Sorry," she says flatly. "I just need you to stay put." While surprise renders me helpless, she swipes my clutch out of my hand. She tosses it to the other end of the room. Inside the fake-leather sleeve, my phone hits the hardwood.

I yank my wrist, trying to free myself, but the desk is heavy, the drawers full of god knows what. It's hopeless, which my half sister undoubtedly knows.

Half sister. It rings in my head, like secrets the world didn't mean to speak.

I recognize her now. Not literally, not from having met her before. I recognize myself in her. The contours of her face, the shape of her eyes. The precision. The unsmiling focus. I don't know how I'm only noticing them now. She's the girl pushed out of the frames of family portraits.

I settle onto the floor with what I hope passes for dignity. The riddle of her engages the rational, magnifying-glass part of my mind. "What should I call you? Abigail or Cass?" I ask.

She blinks. "Abigail," my sister says. "Cass is a third-rate prankster from your high school who you've never laid eyes on."

The whisper of indignation in her voice intrigues me. It's obvious she resents hiding her identity. Needing to.

"Honestly, I did you a *favor*," she insists, spite underlining her every word. "I've devoted *years* to my craft. Understanding every interface. Cracking every code. When your very existence is founded on hidden information," she explains, "you get very good at figuring out how it's hidden."

I watch her, heart pounding. She's absolutely enjoying giving her reveal speech.

"The real Cass just...guessed a couple of passwords and erased a few files for fun. I wouldn't call it *hacking*. When you reached out to her," Abigail continues, "you mentioned you'd never spoken, but you thought she might be interested in a job. I locked her out of her email and have been impersonating her to you ever since." Now Abigail looks impossibly smug. "It was my perfect way in."

I work through the information coming at me, head spinning. There *is* a Cassidy Cross who goes to East Coventry High. And...the proud, venomous girl in front of me isn't her. The real Cass is probably home in Coventry, loitering outside Starbucks. Abigail managed to intercept my communications to the classmate who I assumed— inexpertly—could use the abilities she employed to erase some high school exams in service of The Plan.

And instead of the rebel I intended to hire, I got a *real* hacker.

My half sister.

I reach for questions, feeling as if I'm falling. "How did...how did you even know when I contacted Cass?"

"I've been watching you for some time, Olivia," Abigail says.

The suffocating gravity of her response silences me. With the chrome cuff chewing into my wrist, I start realizing just how early my heist fell apart. I'd failed before I'd even really begun. *Houses of cards.* Without knowing it, I'd stacked mine on a slanted surface.

Except...I have the money.

"You could have easily taken the money for yourself," I say. "You didn't need to transfer it for real."

She huffs a laugh. "Olivia, I'm not after a paltry five million dollars," she replies. "The money in your account is just the proof I need to collect what *I'm* here for."

I feel my eyes widen with realization. "You made a deal with Dash," I say, filling in the details. *The handcuffs.* Left for her. Planned with someone inside this house. Someone who knew I was coming...because Abigail told him. "That's why he was preparing to add you to the will," I finish, darkness opening in my stomach. "You're trading me for an inheritance."

It all fits into place. The reason Abigail couldn't let me give up the heist—it was because the heist was just the first phase of *her* plan. The game within the game. The heist within the heist.

With the new information, I reframe my entire concept of the day. *The Plan. Phase One.* Foolish. Every way I've named my own machinations in my head now feels like the made-up words kids use playing pretend. I was just playing heist.

And Abigail was playing me.

Her jaw clenches. "I never got to know our dad," she says quietly, the hush of contained fury. "My mom signed an NDA and promised never to reveal who my father was to me, for a onetime payment. Enough to make a dent in his liquid assets."

I stay silent, hating the obvious sense of what she's saying. It's exactly coherent with what I know of my dad's fidelity issues. Perfectly consistent with his penchant for pouring money on problems.

When Abigail shrugs, I read the pained resentment in the very not-casual gesture.

"It didn't matter," she says. "My mom didn't know how to make money work for her the way those born to it do. She used up the hush money fast. This"—her eyes dart over the room, the polished wood, the paraphernalia of wealth, the cigars, the chesterfield couches— "was never her world. Which is why Dash was so keen to keep her a secret."

I realize now isn't the first time I've seen the look in her eyes. The peculiar cast of despising your own jealousy. I remember how her scrutiny probed over my copy of *Oliver Twist*, my old clothes, my dollhouse.

Who cares if it's you anymore? I would never give up anything like this.

With gut-churning guilt, I remember everything she's said to me. The way she wants to fit in here. The way she knows she doesn't but reassures herself it doesn't matter.

Insecurities I now know she was dealing with a hundredfold. I feel a pang of pity for her, denied everything I've been denied and more.

"You weren't easy to find, you know," my half sister informs me. "It took intensive investigation through my mom's computer for me to even learn Dash's name. Once I did, it led me to you." She shakes her head in wonderment. "I was shocked to discover how close we were," she says, and I realize she's marveling at Dash's laziness or stupidity. "Just one school district over. When I started monitoring you, saw what you were planning, I realized it was…exactly what I needed. The one way I could get into my father's life."

Her eyes bore into mine.

Handcuffed in place, I hope my face reveals nothing of how I feel. How…intimidated.

"He didn't believe me when I reached out to him. Oh, he knew I was his daughter," she clarifies. "He just didn't believe his *real* daughter would ever turn on him." Her lips purse. "His words. *Real* daughter," she repeats. "He told me to deliver him proof, and then, well…"

She pauses, darkly playful.

"Then there would be an opening in the family," she says.

The words churn my stomach. It shouldn't surprise me, my dad's willingness to replace me. Remove me like I'm an unsavory negotiating point in a deal. Still, he could reject me a thousand times and it would never stop hurting.

I look away. I have no secrets from Abigail Pierce. Not The Plan, not my family. The last stronghold I can keep is the pain putting tears in my eyes.

Of course, I fail.

"Did I hurt your feelings?" she asks. "Imagine how I felt knowing you had everything I was denied. Dad raised you. You have his last name."

Dad. Her use of the innocuous word is quietly resounding. "Believe me, you didn't miss much," I say. Like the day's other lies, it's half honest. Yes, having his last name is what made me want to use his first. He's Dash to me, not Dad, for punishingly fair reasons. Or maybe it's just one more vain attempt to protect my heart. *Dash doesn't love me* hurts a hell of a lot less than *Dad doesn't love me.*

Nevertheless...

On the floor of my father's study, her words force me to reframe my life. I've spent the rueful day walking the lawns and hallways of the house where I grew up, evaluating everything ripped from my grasp when Dash forced me and my mom out. Everything I've lost.

No. Abigail reminds me of everything I once *had.*

Easter egg hunts among the fountains outside. Studying for exams I didn't really need to pass in rooms the size of many apartments. Never *wanting*, except wanting respect from the father whose roof I lived under. Never *wondering*, except wondering whether I was happy *enough* in my dollhouse life.

A paltry five million dollars. Yeah, my objective feels small now— just not in the way Abigail meant.

It's nothing compared to the heist I've already executed, if unknowingly. Years, months, days. Memories and hopes.

I've stolen a whole life from her.

Abigail's mouth twists. "You have no idea what it's like to know your dad not only didn't want you but put himself in debt to hide you from the world. From himself."

"I'm sorry," I say, entirely honest now.

"No." She exhales. "Don't. Don't act like you're not glad you got to have your perfect childhood in this house with your two parents. If my existence had come out, everything would have changed."

With deadening calm, I know she's right. My imagination unwinds the years of my childhood. If my mom had found out about Abigail, she would have left Dash sooner. Much sooner. Dash has shown his willingness to trade one family for another. Maybe Abigail's mom would have been his second wife. My room would have been my sister's.

Partially in defiance, partially, curiosity, I push myself to hold her gaze. It's unnerving, looking into the eyes of the person my father has pitted me against.

No. I won't let Dash control me. Not like this.

"Abigail, we don't have to compete," I plead, hoping she doesn't point out it's not much of a competition when one of us is in handcuffs. "I'm sorry you didn't have the dad you deserved, but you can have a sister."

She is the one who looks away now. The whole room narrows down into her silence. The moment suspends, pillars of glass holding up the fate of everything I've planned. Except, when she speaks, the calm in her voice lets me know I've lost.

"You should have played the long game, Olivia," she says. "Why pull a heist when you can be an heiress?"

She walks out of the room. When the door closes, I'm alone. Really, finally alone.

FIFTY-FOUR

FOR ONCE, I HAVE NOTHING. NO RECONFIGURATIONS. NO ESCAPE plans. I pull on the desk, more frantic now. The metal chews into my wrist, inscribing pink lines on my skin like marks of failure. I get nowhere. The desk is probably hundreds of pounds. It's infuriatingly rudimentary. What's holding me in place won't yield to negotiation or clever lying or fake smiles. It's punishingly physical, hopelessly concrete.

Finally, I weaken. The fight leaves my limbs. I return to the floor, entirely empty. I don't even need to wonder or worry. I know I've reached the ending. I stare up, defeat chaining me in place. From the ceiling, the lights glare into my eyes.

Instantly, inexplicably, they remind me—not of growing up here or revisiting my complicated home. They remind me of the overhead lights in the hallway of my mom's hospital room.

And huddled on the floor of my father's study, I wonder if I've focused on the wrong reminiscences. I've spent the day fighting with flashbacks of this house. Of the Olivia who felt at home here, even close to happy. I needed them. They fueled me.

I concentrate on others now.

In hopelessness's clutches, I remember how horribly *familiar* the feeling is. I've dealt with worse. I've wrestled helplessness in Kent County Memorial Hospital.

What do you do when your mother is lying unconscious, the machines surrounding her the only signs she's clinging to the life she lives for you? You don't give up. You wait, not even going to the vending machine to eat for *fifteen hours* on the off chance she'll need you. You indulge every miserable storybook fantasy saying if you just plead enough, cry enough, hope enough, she'll wake up.

The hours passed. I felt darkness closing in. In case it would remind her that I was waiting for her, I held her hand, clutching hard enough the nurses had to pull my grip free. White knuckles unclenched from motionless fingers. *You're hurting her,* they said.

Don't you think I know that?

Until she woke up.

No words can ever capture the overwhelming rush I felt the moment she opened her eyes—green, like mine. How I wept with relief under the sterile hospital lights.

It was, ironically, impossibly, the happiest day of my life.

Exhaling slowly, I refocus. I don't need rage right now. I don't need vicious mournfulness for memories of idyllic lawn games or illusions of family. I need to remember the joy. The light. The love of what I'm fighting *for*, not what I'm fighting against. The invincible reminder of how hope waits on the other side of pain.

If I give up now, I would give up everything. Everything. Every chance I want for my mom, free of debt, and for myself. I would give in to the darkness, kneeling next to my father's emptily formal desk, prone in failure. Defeated.

No. Hell no.

I change my frustration into furious drive. Why was I even

imagining giving up? The enormity of Abigail Pierce's victory isn't the hardest challenge I've ever faced. The hardest hurt I've ever suffered.

Not. Even. Close.

Every agony is the proof—the *evidence*, laid out with the clarity no courtroom file could ever reflect—of how I've fought past hopelessness for the joy in my life. How if you hold on, the impossible can become the greatest moment of your life. Strength, I decide, maybe isn't measured in what you've won. Maybe it's measured in what you've lost. How you kept on fighting.

Vigor rages in me. It's not the ending. It's *never* the goddamn ending. They're going to have to drag me out of here handcuffed if they want Olivia Owens to retreat.

I search the room for something that can help me. Anything. If only I could reach the clutch with my phone, but it's too far. I have no way of contacting my crew. I have to think *fast*.

On the desk, nothing. No pens, no clips, no materials for improvised lockpicking. I open drawers, every one I can grasp. *Nothing. Nothing. Nothing.* Handcuffed in place, I'm constrained, the rest of the room outside my reach—

The safe.

It's open behind me. *Yes.* I surprised my sister when I entered. In our confrontation, she forgot to close the weighty door, leaving the precious contents in the dark cavity exposed. I stretch, contorting myself so my fingertips just barely brush the files inside. With desperate effort, my shoulders searing, I swipe until the papers tumble out onto the floor.

Quickly, I scour the materials surrounding me. The will. Stock certificates for his various companies. Bonds and treasury documents

I don't know how to interpret. I feel my thoughts bouncing distractedly, panic making me lose focus.

I close my eyes. Breathe in. Breathe out. I think of all the threads I've collected today. Mitchum's revelation about the prenup and Dash needing to be exposed for something. Allen's warning about the debts. Mia's comment about the trust.

The trust.

I open my eyes, inspiration hurtling into me. With fevered fingers, I sweep papers aside until I find what I need. I read as quickly as I can, my heart pounding in my chest so loudly, I almost don't hear the door open and Abigail return.

This time, with my—*our*—father.

FIFTY-FIVE

WHEN DASH'S EYES FALL ON ME, THE COLLISION OF EMOTIONS IN them startles me. He shuts the door behind him.

I don't look away. I stole from my dad. I want him to know it was me.

"I admit, I didn't think you could do it," he says.

I hold my chin high. "Why?" I ask. "You stole my home from me. Money was the least of what I could take from you. I don't regret it."

Fireworks have started outside over the water. Explosions of red and gold light the office. He waves away my words and walks over to a couch, where he sits, legs crossed. I watch him, hiding confusion. His collar undone, his hair imperfect from the wear of the wedding. The defiant relaxation of his posture in his tuxedo. He looks pleased to be here, the recipient of the wedding gift he never expected his daughters would give him.

"No, not that," he says. "Revenge, theft—I understand these instincts well. In fact, they're necessary. You don't get to have this"— he gestures to the room, the house, the imposing everything— "without them. I didn't think *you* were capable of pulling it off, of evading security, of planning something like this. When I heard your scheme, I didn't stop you. I wanted to see how far you'd get."

I feel the slap of his words. "You've always underestimated me," I muster, hearing my retort's weakness, its lack of menace. The entire day, the months of planning, I've imagined myself the defiant intruder in his perfectly smug hallways. Instead, I haven't managed to escape ending up exactly where he wanted me.

Dash smiles. He nods while white fireworks light up his face. Abigail stands, arms crossed, glaring, outside the explosions' glow. The likeness of their faces is otherwise impossible to ignore.

"I suppose I have," my father concedes. "I'll be taking the money back, of course, but I can toss you a couple hundred thousand. You've earned it."

I furrow my brow, not understanding.

Dash goes on cheerfully, clapping his hands together. "Honestly, I feel so much better now. You know, I always regretted not having a son I could pass the empire on to. I figured you were soft. Shallow." He uncrosses his legs and leans forward. "Now I know you're a worthy heir, Olivia Owens. I'm proud of you."

I'm proud of you.

I've never, not once, heard the reverence in his voice when he pronounces my name. It holds me in place like no handcuffs ever could. His is the intonation used for futures forged, dynasties delivered, and queens crowned.

In the shadows, Abigail watches.

My father rises from the couch and pulls from his jacket pocket a key, glinting silver in the light from the windows. He comes over to me, where he unlocks the handcuffs. I don't move. I can't.

"You're my legacy," he says.

I hate how much his approval feeds the fantasies I've spent the day fighting off, racked with the recognition of how I'll always love him, even while I hate him. Even while I steal from him. I'll never escape the dream of the life where he values me.

He's now delivering the reality right into my grasp. Guilty images fill my head of me moving back into this house, not full-time—I would never leave my mom—but half the time, I could be here. I could have this. My dad. *Everything.*

This isn't revenge, a voice in my head whispers. *Is it better, though?* I don't know.

Rubbing my wrist, I stand. I push aside the intoxicating idea of calling every manicured lawn, every palatial room, every strip of crown molding mine again. It is the horrible power of home—how can I rue this house yet yearn for it the instant it returns to my grasp? "What about my crew?" I demand.

"Talented people," Dash remarks without hesitating. "Keep them close, Olivia. You could make use of them in the future."

His measured manner is utterly puzzling. It's like it's the first day of my internship in his footsteps. Nor do I miss what's hidden in his invocation of the future. The life he leads—the life he's leading me into—is one of *using* the people closest to me.

"You won't press charges?" I ask.

He laughs. He's walked over to the drink cart, where he pours himself whiskey into one of the unused glasses. "Charges?" he repeats. "Charges for what? While I'm pleased with your efforts, you didn't succeed or accomplish anything. You can't beat *me*, but you can learn a few things."

Finished pouring, he raises his glass.

In my honor, I realize.

"I can't wait to teach you," he says.

No embarrassed imaginings of how it would feel to return here, under the roof where I grew up, could ever compare to what I feel now. Every hope, every resentful wish, leads here, into the heart of my fantasies. What I wanted was never a heist. It was never a house. It was respect, *his* respect. Recognition. Love.

While I wrestle with myself, my father turns to his other daughter. "Now you. You've done your job sufficiently." His air is dismissive. Painfully professional. "You'll get what you were promised. I'll name you in my will, and you'll receive an inheritance along with Olivia and whatever future children I may have."

The change in his demeanor startles Abigail. I watch her conceal her flinch poorly. In the corner of the room, she no longer looks like my opponent. She looks like the ghost of me.

"That's it?" she replies.

"That was our agreement, was it not?" Dash returns.

With horrible clarity, I realize what he's done here. I recognize his filthy fingerprints everywhere on this conversation. He *implied* he would welcome Abigail into the family without ever intending to honor her expectations. It's perfectly him. Enough promises for you to feel hope. Never enough for you to feel loved.

"But…" With the word, the waver steals further into my sister's voice. "I thought…"

Dash swirls his drink. "Don't tell me you were expecting—what? To move in?" He wanders into the middle of the room, infuriatingly comfortable. It's exactly how he lives, I guess. The man in the center of everything while planning nothing.

"Of course not. I just—" She steps forward, mastering her emotions once more. "So when Olivia pulls off a scheme, you bring her in to the company, but when I do it, I'm just the girl you hired? Olivia didn't even succeed," she points out. "I delivered. Yet you're rewarding *her*. It's not fair."

If the stakes weren't empires and millions, I would find the whole situation perilously close to funny. We just sound like squabbling sisters, pressing our cases in front of our parent, decider of our fate. *She did it first! Why isn't she getting punished? It's not fair!* Of course, the conversation is heartbreakingly far from the sibling drama I'm imagining. The desperation in Abigail's every word leaves me closer to crying, not laughing.

I know exactly what she's feeling. It makes my heart crack. Abigail is strong, stronger than me. It won't matter. Dash will break her anyway.

He frowns incredulously. "Oh, what is *fair*?" He spits the word as if it's poison in his drink. "Fair," he answers himself, "is just a word people use when they want to get their hands on what others have *earned*."

His intonation leaves no doubt which group he considers himself part of. I can't help grimacing. Yes, my father is crafty. Yes, he's charismatic. It doesn't change the fact that he's earned exactly none of the indulgences his life has left him. He carelessly walks in carpeted footsteps. *Fair* is stealing from someone like him.

"You may have my blood, Abigail, but you're not an Owens," he concludes. "I'll have to ask you to leave my property now."

In Abigail's eyes, I watch doors slam shut on hope. The frantic hunger in her gaze withers into nothing. She looks lost, small enough that she could vanish into the shadowy corner of the high-ceilinged study. I could consider it revenge for her betrayal. I even wait for the dark whispers to overtake me. It's what the *Owens* in me would feel, isn't it?

I wait, and they never do. I only feel sad for her. I see myself in my sister. The girl who, years ago, was told to pack her bags and leave.

I can't just watch it happen again.

"No," I hear myself say. "Abigail won't be leaving."

I face my father, who rounds on me. The fires of revenge are burning hot and bright in me once more, reignited by his dismissal of Abigail. I can't overlook it just because he's offered me everything I've privately dreamed of. He needs to pay.

He needs to know how *fairness* really feels—and in the shadows, her dark double, revenge. The same, yet different.

Like sisters.

For once, my father needs to experience what he deserves.

FIFTY-SIX

NO ONE MOVES.

My pulse pounds, my blood rushing in my veins. In my cheeks, my fingertips, my chest, my heart rate is relentless. It isn't frightening or uncomfortable. I'm not the intimidated girl or the mollified heiress the people in the room expect.

I feel good. I feel in control.

At every turn today, I've run into people with their own agendas, who have tried to get in the way of mine. They haven't, though. Each of them has only given me pieces of what I need *now*. My final move.

"I don't want thousands from you," I inform Dash. "I'll be keeping the millions we stole."

He barks a laugh. "You will not. I'm the one in charge here."

I listen close, reveling in the familiar confidence in his voice. I've known wealth. I've known indulgence. Nothing compares to the anticipation of putting him in his place. While I'm not doing it for enjoyment, I will very much enjoy what comes next.

"What you haven't realized yet is," I say, "I'm not the next chapter in your legacy. I'm the end of it."

I don't know what does it. What unnatural calm in my voice, what cold menace in my words, what dark gleam in my glare changes everything. Whatever it is, Dash goes still. Something in the way he looks at me shifts. It takes me a moment to figure out what's different. Then I realize—he's afraid.

For the first time in my life, he knows I'm capable. I'm his equal.

"You don't know what you are. You're just a kid," he mutters, dropping onto the couch as if he's confident.

He's not, though. He's covering his fear. Performing. I would know dishonesty on my father anywhere, grimy fingerprints left on my heart forever. He's lying.

I'm not.

I reach for the documents scattered on the floor and lift the one I need. "I've learned a lot about you today, *Dad*," I say, walking his fate closer to him, conscious of Abigail, our silent witness. "I learned you spent a lot of money to hide your illegitimate daughter from your wife. Were you more upset about the end of your marriage or that I turned all that hush money into a failed investment?"

"You should be grateful for what I did," he fires back, red splotches spreading on his cheeks. "Who knows what your life would look like right now if I hadn't?"

Abigail fidgets behind him, no doubt hearing the dark echo of her own words to me. I know what she's feeling, know what it's like to see yourself in Dash in the worst possible light. To be repulsed by the similarities but unable to escape them.

"Oh, I know how it would look," I reply. "I'm living that life right now. In a two-bedroom house with a mom who loves me. Burdened with medical debts and car-insurance payments we can't afford. *Happy* without you."

Dash snarls. "If you're so happy, then go back to your real home."

I match his snarl with a smile. "I will. First," I say grandly, "I'm taking what's mine." I glance down at the document in my hand, borrowing some of Tom's theatricality. "You didn't have the cash for the hush money, so you borrowed it, right? From your friends. People like Allen Chang."

"How did you—?" he begins, desperation bright in his voice.

I cut him off. "But then it only got worse. You wanted to follow in your great father's footsteps. Be the worthy next chapter of the *Owens legacy*," I say, pronouncing the words so he hears my own dark echo. "So you started your own media corporations. Vanity projects and podcasts that required yet more money to appear successful. But you were spending more than you were bringing in, and so you started selling off Grandpa's companies to try to cover it. It wasn't enough. You needed cash. And what better place to look than the Owens legacy itself?" I pause before I slot the final puzzle piece into the tableau it's taken me hours to construct. "The family trust."

Dash, for once, is silent. He watches me like prey watches its predator, like if he just makes himself small enough, I won't go in for the kill.

"I talked to Mia," I go on flatly. "Apparently, the trust has run dry. Only, it hasn't, has it?"

I drop the trust bank statement on his lap. He makes no move to read it. He doesn't have to. Dashiell Owens, executor of Andrew Owens's estate, knows that there are still ten figures' worth of money in his father's trust. He knows that every year, he is supposed to responsibly invest a certain amount, donate a certain amount to charity, and, of course, send each of his siblings a check.

Except, according to Mia, those checks have stopped coming.

Accusation turns my tone. "Grandpa didn't invest in burying his indiscretions. He invested in what lasted. In futures." I let my eyes drift to my sister, hoping she knows what Dash did was wrong—that she has family who wouldn't rather hide her away. "The trust is fine. You've just been lying to your siblings. Because you're stealing their shares."

Finally, Dash stands, defense mechanisms kicking to life. His jaw is tight, his gaze tighter. "You have *no* idea what you're speaking about," he snaps.

My father is taller than me. He wants to use that on me. To intimidate.

But tonight, I'm in heels.

My gaze is level with his, and I don't blink. "I don't? So if I take these statements down to any of the cousins here tonight, it won't start a war within the family?" I press my question to him like the point of a sword.

"They would destroy you along with me. Please be smart enough to see that," Dash parries, patronizing.

I grin, knowing he's given me the confirmation I needed. My voice is low when I continue, weighted down by the years of hurt and rejection he's left me. "You already did their job for them. If you'd never kicked me out, maybe I'd stand with you now. But I have *nothing* they can take."

My father isn't proud of me now. He's furious. Empires crumble in his eyes. I won't be welcomed back home, won't be given the keys to his castle. I won't be his heiress.

I don't care. I've bested him.

My sister watches me. She doesn't look hurt anymore. She looks avenged.

I face my father for a final time. "Abigail and I are going to leave this wedding *with* the money we stole from you," I order. "I'm aware it cleans out your cash. Maybe Allen will give you another loan, or you can steal more from your dead father." I shrug, unbothered. His debts won't be mine when he removes my name from his will. "As long as my crew and I aren't arrested for this, your family never has to know you're stealing from them, and no one has to know you were bested by the two daughters you cast out."

I notice my sister straighten, surprised to be included. Even touched.

Dashiell Owens watches me for long moments, drink in hand. I hold his gaze, understanding innately that I'm staring right into him, into his rotten heart. The mogul whose fortune is stolen. The host whose friends hate him. The son whose hunger for his father's image has destroyed him.

He knows I know everything. His features warp with wrath. "*Get. Out,*" he orders.

"Happily," I reply. "This isn't my house anyway."

I pick up and fold the accounting statement neatly, creasing the center of the page like I'm choking the life out of the document.

"Do you honestly think you can deceive the family forever?" I can't help asking him. His machinations are risky, even for a man who regularly combines crafty and careless in one move.

He squares his shoulders in petty defensiveness. "Look around you, Olivia," he snaps. "Money isn't about forever. It's about right now. Forever is an afterthought. I needed more," he emphasizes contemptuously, "so I took it."

I say nothing, loathing the echo of my motives in his words. *Why earn when you could deceive? Why inherit when you could rob?* Clinging the paper—my security—and then picking up my clutch from the floor, I join Abigail at the door. She comes closer to me, and decisively, I reach for the knob.

I'm leaving when I hear my father laugh.

Not the showy sound I heard with his groomsmen. No—he's not mocking me. I wish he were. I could easily roll my eyes and forget the insult. Instead, I round, foreboding fixing me in place.

Dash stares into his drink, his demeanor changed. In defeat, amusement has found him.

"Olivia," he pronounces. "You think you aren't part of this family, but can't you see? You *are* my legacy."

He pauses, knowing I'm curiosity's captive. I don't want to hear what he's concluded, yet I wait.

"Like father, like daughter," he chides. "Heiress to an empire of thieves."

His words chill me, shards of silver in my veins. My father glances up, expectant. Waiting for the reward of my retort.

While he may have given me everything, I give him nothing. I shut the door on him, and we leave.

FIFTY-SEVEN

ENTERING THE FOYER, I REALIZE ABIGAIL NO LONGER FOLLOWS ME. I face her, finding my sister hesitating. Walls of white frame her. In her black ensemble, she's a shadow in the well-lit hallway.

"Why did you do that?" she demands.

With heartbreaking clarity, I read her guarded inquisition. She's prying at the edges of generosity, looking for the catch. Waiting for the countermove. I would have done the same. I *have* done the same.

"I betrayed you," she whispers, confessing to herself. "Why did you help me?"

I smile. In a wedding day packed with complicated questions, it's nice to encounter one I can answer immediately. "I guess I've learned some people don't deserve second chances. Some people do," I say honestly.

It is the key in the lock holding up her unflinching facade. Her face twists, tears finally welling in her eyes. "He wasn't who I expected he would be," she offers.

I don't need her explanation. I hear in her words the reprise of everything I've asked myself at night under the rose-patterned comforter in the house I can't *wait* to return to. "I know," I say sadly. "Me neither."

She steps forward.

"I do not, however," I continue, "offer third chances. If you ever double-cross me again, I *will* get revenge. Perhaps I'll plan an elaborate heist on your wedding day. Just for instance." Finally, I grin, dropping my intimidating guise.

Abigail laughs wetly. "I mean"—she nods, the imitation of our negotiating postures—"that's only fair."

In the past hour, I've reminded myself that everything Abigail has done was in service of her plan. Every kindness was orchestrated to win her way into my crew and my confidence. Planning the day required constant vigilance, constant skepticism, constant wariness. I've indulged the instincts, telling myself the person I once considered my ally was my opponent all along.

Except... now I do the opposite. I push myself to wonder whether under her mercenary machinations, she yearned in ways I couldn't possibly understand. Performing friendship out of the fiercest hunger for family.

I can't imagine how painful it was.

She doesn't need to pretend now. "Well, Queen," I say. "Should we go celebrate with our crew?"

Her face lights up, remade in exhilaration. While she didn't get the family she expected from our father's wedding day, she got us. She's not alone.

I wonder where Abigail will go when she goes home. I vow right then—I'm going to know. I'm going to reclaim our entire lifetime of sisterhood. Everything we missed. Comforts and fights, memories and miseries shared, inside jokes and movie nights and double dates. If she wants me, of course.

Interrupting my resolve, security walkie-talkies hiss nearby. I guess Dash shook off his contemplative stupor and decided to set Millennium Security on the hunt for his daughters. "I'm guessing they're here to escort us out," I observe.

Abigail's grin snares a renegade spark. "Only if they catch us," she replies.

In the moment our gazes meet, our impromptu Phase Seven shared wordlessly, I realize my resolution might be very easy. Maybe I'll love having a sister.

We're off without hesitation—running, rounding corners, panting, laughing. I'm pretty certain I hear the guards in pursuit, following our pounding footsteps. It doesn't matter. We're caught up in wild joy, adrenaline making every elegant hall, quiet corridor, and chandelier-lit entryway into our playground. Making every opulence I once considered mine, and mine no longer, into *ours*.

We charge out onto the deck, the air cool on our flushed faces. With security close, we continue hastily down the steps into the tent. Our crew, minus McCoy, is on the dance floor. Jackson is with them. Yes, they may have decided dancing with other guests is clever camouflage. Really, it looks like they're just having fun.

Deonte notices us first. "Everything good?" he asks.

I exchange a quick glance with Abigail, a silent agreement. No one needs to know what happened. Only family.

"Everything is great. Although we're going to get kicked out soon," I say. "Which obviously means we should enjoy this last song."

Deonte needs no convincing. His eyes move from me to Abigail. When he reaches out, she puts her hand in his. He tugs her forward, into the music. In the crush, my crew raises the roof. Celebrating the way *we* deserve. We're walking out of here millionaires.

Instead of joining them, I lock gazes with Jackson. "Hey," he says softly. The hesitant word, wondering where we stand, is far from his exclamation on the day we met, the first word Jackson Roese ever said to me.

"I'm sorry I ever doubted you," I say. "I know you didn't send that message."

"Good," he replies.

I wait for more. "Don't you want to know how I figured it out?" I prompt him when nothing else comes.

He pulls me close in one gently quick movement, lining us up with the precise grace of opportunities seized. I'm pressed to him, chest to chest, tuxedo to dress. "Olivia, as long as I have you, nothing else matters," he says. He stares down at me, his eyes mixing love with confidence in the perfect cocktail he is.

I lean in to kiss him—

And a hand on my shoulder stops me. I turn, finding the bride. She looks *pissed*.

"I don't know how you even got wedding crashers into *my* wedding," she says, nodding to Deonte, Abigail, and McCoy, who is seated nearby, intruders in her crystal-and-lace kingdom. "Abigail isn't even dressed appropriately. I don't want any of them in the background of my photos."

Unbothered, I shrug. "We were just leaving—" I start to say, until one word from Maureen's painted lips snags in my mind.

Abigail. If the chandelier fell onto the dance floor, the surprise wouldn't hit me harder. The final pieces of the day drop neatly into place. *Maureen knows who Abigail is.* The prenup. The short courtship. It's not because Dash is madly in love with his young bride.

It's because she's blackmailing him.

I laugh, earning a concerned yet scathing look from my step-mother. Maureen, who met my father when she was earning her journalism degree. Maureen, who knows how to investigate offhand comments or incoherent details or whatever it was that put her on to my dad's ignominious history. Maureen, who knows how to leverage information. I've underestimated her, I realize. The way people have continually underestimated me. It's maybe my single regret of the day.

I pat her on her diamond-encrusted elbow. "Welcome to the family, Maureen," I say sweetly. "I think you're going to fit right in."

When Maureen eyes me, a door opens down the long hallway of her gaze, as if she's recognizing something. It's almost a shame, I decide. If Maureen weren't my stepmother, I feel like we actually could have been friends.

I face my crew, ready to usher us out.

"Who the hell is Abigail?" Tom asks.

My sister and I exchange glances. Promptly, we burst into giggles.

FIFTY-EIGHT

SISTERS?" JACKSON REPEATS.

On the dance floor, my crew is comically awestruck after I've succinctly explained the situation. Wide-eyed, they're motionless among the crowd of wedding guests while the music pounds in our ears. Jackson looks at me, searching for some sign of how I really feel about this revelation.

I don't entirely know. I'm not endeared to the idea of more kin on the Owens side, not with my family history. Deceit, larceny, infidelity, corruption. Why couldn't we just get into playing Uno or visiting national parks instead? But I meant what I said about second chances. I'm going to try. I smile reassuringly to Jackson, who nods, placated.

"I think we're missing, like, seven parts of this story," Tom says.

"We'll explain everything later," Abigail promises, her authoritativeness returning. Her eyes dart past the tent, where Maureen is pointing her out to security. "Right now, I'm about to be officially kicked out of this wedding."

"Where one of us goes, we all go," Deonte replies unhesitatingly.

"Let's make our triumphant getaway," Tom concurs.

Together, we walk off the dance floor, grabbing McCoy. We're reaching the lawn when Deonte halts.

"Hold up. We gotta get the cake!" he declares.

He's right. Of course he's right. Security or no security, we won't leave the wedding without one final heist. No one hesitates. We make a dash for the cake table, each of us grabbing a plate laden with one of Deonte's decadent slices and running off into the night. Everyone's exhilarated laughter joins into one chorus while the din of the party recedes, the damp grass soft under our feet, the hushed house drawing nearer.

"I grabbed a slice for Kevin," Tom shouts. "Somebody give that kid a call."

"On it," McCoy responds, handing his cake to Deonte so he can take out his phone.

We race to the front of the house under the stars. When we hit the driveway, Kevin is waiting for us. In his father's Lamborghini.

Honestly, I understand Kevin's ransom demand now. In the largely vacant driveway, under the gazes of the valet attendants, the engine hums with power. Dark-walled wheels contrast with the electric-teal curves of the SUV's exterior. When Kevin pops the passenger door, it opens upward.

"Oh shit," Abigail utters.

"Yeah," Deonte agrees.

We pile in. McCoy pushes Kevin out of the driver's seat while I sit on Jackson's lap in the front. The interior smells like cologne-soaked leather. We tear out of the property, the pavement noiseless under the vehicle's prowl, the headlights cutting dazzling swaths in front of us.

Our joyride lasts about thirty seconds. McCoy stops the car in the parking lot next to our van. "We're absolutely not getting on the road in a car without enough seat belts for every minor I'm driving," he says firmly.

Everyone grumbles but obeys. We file into the van, the reprise of when we got here earlier today. Was it only hours ago? I'm immeasurably grateful for the differences. Next to me, Jackson puts his hand in mine. Abigail's eyes dance. Kevin looks as if he'd prefer this van with his friends over the nicest Lamborghini in the world. McCoy pulls out, leaving the Owens property while the crew eats cake, and Tom is finally permitted to put on his heist playlist.

"Cake is fire," Kevin comments.

"Yeah. Seriously, Deonte," I say, chewing.

Deonte takes a huge bite, rightfully pleased with himself.

"We're rich!" Tom hollers out the window.

In the middle row, Kevin pauses with his fork held over his cake. "Wait, what? You said you were only giving me five thousand?"

Oh. Right. When I was negotiating with Kevin, I didn't anticipate actually liking him at the end of the day.

"Don't worry," Abigail chimes in, "I maybe stole a little extra to cover new crew members."

I whirl to face her in the back. "You did? When?"

"Okay, when I stole it, it wasn't exactly with the intent to share it with any of you, but I've had a...change of heart," she confesses, her eyes meeting mine.

"Does that mean I get a cut?" Jackson asks.

"Dude, no way," Tom objects. "You didn't do anything."

"He did distract some guards," Kevin points out, coming charmingly to Jackson's defense despite having only just met him. His superpower possibly isn't resilience in the face of rejection. It might be his open heart. While it's not a conventional virtue in a heist crew, we're not exactly a conventional heist crew.

"He also dutifully served as a groomsman," McCoy says from the driver's seat.

Deonte evaluates Jackson, unconvinced. "I don't think dating the boss is enough to get a cut." He decides. "No offense."

Jackson shrugs. "I had to ask."

"Maybe next heist, pal," Tom offers.

"Oh god, don't even joke!" McCoy exclaims. "I'm never doing this again."

I catch Tom's eye. Despite my sympathy for McCoy's stress, I don't feel the same way. We did it once. We *could* do it again. I feel the urge in me to chase my abilities until they break under my ambition. I know Tom understands. Maybe *only* Tom understands. His lips purse in restless contemplation, not smiling. Closer to concealing unspoken plans.

It's reassuring in ways I wouldn't know how to express, realizing even just one other person wants to walk the edge of everything. I've worked in the dark for months, lonely in my vengeance. The idea of someone, anyone, getting close was dangerous. Which makes it intoxicating now. Maybe we'll all do it again someday. I know with certainty I would only ever pull my next heist with the people in this van.

I can't help laughing while the music plays and wind whips in the open windows. I thought stealing from my dad would be the revenge I needed—and it was. It wasn't my lesson to learn or my flaw to outgrow. It was vicious, and it was necessary, and it was good.

But revenge isn't something that ends. It's a living thing that needs to be fed within you every day. It's bigger than just stealing from my dad, even bigger than embarrassing him. Revenge also means filling the place in my heart he vacated.

It looks like being happy and having friends and the life Dashiell Owens won't ever have. Not for real.

FIFTY-NINE

WE START SPENDING OUR FORTUNE IN A GAS STATION AT MID-
night. Everyone in the crew walks down the aisles, grabbing
anything and everything we want. Under the fluorescents, arms full,
we feel like royalty. No—royalty isn't earned. Nor does it celebrate
with snacks. I'd rather be masterminds.

I check out at the register and meet my crew outside, where they're
waiting for their own rides home holding more Pringles, Skittles, and
Gatorade than anyone in formal wear probably ever has. In the white
aura of the gas station light on the inky abyss of the pavement, the
portrait of them is perfect. Waiting shoulder to shoulder like a police
lineup or a wedding party. Collars loosened, cheeks flushed, eyes
wide with exhausted joy.

Queen—

No. No more code names. Not for friends. Heart full, I correct
myself.

Abigail. Deonte. Tom. McCoy. Kevin. Jackson.

Kevin's rideshare arrives first. He's returning to the wedding,
where Mitchum will expect to find his son, waiting in the Lamborghini in punishment for his fancy-watch stunt. With misty eyes, he hugs
every member of the crew. I pat him on the back when he reaches me.

"We're hanging out next weekend, right?" he asks.

"I'm not sure I'll be recovered by next weekend," I say honestly. "I feel like I could sleep for days."

"Yeah, yeah, of course," Kevin replies. "Only thing is, Saturday is my birthday, so..." He trails off hopefully.

"Are you inviting us to your birthday party?" Tom asks.

Kevin smiles, sheepish. "If you think it's cool, then yeah. Or not, whatever."

I laugh. "We'll be there," I promise him.

"Yeah, man, I'll make cupcakes," Deonte adds.

Kevin brightens. "For real?"

"Wouldn't miss it," Tom assures him with real warmth.

Kevin nods in gratitude. While he walks to his waiting UberX, I'm pretty certain I hear him sniffle.

Next is Deonte. His car pulls up in the midnight fog starting to drift over the highway. "Congrats on your first of many," I call out to him.

He furrows his brow doubtfully. "I'm good on heists for a bit," he replies.

I shake my head. "First wedding where you provided the cake," I clarify.

Now pride steals into his slow smile. He climbs into the car, waving his goodbye. The million dollars going to his bakery is probably the best use any of us will make of my father's fortune. It's practically a public service.

While I watch the car drive away, I feel a hand on my back. Tom stands beside me.

"I'm off," he says.

I feel a little sad how quickly the crew is separating. In my heart,

I know it's not only the comedown, the dizzying effect of the plan I designed disassembling itself into the fond recesses of shared memories. If I'm really honest, I'm also a little scared. When you hold people close, the connection isn't durable like diamond. It's fragile like glass.

"Don't be a stranger," I say, hoping my voice hides my vulnerability.

His lips curl in a half grin. "To you? How could I?"

I hear his unspoken undercurrent. We're too alike to ever be strangers to each other.

He walks to his waiting car, the light emphasizing the lines of his figure. "Feel free to give my number to your cousin anytime," he calls out over his shoulder.

"Hilarious," I reply flatly.

He shrugs. "With the return of golden boy over there, I'll need a new date to the next Owens heist."

Something squirms in my stomach. Not exactly jealousy, not exactly *not* jealousy. More like anticipation. No matter what I do next, I know Tom will be with me.

I face the remainder of the crew. Except it isn't the remainder of the crew. Jackson waits with his hands in his pockets. McCoy stands with him, visibly exhausted. Abigail is gone. With my heart pounding painfully, I pass my gaze down the road and finally find her, walking on the side of the highway, nearly out of sight.

It hurts instantly. I feel naive, remembering my excitement to have her in my life without ever considering whether she wanted me in hers. Of course she wouldn't. Whatever distrust I feel for the Owens family, she must feel a hundredfold. I have to respect her instinct for wariness, even if the rejection hurts. It's the problem with the fragility of glass. It cuts deep when you're not looking.

I could chase her. I could probably catch her easily. What holds me in place is knowing she *doesn't want me to*. It's devastatingly important. Learning who Abigail is left me reckoning with what my father really robbed her of. It wasn't just my life on the Owens estate, or hers. It wasn't just luxury or loneliness. It was deeper. He decided our lives for us. I would live in the house. Abigail Pierce would not.

Revelation came over me while we ran from our coup in his office. Every step felt like life reclaimed. I missed one crucial point of the day, I realized. I wasn't only stealing millions. I wasn't only stealing revenge, or what I deserve, or what my mom deserves. I was stealing freedom.

I won't deprive Abigail of it now. If my sister wants to leave, I won't force her to stay.

The closing of the van door distracts me. I find McCoy has returned to the driver's seat with the windows rolled down. He'll drive it to the rental tonight. I walk up to the door and hook my fingers in the open window. "You good?" I ask him.

"I'm good." He hesitates, weighing his next words. "I'm proud of you, Olivia," he says.

The emotion lodged in my throat surprises me. "Proud of me for embarking on a successful life of crime?"

He doesn't drop my gaze, his expression serious. "Proud of who you are."

I fight the wobble in my lip, the water in my eyes. "You better drive off," I say, "before I start crying like Kevin." I hardly manage to get the sentence out.

McCoy laughs and starts the engine.

"Thanks," I add, unable to say more. It's a little overwhelming, realizing how much I needed to hear pride from someone like him—someone, I guess, like a father figure in my life. I needed it desperately. My dad was proud of me only when he thought he could use me. Knowing someone appreciates me for me... It's funny, how the most precious rewards are sometimes found in gas station parking lots instead of in safes or secret accounts.

McCoy drives off, the van's red lights disappearing into the night fog. It's finally just me and Jackson.

He holds his arm out, and I walk into the embrace and cling to his side for warmth. When he speaks after a moment, I feel his voice vibrate against me.

"I can't believe I ran through your house evading security," he complains playfully, "and I'm not even getting a cut."

"It's not like you're walking away empty-handed," I point out. Withdrawing from his arms, I entwine my fingers with his.

He grins. It's dazzling. "You're right," he says. "I made the biggest score of the night by far."

I'm smiling when he kisses me, capturing me with lips I doubt I'll ever stop longing for. When he pulls back, he takes something out of his jacket pocket. I glimpse metal reflecting cool light.

"I did, however, steal one thing tonight," he says.

He opens his hand, revealing my necklace.

I'm speechless, my gasp caught in my chest. It means, quietly, everything. Weeks ago, Jackson refused to steal anything under any circumstances. The fact that he did now, and it was this, the pendant-shaped piece of my heart, robs me of words. I recognize what it really is—the work of someone who deeply, irrevocably cares about me.

He drapes it around my neck and lets his fingers linger as he secures the clasp. I shiver—and not from the cold. His caress feels impossibly real, and with it comes the pleasant shock of realizing, while I can't trust everyone, I can trust my own heart.

EPILOGUE

ONE WEEK LATER

I SIT IN FRONT OF MY MIRROR, DOING MY MAKEUP AFTER MY SHIFT at Vive. I decided not to quit my job despite my newly won financial resources. It reminds me of what my circumstances looked like until very recently, and it helps me keep up the appearance of having not just stolen a million dollars... even if I can now indulge in one of the pricier handbags.

In my closet sit my heels, clean of the mud and grass I wiped from them a week ago. Everything is the same, except in the important ways.

My mom knocks on my door, then enters. She looks happier these days, ever since I sold her on the story that friends and family pressured my dad into providing more support to "his only daughter," resulting in me receiving a substantial monthly allowance. Enough for rent, medical bills, and other expenses, with plenty left over.

It's helped my mom return to herself more. She's started painting again. Without the constant pressure of multiple jobs, she has the chance to find out what she really wants to do with her life. Once, over dinner, she even mentioned getting a degree in counseling.

I don't know whether the cover story for the money has her completely convinced, knowing the kind of man my father is. I don't know if she cares. The hope in her eyes, the spark in her smile—they're precious beyond words, beyond dollar signs, beyond the precarious variables of The Plan. She no longer looks lost in unfamiliar hallways. She looks like she's home.

"Will you be out late?" she asks.

"No, Mom," I say, finishing my lipstick. "We're just watching a movie."

Her forehead creases in puzzlement. "Your chess club is watching a movie?" she repeats. "Do you...play chess ever?"

I laugh. It's a fair question. "We're between, um, chess games right now. I hope we'll start again soon," I say. In quiet moments, I've found myself missing the weeks when designing every facet of the wedding heist occupied my focus. It gave me a gift you can only find and never steal—purpose.

I can't just rob my father again, though. It's not as if he has much for me to take anyway, and besides, he's no longer a challenge. Instead, I'm waiting for the perfect opportunity to arise. The perfect mark.

I want more. No, not more. I want *everything*.

The desire makes my father's words repeat in my head. *Like father, like daughter.* I've decided he's wrong. Heiress to an empire of thieves? Perhaps. Like him? No. I won't steal everything from just anyone. If my future holds other heists, I'll steal from people who don't deserve what they have.

"Well, have fun," Mom replies, placated. "Jackson just pulled up."

My phone hums on my desk. I check the screen idly, confident of what I'll find. Yes, once more it is Kevin, sending the group chat his favorite Master Oogway meme. We re-created the group chat on our own phones with one very obvious rule—no references to the heist—except for one. Privately proud of my code names' endurance, I permitted Kevin to name the chat "Chess Club."

I give Mom a quick hug on my way out, then fly down the narrow, creaky hallway. Yes, with the million dollars, I could probably convince my mom to buy something bigger, but I've grown to like this house and the ways it makes me feel *not* like an Owens.

At the door, I notice mail has been dropped in the mail slot. I recognize a postcard from London on top. Grinning, I pick up the glossy image of the River Thames. McCoy promptly used his million to visit the UK and "see Shakespeare the way it was intended in the Globe."

I hold on to the postcard to show the crew. We're meeting at the Webbers' mansion for a promised cornhole rematch and a *Kung Fu Panda* marathon.

Everyone else is coming except Abigail. I've given her space, holding on dearly to the email I received the day after the wedding. I didn't recognize the sender, obviously. It was no ordinary email address, composed instead of random letters and numbers. Encryption, designed not to be replied to. *See you soon, sis,* the message read.

While she hasn't opened up to me, she hasn't exactly closed the door forever, either. It's more like she's locked our relationship with a code or a key. Not impenetrable—just complicated.

Under the postcard, an embossed envelope catches my eye. It's trimmed in heavy black lining, the address in handwritten calligraphy. *Olivia Owens*, it reads. Of course, I open it.

I read the cream-white card inside once, twice, three times. With every mechanism in my head starting to move, I calmly return the card to the envelope. Clutching it in my hand, I head out the front door.

Coventry greets me outside, the wonderfully familiar panorama of cracked cement and chain-link fences. My heart rate picks up as I walk down my driveway to Jackson's waiting car. I lean over to kiss him when I get in. He smiles, catching my chin to make the kiss linger.

I can't help letting his lips divert me from the envelope in my hand. Being with Jackson is the only time I don't hunger for the next heist. Instead, in his arms, I want other things. Things I could imagine distracting or satisfying me...possibly forever.

He pulls away from the kiss finally, as if he's forcing himself. "Whoa, what's in the envelope?" he asks enthusiastically. "Looks fancy. Whoever did the lettering kind of went hard."

"I got invited to Switzerland," I say. "It's my grandmother's seventieth birthday."

His face clouds with confusion. "Your grandma who you haven't spoken to in years?"

I nod. "It's going to be an Owens family reunion," I say quietly.

Jackson's gaze narrows.

I wait. He's feeling me out. Intrigued. "Don't tell me you have to go," he ventures.

"*Have* to go, no. I don't have to," I reply. "But..." I fall silent while Jackson watches, no doubt perceiving the gears moving in my eyes. Dash is nothing compared to my grandmother, who has *generations* of inherited wealth under her command, even royalty. *Empire of thieves.* Dash wasn't referring only to himself. It's impossible my grandmother's dynasty claimed their fortune without a little filth.

What if the vengeance I wrought on my father's wedding day was only the opening overture of my ruination of the Owens family? Empires fall as they rise—in pieces. What if I have more ruining to do?

The queen of endings.

It's perfect. *She's* perfect. *The perfect mark.*

Jackson laughs, shaking his head. "Do I even want to know what you're planning?"

I settle into my seat, a smile playing over my face. In my head, a new scheme begins to unfold.

"I don't know," I say. "Do you?"

ACKNOWLEDGMENTS

Stealing millions of dollars is risky. Switching genres with an idea we weren't sure we could pull off felt only slightly less risky. We have the utmost gratitude for our very own heist crew who made it happen.

Katie Shea Boutillier, your faith in and inexhaustible support of this story is why it exists. We are ever grateful for your encouragement, your insight, and your incredible drive—in everything, and especially in this. You remain one of our oldest, dearest publishing friends. Thank you for being our mastermind.

Samantha Gentry, we're immeasurably grateful for how you've guided and overseen every single aspect of *Heiress Takes All*. From your perceptive notes to your careful and insightful positioning to understanding our *Succession* references, working with you has been a dream. We're very fortunate to call you our editor! Very (*very*) special thanks to Caitlyn Averett for championing and welcoming the manuscript to its home. We're forever in your debt for making us LBYR authors. Thank you as well to Alexandra Houdeshell for your very kind feedback and all your help along the way!

Jenny Kimura and Howard Huang, the word this cover evokes is our favorite word to describe covers—*iconic*. We knew it would come out heart-stoppingly good from the moment we saw the first concept of the wedding cake. The final result is even more dazzling, exactly the unforgettable portrait we hoped for. Every inch of these pages' design manages to match it for style, and we couldn't be more grateful for how the whole masterpiece shines.

Little, Brown Young Readers was our dream home for this story from the start. We're very honored to work with the entire team.

Elizabeth Starr Baer, in addition to your keen-eyed copyediting, we appreciate and applaud your keeping us honest on timelines and Rhode Island driving laws. Reading your impeccable heist schedule on the style guide was one of the very coolest parts of the process! Lindsay Walter-Greaney, we can hardly keep the pair of us organized—we're in awe and very appreciative of your fitting every piece of this production together perfectly. One of our favorite experiences in publishing is holding this book in our hands. Kimberly Stella, it wouldn't happen without your coordination. We're deeply grateful.

We owe it to our fabulous publicity and marketing teams for helping us reach the readers we dream of with every word we write. Kelly Moran, working with you is a delight, as is witnessing every way you share Olivia's story with the world. Stefanie Hoffman and Alice Gelber, thank you for getting out the word on this book. Savannah Kennelly, it is a joy watching you light up the LBYR socials—and even more so to be part of your work! Christie Michel, we grew up in school libraries, and your care in connecting this story with young readers means everything to us.

While Olivia Owens and her crew are thieves, they're also friends. We couldn't imagine publishing without ours. Bridget Morrissey... there are no words. You inspire and encourage us in literally everything. EBA always. Forever grateful to have you at our side in both the lows and the highs in this industry—the ghosts know that there sure have been plenty of both! May we always have encyclopedias and deep conversations at the Waffle House.

Maura Milan, our forever accountability buddy. Thank you for asking the questions that make us figure out things and for watching action movies with us. Gabrielle Gold, our oldest friend and first confidante. Thank you for fifteen years of friendship.

The writing community is one of the best parts of this career. We are so grateful to publishing for bringing into our lives Rebekah Faubion, Lindsay Grossman, Kalie and Jody Holford, Derek Milman, Kayla Olson, Farrah Penn, Jodi Picoult, Gretchen Schreiber, Alicia Thompson, and Brian Murray Williams.

Of course, thank you to our family. We promise the Owens family is not at all inspired by you.

Our final and deepest thanks go to every bookseller who has championed our work—you all are the lifeblood of this industry—and to you, our readers. With every release—and every message, Instagram post, and kind word—your encouragement keeps us going and inspired. We write for you...always. Happy heisting.

Mike Yoon

EMILY WIBBERLEY & AUSTIN SIEGEMUND-BROKA met and fell in love in high school. Austin went on to graduate from Harvard, while Emily graduated from Princeton. Together, they are the authors of numerous YA and adult romance novels. Now married, they live in Los Angeles, where they continue to take daily inspiration from their own love story and would join each other's heist crews in a heartbeat. They invite you to find them online at emilyandaustinwrite.com.